"Emma?"

"I'm back here, Bucky. I'll be out in a second."

I noticed something by the far edge of the shrubs, an odd break in the shadows. It resolved itself into a patch of mottled pale light and utter black, far too definite to be a shadow. Then I realized that the mottled white was actually part of someone's lower leg, the flesh that showed between a dark sock and where the trouser leg rode up. . . .

"Emma, where are you?"

The leg continued and I realized that someone was lying face down, a hand palm up, fingers slightly curled. A sweet, sickly smell hit me. And then I realized that the sound of buzzing insects was not inside my head. . . .

"Emma? Do you need help?"

And then I saw the darkened stains in the soil around the man's fair hair—and was glad that I couldn't see the rest of his face. . . .

Also by Dana Cameron

SITE UNSEEN
GRAVE CONSEQUENCES

DANA CAMERON

PAST MALICE

AN EMMA FIELDING MYSTERY

AVON BOOKS
An Imprint of HarperCollinsPublishers

This is a work of fiction. Names, characters, places, and incidents are products of the author's imagination or are used fictitiously and are not to be construed as real. Any resemblance to actual events, locales, organizations, or persons, living or dead, is entirely coincidental.

AVON BOOKS
An Imprint of HarperCollins*Publishers*
10 East 53rd Street
New York, New York 10022-5299

Copyright © 2003 by Dana Cameron
ISBN: 0-380-81956-2
www.avonmystery.com

First Avon Books paperback printing: June 2003

Avon Trademark Reg. U.S. Pat. Off. and in Other Countries, Marca Registrada, Hecho en U.S.A.
HarperCollins® is a registered trademark of HarperCollins Publishers Inc.

Printed in the U.S.A.

10 9 8 7 6 5 4 3 2 1

Dedicated to the memory of my uncle,
Bob Cameron,
who was curious about what went on
behind the scenes at museums.

Acknowledgments

FIRST OFF, DIEGO, YOU'RE THE BEST, ALWAYS. I AM also tremendously grateful to the following people, who supported my efforts and read and commented on all or part of this manuscript: Beth Krueger, Ann Barbier, Pam Crane, Peter Morrison, Heather Stewart, my agent Kit Ward, and my editor at Avon, Sarah Durand. Every one of them gave me excellent advice. Detective John Bianchi of the Beverly Police Department was particularly helpful in answering my questions about procedure, and he directed me to several excellent resources, and Jerry Smith of Cabot Records, Beverly, helped me shop for a birthday present for Brian—although they pointed me in the right direction, if I've strayed off the path, it's my own doing. And thanks to Kate Mattes of Kate's Mystery Books in Cambridge, for her support of mystery writers everywhere over the past twenty years.

PAST MALICE

Chapter 1

To most people, I'll bet the old place looked nothing at all like a battlefield. To most casual observers, the Chandler House was the epitome of what they imagine the past to have been: a big colonial house by the ocean, a wind-swept lawn leading down to a dramatic cliff, romantic to the nth-degree. The reason that so many people think the past really was the good old days is because of the fine, lovely things that survive. These are the very best, the very richest things that would have inspired pride and a desire to preserve them. Seeing these objects causes people to confide in me how much they've always loved history, how they've always wanted to be archaeologists, how they would have loved to have lived "back then," whether back then was ancient Egypt, imperial Rome, or, as it was in this case, colonial New England.

I have to smile when I think that they're imagining big skirts, wigs, and courtly manners. They are not imagining a world without antibiotics or indoor plumbing or the hope of democracy and equal rights. They are forgetting that they might be lost without supermarkets or instantaneous global communication or electricity. They are not thinking of a world where, to paraphrase Monty Python, the king was the only one who didn't smell like crap, which isn't such a bad summary for most of history.

It wasn't even the neat row of trenches by the side of the house that reminded me of a battlefield: I would never have allowed my students to let things get that messy. No, our trenches were orthogonal, hell, even the back dirt piles were clean, made of well-sifted loam, filled with fat worms and sorted pebbles, the sort of thing that sends gardeners drooling. If we didn't have to put it all back when we were finished, I would have brought it back home with me myself. And it wasn't the fencing we'd put up around the site to keep the unwary, the unthinking, and the dim-witted from falling into one of our nice, square units and breaking a neck, or worse, disturbing my carefully exposed stratigraphy. We'd even deliberately chosen the portable wooden fencing to blend in with the scenery, so you couldn't even claim that it resembled a military picket. No, I'm afraid it was the general background hum of negative emotions that made me feel like I was digging in for my own protection as much as I was trying to learn about the Chandler family.

I'm not usually so misanthropic; it's just that I was tired of trying to fight to do my job properly and we still had another two weeks of work to go. It would have worn the patience of a saint down to a nubbin, and I'm no saint for all my sister claims I am a Puritan. I just knew that I had to bide my time and pick which battles to fight, and which ones to avoid. Anyone who tells you that the Ivory Tower is a quiet retreat from the dirty old "outside world" doesn't know what she's talking about.

I sighed and stood up from the bench, telling myself that

I would be better off for another walk around the property, and another long look out at the ocean behind the house. I was waiting to be invited into the Stone Harbor Historical Society's board meeting to tell them all about the archaeological research I'd talked them into letting me do on their property at the Chandler House. I figured there'd be another half hour or so of their private business—to which I was pointedly not invited—before I had to go in.

The main part of the Chandler House was an early example of a brick Georgian structure, two floors with four rooms each, and an attic with dormers. As I faced the front, there was a small brick addition to the right; there was none on the left. When I walked around to the rear, there was another, later addition, also in brick; its two large cube-shaped rooms faced the ocean that relentlessly crashed against the Massachusetts coast.

I picked up a flat pebble from the path and slung it sidewise, making it skip three times before it lost momentum and sank. The one that followed it only brushed the water twice, then hit a wave with a plop. The next pebble I picked up ached to be thrown at the fat seagull I saw perching on a white-stained piling not too far away from the shore. I told myself that I could hit it, if I wanted to. But my aim is pretty bad and I didn't really want to wreck my karma by taking out my bad mood on the poor bird, no matter how nasty I think gulls are. Besides, my veterinarian sister was staying with me and any slight I inflicted on the animal kingdom would be immediately telegraphed to her, and she would instigate a massive retaliation. So I dropped the stone back on the path and walked up the lawn to the house. After another half-perambulation around the building, I heard the sound of footsteps on the gravel in front of the house.

"Evening, Professor."

I looked up to see Justin Fisher, one of three security

guards who worked here. A nice kid, maybe twenty-four or so, who looked like he was five years younger. He had straw-colored hair that was cut fashionably short and close to his head, a crooked smile, and a youthfully eager presence that was made positively gawky by the authority of his uniform.

"Evening, Justin. You know you can call me Emma, right?"

"I know, it's just that I made the mistake of calling you Emma in front of Mr. Fiske, and he wasn't thrilled. So I figured I'd just better. . . ." He shrugged. "You know."

"Just to keep on the safe side." I nodded and we both smiled uncomfortably, trying to find a topic that was a little less awkward.

"Hey, that book you told me about, for my paper?" Justin was taking classes at night, trying to earn a graduate degree in history.

"Was it helpful?"

He rocked his hand, mezzo-mezzo. "Kind of. It was a little off from what I needed, but there was an appendix with a whole lot of references that really paid off. Archaeologists really do look at things differently than historians, don't they?"

I shrugged. "Well, I think the main differences are in the scale and focus of what we're looking at—historians tend to look at major events on a global scale, and we're more often looking at individual families or communities. The materials are different, but I wonder if the distinctions aren't really just academic."

Justin's face showed he wasn't convinced. "Feels different to me. But I like getting the alternative perspective."

I couldn't help smiling and waved a finger at him. "Ah, that's the first step down the slippery slope, though. First it's getting an alternative perspective, then you'll start looking at houses—looking to see what was original, what was added on later—and you'll tell your friends you can stop any time you want. Except then, architecture won't be enough for you. Your family will start to worry. You'll begin to ask about old photographs and paintings and how Stone Harbor used to look before the war—Revolutionary War, that is—and then it will get worse. You'll start walking with your head down, looking for broken bits of pottery that might have washed out of the fill they're using to make the new sidewalks downtown. There'll be an intervention—your girlfriend crying, your grandparents shaking their fists at the sky—but it will be too late. You'll be an archaeologist and there's no cure for that."

"Yeah, except for the bad pay. Except for the snakes and spiders and worms and all that manual labor. Nice try, but no thanks. I think I'll stick with teaching grade school history."

"Okay, okay, but do let me know if you need any more help—oops, it looks like I'm on."

We looked over to the house, where an older woman was waving to me.

Justin raised his hand in farewell. "Good luck. I'm going to walk down along the seawall and make sure there isn't some threat coming to us by water."

The woman called, "We're just about ready for your presentation, Professor! Come on in!"

I went up to the front door and tried to banish my embattled feelings. I wasn't particularly fond of Fiona Prowse—"call me Fee" was what she told everyone—but I did want to try to get along with her. Problem was, she saw my work as an unnecessary expense and kept trying to find ways to make it either vanish or make it pay into the coffers of the Chandler House, neither of which was likely to happen.

She clapped her hands to get me to speed up, and although I knew from the big grin on her face that she thought she was being funny, I gritted my teeth against her false cheeriness. I decided that if she'd only loosen up, I wouldn't feel quite so put off. She led me through the front door; the two rooms on the left-hand side of the hall were devoted to office space. The central hall held a small ticket area and a display of postcards and books on local history for sale; the rest of the rooms on this floor and the second were open to the public. The addition held an education space downstairs and a hall/auditorium upstairs. The education room was set up like a kitchen for demonstrations in colonial cookery and dyeing and other household activities, complete with period utensils like a mortar and pestle, earthenware bowls of various sizes, and big wooden spoons. There were herbs hanging from the rafters, and a string of dusty dried apple slices over a working fireplace, thankfully unlit during the summer. Fee Prowse led me into the central hall, and up the front staircase.

Fee was a tall, big-boned woman with old-fashioned posture that spoke of determination or at least a capacity for endurance. She had a round face with cheeks going a little soft and sagging and her mouth was hard but not quite pursed, her jaw always set behind her smiles. Her hair was a carefully molded bunch of short, dark mahogany curls that in the back brushed her collar; maybe her hair had been close to that color in her youth—darker red than mine now—but at this moment, the gray in her eyebrows seemed much more authentic and I reckoned that both the curls and the color had come out of a box. She was the kind of woman who never lost an argument, at least not in her own mind. All of the dresses I'd ever seen her in were below the knee, short-sleeved, sensible professional prints. Low heels, because a lady didn't wear anything else to work, but not too high, because that would give people the wrong idea and besides, they were so bad for your feet. Practical and thrifty and singleminded, Fee had good qualities for someone in charge of the account books.

She gestured to a chair outside the meeting room. "If you just have a seat here, we should be ready in just a minute."

"Thanks."

I sat outside the room, which had been converted from the big upstairs room in the addition, and pushed my seat back so that it was leaning against the wall on two feet, evidence that I really was in a bad-girl mood. The door didn't catch closed all the way, and I could hear the conversation as clearly as if I'd been in the room myself. Always good to get a feel for what was going on, I rationalized.

"—the police haven't been able to do much. Though, honestly, what are they supposed to do?" I recognized that voice: It was Aden Fiske, who was the head of the Stone Harbor Historical Society and manager of the Chandler House site. "They can't exactly do anything with a brick and a pile of rocks, or analyze the handwriting from a spray-painted wall."

"The question isn't what they can do now, the question is, where were they at the time the vandalism took place?" a cross-sounding man's voice groused. I thought it might be Bradley Chandler, who was the manager of the Historical Society's other property across town, the Tapley House. "As homeowners, we pay a lot of tax money and then this—"

I'd heard about the vandalism but didn't know any of the details; I'd have to ask my husband, Brian, if he'd seen anything in the paper when I got home. There certainly seemed to be something about the historical district in Stone Harbor lately, I thought, and it wasn't doing anything to dispel the notion of a place under siege.

"Now, Bray, I understand your frustration, but they can't

be everywhere at once. They got there as soon as the neighbors called." That voice was a younger man's, quite arresting.

"And I suppose we should be grateful that anyone bothered to call in, the way things are going now. I thought that Perry was supposed to—" That was Bradley Chandler again, grousing.

"She is very late, isn't she, Bray?" said Aden Fiske. "Has anyone tried her house?"

Fee spoke up then. "There was no answer. I think that we should just continue on so we can all get home."

"All right then, if you would call in our guest, then."

That was my signal to stop eavesdropping and straighten out my chair as quietly as I could. By the time Fee came out for me, I was carefully going over the notes I'd penned on a yellow legal pad.

"Professor?" She smiled and raised her eyebrows, too full of glee for my taste. Sunday nights were for watching television while folding the laundry, and that's what I wished I was doing right now.

The room was filled with about twenty people, four sitting at one table set with water glasses and notepads for five. Aden Fiske was seated at the center of the table. He was slight and trim, in his sixties and a working definition of dapper, with white hair brushed back off his narrow pink face; his nose was straight but came to a sharp point, giving him a faintly comical air. He stood up and introduced me.

"Well, Fee and I both know what Professor Fielding is up to, but I think it would be useful for her to give us a little overview for the rest of you about the absolute mess she's been making in our backyard!"

Everyone giggled at Aden's naughty behavior, and I smiled. He really was helping me to disarm any more potential nay-sayers.

I briefly summarized my goals, to identify any archaeological remains that might be affected by the proposed gift shop and restroom facilities, and to learn more about the early eighteenth-century Chandler family from their own artifacts and documents. Most people nodded, interested, a few smiled politely, a handful remained unconvinced.

Aden thanked me. "I've been following the project from its start and I for one am very excited about what we might learn. And, who knows? Professor Fielding's expertise might be needed elsewhere on our properties, as we hope to expand their facilities."

"Well, I hope it won't become too much of a habit. Fee says it is very expensive." I got a good look at Bradley Chandler then, a sloppy-looking man, carelessly dressed in business casual, his graying blond hair and a short, curling beard making him look like an overweight and annoyed garden gnome.

"Bray, when will you stop being so damned cheap! It's not like it's your money we're spending, anyhow!" Aden said this in such an overstated way that the rest of the board members laughed. Bradley, or Bray, as I guess he was called, looked put out, but then relaxed when Fiske continued.

"Oh, I know you're just being careful. We couldn't be managing so well without your caution, but I think a little spending is called for here."

I nodded, ready for this complaint at least. "It is an expense, but when you consider that you are getting a team of professionally trained people to conduct research for you, answer questions to inform the public, and pave the way, legally speaking, for you to build a snack shop and toilets to upgrade your facility . . ." I paused to smile, "it's really not that bad. Plus, I think the publicity is good for tourism."

"I know Aden thinks so," Bray answered carefully, "but there's nothing to indicate that our visitorship is up in the past week."

I nodded again. "These things do take time. But the way I figure it, the more people talk about the project, the more we get nice little articles in the paper like the one last week, the more interest is generated, the more people will stop by for a tour or to buy a book and the better that is for everyone."

There was general murmured agreement from the rest of the board.

"You know, I was thinking," Fee chirruped. "Those little bits of things you dig up?"

I frowned. "Artifacts? Potsherds, glass, that sort of—?"

She nodded. "Right, the little bits of pottery. I was wondering if we couldn't scrub them up all nice and clean and then sell them, you know, as souvenirs? Fifty cents or a dollar, and the visitors can take home a little piece of history with them."

I blinked and then decided that she really was serious. Sell the artifacts? "Uh, well, can't do that, I'm afraid. The laws are pretty strict about these things and the fact that the house is on the National Register means you've got to preserve these things for the future."

I didn't expect the help I got, but it came from the best source possible. "And besides, Fee," Aden said, "we discussed maybe having a little exhibit, one of those glassed-in table cases, to show the visitors what we've been finding. The Chandler family descendants are very keen on preserving the historical trust, as well." And when Aden Fiske said something, you could pretty much count on it being the final word.

Everyone around the tables nodded, even Fee, who still didn't look convinced. She shrugged and bobbed her head up and down in an effort to put distance between her and the idea. "It was just a thought," she said.

I went on. "Well, as some of you might have observed, we've started opening a few test pits beside the house, the proposed location of the restrooms and gift shop. From what I've seen of the maps and documents I've been studying, this was the location of the wing of the house that burned down in the early part of the eighteenth century. It doesn't look to me like it was ever rebuilt, which I think is strange—"

"Why is that?" A man, the youngest person in the room besides me, probably in his thirties, spoke up. He had eye-catching good looks, very slim with brown wavy hair. I tried to remember his name from the short list Aden had rattled off for me: Daniel Voeller. It was worth remembering, I decided. I vaguely recalled that he was connected with the factory in the northern part of Stone Harbor up the coast from the Chandler House. It was a modern concern that had done a lot to bring employment to Stone Harbor by bidding for the assembly jobs of larger electronics companies—fairly low impact on the environment, lots of different work for the employees, and so far, very successful.

"Because a house as high-style as this one, belonging to people as wealthy as the Chandlers usually was built with elite English ideas about classical symmetry," I said. "There probably would have been wings on both sides of the house, the same number of windows on each side of the door, lots of geometry. You know, like Mount Vernon and Monticello were built later on in the century? Anyway, I'm surprised the Chandlers didn't rebuild it, but maybe I'll find out why as we work. We haven't yet reached the burn layer in every unit—the depth at which we could actually observe fire-altered soil, a layer of ash and charcoal, things like that—but we are closing in on it. And we'll also find out whether they had outbuildings of any sort nearby—barns, storage sheds, and the like. On one hand, the road has been in its present location since the house was built; the Chandlers needed a way to get into town and to get guests from their small dock up to the house. On the other hand, that side of the house would still be visible from the common, and therefore, the issue of aesthetics would certainly have come into play."

There were a few throats cleared here, and glances were being exchanged. I wondered what was going on.

Aden Fiske filled in lightly, "As there seems to be today as well. Our only neighbors to the south of us, the Bellamys, have again voiced concerns about the, ah, 'visual disruption' that they claim your work presents. In point of fact, they've asked whether you can't fill in your units and get rid of the blue tarps while they have their guests over next weekend."

I could feel myself slump; I'd met Mr. Bellamy once, and his complaints had been a nuisance as well as irrational, but this new one took me by surprise. Fill in the units, before the work was completed? That would be like gluing the marble chips back onto an unfinished sculpture. "I . . . really, it just isn't possible—"

Aden raised a hand. "No, of course not, and we would never ask you to. I have told them that we will put up some bunting or potted plants along the inside of our fence, as a neighborly gesture. But they do not seem to understand that we are well within our rights and their backyard doesn't even line up with ours, so there isn't really much to complain about."

"But you forget, Ade, that these are the people who wanted to live here for the view and the historical nature of the area, and then complain that there are tourists that want to come here in the summer for exactly the same reason." Bray Chandler showed a rare bit of humor and the smile did a lot for him. "They're capable of complaining about anything."

"First they were upset because they thought our old wooden fence—which would have shielded you from their view admirably—blocked their view to the north," Aden explained to me. "So when it came time to replace it, we discussed it with them and went for a coated chain link fence.

Nicer view, but now they complain because they can see the visitors on the grounds and insist that they didn't move here to have herds of people outside their front door, which is actually nowhere near our grounds. So don't worry about them, just be aware that they exist to make your life unpleasant."

This brought universal laughter, and I guessed that there was no love wasted on the Bellamys. I went on to explain that my work would be going on for another two weeks, that the finished report would be prepared within a few months, and that we were preparing a flyer to hand out to curious visitors. "If your guides are interested, we'll keep them updated with what we find, so that they can answer any questions about the site."

"I'm sure I speak for everyone when I say that we're all looking forward to learning about your discoveries and adding to what we know of Stone Harbor's history. No doubt this relationship is to our mutual benefit—" here Aden glanced around at the other board members, who nodded agreement "—to have someone of your caliber interested in our sites: We know we are getting the best for our properties, and it's possible that as work is needed on Stone Harbor's other historic properties, you'll be in a position to get some real professional benefit from the job."

I smiled and nodded thanks, but inside, my thoughts were racing—and so was my pulse. Was Aden really doing what I thought he was doing, essentially establishing me as the go-to person for conducting archaeological research in Stone Harbor? If he was, and it was clear to me that was exactly what was going on, this could be the basis for research not only on the level of the Chandler household but of neighborhoods, and the whole community of Stone Harbor, longterm research that could cover the whole range of questions, from first settlement to industrialization, and the whole population, from the lowliest fisherman to the wealthiest landowner.

Considering the number of two- and three-hundred-year-old structures still standing in Stone Harbor, with a good possibility of intact surfaces left to explore, this was a gift with a big red ribbon on the box. And although every archaeologist thinks that every project could potentially be the start of something big, longterm, and revolutionary, this really could be a shiny brass ring.

"Thank you, Aden. I'm certainly looking forward to working with you all." Which was a nicely ambiguous statement, possibly referring to either this project or the hypothetical projects to come after.

"Right," Aden announced, looking around. "I think that's about—"

Fee cleared her throat. "I think we have just one other issue to discuss, Aden? The one I brought up the other day?"

Aden made a face. "Oh, Fee, do you think it's necessary?"

She bit her bottom lip and faced his obvious reluctance. "I really do."

Aden turned to the others. "Fee is concerned about the security here. She thinks that our present security is insufficient and that our most recent hire, Justin Fisher, is not up to the job. Any thoughts?"

Daniel Voeller spoke up, his eyes hard and his words deliberately chosen and provocative. "And why is that, Fee? He's been on time or early every shift, there've been no incidents. Why, exactly, do you think he should be replaced?"

She didn't meet his glance. "I think he's just too young, is all, Danny. Not enough of a presence."

Aden looked around impatiently. If there were any others who came down on Fee's side, they were not speaking up. "Well, perhaps we'll give him another month, and see how he shapes up, shall we? That's enough for tonight, people. I'll see you all next week for the Chandler reunion meeting. Go home, get a gin and tonic, for God's sake!"

Everyone laughed, got up and stretched and shook hands, arranged to meet elsewhere, planned to get together for drinks, the way that people do who've been working familiarly with each other for years. Aden was in the thick of this, and as I packed up my notepad, I could hear him arrange for two cocktail parties and several barbecues. I noticed that his jokes, sometimes bawdy, sometimes barbed, were taken as marks of affection.

"Good evening. I'm Bray Chandler." The garden gnome introduced himself to me. "I found your talk of particular interest as I'm descended from Matthew Chandler."

"Really? And your family's been here ever since? That's so neat," I said. "Which one of his children are you descended from?"

"Nicholas Chandler."

I frowned, not remembering the name right off. "I'm not sure I. . . ."

"There are some sources that list him, some that don't." He waved his hand airily. "You know how these family genealogies can be."

"Oh, sure. I'll go back and check my notes. It's very nice to meet you, Bray."

Bray said he'd see me later, and Aden caught up with me in the hallway. He tried to speak, and then was interrupted as departing board members passed us calling good night. He waved but with an overexaggerated shrug gestured that I should follow him into the next room, where we could speak privately.

"I just wanted to catch up and tell you how much I am looking forward to watching you and your crew at work. I'm sure everyone tells you how they always wanted to be an archaeologist—"

"Yeah, but it's okay, it's nice to know people are interested in what you do," I said.

"—but I actually worked on a dig when I was in college, many, many years ago. In Greece, gorgeous place, all blue and white . . ." He grimaced and sighed, as if remembering just how many years ago it had been. "So while I would never want to get in your way, if there was a moment when I was free and there was some dirt to be sifted, well, I'd be delighted if you'd let someone show me what to look for. It would be a treat."

I nodded: The more he felt a part of the project, the better for us all. "I'd be happy to."

"Great." He rubbed his hands together. "I didn't want all the others pestering you, but I am glad I might be able to sneak in and help a little. RHIP—rank hath its privilege, you know, and I damned well make the most of it! You're only here for a few weeks. Do you have other plans this summer? More work, I mean."

"I'll probably be going up to Maine for a few weeks later on, to work on Fort Providence. It's an early settlement I've spent some time on before."

"Yes, now I remember the name from looking at your vitae." He frowned. "I seem to recall that there was some real unpleasantness up there. A news segment, some time ago."

I kept my face blank and looked out the window at the boats moored far out in the harbor. "A good friend of mine was killed. It wasn't really anything to do with the site or my work, not really." I still had trouble convincing myself of that fact, on some days. I swallowed. "Still, it's good to get up there, remember her and why she loved the place."

Aden was instantly contrite. "Of course, of course, I didn't mean to bring up any bad memories. I'm sorry I asked. In any case, it's good to know you've got lots to keep you busy this summer."

There was another awkward moment and then Aden led me down the stairs. "Oh, about the Chandler family reunion, on July Fourth? They would absolutely love it if you would do a little talk about your project here, before the big party. Now, you don't have to, of course, but I know they would just be delighted—"

"Oh, no problem, I'd be happy to," I said. Aden locked up the house with a key he returned to his pocket. He immediately lit up a cigarette and inhaled greedily.

"And you and your husband will join us for the dinner after. It will be a great feed. The Chandlers don't skimp when it comes to their food."

"Oh, thanks," I said. We were back outside now, walking the parking lot in front of the house. "Say, Aden? Can you tell me who owns the Mather House, offhand? You know, the abandoned place just to the north of here? I haven't found out who the present owners are, and I'd like to talk to them about doing some work there, sometime. You know, comparative stuff."

"I couldn't say, Emma, but if you—"

A car pulled up to the lot, and we watched a young man get out. He waved to Daniel Voeller, who, upon seeing him, quickly said good-bye to the remaining board members and brushed past us.

Aden leaned over to whisper in my ear. "That's Danny Voeller's Charles. Love's young dream." He rolled his eyes.

"I would really love to stay for the Chandlers' dinner," I said, ignoring his unspoken comment, "but my sister is visiting and I promised her fireworks on the Fourth. But the talk, that's fine."

"Bring her too, if you like, and we'll have fireworks here. Won't be a better seat in the house, unless you are on a boat."

I suddenly realized that Aden relished playing lord of the manor, and his humor and teasing were all part of that larger-than-life image.

"Okay, great, thank you, I'll think about it. Good night, Aden." I shook his hand and dug out the keys to my Civic, which I wished looked a little less rough than it did. A wash, at least, would have made me feel a little more respectable, even if it wouldn't have done any real good.

"Good night, Emma." He rapped the hood of the car with his knuckles as he walked by and called out to Justin, who was running up to us. "I'm heading out, Justin. You can finish closing up and set the alarms before you head out."

Justin was out of breath and looked unhappy. "Yes, but Mr. Fiske, I was trying to find you. I just took a call in the main office. It's Perry, ah, Ms. Taylor."

"What's wrong?"

I froze: Something in Justin's face told me it was bad.

"She's in the hospital. She was hit by a car!"

Aden went ashen. "My God, Perry! Is she hurt?"

Justin nodded, still winded. "Broken bones and bad bruises. But you don't know the worst of it."

"What worst, what's happened?" I thought that Aden wobbled a little where he stood.

Justin gasped out, "Ms. Taylor says . . . the car swerved toward her. Someone tried to run her over."

Chapter 2

I PULLED UP INTO THE DRIVEWAY OF THE FUNNY Farm, our nineteenth-century house, which, with all the renovation work we were doing, was getting funnier by the day. My heart rate had slowed down over the course of the drive across two towns, and seeing the old white farmhouse with its connected buildings, only about two years in our possession, had a lot to do with it. "Big house, little house, back house, barn," was the way the rhyme went, and the structures formed a courtyard on the driveway, with doors to each building leading out onto the gravel. It felt like a family compound, and that sense of security was what I needed most at the moment.

Relieved to see that the students hadn't come back from their weekend yet, I grabbed my briefcase and headed toward the back door of the main house when something made me stop. I couldn't shake the feeling that I was being watched, and when you live on a tertiary country road with no neighbors within a quarter mile, that is a very spooky feeling indeed.

I looked around, saw no one, then began to cross the drive when I felt compelled to stop again. Something drew my eyes down to the bushes by the side of the house and I saw what was disturbing me. A single yellow eye, bright as a lamp, was following me from the shadows; farther back I could just make out the slow twitch of the end of a tail betraying its owner's interest in my progress.

I relaxed, but only a little. "Evening, Quasi."

The big black and white coon-cat-mixed-with-who-knows-what didn't say a word, of course, but now that I was aware of him, I could hear his tail rustling the dead leaves under the shrubbery. Even though it had been a good long while since Quasimodo, a stray Brian had rescued a year ago, had actually tried to claw a chunk out of me, I watched him as I began to step onto the low back porch. He stared right back, his one good eye intent on holding my gaze.

Something was definitely wrong: I could swear that Quasi was grinning.

That in itself was warning enough, and I looked down just in time to avoid stepping in the remains of a squirrel left on the step. Whether it was deposited there as a tribute for Brian or simply messy eating, I couldn't have said, but I was ninety-nine percent certain that the cat was also hoping I would step in his leftovers. We have that kind of relationship.

"Nice try, Quasi," I called back to him, but all I saw was the disappearing snake of his bushy black tail as the cat slunk off into the undergrowth, thwarted. I nudged the former squirrel off the step for Quasi to finish later.

"Hey, Sugar!" I called, once inside the house. "Brian? Bucky?"

There was no answer, either from my husband or my sister. The red light on the answering machine was blinking and when I hit the play button, I heard my trainer's voice. "Good evening, Dr. Fielding. While you told me that you wouldn't be in for a few weeks, I would like to remind you that Krav Maga requires practice as well as mental preparation. I trust you are at least thinking through your moves during your break, and if you would like to join me for a session, here in the real world, I would be delighted to see you."

I frowned: Fat chance, Nolan. I already felt defensive enough on my own, at the moment, without more of the Israeli army's fighting techniques. I flung my case onto the table and promptly made myself a G and T with two lime wedges, and then found my way out to the front porch and the swing. It was practically the only part of the house that wasn't under construction or covered in power tools, sawdust, and dropcloths. Or graduate students, for that matter.

The cold condensation on the glass felt good against my forehead and after a healthy sip, I bit into the extra piece of lime; the sharp citrus bite helped clean out the bad taste the evening's events had left in my mouth; I pitched the lime skin over the porch railing—it might go well with squirrel—and rocked gently back and forth on the swing, letting myself relax and staring at nothing in particular in the field across the street from us. There were sturdy green stalks more than a yard tall coming up in the neat rows of furrows, and I realized the corn would need a lot more rain if it was going to make it through the season.

That was one of the things that I liked about Lawton, Massachusetts, where our soon-to-be-a-dream house was located. Wedged in between Stone Harbor and Boxham-by-Sea, it had most of their good qualities with few of the drawbacks. Although it was within commuting distance to Brian's work as a chemist at a pharmaceutical lab in Cambridge and mine at Caldwell College in southern Maine, it was still largely a matter of a central downtown and outlying farms, which gave it a country feel. It had been created as a town in the late eighteenth century, made up of former chunks of its two neighboring towns, but because it had only the tiniest of waterfronts, it was still quite rural. While they fought over tourist trade and waterfront attractions, people lived in Lawton at a slower pace, with just the first signs of gentrification starting to show. Brian and I only hoped that the fields that surrounded us would continue to provide fresh produce for the chic restaurants in those two towns, had for the ships in their harbors during the seagoing days, and wouldn't start to sprout condominiums or deluxe McMansions in the faux colonial style. Selfish, perhaps, but in spite of that hope, it was the long history of change with incoming waves of immigrants, from twelve thousand years ago to the present, that drew us to the area. Despite the increasing crowdedness downtown, it still felt as though there was room for everyone and everything, Vietnamese groceries next to the 1930s Federalist-style post office next to an eighteenth-century storefront housing a German deli that replaced a dry-goods store in the 1890s. Maybe that was an idealized notion—and heaven knew that the towns weren't without their strife, even ugliness at times—but I had hopes for the place, and what was the point of living somewhere if you didn't believe it would grow into your ideal?

It was really nice to be so removed from everything, listening to the early night noises begin to pick up, smelling clean dirt that I hadn't dug myself. And after what I'd heard about Perry, I was glad to be well away from people. Quasi might be a terror to the local fauna, but I wasn't so particularly fond of my own species at the moment.

Who'd want to run down poor Perry Taylor? Thank God she wasn't badly hurt, a broken arm and some bad bruises, but still. . . . I couldn't imagine what it would take for someone to intentionally point a pickup truck at a young woman and drive toward her with every intention of harming her, maybe even killing her. But I couldn't believe it was a drunk driver, not from what Justin had told us. It seemed to me that drunks were more likely to hurt someone out of some misjudgment, rather than actually aiming for you.

At that moment I heard car horns honking; the students were coming home to roost and it was time for me to put aside such morbid brooding. I waved and smiled, but inside, I sighed. Rather than have my crew drive down from Maine every day, about an hour each way, I had suggested that they camp out in the back part of our house. I didn't resent saving them the time—there's nothing like the grinding misery of a long drive after a hard day's work before you get to a shower and a beer and dinner—but I did rather regret giving up my privacy after work. It was my chance to unwind, forget about the day, to let my hair down, literally and figuratively. They'd all been grateful and good about taking short showers and keeping the crowded conditions as tidy as possible, so I couldn't really complain. They also seemed to be having a lot of fun.

Maybe it was just that I felt unable to get into the slumber party atmosphere that they were able to foster. I felt like I was like the mother who hears the kids' voices fade away and die into suspicious silence every time she goes into the party room to see how everyone is doing. Ugh.

I sauntered off the porch and across the drive to where they were unloading their gear.

"Hey, Emma! Good weekend?" Meg said. I could only tell it was Meg Garrity because I could just make out the platinum blonde spikes of her hair over the two big brown grocery bags she was carrying in addition to a bulging duffel bag with a broken zipper. "You had the meeting tonight?"

I took one of the bags from her and walked her into the back house, which was serving as a bunkhouse for the next couple of weeks. "Yep. Not everyone's convinced of the necessity of our work, but that's getting smoothed over. And the end . . . the end was a little more exciting than I think anyone expected."

I told her about Perry having been hurt. She frowned.

"Perry? Is she the older lady with the scary smile and the too-tight clown curls?"

"No, and a little charity please, if you don't mind. That's Fee you're thinking of. Perry's younger, a little preppy, brown hair always in the headband. I think you met a couple of times."

Meg grimaced as she set down her burdens. "Right. She was the one who said she thought the archaeology would be more interesting. More than just holes in the ground."

"That's the one. Well, Justin told us that she was out checking her mailbox before she was supposed to come in for the meeting and this truck came bearing down on her. At first, I guess she thought the driver was just pulling over to ask for directions—she lives in a big old place way out past the farmstand—but then she realized that the truck was speeding up and not slowing down. She got out of the way just in time, escaped with a broken arm and bruises."

"Shit." Meg stared. "Did she get the plates, see the driver, anything?"

"No, it was too quick. She only thinks it was a dark-colored pickup. Maybe an SUV, maybe blue."

"That's not much. Must have been a drunk driver?"

"Yeah, I guess." I didn't tell Meg about the discussion of the graffiti and the vandalism at the Tapley House. Without further proof, I had to assume that these were still coincidental. "Everyone else coming in?"

"Yep, just sorting out the various bags of clean laundry and whose junk food is whose. We stopped by the state liquor store on the way down—too bad they don't sell beer, it would save a stop—but we picked up some clear and some brown." Meg pulled out a large pour-size bottle of gin and another of bourbon and set them on the counter.

"That should last us the rest of the dig," I observed. "Not too much partying going on." Again I felt a pang of disappointment; everything seemed so tame, which was fine, but I couldn't shake the notion that I was an inhibition.

"No, not that kind of crew, this time," Meg agreed. "Everyone's pretty mellow. It's nice, for a change."

I was surprised to hear her say that. "How's Neal doing? Everything going okay up at the lab?" Meg and Neal Fenn had been living together since they'd met at the dig on Penitence Point a couple of years ago.

Meg smirked. "Just ducky. He's eating his heart out, stuck doing analysis up at Caldwell when the rest of us are digging. Especially when the weather is so nice."

"Well, that's a part of the job too," I said, not feeling a bit sympathetic. "You don't just get to dig up the goodies, you have to study them, or people will get the wrong impression. Think we're just greedy." I looked at Meg. "But you did encourage him, I hope, tell him he's on the road to his degree, all the hard picky work will pay off, etc.?"

"Nope. I rubbed his nose in it. Told him how gorgeous the site is, how all the contexts were perfect, and how we were finding the most amazing stuff."

"We haven't gotten far below the nineteenth-century levels yet," I reminded her, "but if you like whiteware, we have tons of really nice transfer print. That brick feature looks promising, though; it may be a foundation. But I suspect you didn't mention the ogling tourists, the cold scrutiny of the historical society members, and the crabby neighbors, right?"

Again, Meg made a sour face and shook her head. She unloaded another bag. "No. He wants to experience the field, he should be in the field."

"I can't wait until you start work on your thesis. It will be payback time for Neal, then."

"Who says we'll be together that long?" She tossed her head so that her rows of silver earrings clattered, but Meg's breeziness indicated to me that she said so, or believed so, and nothing was going to change that. The others came in, depositing backpacks and bundles of food on the floor.

I'd worked with them all before and had to admit, I had it pretty good as far as crews went, on this project. Dian had been at Penitence Point with me as well, and was almost ready to start her dissertation work next year. A little taller than Meg, and all dark curls and curves, Dian, although a fair student and a very nice person, always made me imagine that all she ever thought about was sex. She had a permanent grin that was half lazy leer and half cat-that-ate-the-cream. It was unnerving at times.

The two guys working with me were a little more innocuous than Meg's aggression or Dian's lasciviousness. Rob was a compact and jovial little gorilla whose on-again, off-again relationship with Dian didn't seem to worry either of them too much. Joe was tall, fair skinned, and vague, a dreamy first year whose black hair and eyebrows were the most definite thing about him. They followed us into the back house and dumped down their clean laundry and groceries onto the floor with all the carelessness of youth.

I looked around at the room in the little house where they were sleeping, instantly made less tidy by the mere presence of the students. "I'm sorry you're all out here in the boonies. I'd let you into the house to sleep but—"

"But you haven't got a floor in the dining room, and the living room is full of the stuff from the dining room, and your sister's in the spare room." Dian patted my arm. "Don't keep sweating it, Emma, we don't perceive it as some kind of political statement, with management sleeping in the big house and labor in the outbuildings."

I tried unsuccessfully to suppress a grin. "But Dian, that's actually how I meant it."

Meg waved my worries away. "We're fine. No bugs, no rain, fifteen minutes to work, no problem. We're going to get the grill started. Can we cook you anything?"

We had an old stone barbecue with a chimney out back. "No thanks, Meg. I think I'll wait for Brian and my sister to get home."

"So we're actually going to get to meet her?" Rob took a beer from the cooler and opened it. "What's your sister like? Do you guys look alike?"

"No, not at all. Bucky's a lot younger than I am, almost eight years." I was at a loss to describe her politely. "She's . . . more compact and athletically built."

"Shorter and flatter," translated Dian.

"Well, maybe a bit, five-five or so. I guess our faces aren't too different—my nose is way cuter, though, if anyone asks, and she's got that stubborn chin on her. Same hair and skin color, and freckles—neither one of us can be out in the sun without scorching—but her hair is short, it was shorter than Meg's at one point, but now it's down to her ears. It still looks a trifle rad, but Mother is delighted."

"And she's spending her vacation here because . . . ?" Meg was piling packages of ground meat, hot dogs, condiments, and buns onto Joe until he didn't have any arms left.

"She claims she wants to know what it is I do for a living. She's going to help out a couple of days." I frowned. Bucky had never been all that interested in archaeology, and I suspected there were other, more personal matters at hand that she would bring up only when she was good and ready.

"We'll see how that goes. Anyway, I suspect it's because she thought it would be nice if we fed her for a week or two. Cheaper than a real vacation."

"Way cheaper." Dian frowned. "Why do you call her Bucky?"

I fished the other wedge of lime out of my drink and worried it for a while. "She didn't like her real name when we were kids, so I gave her a new one. Too bad for her; I think I was looking for something that would reinforce what I perceived as her sidekick status."

"Does your mother call her that?" Joe asked from behind the pile of food.

"No, she calls her by her real name."

"Which is?" Dian was getting impatient with me.

"You'd better ask her that." I grinned. "I wouldn't want to give away any state secrets."

The students exchanged a glance, making faces. "Must be something awful."

"I'm not telling. She'll tell you if she wants to."

"Hey, guess who I saw this weekend?" Rob announced.

"Who's that?" I said.

"Alan Crabtree. He's working at the library again; I think he's going to go for a degree in library science. He said to say hi."

"How's he doing?"

"He looks real good. Seems happy. He doesn't miss the fieldwork at all. Likes air-conditioning in the summer." Suddenly Rob hopped up and began rooting through a backpack. "Before I forget, Em, I got the flyers photocopied like you asked."

"Thanks. We'll use this bunch, and if we need more, we'll get the Chandler House people to do more for us." I looked over the sheet and handed one to Meg. "So what else should I have put?"

Meg read, nodding. "You've got a nice summary of the site and what we're doing. What about a FAQ?"

I shrugged. "We can do that on the next batch, I guess. Top Ten Answers to Questions Archaeologists Get Asked. Anyone?"

They all chimed in, in varying tones of boredom and sarcasm because there were some days it felt like there really were only about a handful of questions we ever got asked.

" 'No, we didn't find any gold.' "

" 'No, we're not looking for dinosaurs.' "

" 'No, we don't get to keep what we find.' "

" 'No, we probably won't find any bodies—ah, skeletons, I mean.' "

Meg smacked Joe in the arm and they all looked at me, the giggling turning nervous and dying away. Everyone in the department remembered what had happened out at another site I'd worked on where there were actual bodies. Meg especially.

I shook it off. "Nope, not a chance of it. Sorry to disappoint you all. I don't suppose anyone has another lime, do they? I've just about killed this one."

It worked; the mood lightened, I got another chunk of lime to torture, and the students finished unloading the cars. They all went around back to start their dinner.

Just then Brian and Bucky came back from the grocery store. I suppose that it would have been easier to say simply that Bucky and I look a lot alike, but the truth of it was, I just couldn't see what other people did of our resemblance. Brian Chang and I have been married for almost seven years now, and even though he is a couple of inches taller than I, has dark brown hair that always needs cutting, and is almost always in a good mood, I really felt he and I were more similar looking than me and my sister, though no one else would ever have suggested that resemblance in a thousand years. I guess it's just the way that people who have been together for a long time start to rub off on each other.

I ran over, ostensibly to help with the bags, but it was really to kiss Brian. He tasted saltier than usual. I kissed him again, trying to figure out what it was.

"Hey sweetie, where you been?"

He knew what I meant. "We got pizza down by the supermarket."

That's what I tasted: sausage. "And you didn't wait for me?"

"We didn't know how long you'd be." Bucky dug a couple of plastic-handled shopping bags out of the back of the pickup.

"Still." I grabbed a couple of bags, and we walked up to the house.

"Next time," Brian said. He looked down at the side steps. "Bogus. Squirrel tartare."

"I know. Quasi left it as a booby-trap for me."

"You don't understand him. He's just a big muffin," Bucky said, closing the kitchen door with her foot.

"You can say that, you and Brian are the only ones who can get near him." I began unloading the groceries onto the counter, handing things to Bucky to put in the fridge. "When God was making nasty, scary animals, he came up with Quasi, but decided that cat was too damned mean. So then he came up with the Tasmanian Devil and thought it was much sweeter."

Bucky frowned, trying to make room amid the leftovers. "Naw. He's just a little, you know, territorial."

"Did you bring your stethoscope with you? I'd love it if you could check him out." Quasi and I had opposing ideas about going to the vet but had come to a compromise in the past year when he'd grown beyond even Brian's ability to wrestle him into a carrier: I wouldn't make him go to the vet and he wouldn't try to tear my spleen out. We settled on having Bucky check him out and give him his shots when she came up to visit. "I know you're on vacation and all. . . ."

"Sure, but I keep telling you: The day he lets you take him to your real vet, you'll know he's really ill."

"And that's your considered professional—" I went to pass Bucky the milk and suddenly a small bottle of water went whizzing past my face: Bucky had thrown it behind her without even looking. "Hey!"

I looked over and Brian had snagged the bottle handily. Neither of them had said a word to the other. "Hey," I repeated. "Someone could have gotten hurt!"

"You want some water, Em?" my sister asked.

"No . . . but take it easy, will you? We just patched up the walls in here and I want one room without big, gaping holes in it."

"Relax." Bucky opened her water. "You always worry too much."

She knows I hate being told to relax.

Brian drank some of his water and then came over to rub my shoulders. "Have you eaten?"

I was in no mood to be mollified. "No. I was waiting for you guys."

"Good thing I brought this for you then." He pulled out a small box from the last of the bags, marked Mario's. I could smell the sausage and snatched it away from him, all forgiven. "Let's go sit on the porch then?"

The porch was really the living room, this summer. Bucky finished in the fridge and then ran past me, so that she could claim a seat on the swinging bench. Brian sat down next to her and I found myself annoyed with both of them again. Then Brian reached over and poked Bucky in the side, and said, "Shift it over to the steps, kiddo. I want to sit next to your sister."

My storm clouds evaporated and I sat down next to Brian, who pulled me closer. Bucky made a face and sat on the stairs.

"How'd the meeting go?"

"Oh." I stopped smiling and felt my shoulders slump. "Okay." I told them about my presentation, that it had gone well, and then paused.

"What else?" Brian nudged me.

"Something happened to one of the board members. She was hit by a car." I fished a piece of onion from the bottom of the box.

"What?"

"Holy snappers!" Bucky gaped, then sat back and stared at the birds hopping around the field on the opposite side of the street.

I gave them a brief account of what I knew. That little furrow between Brian's eyebrows got deeper. "It doesn't sound like it's a good time to be on the Stone Harbor Historical Society board, does it?" he said.

Bucky looked up at us. "Why do you say—?"

"The vandalism at the Tapley House?" he said. "I read about it in the paper. And the flap about the bus route? Everyone in town is up in arms about that. That was in the paper too."

I thought about the proposed rerouting of the local bus, the one that took tourists from the train to the downtown and commuters from downtown to the train. If it moved to "preserve the aesthetic and historic qualities of the historic district," a lot of people were going to have to find another way across town to get their bus to work. And that included the workers at the Voeller assembly business. "Hmmm."

"This is where we're digging tomorrow, Em?" Bucky looked more interested than worried.

"No, we're at the Chandler House. None of this has anything to do with us," I said, as much for Brian's benefit as for Bucky's. I put my thoughts that had run along similar veins aside for the moment. The sun was taking its time setting and the bugs still weren't out yet. It was the perfect time to let your cares seep away.

Brian sighed and raised his bottle halfway to his lips when a thought struck him. "Ah, Emma? You did speak to Meg about leaving her you-know-what at home, didn't you?"

Brian was referring to the fact that Meg owned at least one handgun, something he wanted to keep as far from our house as possible. "Yep. She had no problem with it. We're going to be fine, hon."

"You girls be careful out there, tomorrow. That's all."

"Ha!" Bucky said. "I defy anyone to take on the Fielding girls and walk away with their full complement of body parts!"

"Or an unbruised ego!" I added. "Speaking of which, Brian, I left a copy of my book out on the table last night and I can't find it now. You seen it?"

"Nope. Try your office." He pushed back on the swing. "Hey, Bucks, did Emma tell you what I've been working on lately?"

"No. She doesn't know a Suzuki reaction from an Erlenmeyer flask."

"I do so know the difference," I said, but I didn't really. One was some kind of procedure and had nothing to do with the admiring glances one gets from a new motorcycle, and the other was a piece of glassware. "I'm just happier working on a cultural level than the molecular."

"Well," Brian said, "the biologists screened the natural products library against a protein implicated in Alzheimer's, and they found something that looks good. All they want from me now is to resynthesize the molecule in sufficient amounts to test in animals."

"Sounds like a bitch," my sister said.

It sounded like magic to me. Even though when Brian explained what he did to me, I still couldn't imagine manipulating nature like that. It left me in awe of what he did for a living.

"Yeah," Brian said. "It's gonna keep me and Roddy off the street for the rest of the year, that's for sure—"

I worked on my pizza, trying not to feel left out while they talked about things that were far beyond my ken. I nudged Bucky in the butt with my foot when she made a grab for the slice I wasn't quite done with. "Knock it off. Jeez, some day I'd like to be able to eat something without finding your paws in it."

"I thought you were done."

"Likely story. So, you gonna be ready to leave when we go tomorrow? And don't forget to bring your inhaler, just in case; the work's going to be hard. I don't want you to collapse and have an asthma attack."

She groaned. "What time again? Zero-dark-hundred hours?"

"Tch, we leave here at seven-thirty. Sun's up for hours by then. Wimp."

Bucky leaned against the railing and scrunched closed her eyes, pouting. "Wah. Yes, I'll be up then, just wake me when you get up. You never used to be such an early bird."

"When you get to my age, you learn a few virtues," I replied, primly. "Including how important it is to get a jump on the day."

Brian stared at me, incredulous. I put my finger up to my lips; I was still the polar opposite of a morning person, but Bucky was worse. And there is no point in having a sister unless you can torment her.

Chapter 3

I GOT UP EARLY THE NEXT MORNING ONLY BECAUSE I knew I needed five minutes by myself before the general rush hour. Most everyone in my acquaintance knew not to speak to me until the second or third cup of coffee, but there was no sense in needlessly taking risks. In the bathroom, I brushed my teeth and looked out the window blearily; I thought I saw Dian skulking across the yard, hair trailing wet tendrils, with something clutched in her hand. A towel. Although they had the use of our bathroom, the grad students had also rigged up a camping shower in the back yard where we had plenty of trees to ensure everyone's privacy. Just from the way she was moving, I knew something was up.

Sure enough, I heard a squawk and saw Joe, fully dressed, come shooting out from the woods, yelling, "It wasn't me! I didn't mean to see you!"

Meg followed, uninterested in Joe, dripping wet, utterly naked except for a pair of work boots, and completely unselfconscious. I would have run too, if I knew myself to be the cause of the look on her face. "Where is it, Dian!? I haven't got time for this shit!"

I rapped on the window and raised the sash. "Um, Meg? If you don't mind? It's a little early in the season for dryads."

The student peered up at the house, hand shielding eyes that were squinting against the sun. "Morning, Emma. It's Dian's fault, she stole—"

A towel came flying out from the underbrush and Meg caught it, wrapping it around herself, shaking her head. "You'll get yours, Kosnick!"

I heard a giggle come from the shrubbery and realized that I was struggling against the gravitational pull of no coffee. I shut the window and headed downstairs, where I could smell the coffee brewing. Brian handed me a mug and I drank, waiting for everything to come into focus.

"Good morning," I said at last. He came into focus and looked cute, for all he was awake already.

"Hey there. What was the noise outside?"

Good, he hadn't seen Meg. "Kids were fooling around. I told them to knock it off."

"You wake up Bucky?"

"No, I'll do it now. Give me another—"

But Brian had already filled another cup from the pot.

"You're so good to put up with me. With all this."

"I know. But the secret is that all you require is equal parts coffee and sex, so it's really not too difficult for me."

"Hmmm, I never thought of myself as quite that simple. Well, now that I've had the coffee part. . . ." I kissed him and gave him a friendly pat on the butt. "Good morning. Have you decided what you want for your birthday, yet?"

"We already got the presents—is yours charged up, by the way?"

"No, I'll go plug it in when I wake up her nibs."

"Good, just don't forget it when you leave. There's no

point in having a cell phone for safety if you keep leaving it home."

I nodded exaggeratedly. "Right, I get it already. I meant, what do you want to do for your birthday? Party? Dinner out?"

"I don't know, maybe. I'll think about it. Go on, now."

I could hear the students clambering into the kitchen and pause in silence until Brian said, "It's all right. She's had a cup and is making sentences." Then conversation began and I heard the fridge door opening and the tap running as breakfast was made.

I didn't bother knocking; I knew what would be waiting for me on the other side of the guest bedroom door. The door opened about halfway before it jammed on something, but I was able to squeeze myself in through the crack. Jeez, she'd only been with us two days, and already my sister had turned the guestroom into a pigsty. Clothes—clean ones, I presume—were strewn about the floor and chair, and my sister herself looked like she was strewn on the bed: on her belly, face nearly buried in the pillow, mouth open, one arm flung across her back, the other still resting over a book. I got a closer look and realized that it was my book, the one I'd been hunting for the night before. Bucky was drooling onto it.

"Jeez, Bucks! Have a heart!" I said out loud, but my sister sleeps like the dead, just like me. I kicked at the side of the bed and got a moan for my trouble. I set the coffee down on the nightstand, and carefully tried to lift Bucky's head from the book, but the pages were stuck to her face. I peeled the book away and dropped Bucky's head back onto the pillow; this time, I heard her snort and she pried one eye open, which gazed at me, full of resentment.

"—'acation," she mumbled.

"If you wanted to take a real vacation, then you shouldn't

have said you wanted to hang out with me." I looked at her, almost moved to pity. Almost. "You don't have to do this, you know."

"No, s'good, I'll—" Bucky suddenly pushed herself up, the other eye open now. Presumably her sense of smell had just woken up. "Gimme."

I handed her the mug as she groped for it, doing a pretty fair imitation of young Patty Duke at the dinner table in *The Miracle Worker*. "Well, look, whatever you decide, I'm leaving in about half an hour."

"N'kay."

"And Bucks?"

"Nnnnh?" came from behind the coffee mug.

I frowned and brushed at the damp spot on the crumpled page. "Lay off my books."

Twenty-five minutes later, Bucky came downstairs, which might be an overstatement of her active participation in the matter. At first I thought she was just treading heavily on the steps, but then I realized that she was really smacking into the wall on one side of the staircase, then into the railing on the opposite side. "Bucks? You up for this? Why don't you just stay in bed?"

She waved away my suggestion. "No, no, I'm good."

I would have believed her more if her eyes had been open, but she was dressed—after a fashion—in khaki shorts, an oversized sweatshirt, and sneakers. She was, however, using real words now.

"Coffee?"

"What happened to your other cup?"

"Gone." She shrugged. "I dunno."

I handed her another mug without a word as she slumped

down into the kitchen chair. She took a sip and mumbled something.

"Didn't catch that, kiddo. Got to open your mouth more."

"Least it's strong." She leaned back, the cup clutched precariously to her chest, eyes closed again.

Rob came down from the bathroom and looked at Bucky, and then at me. "Man, there couldn't be two of you like this in the same household, could there? How'd you ever get out the door in the morning to get to school?"

"Mother's voice was enough to propel us out the door," I said. "There was always the bus, homeroom, first, second, and third periods for napping. . . ." I took the coffee cup out of Bucky's hand. "Come on, if you're coming with me, you're coming now. Last chance to crawl back up to bed."

"No, I'm good, I'm coming."

"Don't be too far behind, you guys," I said. "Brian, I'm leaving."

"I'm right here," he said, popping up behind me. "I was just outside having a look at your car. It looks like it's leaking coolant again."

"Oh, man. Will it be okay to get to the site for a couple more days?"

"Yeah, I topped it off, so it should be fine. But we might have to accelerate our plans to shoot ol' Bessy sooner than we thought and find you some new transportation."

"Thanks. Just so I can get through the next week or two." I kissed Brian, then got interested in the procedure and stayed around for some more.

"Ahem." My sister was starting to sound impatient.

"Okay, we're off." I patted Brian's hand and went out. Sure enough, there was a puddle of green stuff under the car; Brian had thrown cat litter on it to clean it up before any of the local critters ate it and were poisoned. I threw my stuff into the back and waited until Bucky got her own seatbelt fastened.

My sister shook her head hard, as if she was trying to clear up her reception. "So, you going to give me the lowdown on what to do? What we're looking for?"

"Well, we can start with that. It's not something specific we're looking for, at this stage, it's more like we're trying to identify what's there. We will probably be finding the foundations to a wing that burnt down a couple of years after the place was built, and maybe we'll find out why they didn't rebuild it after. Other than that, we're identifying what remains are still present, whether the construction of a small restroom facility will destroy anything important. If we're lucky, we might find some neat information about the family."

She scratched her arm and yawned. "And you didn't get any of this from the documentary research you did? Didn't you tell me you'd spent a lot of time in the library and at the archives?"

"Well, yeah, but the archaeology gives a totally different perspective on things. You might find discrepancies between what they say they were doing and what they were really doing. For example, if we found that the Chandlers paid their taxes during certain years, but we find really cheap pottery that dates to those same periods, it might indicate that they were just scraping along, trying to keep the household going. You only get one side of the picture looking at one set of data or the other. Also, the documents usually only tell about significant situations or people, and in the case of Massachusetts in the eighteenth century—or anywhere else, for that matter—it would have been mostly what men were doing. Women generally only show up in the documents when they hit a life event—like being born, giving birth, dying, breaking the law—"

"I'm looking forward to that one myself," Bucky said.

"You know what I mean. You never get a whole lot about them, unless you are very lucky. The documents also tend to favor the very rich, the literate, the socially or politically powerful, and so on, so archaeology is also the best chance we have for learning about the poor, servants, slaves, children, the illiterate, and the like."

"Yeah, but why would you want to?"

I turned quickly to look at Bucky, but she was smiling. I looked back at the road, hitting the signal for the turn a little more vehemently than I usually would, and gnawed at the inside of my lip.

Driving and, more importantly, parking, were perennial problems in the coastal towns of Boston's North Shore, and Stone Harbor was no exception. The streets were for the most part narrow and twisting, built when most people went on foot or horseback or by water. Even on the main roads, the houses were pressed in close together, built when it was imperative to be as close to the center of town—and trade and business—as possible. The modern demands of the tourist trade and upscale housing with a water view had done nothing to diminish the competition for the best spaces down on the waterfront. I let these thoughts occupy me while I tried to think of a response to Bucky.

She tried to placate me. "I'm serious, Emma. Well, half serious. Why is it so important?"

"How about getting the full picture? How about knowing how the bulk of the population lived?" I paused to let a minivan take a left turn, then continued on, trying to transmute my fervent feelings into convincing reasons. "I mean, most everyone wasn't literate, male, white, well-off, right? Even if we only learn a little at a time, it adds to what we know about the past by a huge percentage, as far as I'm concerned. I mean, take the Chandlers. We know scads about *him*: Matthew Chandler was a judge and a magistrate, literally a bigwig in town. We know he was not trained as a military man, but he went on scouting expeditions with the other leaders in the town. We know something of where his commercial interests were and I suspect that they not only paid their taxes on time but also ate off some fairly high-falutin' dishes too. I don't know for sure, but maybe we'll find out."

I pulled onto the main street by the common and made the last turn onto the road for the site. I noticed that most of the houses were typical New England colors: gray, white, and yellow clapboards, with the occasional brick house thrown in for good measure. There was one, however, on the far side of the common, that always caught my attention. That was because it was striped with every color you could see on the other houses, and then some. I shook my head and resumed my lecture.

"But we don't know much about his wife, Margaret. She had, like, nearly a dozen kids who survived. Think about that, in a time when the leading cause of death for women was childbirth. We know she died when she was eighty-six, a tremendous age for anyone at the time. There's a chance she was literate: The town library has a book with her name in it. But what else? Was she a decent person? How did she use her position in town? Was she a hostess of renown or a shoddy housekeeper? Was she religious, how did she treat her servants, did she like living in Stone Harbor or did she wish she was back in England every day of her life? There are so many questions I could ask, and yes, it is important to know these things."

We made it down the long, tree-lined avenue, heading for the large colonial house at the end of the road, and I turned into the parking lot off at one side in the front and killed the engine. If I'd rolled down the window and listened carefully, I could have heard the waves crashing on the other side of the property.

"The best reason I can give you, Bucky, is that when you are studying anything, I don't care if it is history or archaeology or chemistry or whatever, you don't ignore more than half the population. You can't only look in the light for your lost keys, you have to forage a little further afield than that. What you don't know is going to shape what you do know. You see what I mean?"

She didn't. Bucky was fast asleep, her head against the passenger side window.

I thought about waking her, even thought about whispering "Ma's here" in her ear—that was always good for a reaction—but decided to let her sleep. I got out, got my stuff, and, after a moment's hesitation, shut the door quietly behind me.

I crunched down the gravel of the parking lot toward the house, waving to Fee as I walked by the window to her office. She didn't notice me at first, and I saw that she was talking on the phone; she looked distinctly worried. I paused, wondering whether anything was wrong, and then she saw me and a huge, false smile split her face. It was like watching a curtain rapidly descend as another set magically transformed the stage. I waved again and walked around the right side of the house, unlatching the gate and letting myself in.

This was one of the perks of the ungodly early hours that archaeology demands: seeing the site before everyone else arrived, being on the property when it was still quiet and largely deserted. I took a sip out of my travel mug and took it all in: the back of the house, with its small ornamental garden directly outside it, a slight drop-off, following the natural slope of the ground, cut by a short, wide staircase that led to the lawn below. The lawn was mown and well-trampled by the visitors who wanted to get the great view of Stone Harbor's harbor, to my right, and Sheep's Head Island, a little lump of rock and scrubby bushes, about a half mile from the shore and directly in front of us. I was pleased to see that the Chandler House people had put a sturdy picket fence well in from the bluff's edge, to keep visitors from straying too close to the edge. To my left, looking northwest up the coast, was a bit of empty wooded coast before you could see the jutting point of Lawton, which was like a splinter stuck between the larger harbors of Stone Harbor and Boxham-by-Sea. It was in this area that the Mather House was located. Now abandoned, it had been built by the Chandlers some time after their house, and it had taken on the name of the owners during the nineteenth century. I was eager to find out who owned it now, as it would be a real opportunity to compare two households from roughly the same period, especially as the first few occupants of the Mather House had been members of the Chandler family too.

To my right, only a meter or two from the side of the house, was the collection of squares and regular rectangles of blue tarps that covered my units, held down by rocks. These were on the right side of the house, and at the edge of the property, demarked on that side by a coated chain link fence. I could just about make out the infernal Bellamy's house across the street through the trees on our side. Ruin their view, indeed. I could hear the sound of dogs barking.

I took another sip of my coffee, walked back, and began pulling the tarps away to get a look at the units. I had to reach down into a unit and fish out one anchor rock that must have slid in overnight. Meter-square holes in the ground, at most maybe half a meter in depth, the different layers of dirt stacked up, the oldest at the bottom, the newest at the top, looking like an uneven sort of layer cake. Imagine a laundry pile, I always told my freshmen, where the things on the bottom are what got thrown in first, on Monday, and the things on the top were thrown in last. Now in archaeology you might not know how much time has passed between one layer and another, but you can usually assume that the stuff on the bottom is older than the stuff on top, unless there's been some catastrophic event—like landscaping or an earthquake—that's moved things out of order. Kind of like me rooting through the laundry on Thursdays to see if I have already worn my favorite shirt. By the way things looked here, based on the artifacts we were finding, we were probably looking at a late-eighteenth-century living surface in this unit, and Meg, as usual, was a bit farther down from that, possibly to the mid-eighteenth century, right above the burn layer that we knew was the result of the fire in the 1730s. We also had a brick feature there that looked suspiciously like a house foundation; perhaps it was the foundation of the wing that had been here once upon a time.

I squatted down to stare at one particularly interesting stratum, a layer of soil that looked like clean sand, and tried to figure out what it could be, when I heard something that I thought at first was a seagull. I then dismissed that notion in favor of a slipping fan belt, but was forced to the realization that it was a woman's voice. It was directed at me.

"Look, I can see you over there! Don't you think it's a little childish to be avoiding me like this? I really think we need to talk about this situation."

Situation? I looked around to see whether she wasn't actually speaking to someone else.

"Yes, you. Come on over, I'm not going to bite."

Maybe not, lady, I thought, but I might. I couldn't help myself; I didn't have any idea of what the problem was and I was already predisposed against her. I hadn't gotten a good look at her before now, but that didn't help either. Her demeanor was one of aggression uncomfortably married to cuteness. Her hair was a frizzy, nondescript brown, cut short in a way that did nothing for her round face; some of it was caught up in a pink scrunchy on top of her head. Her stocky posture was like that of a bulldog, her jejune bangs and top-knot reminded me of a Shih Tzu, and the way she couldn't quite keep her mouth closed, showing her pointy little teeth, was distinctly puglike.

I got up and dusted myself off automatically even though it was still too early for me to have gotten dirty. "How can I help you?"

"Claire Bellamy." She didn't offer her hand, but jerked her head back toward the house across the road. The sound of large dogs barking loudly seemed to continue nonstop. "I live across the road there, and your students have been caus-ing a real disturbance."

"I beg your pardon?"

"You're the archaeologist, right?"

"Yes, I'm Emma—"

"The way your students were carrying on out here this morning really is unacceptable. It's starting to affect my quality of life, more than that, it's beginning to take a toll on my children."

"I beg your pardon? My students? My students haven't even arrived yet, they were still at home when I left, maybe twenty minutes ago."

"Well, I don't know who else you think it could possibly have been. All I know was that there was all sorts of racket out here about five-thirty, by this side of the house. Where you've been working. Then there was all this noise, tires squealing, and by the time I made it to the window, I saw a dark car taking off down the road. If it wasn't your students, who else could it have been?"

She was nuts. "Mrs. Bellamy, it could have been anyone." I recalled that Perry had been hit by a dark-colored vehicle. "This is a public road—"

"And I still don't understand that, if ours is the only house on it—"

And yet you'd probably complain if it wasn't plowed first thing in the morning during the winter, I thought. "The Chandler House is on it too. Maybe someone got lost and was trying to turn around; it could have been kids fooling around, it could have been a lot of things, but I know for a fact it wasn't my students. None of them has a dark car, none of them is even here yet." And fully one-fifth of my crew was stark naked at that hour, so I know she didn't even have her car keys on her, I concluded to myself.

Her eyes welled with tears, reminding me of those pictures of sad clowns. "You don't understand, this is just not acceptable. We moved here for the quiet and all we get is noise and trouble. It's not fair. If I'm not even allowed to sleep in my own house—"

I watched her chin quiver and I bit my tongue, trying to keep from saying what was really on my mind, that her dogs barking and her attitude were probably more than half the problem. "I'm sorry you were upset, and I'm sure that it was vexing to be woken up, but I assure you, it was nothing to do with me. Now if you'll excuse me, I have to get back to work."

"Wait!" she called after me. "You've been told, haven't you, that you'll have to get rid of all this mess by next Saturday, right? I can't have my guests over with *this* going on over here."

I recalled the discussion about this topic from last night's meeting, and decided to pretend I hadn't heard her. That wasn't an option, however, as I was rapidly learning what was meant by the expression "shrill as a fishwife."

She pressed on. "You are going to close up these holes, right?"

"I haven't been told anything of the sort. As far as I understand the matter, the board is quite pleased to go along with our original agreement, which means that I'll close up here when I have finished my work, in about two weeks. That's not a very long time and in any case, you really wouldn't want to burden yourself worrying about what is going on with someone else's property. Unless your guests are going to be hanging out in your side yard, next to the trash bins, I doubt they'll even notice that there are holes in the ground over on this side of the street. And if they did, you could use it as a conversation point. They might find it interesting."

She put her hands on her hips. "You know this conversation is really pointless—"

Hallelujah. My thoughts exactly.

"—and I'm just going to have to bring it up with your boss."

She paused and waited to see how I would react and then I realized that she was talking about Aden Fiske and not the dean or someone at Caldwell College, where I teach.

I nodded solemnly. "I think that's really for the best. I'm sure you and he will work something out. But in the meantime, what are you going to do when the real disturbance starts? What are you going to do when they start construction on the gift shop?"

Mrs. Bellamy looked suspicious, as though her victory had just been snatched away from her. "What do you mean?"

"If you're upset now, what will happen when a construction crew comes in here and starts putting together a little shed for gifts and restrooms and that sort of thing?"

Her mouth moved for a few seconds before she could make the words come out. "They can't do that!"

"Why not? They seem to be doing it now; you didn't get

a notice about this from the city, to come to a planning meeting and discuss it?"

"There was something—but no one said that *this* was going to happen! This is incredible!"

That's how houses get built, I thought. I shrugged. "I guess you should have spoken up then."

Trembling anger made Claire Bellamy resemble an irritated Shih Tzu even more, and when I turned away to get back to work, I could feel her eyes boring little holes into my back before she finally huffed and went away. I was just glad that Bucky was in the car asleep, or that wouldn't have gone as smoothly as it did: Bucky had no sense of tact. Then I was kind of sorry that my sister wasn't there for the show; I always envied her ability to combine wit with her sharp tongue. It would have been fun to watch, even if it wasn't good politics, an immature part of myself complained. Nice fireworks before Independence Day.

I squatted back down to look at what Meg was in the process of uncovering, swallowed the last mouthful of my cold coffee, then stood up again with a frown. If there had been someone out here, early in the morning, causing a "racket" as Mrs. Bellamy called it, what were they doing by the side of the house? More than that, had they been doing anything to the site?

I pulled the rest of the tarps back, but nothing appeared to be amiss, apart from the unit where Joe was working. There were two slight concavities in the side of one, near the top, and I realized that Joe had been sitting on the edge of his unit to take notes, compacting the soil underneath him and leaving an impression of his bum. There was no real harm yet, but I'd warn him to sit outside the unit, so the wall wouldn't collapse as the soil dried out. Nothing wrong here, so I strolled around the side of the house, where there were some trees and bushes planted to conceal the maintenance

shed and trash bins. This was where we'd located our spoil
heaps, but there was nothing wrong there either, no trash, no
beer bottles that might have been flung by teenagers partying down by the water, no sign that the shed had been at all
tampered with, which was good, because that's where we
were storing our tools and screens at night. I heard Bucky
call my name, her voice coming from in back of me, by the
units.

"I'm back here, Buckminster. I'll be out in a second." I
noticed something by the far edge of the shrubs, almost to
the front of the house. It wasn't anything more than an odd
break in the shadows, a little more solid than I expected to
see there, but I thought I'd have a look in any case. As I
walked past, dozens of little sparrows flew out of the bushes
where they'd been hiding, nesting, sleeping, whatever.

"Sorry guys," I said. "I didn't mean to get you up at this
ungodly hour too. Though technically it's in your contract to
be awake by now."

The break in the shadows resolved itself into a patch of
mottled pale light and utter black, far too definite to be a
shadow, the breaks too regular. Then I realized that the mottled white was actually part of someone's lower leg, the flesh
that showed between a dark sock and where the trouser rode
up. Even at that point, it took a moment before I really understood what I was looking at: the laced black shoe, the
sock, the skin of a man's calf, the hem of a trouser leg.

"Emma? Where are you?"

—The leg of the man continued and I realized that someone was lying face down, a hand palm up, fingers slightly
curled showed now. A sickly sweet smell hit me and then I
realized that the sound of buzzing insects was not inside my
head—

"Emma? Do you need help with the tools?"

And then I saw the darkened stains in the soil around

Justin's fair hair and was glad that I couldn't see the rest of his face, concealed in the underbrush. I stepped back, swallowed, swallowed again, and thought about being sick—What should I do?

"Emma, cut the crap, where—?"

That woke me up when nothing else might have. "Bucky! Don't come back here!"

"What?" I could tell that she'd stopped; it must have been something in my voice.

"I mean it! Don't come back here!" I turned and stumbled back past the bushes, startling another flight of sparrows from their roosts with a rustling and low whistling. My legs felt rubbery, as if they hadn't gotten the message that I wanted to be out of there and wanted above all else to keep my sister from seeing what was back there. A breeze picked up and I shivered, all of a sudden realizing that I'd broken into a sweat. I couldn't feel my hands and my mouth felt as though it was stuffed with cotton. I swallowed again and picked my way across the spoils heap, catching my foot on a large cobble and almost tripping into Bucky. I saw my sister's eyes go wide and wondered what I looked like.

It took me a moment to articulate anything of the horror I'd just seen. "Bucky, you . . . don't go back there."

"Emma, tell me what's wrong!"

"There's a body . . . a security guard . . . Justin. He's back there."

I couldn't actually say the words out loud. Bucky looked at me, forehead wrinkled with concern, chin pulled back with reluctant realization, eyebrows arched, asking the question.

I nodded. "We have to call the cops. Right now. He's been killed."

Chapter 4

I'D SAID THAT I THOUGHT JUSTIN HAD BEEN KILLED
before I could figure out just how I might know that he
wasn't simply dead. I didn't have time to go back over what
it was that I'd seen that made me choose that word rather
than another, because it was exactly at that moment that the
graduate students arrived; I could hear them chattering and
the sound of car doors slamming. Gathering myself, trying
to keep a bad situation from getting worse, I turned to Bucky
and held her by the shoulders.

"Stay here. Don't let anyone else through, and for God's
sake, don't go back there yourself. I'm going in the house to
find a phone."

Bucky was ashen. "Okay."

I hustled around to the other side of the house, thinking
how I hated seeing my sister look like she did, and almost
ran into the four members of my crew. "Hey, Meg, you guys.
Do me a favor. Could you wait out by the cars for a minute?
There's . . . there's been an accident." Even as I said the

word, I knew it was an easy mistruth. "I think it would be a good idea if we didn't start right in to work. It might be a lab day, today."

"But the weather report didn't say anything—" Meg began, frowning. "Emma, what is it?"

The smiles froze, then melted off the faces of the rest of the crew as they realized that something was really wrong.

"It looks like Justin. I'm pretty sure he's dead. I'm going to call an ambulance and the police."

"You're joking," Meg said, in a tone of voice that suggested she knew otherwise.

"Oh, man," Rob said.

Joe didn't say anything, but swallowed hard.

There was a short silence. "What do . . . what should we do?" Dian asked.

"Just don't go back there. Wait for me by the cars. I'll be with you just as soon as I know what's going on. I've got to—" I gestured toward the house.

"Right, yes, go."

I went in the front door, which was, thankfully, unlocked, and headed straight for Fee's office. She greeted me with another bright smile, and it made me tired to see it, as it felt so much more like a barrier than a welcome.

"Good morning, Emma—" she trilled.

"Fee, I've got to use the phone right away. There's an emergency."

Bless Fee, she shoved the phone right toward me without a second's hesitation. "What is it?" she asked as I began to dial.

"I think Justin is dead."

"You can't be serious." She put down the file she'd been reading.

"Yes."

"Dear God." Fee crossed herself. "Where is he?"

"He's—hello? I need some help, right away!" I told the 911 operator. "Police and an ambulance—I think he's dead. Pulse—no, I didn't get a chance. Stone Harbor, the Chandler House, two Chandler Street, the far end of the common off Water Street. I don't know how. I don't know when—what? Well, it's"—here I snuck a look at Fee, then turned away slightly—"it's the smell that makes me think so. Emma Fielding. Right, I'll be here. Please. Hurry."

I hung up and saw how strangely Fee regarded me. "I'm okay," I said. "I guess I'd better go wait outside, for the police." I lowered and rubbed my head, trying to collect my wits, trying not to think about poor Justin.

"Emma!" Fee almost shouted. I looked up, alarmed.

"What?"

"I'm sorry," she said quickly. "I thought you were—" She darted forward and closed the file that had been sitting open on her desk, sweeping it away from me, keeping her gaze level with mine the whole time. "I thought you were going to pass out there, for a minute."

It was such an obvious lie and she was so clearly trying to keep me from seeing what was in that file that I was at a momentary loss how to answer. "No. No, I'm fine. I'll just go. . . ." I hooked my thumb toward the door and tried not to stare at the file that she held, awkwardly, casually, behind her hip. "I guess you'd better call some folks. Aden, I suppose, and—"

"Oh no! Aden won't like this at all," she said quickly. I was struck by the dread in her voice, which seemed to be more fear of Aden himself than a reluctance to share the bad news.

"I don't think anyone will like it," I said. What was up with her? "But I think it's best."

"No, of course, you're right." She began to well up. "Goodness, Justin. This is so—"

"I know. I'll be outside."

As I shut the door behind me, I could already hear the sirens in the distance. As I made my way out the front door, I wondered what in the file was so secret. Concentrating, I recalled an unclear image of names and numbers, but I hadn't been thinking about it, hadn't been focusing on it. Was it telephone numbers? Social Security Numbers? Street names or people's names? I shook my head; I had no idea what it was Fee was trying to hide from me. I looked over my shoulder and saw her place the file into a buff-colored filing cabinet, which she locked before she picked up the phone.

The sirens drew closer, and I could see a flash of blue lights as they came down the long avenue to the house. I held up my hand, as if they wouldn't find their way to the imposing brick structure on their own, and waited for it all to begin.

It seemed to take an eternity. I had the most unappetizing sensation of dissociation; my head felt as though it was about ten feet above and to the left of the constricted knot of my stomach, all stretched out and like one of the drawings of Alice in Wonderland by Tenniel. The dizziness that had been creeping up on me was firmly situated now, a feeling that my bones had shrunk away into nothingness, leaving a hollow core that would not support me if I stopped concentrating on standing upright. I rubbed my fingers together, trying to chase the cold out, but they were slick with sweat and I couldn't generate any friction to warm them.

Bucky was still back there.

The police cars were parked, and I was aware of someone getting out. All I knew was that I couldn't leave Bucky alone any longer, so I said, "I called, he's back here," and hurried around the house the long way around.

Bucky was where I left her, now fully awake, gray as the oversized sweatshirt she clutched around herself, and staring fixedly at some point past the spoils heap. She started when I called her name, and I knew I shouldn't have left her by herself for so long.

"Are you okay?" I asked.

"Yeah. Fine." She frowned and shrugged my arm off her shoulder. "Cops here?"

I stepped back and stooped to check the knot on my bootlace. "Yeah, right behind me. I just wanted to make sure you were all right."

"Yeah, well, I didn't see anything, I didn't do anything. I just did exactly what you said."

I straightened up. "Good. That was good."

"You're okay?" she asked.

"I'm not hurt or anything."

"Good."

"Okay, which one of you put in the call?"

It was then that I got a look at the officer for the first time. He was young, with a blond crew cut that would have made him look even younger if it weren't for the nearly palpable aura of authority that he radiated. That reminded me of Justin and I felt my eyes start to well up. I tried to focus and looked at his nameplate: Officer Lovell.

I raised my hand when I had gotten a grip on myself. "I did. Justin's back there, past the spoils heap—"

"The what?"

"The . . . pile of dirt right there. He's past that, under some bushes."

He gave me a stern look. "Did you touch anything?"

"No, nothing."

"Is this the only way in?"

"Pretty much. We have to walk all the way around the house to get here; we used to just cut through a space in the shrubs at the front, but they asked us not to do that. It detracted from the experience, was what Fee said."

Lovell glanced at the space I indicated, which was just narrow enough to slide through sideways, if you really wanted to. Most people wouldn't want to. "Okay, that's still a possible entrance though. Did you check his pulse?"

"No, I didn't get close enough. I . . . the smell. . . ."

He cut me off with an abrupt gesture that suggested he was afraid that I might throw up or start crying or something worse. "Okay, okay, never mind. Stay put. You," he indicated Bucky. "Give your statement to Officer Hill over there. I'll be right back." He picked his way carefully across the uneven mounds of dirt and was lost in the shrubbery.

It was then that Ted Cressey showed up for work. He was about five ten, narrowly built, tidy little hands, and a head full of graying hair. His brown trousers and white shirt were both pressed, and the shirt was tucked in with care. His face reminded me of a wood carving that hadn't been sanded all the way down, a little rough, a little lined, with good teeth that showed when he smiled. When he saw the police, he stopped in his tracks and almost turned around, then caught himself, and asked Officer Hill what was going on. He looked over at me and said something I couldn't hear.

Lovell returned from Justin, looking sober.

"Do you know who he is?"

"His name's Justin Fisher. He's a security guard here at the house."

"Know him well?"

"No, just to say hi to, talk to. I gave him some advice about a paper he was working on in one of his classes."

"Who are you? You work here too?"

"My name's Emma Fielding. I'm working here now, contracting, as an archaeologist, but I teach full time at Caldwell College in Maine."

Officer Lovell looked up from his notes. "You live in Maine?"

"No, I wish. I live over in Lawton."

He frowned. "And what's wrong with Lawton?"

I was surprised by this. "Nothing, nothing's wrong with Lawton. It's just . . . my husband and I moved here almost two years ago, it's halfway between our jobs. We like Lawton fine, but it's still a long haul to work."

Lovell returned to business. "Right. What time did you find . . . Justin?"

"I got here about seven-forty-five. It was just after that." Then I remembered my conversation with Claire Bellamy. "No, it was a bit longer, say five minutes or so? I was having a look at the units, I had a talk with the neighbor—" Not a very nice talk, I recalled, but that put me in mind of something else. "She was complaining about the racket that my students and I were making out here at five-thirty, but I had to tell her no one from the project was out here by then. It had to be someone else."

"Where's the neighbor live?"

"Just over there, across the road."

He followed the direction of my hand pointing. "Okay, well, the neighbor will be our next stop."

Officer Hill joined us as he said that, leaving Bucky where she was and having sent Ted to wait out front. I realized that these two would be the first two in a long line of official visitors to the site today. I also realized that Claire Bellamy would not thank me for directing the police to her. It would negatively affect her quality of life. I found myself hard pressed not to take a little satisfaction from that.

"Oh, I know them," Hill said. "She's got us on speed-dial."

"Yeah?"

"Like you wouldn't believe. Every little thing. They've got a couple of big dogs over there, poodles or something."

"Poodles?" Officer Lovell didn't look convinced.

"I'm telling you. Big mothers, and jumpy, too. Keep an eye out, is all I'm saying."

Lovell turned back to me. "Okay, a few more questions here."

After he finished, I gave him my address and telephone number. That's when the ambulance arrived and the crime scene unit and things started getting crowded around the site.

A detective in plainclothes also arrived, conferred with the two uniformed officers for a minute, and looked my way. They talked a little more, and for the sake of not asking Bucky again if she were all right and for something to do, I began to size up the detective. He was a big man, over six feet and built like a tree trunk. He was wearing a sports jacket in a nice summer weave of light brown wool over a yellow shirt and tan trousers, with shoes that spoke of careful selection. I wouldn't have noticed that he was just starting to get a little thick around the middle but he pushed his jacket back to rest his hand on his hip. I guessed the clothes weren't really expensive—they weren't on the first line of fashion, but fit well and suggested an interest in a stylish appearance that didn't seem to match the workaday wear that I was expecting. His face was long, broad, ruddy, and creased with wear and care; a wide brow gave him a look of concentration and disapproval, or at least skepticism, and the lines alongside his mouth hinted at jowls that might come with another fifteen or twenty years. He was probably in his late forties or thereabouts. His hair was dark brown with a lot going to gray; there was plenty left though the widow's peaks were probably getting higher every year, but there was no need of a comb-over yet. A few locks that fell forward suggested a boyishness that wasn't present in the rest of his demeanor.

He caught me staring and came over. "I'm Detective Bader. I understand that you were the one to find the body?"

"Yes." It must have been nerves on my part, because I

blurted out the first thing that came into my mind. "I've got my crew out front, waiting to work."

He shook his head and I felt stupid. "I would make other plans, if I were you, for today at least. I've got some questions for you."

"Okay."

"You got here about seven-forty-five? Did you notice anything unusual? Anything out of place?"

"Mmm, no." I frowned. "One of the rocks we use to hold down our tarps had slid into the unit, that's all."

"Oh?"

"This one." I indicated the rock with my toe. "Well, it had been fine last night. There's no particular reason it should have moved. Sometimes dew or rain will weight down the tarps and drag them in."

We all looked at the rock. It was a big rounded cobble that wouldn't have moved easily on its own.

"Who is allowed back here?"

"Back here? The grounds are open to the visitors during the day, there are landscapers who come—"

"During the day, right. I mean, who is allowed in this fenced-in area?"

"Well, no one, really. My crew—they're all out front— sometimes some of the staff come back here, while we're here, to see how we're doing. And sometimes they bring VIP visitors, to show us off. So besides them, the staff, and my crew, no other visitors, as a rule." I started thinking of the multitudinous footprints, and wished the crime scene specialists good luck: The soil was dry and dusty and might have held a clear track for a short while before it was disturbed by someone else, or a breeze, or the squirrels.

"Was the barrier secured when you arrived?"

"Secured might be too strong a word," I said. "We pull the sawhorse across the gap to keep the tourists out during the day; at night, the place is about as sealed off as the rest of the grounds—"

He looked around at the low chain link fence and grimaced. "Which means anyone interested in getting into the yard could just hop the fence."

"Well, there's really nothing in the yard that anyone would want. Most people looking at our work mistake it for gardening or drainage or repairs or something; they generally think of archaeology in terms of huge areal excavations near pyramids. The Chandler House is alarmed, as far as I know. I don't know whether that was tripped or not. Fee would know."

"Fee?"

"Fiona Prowse. She's one of the employees. Does some tours, mostly does the books, does a bit of everything here. Her office is in the front of the house."

"She was here when you got here this morning?"

"Oh, yes. She was on the phone; I waved but she didn't see me at first." Didn't see me because she was too upset, I thought, and then she smiled that big phony smile of hers.

He nodded and scribbled down something on his pad. "She's here now?"

"Yes, so far as I know."

We went on and on, mostly about our schedule, when I'd left last night, that sort of thing. Finally, we came back to what I knew about Justin.

"I didn't know him well. I knew he wanted to be a history teacher. He was a really nice kid." I felt around in my pocket for a handkerchief.

"Some would say you're not much more than a kid yourself," he pointed out.

I wiped my nose. "I'm at the age where I savor getting carded at the liquor store."

At that moment, the crime scene technicians showed up,

a few casting wary glances at me, curious looks at the excavations and bunched-up tarps. One stopped, telling the others to go ahead.

"You an archaeologist?"

I was taken aback. "Yeah. How did you—?"

"Stuart Feldman." He pointed to the trowel I had stuck in my belt loop. "I worked on a couple of digs during undergraduate, out in California. I was going to be an archaeologist for a while, when I was a kid, but that was before I got caught up in the technical side of things. Do you know Dick Johnston?"

"Only by reputation. His work is a thousand years earlier than mine and three thousand miles away."

He shrugged. "Well, it was a shot. What are you working on here?"

Detective Bader answered for me. "She's working on answering questions for me. She's the one who called us in."

Feldman snapped his gum. "No kidding? You take any pictures at the end of the day yesterday?"

The light dawned on me. "Yes, I think we did! We were just starting to show up the top of the brick feature—I think it's a foundation wall—and we shot a couple because the light is at its best here in the late afternoon. I dropped them off to get developed last night!"

Bader looked startled. "You have pictures of the . . . site? From late yesterday?"

I nodded excitedly. "I even have a couple of record shots of the surface from before we started, if that helps."

Feldman explained to Bader. "They do that sometimes, just as a matter of course, to record what a site looked like before excavation. They also take pictures throughout the process of the dig, but especially if there was something there worth recording. They might show anything that changed since they left last night."

Detective Bader turned to me, with something an optimist might have taken as approval. "Good. Can you get them to me as soon as possible?"

"They'll be ready tomorrow morning," I said.

"Why don't you stop by here tomorrow?"

I said I would, and asked if it was okay to dismiss the crew.

Bader nodded. Lovell returned and began to cordon off the site; Hill went across the street—to talk to Claire, I assumed. Good luck to him.

Bucky and I walked around to the front, where the students were hanging around the truck they came in. Today it was Meg's big red Chevy, the one with the personalized TRK GRRL license plate in front, and since it was registered in Maine and not Colorado, where she'd come from, it made me think she was planning on sticking around for a while with Neal, no matter what she said. The truck was as big as Meg's attitude and all out of proportion to her actual height, which was just five foot four.

"What's the scoop? What's happened?"

I filled them in briefly. "So here's the plan. You're going to head back to the house with the artifacts we've found up to today—the rest of the bags are in the backhouse at home. It's a wash day, for now. I'm sorry we have to waste the sunshine, but I'm hoping we'll be able to be out here again tomorrow. I'm going to stick around for a bit, see what they need from me, keep an eye on the units, and then run some errands. Bucky, you head back with them, okay? You can either hang out, go to sleep, or work on the sherds if you want."

"Why can't I stay here?"

"There's nothing for you to do here. I probably won't be long in any case."

"Whatever. I'll work on the sherds then."

This brought a murmur of surprise and approval from the crew. The work was dull and tedious, and it took a far better attitude than we collectively had now to do it happily. Another set of hands—and fresh, unjaded ones, at that—was something to celebrate.

"C'mon, Bucky," Meg said. "I'll show you how it's done."

I could see Meg getting a slight dose of the Chin; when Bucky stuck out her chin at that particular angle, it took me right back to our childhood; she was digging in, ready for conflict. "Great. But call me Carrie, okay?"

"Emma calls you—"

"Yeah, well, she's the only one and someday God will punish her for it."

"What's Carrie short for?"

Bucky shook her head, making a face like someone who'd just stepped in dog mess. "It's short for Charlotte, but just call me Carrie. I think my name is really gruesome."

"Okay, Gruesome. I'll show you how to do the lab work."

They collected their tools and lunch bags when another large truck pulled up next to us, also filled with tools and young people dressed for outdoor work. I noticed that Dian and Meg brightened considerably and that Rob and Joe rolled their eyes. Bucky looked over as two guys in cut-off jeans, company T-shirts, and work boots hopped out of the cab. For the first time that morning, my sister smiled with genuine pleasure. The landscapers were here.

"Morning Emma," the driver called.

"Morning, Jerry." I hustled over to the truck before they could start unloading, and explained what was going on. "You might want to check with the cops first," I concluded.

The smiles faded from their faces, replaced by stunned looks. "You're kidding me. But he's such a good kid—" Jerry said. He rubbed his hand over his face. "Okay, thanks. We'll go see what we can get done today."

"Get his phone number, Emma?" Dian asked as I returned to where the crew was standing.

"Not exactly."

"She's completely oblivious to other men since she got married," said Bucky.

"I'm not actually shopping," I said. "Especially not for landscapers." I left the field wide open for Bucky.

"Just leafing through the catalogue," my sister shot back.

"But I wouldn't go for a rake like Jerry," I replied.

"Too much of a weed," Bucky said.

"You're the one who likes her men so seedy—" I announced.

Meg finally couldn't take it anymore. "Enough with the puns already. Dear God, it's not fair."

I felt a little guilty about making jokes, but the speed with which Bucky responded assured me that we both needed to think about something besides the morning's events. I sent them off and then returned around the back to see if there was anything else I could help Detective Bader with.

He started right in again, as if there had been no interruption. "Have you noticed anything around here that might suggest why Mr. Fisher was killed?"

"There've been a lot of, well, I wouldn't call them problems, but let's say issues between the Historical Society and the town, lately."

"Like what?" Detective Bader appeared as if he knew the answer already, but I told him what I knew of the vandalism at the Tapley House, the proposed rerouting of the bus, and the friction between the Bellamys and the Chandler House. I also mentioned what I'd overheard in the board meeting, about Fee not thinking that Justin was suited to the job. I didn't think it was related, but he wrote it down anyway.

"You never know," he said as if reading my mind. "It

could be anything. We won't know until we dig around a little."

I guess that makes two of us, I thought. I was starting to lose my focus.

"It might be something to do with Mr. Fisher here, nothing to do with the Historical Society."

"Oh!" I remembered Perry's broken arm and told him about the incident. He frowned.

"That's rather more serious, isn't it? I'll look into that. Here's my card; call if you think of anything else."

I looked at the card: Detective Sargeant Douglas Bader. I realized that he used the Americanized pronunciation of his name, rhyming the first syllable with *fade*. Maybe his family changed it during the war, maybe it was something they adopted right away, when they came to this country to better assimilate—

"Thanks very much, Ms. Fielding."

I looked up; I'd gone into my own little world again.

"Officer Lovell has your number? Well, until tomorrow, then."

And with all due courtesy, Detective Bader dismissed me from my own site.

Chapter 5

I WAS ABOUT HALFWAY BACK TO LAWTON WHEN I REalized that the camera I had with me actually had the shots I'd taken of the site yesterday, so I went to the photo place to get them done as a rush order. The nuisance was that I'd have to come back after that to pick up the shots that weren't a rush order.

After I'd dropped them off, I figured I might as well stop by the Stone Harbor Library while I was nearby, to look up Bray Chandler's ancestor, Nicholas. I looked in the birth records and found what I remembered and expected: Over the course of fifteen years, Margaret Chandler had eight children who lived and two who died, one at childbirth, one as a toddler. There was no mention of a Nicholas Chandler anywhere. I checked the death records and there was a Nicholas Chandler listed as having been deceased in 1738, the same year as the fire downtown. While that didn't necessarily indicate that he was a son of Margaret and Matthew's, my curiosity was piqued. I looked in the marriage records and found that he married Abigail Bradley in 1736 and had two young children with her at the time of his death. I realized I would have to double check the records at the courthouse to see if there was any information there that might confirm that he was one of Margaret's children. Birth and death records, though, were subject to mistake, just as Bray had said, but usually there were ways of corroborating your information.

I was glad when I finally pulled into the driveway a couple of hours later. I'd just put on the brake when my phone rang, scaring the hell out of me. I answered it once I realized that the ringing was coming from deep in my backpack. I fumbled with the buttons until I hit the right one. "Hello?"

"Hi, it's me," Brian said. "How you doing?"

"Um, good. How about you?"

"Real good. Where are you?"

"In the car—"

"You're not driving and talking on the phone, are you?"

"No, of course not. I just pulled into the driveway."

"Is something wrong? What are you doing home?"

"There was some trouble out on the site today. One of the security guards died." I took a deep breath. "I found him."

"Are you okay? Are you hurt?"

"No, I'm fine. I think, I don't know, but I think he was shot. There was . . . an awful lot of blood." I told him the rest of the story.

There was a long silence from Brian's end before he answered. "Okay, is Bucky home with you?"

"Yes, of course. Everyone's here. Everyone's okay. It happened long before we got there." That didn't sound as reassuring as I meant it.

"I'll come home right now."

The urgency in his voice worried me. "Brian, there's no

need. I'm fine, there's no emergency. Don't get yourself wound up over nothing."

"Only if you're sure. I'm glad we got the phones. I'm really glad."

I didn't have the heart to tell him I'd run into the office to use Fee's; I hadn't even thought about my cell phone. I'd have to get the hang of using it. "Okay, I'll see you soon. I love you."

"I love you too."

I stared at the keypad for a moment until I found the off button; the battery was low. I'd have to recharge it tonight.

The students were out by the tree, having set up the rudiments of a lab at the house, washing outside and drying and labeling inside. "I'm glad we have a few things to work on," I announced. "Looks like tomorrow is lab day too."

The groans that usually accompanied this sort of news were absent; they were all understandably quiet and Joe was downright stricken.

"Any news, Emma?" Rob asked.

I shook my head. "Maybe tomorrow. I'm not first on the list to be told anything in any case."

As much as I wanted to head up to my office, I decided that I'd keep an eye on everyone to see how they were doing. None of them knew Justin all that well—being on the site early and late was how I got to know him—but it never hurt, in the face of such news, to be part of a group. Realizing that Justin wasn't so much older than them, and that he was involved in the same sort of academic endeavors, had been sobering.

I had a look at what everyone was washing—mostly nails and a few sherds of redware, creamware, and stoneware—and noticed that there were a lot of seed fragments showing up. It would do to pay attention to the stratigraphy here to see if this stuff was coming from before or after the fire. When I got to Bucky, I saw that she was engrossed in trying to get all the corrosion off a nail.

"Hey, Bucks, just get the dirt off. The corrosion is there to stay."

"You won't remove it at all?"

I looked at it; it was pretty clearly a cut nail, with a bit of pebble stuck with the rust. "Nope. Just clean it up as best you can. If it looked like it might not be a nail, we'd spend more time on it, but don't get hung up on them. You'll get too many to worry about them or the brick chips."

"Okay." She scowled at the nail and put it aside, not liking to leave anything half done. "This isn't nearly as interesting as I thought it would be. I mean, I could go and look in the street and find pieces of brick and glass and nail. It doesn't seem all that different from today."

"And just think if you had a thousand bags or more to go through," Meg said. "All by yourself."

Bucky looked at Meg like she was insane. "Are you kidding me? I'd rather express the anal glands of fifteen cranky Great Danes every day for a month."

"Good God, Bucky!" I thought Meg was going to pass out at the image. "That's a bit much, isn't it?"

She shrugged. "Hey, Em, welcome to my world. No guts, no glory."

"Well," I said queasily, "at least by going over the bags yourself, you get to know the entire collection though, and that's invaluable."

"I always worried about you," my sister said. "There's something scary about this kind of obsessive attention to detail, when there's no life at stake."

I smiled, showing as many teeth as I could. "Yeah, there is. Welcome to my world."

* * *

Brian pulled up a short while later. By this time, it was late afternoon and we'd put away the artifacts and broken out the beer. Everyone seemed to be doing tolerably well, although the atmosphere, which usually might have ranged from the jovial to the scatological or the just plain silly, was muted. I couldn't blame them a bit.

"How you doing?" Brian whispered, when I ran up to greet him at the car.

"I'm good. I'm fine. I was glad to come home, though, after. I just wanted things to be normal."

"She's fine," Bucky announced, rudely appearing behind us and breaking up what would have been a rather nice moment. "Perfectly well behaved. Well, except for that one thing. . . ."

I shot her a look; I hadn't done anything at all, and there was no use in playing on Brian's nerves, not at a time like this.

Brian didn't look too concerned, however, as we went into the house. "And what was that, I'd like to know?"

"She was totally eyeing the landscapers out at the Chandler House. You might want to watch out for that, Brian. They were young, tanned, and had extremely well-defined leg muscles."

Brian snorted. "I'm not worried. She'd never leave all this." He gestured to the newly plastered but still unpainted kitchen, the stripped hallway, and the dining room with no floor.

"I wouldn't count on it." I stuck my tongue out, making sure he could see me.

"Landscapers aside, you're going to be careful, right?" he said to me.

"Yes, of course. I'm always careful."

"Okay." He let my hand go. "What do you girls want for dinner tonight? Anything you want, as long as it's meatloaf, because that's what I've got stuff for."

"That sounds good. Want some help?"

"Get the dishwasher unloaded, would you? Want it crusty or not so crusty?"

"Extra crust," I said.

"Yeah, it makes your coat glossy," Bucky added.

"All right, then." He began to pull out the ingredients. "I'm glad you had your phone on you. It's not like you were out in the middle of nowhere, but. . . ."

I caught Bucky's eye and shook my head slightly. "Yeah. It was a good idea on your part." He didn't need to know that I'd never even thought of using it. I had to get into the habit.

Bucky let out a beer belch in response to my half-truth.

"Gross," I said.

"My God," Brian said. "I've married into a family of Yeti."

Joe came in from the little house, shaking an alarm clock. "Emma, have you got another battery? This one is dying and I wouldn't want to be late for work."

"Heavens forefend. Give it here." I rummaged through the junk drawer until I found a new battery and took off the back. The dying battery was stuck in good, and I couldn't wiggle it out no matter what I tried; I attempted everything that I thought wouldn't damage the old clock. "Brian, is there a trick to getting the battery out?"

"Yeah, there's a trick." He pulled a screwdriver out of the junk drawer and slid it under the battery. He tried to pry it out with no success, then tried again. This time, with an alarming creak of plastic, the battery came shooting up and he grabbed it in midair. He handed it to me with a self-impressed grin.

"That wasn't a trick, that was brute force," I protested. "I could have done that."

"Ah, but that *is* the trick: knowing when to use brute force." He smiled and replaced the back of the clock, then put the battery away for recycling and the screwdriver back in the drawer. "Hey, you guys want meatloaf? I'm making a double batch."

"Hon, they don't want to be stuck with us," I said hurriedly. I didn't want to force them into anything.

"Meatloaf sounds good," Joe said. He hollered out the back of the kitchen. "You guys want meatloaf?"

A chorus of approval came from the side of the house. "Yes, please," Joe said. "We'll finish getting the artifacts put away."

Dinner was a lot of fun, and I was surprised to find just how pleased I was at the students' willingness to join us. We sat around the table for two hours after, trading stories, and it went a long way toward blotting out what I'd seen that morning. It surprised me, too, to see how much that community meant to me, how badly I needed to be surrounded by people like my crew.

Brian, Bucky, and I sat around a while after they excused themselves and withdrew to the little house. "So, spill it," I said, handing Bucky another beer. "Anyone new on the horizon?"

She shrugged and took the bottle. "Not really."

"What about whatshisname? Joel, wasn't it?"

"You know perfectly well what his name is." Bucky began to peel at the label on the bottle contemplatively and I was pretty certain I'd just hit on the reason Bucky was visiting us. "I've told him I'd like a break. It was about a month ago."

"What on earth for?" I'd had hopes for Joel. More than that, my sister's abrupt desire to spend time with me suddenly made sense. Not that she would have ever admitted it.

Again came the shrug, with just the merest hint of the Chin. "Ah, I don't know. He's too much of a geek for me. He was boring." It was as if she was looking for backup on her decision, but she would find none here.

"Nothing wrong with being a geek," Brian said. "Geeks and nerds make very good mates." He and I clinked our bottles together.

"Besides, what would you call a person who didn't take summers off from college?" I said. "Who was busy racking up the college credits even before she finished high school?"

"Eager to get where I was going," Bucky said, peeling the label off her bottle with real concentration now. "It's not just that. He's got all these plans. He wants, you know, a house, he wants to figure out how he can save up enough money to travel when he retires. That kind of stuff." She paused as if unwilling to confess the rest. "He wants all sorts of things."

"The bastard," Brian whispered in mock horror.

"Yeah, come on, Bucks. Those all sound like positives to me."

"Well, he was crowding me, so I told him to back off. Talked to Ma lately?"

I knew I'd touched a nerve there; the subject of our parents seldom came up unless we were planning how to cope with them, tag-team style. Bucky had retreated into her shell and would only reappear when she was good and ready to. "Yup. Her study group is going to Paris this year, for a week, end of July. They're going to do twentieth-century poets. She's worried about the garden while she's gone, so I volunteered you to go over and water it a couple of days."

"Gee, thanks."

"And Dad called the other day. He and Beebee are already in Nantucket, but they said they would stop by here Labor Day for a visit."

"Well, maybe I'll stop by then too. Get it over with." She finished her beer and put the bottle on the side of the sink; she left the shredded label on the table. "I'm for bed. We working on the sherds tomorrow?"

"Yes."

"Maybe I'll do that for a bit and then head into town."

"I'll be gone for the morning, so plan on taking the car in the afternoon."

"Okay. Night, Brian."

"Night."

The next morning, after ensuring that the crew had ample work to keep them occupied through the day, I tore off down to the photography place in Stone Harbor to pick up the rest of my prints. There were two main roads in Stone Harbor, and both roughly followed the coastline. The first, the oldest, ran directly along the waterfront, and I knew from hard experience that in the peak summer season it was worth parking as far away as possible and walking in. The traffic was incredible. It was complicated by campers and motor homes for which there was barely room, the proliferation of tourists who ran back and forth across the street from the view of the harbor to the photo-opportunity stocks that seemed to be obligatory in any Massachusetts town older than two hundred years, and yet another T-shirt stand wedged into an eighteenth-century shop space. The riot of color and noise, set against a background on one side of white sails and blue ocean and on the other by low buildings of stone and wood, modestly painted in muted colors, was sometimes a little tough to take. The second road was newer and therefore slightly less twisty. It was about a quarter of a mile inland and ran past what was now the main business district.

It was still early, so I made good time. As I entered the photo place the owner, Roger, greeted me warmly, and with good reason. I kept him in electricity for months at a time with the bills I ran up with my slides and prints, but it was worth it. He always got the color and the sharpness right and those were the main things.

"Morning, Emma."

"It is morning, isn't it?" I said, a little more cheerfully than I am usually able to manage. "How's things, Roger?"

"Not bad. Last trickle of prom and graduation pictures, now we're heading into vacation shots. I always look forward to yours, though; I never know what I'm going to get. Sometimes it's old maps, sometimes it's buildings, sometimes it's broken pieces of things, sometimes it's great scenery—"

"Those last ones are probably Brian's fault. He made me take a vacation last year. My system still hasn't recovered from all that lying around on the beach in Jamaica."

"Well, they were pretty shots," he said approvingly. "And this time I have—what? Dirt. Rocks. I have to tell you Emma, I wasn't thrilled." He smiled and handed me a couple of envelopes.

"Ah, but these are special rocks and dirt. These are historical rocks and dirt." As always, I opened them right then and there, to see how they came out. "See here? That's the foundation of a house that was built in the seventeen-twenties, part of it burned about fourteen years later. And that," I pointed to a shallow depression in the ground, "I'm thinking that looks like it was a planting hole, maybe to put in a small tree or a bush. It could also be something related to the destruction of the house, but we're finding more of them and I'm wondering if there wasn't a garden there at some point after the fire."

"Emma," Roger said. "It's dirt. It's a hole in the ground. This makes the usual stuff I see, like thirty-six exposures of kids with the family cat, all of them wearing party hats, look like fine art."

I clucked. "Some people have no appreciation for science. I'd like to oblige you with cute cat pictures, but I'm not sure ours would register on film—there's something demonic about him."

Roger rang up the total. "Thirty-four fifty please."

"Ouch."

He smiled. "Remember though: That's historic dirt in those photos."

I made a face as I handed him the cash and took my receipt. "Take it easy."

"Whenever I can."

Pulling up the drive to the Chandler House took a little of the wind out of my sails; it was hard to enjoy the beautiful day knowing that Justin had died in such an ugly fashion just the day before. It was still early when I arrived, and the historic house was in a state. The fact that Fee bustled about so briskly rubbed me the wrong way, and I wondered if I was being too cynical in imagining that the spreading news about Justin's death mightn't goose the ticket sales for the house tour, when they eventually resumed. Surely that was too base a thought. . . .

I walked into her office. "How are you doing, Fee?"

"Well, it's all just a little sad and disturbing, isn't it? I'm glad I have my work to keep me busy, else I don't know what I'd do with myself."

I recalled that she hadn't thought much of him when she'd voiced her opinions at the board meeting. She thought he was too young, though the way she seemed to challenge Daniel, I wondered whether there wasn't something else going on there—a power struggle, perhaps? Something that wasn't obvious to everyone else.

"Is there a new guard coming soon?" I said.

"Oh, yes. We called the person who was second in line for the job, my first choice, actually. He said he was still free and happy to start work."

"Suited for the job, is he?" I said, not quite certain how to phrase a more direct question about what Fee thought of Justin.

"My, yes. Nice older gentleman. Married. Not so flighty as a lot of the younger people we spoke to. You never know what they're getting up to, or how long they'll stay. You want someone solid, responsible."

I thought about Justin's goal of being a history teacher, the way he told me he went about his work toward his master's degree. "Justin seemed pretty responsible to me."

"I'm sure he was, in his way," she said quickly. "But he's gone now, and who knows under what circumstances, and now we have to carry on, don't we?"

There was something almost happy about her brisk manner this morning that sent a shiver down my spine. "Is Aden in?" I asked, if only to try and collect myself.

"Yes he is. He's back in his office, if you like."

I rapped a knuckle against her desk idly. "I guess I'll stop up and check in before I head back home. Any idea when the police will be back?"

"I haven't the least idea. Later this morning, I imagine."

She seemed singularly uninterested in the events that were virtually taking place right under her office window. Most people would have given in to guilt-tinged curiosity of some kind.

"Do you know if there's going to be a service for Justin?"

"I don't know. I'm sure we'll be told." Emotions fought

across her face and she eventually decided to tell me: "From what I know of Justin's . . . people . . . they stick close together. It's possible they might only have a private ceremony. They tend to be clannish and quiet."

"You know them well?" I was assuming she meant his family, but why should she hesitate over that?

She colored. "I wouldn't say that."

That was interesting; how was it she knew so much about Justin's family? I didn't know whether Fee was from around here.

"I guess I'll head back and find Aden."

"All right, Emma."

The door to Aden's office was ajar, and he was seated by his desk with his back to me, looking out the window at the harbor, with his feet up on the sill, talking on the phone. His office was exactly what you'd expect for such a room. It was more like his personal library, with a couple of nice pieces of period furniture, well-worn wool carpets, and a framed antique map of Stone Harbor and Boxham-by-Sea on the wall without a window. Only the open files on his desk and the computer betrayed that it was a place of business.

At my knock, he craned his head around to see who it was and waved me in.

"—very good then. I see we're all on the same page. Just one more thing before I let you go—"

I walked over to the wall to look at a framed photograph crowded with men dressed in hunting garb and armed with rifles, standing over a couple of bucks. In the corner, someone had written in ink 1972 STONE HARBOR HUNTING PARTY. Some of the faces looked familiar, although the only one I could definitely identify was Aden himself. Same grin, more hair, more flesh on his bones.

Aden hung up and with a little difficulty swung his legs

down to the floor, before he swiveled around to face me. He grimaced with the effort.

"Isn't that the first thing they teach you in school, Emma? Not to tilt your chair back, not to put your feet up?"

"I'm pretty sure it is."

Aden rubbed at his back. "I know I shouldn't do it, but I do it anyway. It's terrible for me, the ruin of my back, and yet I do it anyway. Why is that, do you think?"

What I thought was that Aden didn't seem to be much concerned with what had taken place just outside his office and only the day before. No one was expressing the sadness, confusion, or anger that one might have expected; hell, that I was experiencing myself. "Maybe you aren't much for doing what people tell you to do," I offered.

Aden tapped the desk with his middle finger. "Well, I'm not at that. I see you're interested in ancient history there." He indicated the photograph.

"Yes, it looks like a classic."

"We used to go every year. That was the last time we were all together." He got up and pushed his nose close to the photo. "There I am, of course. Couldn't miss that puss, could you? And there is Burke Chandler—that's Bray's father, he's gone now—and that one is Keith Prowse, Fee's older brother. That one there is Raymond Taylor, poor bastard."

"Is he related to Perry?"

"Oh, God yes. Don't you know, we're all related to each other, we old families?" He cackled. "But Raymond was Perry's father. A great man for hunting, was Ray, but then the cancer got him, and took its time too." Aden sighed hugely, then he looked at me slyly. "But there's someone else you know in that party."

I had another look at the picture and then shrugged. Time had changed too much for me to recognize who I might know.

"I'm actually asking you a trick question. Teddy Cressey is taking the picture."

"He went hunting with you?"

"Well, he kept pestering me to go with us, so I let him come along. You know, to look after us, help with the dirty work. No one really liked him, but it was useful to have an extra pair of hands along. It was a good time." He sighed again. "But you're not here to discuss that long-forgotten trip. I'll tell you, I really wish that I could be anywhere but in this miserable office today." He went over and sat back down at his desk, swiveling toward the window again.

"I can believe it. It's going to be a tough one."

"I'm going to imagine that I'm out there on the water. Nothing can follow you out there, Emma, or at least, you're given the illusion of that, which is almost as good. Do you know what I mean?"

I nodded. "It's been a while, but I grew up sailing."

"There you are. No noise, you have only the immediacies of what you're doing, and if those are taken care of, you're free to watch the scenery, ignore the rest of the world." He cast another longing glance through the window behind him, smiled sadly, and then resigned himself to being where he was. "What can I do for you this morning, Emma?"

"Not much. I guess I wanted to know whether you'd heard anything from the police. About Justin, about what their plans are for the site."

"I don't know much. They'd only say that he was shot, but of course, they wouldn't say anything more than that. We didn't find anything about the locks or alarm to suggest a break-in, but what I'm willing to guess is that poor Mr. Fisher startled someone who intended just that. I can't guess why, though. We don't keep a lot of cash on the premises, ever, and anything that might be of value in the house is generally too large to be carried off easily or too recognizable to be easily disposed of."

I had to agree; there wasn't much in the house that was fantastically valuable. Most of the rooms were decorated to illustrate different periods of the house's use, and most of the objects weren't actual belongings of the Chandler family but things accumulated along the way to furnish the rooms and give an idea of how each space was used through time. The furniture was good, but there wasn't anything that would make a break-in worthwhile. Or make killing poor Justin Fisher worthwhile either.

"I'm betting it was just one of those unhappy accidents that plague our society these days. Stupidity that is complicated and escalated by the use of violence. But that's something you'd know something about too, isn't it?"

"I beg your pardon?" I instantly knew what he was talking about but couldn't believe that he would mention again. It was a ghoulish prying that was in the poorest taste, as far as I was concerned, especially after I'd made it clear how much the topic bothered me when he brought it up after the board meeting. Anger made a mask of my face and I could feel my jaw muscles tighten. "What is it that you mean, Aden?"

"I mean that you've experienced this violence I describe firsthand." His words were as hard as I felt my face going. It was an aggressiveness that was totally inappropriate to the situation, bringing up what had happened at Penitence Point, as he seemed to know about it.

"Yes. So have many people."

"It just occurs to me that you might feel Justin's death more keenly than others of us, because of that. I mean, we knew Justin well, but I could see how his death, the very fact of finding his body, would have a profound effect on you."

Although his words sounded like sympathy, they struck

me as being more of a probe, and I found myself disliking Aden intensely. He might as well have asked "What makes you tick?" and been no less offensive, as far as I was concerned. It was the pain from my teeth clenching that reminded me to relax a little before I chipped a tooth or said something I shouldn't.

Before I could figure out what to say in response to this, Aden withdrew. "Look, I'm only trying to say that I know you had an awful shock yesterday and that you must be feeling it acutely. I'm an oaf: I try to be sympathetic and end up trampling all over the sensibilities of the other person. I'm sorry if I offended you."

I wasn't satisfied; it occurred to me that Aden always knew exactly what he was saying and how it would affect the other person. His behavior was that of a curious kid with a dissecting kit, scalpel in eager hand. His persona as a jovial eccentric was a mask for something far less amusing or attractive.

"While you are here, working on the site, I do feel responsible for you, so I hope you'll let me do anything I can to help you with your work. Through all this."

And if I wasn't completely mistaken, he was reminding me that I was working here on his say-so and was there just a hint of admonishment should I decide to speak my mind? Maybe I wasn't in the best state, but my instincts are good and getting better all the time, and I was pretty certain that was exactly what was going on.

"Well, unless you can speed up the police investigation, so I can get back to work out there, I guess there's nothing you can do," I said lightly. "So I'll just have to pretend that I'm out there for a sail too, while I head for the library today. Actually, if I were out there, it wouldn't be a bad way of studying the site. I mean, when you get down to it, so much of the traffic along this coast was conducted by water that it's like the houses along the big rivers in the south, where you have two front doors; one for the road side and one for the water side."

"That explains so many of the narrow, twisty little roads we have around here—highways included," Aden agreed, looking thoughtful.

"I'm sure the Chandlers would have had a jetty or a wharf, if not by their cliff, then close by, for people to reach them that way too." All I had to work from was one reference in a diary and the tax records, so I didn't know the actual location of it yet.

"Well, I might not be able to take you out on the water myself today, but maybe I can help. You say you haven't been sailing for a while, but how would you feel about taking my outboard? It's tied up at the marina on the other side of the point. The currents can be pretty strong along the point, but if you're up to it, you're welcome to take that out and have a look at the historic site from the water today."

Actually, as little as I liked the idea of being beholden to Aden at this particular moment, it struck me as a great idea. No one expected me back at the house much before noontime, and the thought of being on the water was beguiling, especially if I could rationalize it as being in the name of work. "I'd love to, as long as you don't. . . ."

"I'm tied up here for the rest of the day. Why don't you?" He grinned, a nasty little imp's grin. "I can see you want to."

Aden seemed to be able to see a good many things and I was beginning to think that it wasn't his most appealing trait. "Okay, thanks, I'll do that."

"Here's a note." He began to scribble on a piece of paper and handed it to me. "I doubt that anyone would give you any trouble, but just in case, give them this. But you shouldn't have any problem." He reached into a drawer and then handed me a key, "This is for the padlock."

I took it and put it into my pocket. "Great, thanks. You're sure you don't mind?"

"Like I said, there's no chance of me getting out of here today. I'm a slave to the phone and will be for a while." He made a sour face. "Not the least of which will be the Chandler family reunionistas, when they hear that there's been a death here. It is a big fundraiser for us and I can't let it get away from me . . . us."

"I'll be sure to let you know what I see, if there is anything." I heard the sound of the scene of the crime squad arriving, and Aden and I both turned our heads instinctively toward the noise. "I've got to give Detective Bader the film and then I'll be off."

"Film?"

"He wanted the pictures I took of the site during work yesterday, in case they show him anything useful that might help with the investigation of Justin's death."

Aden stared at me for a long moment, and I couldn't fathom the expression on his face. Instinctively I tightened my grip on the strap of my handbag which held the photos. Finally he smiled humorlessly. "What a very curious profession you're in, Dr. Fielding."

I nodded, not smiling. "Some days, it's a little more curious than I like."

Chapter 6

ON MY WAY OUT TO MY CAR, I STOPPED BY THE site—which was now part of a crime scene. It was no more secure than it had been when I was working there, nothing more than the chain link fence on one side, the house on the other, the shrubs at one end, and a sawhorse and snow fencing at the other by the back of the property, but the addition of police tape certainly made a pronounced difference. I hesitated even to approach, but I guess my sense of self-restriction is a little stronger than most people's; Bucky wouldn't have blinked. Maybe it was an indication of birth order or something; whatever it was, it was a good summary of our personality types.

I didn't have to do much more than pause by the tape when Detective Bader was at my side. "Good morning."

"Good morning. I brought the pictures. I picked out these," I handed him the ones I'd sorted out in the car, "because they show the site the night before the murder, and they are specifically of the areas you're interested in. I didn't figure you'd want to see the ones we'd taken of artifacts, but if you want to see them too—"

"No, probably not. Do you mind if I take these for a while?"

"Keep them. I always get duplicates made. In my field, order and redundancy have their rewards."

He looked as though he were about to say something, but then thought better of it. Before he could speak, however, Stuart Feldman from the crime scene team hailed me.

"How you doing today?" he asked.

"I'm not too bad," I said. "It's just kind of horrible to think of someone just . . . shooting . . . Justin like that. He was a nice kid." I caught a glance exchanged between Bader and Feldman. "I mean, he seemed that way to me, the times we talked."

"No reason to think otherwise," Stuart said. "Don't worry, we'll get whoever did this."

"I know."

"And I don't think we'll be too much longer than today." He glanced at Bader, who nodded. "The work is going pretty smoothly. Unless something wildly untoward happens, I'm betting you can get back to work tomorrow, if you like."

"I guess I would, if you're sure it won't be impeding your work."

"Don't worry. We wouldn't let you, otherwise. Say, any interesting finds so far?"

"Not much that's unusual," I said. "Mostly household trash—glass, pottery, bone, that sort of thing. But of course you know that we never really focus on the artifacts. It's the stratigraphy and what it can tell us about what was going on at the site that's really important." I grinned at him; the statement was as true as it was false. Understanding the stratigraphy was the most important part of our work, but the artifacts would always be the principal lure.

"Oh, yeah, right. Dr. Johnston told me that one too. I didn't buy it from him either."

I turned back to Bader, aware that he hadn't said a word through this conversation. I couldn't tell if he was interested or not. I suppose it didn't do for him to get too chatty with anyone in my position. I mean, he didn't know me, didn't know that I had nothing to do with Justin's death.

"Well, if you have any questions about the pictures or you think there's something else I can help you with. . . ." I trailed off; of course he'd find me if he had questions. "I'll be going."

"Thanks, for these." He waved the envelope. "I'll get them back to you if it turns out that they don't help us. Wouldn't want to break a link in your chain of evidence," he said, and almost smiled.

I turned to go.

"Dr. Fielding?"

I turned but Detective Bader jerked his head, indicating that I should follow him along the chain link fence, a little away from the ongoing investigation.

"I'm . . . I have a question for you."

Gone was the curt assurance that characterized the questions he'd asked me yesterday. This was different, I could tell; it had nothing to do with Justin.

"Sure, what is it?" I was more than eager to help.

"I'm interested in history. All sorts."

My heart beat a little faster, as it always did with the anticipation of a question that I might be able to answer. "Okay."

"I've just started reading about the U.S.–Mexican War, and wondered whether any volunteer units were sent from around here. Can you help me out with that?"

Damn, I thought to myself, let down. I vaguely knew that it was in the mid-nineteenth century, but that was it. "I'm sorry, that's something I know nothing about. You probably already know to check with the library; they'll often have a section dedicated to town history, or you could check the state archives. At least they'd be able to tell you where to start looking, if they haven't got an answer for you themselves."

Bader's mouth moved slightly to the side, something that wasn't quite a grin or a frown, and he blinked slowly. "Thanks anyway," he said and returned to the site.

I made for the parking lot, wishing that I'd been able to answer the question. I don't know exactly why, I suppose that it was the faint hope that I could make myself stand out a bit, be trusted, maybe learn a little more firsthand about what had happened to Justin. I reached for my car keys, then thought better of it. The parking would be abominable downtown, and I could just as easily walk to the wharf and leave my car here.

The view from up by the Chandler House was really spectacular, and as I followed the coast road, I could see the whole harbor below. The elevation of the Chandler House wasn't very high, maybe twenty or thirty feet above sea level, but it was enough to give the place a great vantage point, looking down on the edges of the rest of the neighborhood about a quarter of a mile away. The town was more built up down there, where the land was flatter. I wondered whether there had been a watchtower up this way, at one point, or if it had been on the other side of the harbor, which actually stuck out farther into the ocean. I made a mental note to check the town histories. Not only had the Chandlers had a tremendous view, but they would have also been on view themselves, from nearly every part of town.

I played a little game that I often played while walking

around: What would it have looked like here in the seventeenth century? What would it have looked like fifty years ago? A thousand years ago? Twenty years from now? I tried to put myself in the mind of someone walking into town having just visited Margaret Chandler. Okay, the guardrail wouldn't have been there, and neither would the pavement and sidewalk. There would be fewer trees; I was guessing that like most places in Massachusetts and elsewhere, the use of trees for fuel and shipbuilding and everything else would have left it denuded around here pretty early on. Okay, the wharves I could see down below me would have been there, but of timber and not concrete, and the ships would have been wooden and not fiberglass; more working vessels, certainly, and few or none devoted solely to pleasure. The beach might have been busier, filled with fishermen repairing nets or selling fish, maybe, and perhaps someone collecting driftwood or clams. There would have been the same crowd of shops, only selling what was coming in on the ships—sugar, textiles, and china—or what was needed to outfit them. Now there were snack joints, souvenir shops, and art galleries—mementoes of journeys and refitting stops, to be sure; the same but different on the face of it all.

Scratch a little deeper into the social history, and, well, that was a different story. I certainly wouldn't have been striding along alone, the outline of my lower limbs embarrassingly visible to the entire world, pursuing historical research on my own. Actually, if I was very, very lucky, I might have had the privilege and the leisure to read a bit about history, perhaps even travel to see the sites of the classical world, but not much more than that. Most women, most people, weren't so lucky though, and the odds were that I would have been cleaning fish, or weaving, or stuck with my head against the side of a cow someplace, six kids hanging off my skirts and crying for their dinner or because the chickens were pecking at them.

I grinned at that and decided to save that particular thought for Brian to laugh at later.

I continued as I followed the road past the common: get rid of the Victorian houses and the telephone poles. Lose the cars and buses and insert a horsed rider or two, maybe a carriage. Add some sheep and some cows and a couple of kids to watch them. Add a lot of mud—the common is a working place, not just a gathering place—and maybe make it market day instead of drill day for the militia. Away from the common and the strictures of the modern-day Stone Harbor Historical Society, there are small houses, maybe eighteenth-century houses underneath the vinyl siding—good against the salt air but bad for my imagination, so away with it. The houses are crowded together, there aren't the same zoning regulations, but there is the constant worry about fire, especially here, in a place that had been scarred by fire on several occasions, so keep an eye on the smoke coming from the chimneys, smoke that is scented with food and blacksmithing and tar and fish. That might have been a pleasant smell, mingled with the salt air, or it might not have been a happy substitute for the exhaust of the tour bus that passed me, making me cough at its diesel exhaust. The exhaust lingered for a moment on the warm air, then a little breeze dispelled it.

Okay, it's all a trade-off, I decided. As long as I can visit the past in my work and my imagination, I'm probably better off in the twenty-first century. At least there's indoor plumbing that doesn't involve something that looks like a large coffee cup with an extra wide rim.

As I found my way onto the leveler ground of Water Street, I paused to pick a piece of gravel out of the tread of my sneaker. I pulled it free, dropped it to the side, and retied my laces. The marina wasn't too far now. . . .

I found Aden's outboard, unlocked the padlock at the ring at the bow, and removed the tarpaulin cover. The feeling of the boat shifting under my feet brought back a flood of memories that were as situated in my muscles as they were in my brain; it only took a moment to steady myself, get the feel of the boat as I seated myself in the stern. Every time I get this close to the water, I feel like I am getting away with something, getting away from something. It had been far too long.

I checked that there was a life jacket and a fire extinguisher; no problem, but there were no oars. That was no problem either; I wouldn't be going too far from shore, and my trip today would be a short one. The red gas tank connected by the hose to the engine was nearly empty, but the spare was full; I'd be able to run for a while and then could switch the tanks.

After I put on the life preserver, I squeezed the priming bulb, opened the vent on the top of the gas tank, and pulled the rope to start it. Although I had been prepared to spend the traditional hour of yanking, amazingly, after only two tries, the engine caught. Blue smoke drifted up from the water; I saw the trickle of water under the engine head and knew that water was circulating through the engine. I opened the choke slowly until the engine began to warm up and smooth out, then unhitched the bow and stern lines from the dock and set out.

The boat was vintage and nicely made—I wouldn't have expected anything less from Aden, who struck me as a man who knew what he was doing and had the money to pay for his pleasures—and I made better progress than I might have expected, given the onshore wind and the chop. I soon fell back into the rhythm of navigating, keeping one eye over my shoulder and watching out for other craft. I giggled, never imagining that the smell of gasoline and salt air would be so intoxicating. I opened her up and felt the breeze blow my bangs back. The sun was warm, the salty air cool enough to be comfortable, and if I couldn't be on dry land digging and getting work done, then this was a more than satisfactory alternative.

It took me about fifteen minutes to come around the point, and as I did, I briefly saw the Chandler House before the weeds and shrubs blocked out the sight altogether. I angled back and then cut the engine for a more leisurely view. It was an imposing image to be left with, and put into the context of motorless transport and construction that was based on human brawn and animal traction, impressive. The house would have made a vast statement from land or sea, especially after the back addition was built. I made another note to check where the wharf would have been at the top of the cliff.

I found myself drifting a little too close to the rocks, so I started up again and backed off, heading closer to where the road ended in the cliff. It was just then that I saw it—there!

There was a spot where the ground fell away a bit and was a little lower; with a good set of stairs and a float, there would have been access to the property from the water side. I shivered, not fancying the thought of how the guy building the stairs would have been precariously dangling as he started on his work; the face of the cliff was fairly straight and the water just below it was dark and not particularly calm.

I cut the engine and took the opportunity to switch to the second gas tank. I squeezed the priming bulb and opened the vent on the top of the gas tank, and then realized I should find some landmarks to see whether I could locate the place

again from up on the road. After a couple of minutes of ori-
enting myself, I pulled the rope again. The engine didn't
catch, and, cursing, I tried again, but then stopped: The
smell of gasoline was far stronger than it should have been,
and that always warrants attention. I couldn't see anything
amiss but the smell was so strong now that I started hunting
for it in earnest, worry beginning to build in me. I pulled up
one of the floorboards and saw that there was a puddle of
gasoline sloshing around beneath me, one that appeared to
be increasing in size. A prickle of fear made me shiver, and I
saw where the gas was leaking from: There was a puncture
in the second gas tank.

A closer inspection gave me a sickening jolt, as I could
see that there was no way that the puncture could have been
made by accident. The hole looked as though it had been
made by a screwdriver, the ragged edges of the hole forced
inward. I realized that gas had only stayed in the tank as long
as the vent on top was closed. I closed it again, but it didn't
make me feel any better.

I sat back in disbelief, panic at what I'd just seen, what
I'd just had to do, making me a statue. Well, not quite a
statue; hyperventilation isn't usually an issue for cold mar-
ble. But the reek of gasoline told me that it was all true.
Someone had deliberately pierced the fuel tank on Aden
Fiske's boat.

Chapter 7

I HAD A CHOICE. I COULD STAY IN THE BOAT, HOPING someone else would be by soon to pick me up—and that thought reminded me of my cell phone, which I'd carefully put in the car in case of emergencies. Damn it. And flares? Not even an option. And even if I'd had oars, the boat was a little too big for me to row all the way back. But I didn't want to stay and wait. The smell of gasoline was making me gag now, and the thought that someone, possibly aware of Aden's smoking habit, had sabotaged his boat, made my skin crawl. I felt very alone, terribly exposed, and downright scared.

I decided I wasn't going to sit there, with the gasoline sliding around beneath me and someone out there who hated Aden enough to try and kill him, not when I was so close to the shore. I hated the idea of waiting until someone saw me: I'd climb up the cliff. I dropped the anchor, and waited until a fortuitous wave smacked the boat up against the smooth, seaweed-covered rocks at the base of the cliff, making an ugly grinding noise. I found myself in the unpleasant situation of having to jump without a firm base to support me: As soon as I tried pushing off, I shoved the boat farther beneath me, which reduced how far up the rock I could land.

I managed a sort of awkward frog hop that splayed me across the rock for just an instant. I felt a pain in my abdomen where a section of the rock stuck out, and grabbed frantically at the seaweed that clung to the rock. I was just another piece of jetsam. Then I began to slide down into the water, becoming soaked to the chest and weighed down by my clothes. I kicked and pulled myself up at the same time and managed to scramble all the way onto the jutting boulder. Salt water stung my hands and lower chest where I had been scraped down the side of the rock, which was covered with barnacles. Sitting for a moment to catch my breath, I watched as the boat bobbed on the waves.

I was safe for the moment, but how the hell was I going to get up the face of the cliff? It didn't seem like such a great idea, now that I'd passed the point of no return.

I didn't dare risk trying to swim around, that was for sure. It was just too deep, too rocky, and too choppy. There weren't enough of the lower, half-submerged rocks to consider leaping between them. It looked like the only way out was up.

As soon as I shifted my weight, I knew this was going to be trickier than I thought. Trying to stand up immediately reminded me of what I now faced: The rock was slippery, damp, and covered with slick seaweed bladders that gave off a noxious smell when they broke under me. I turned myself around so that now I faced the cliff itself, and after slipping and dunking my foot back into the water again, I managed to stand upright, leaning against the main wall of the cliff.

I shivered violently—the wind renewed the shock of the cold wet against my skin—and studied the wall of rock and seaweed for a possible route up. It wasn't sheer, and I could tell that it was possible to climb up—there were plenty of hand- and toeholds—but it took me a moment to decide that this really was what I had to do. I hadn't been near this kind of rock climbing for nearly twenty years, and even then, that had only been the sort of thing one does as a kid in suburban woods. There had been nothing trained or skilled about that kind of scrabbling, and I was such a cautious kid that I never tackled anything that didn't look pretty manageable. I also hadn't just bailed out of a sabotaged boat in a dangerous part of the harbor with little choice in the matter.

I swallowed and could feel my heart pounding away. A sick feeling pervaded me as I realized that I would have to ditch my life preserver if I wanted to get the best holds possible; clinging was now high on my list of priorities. It was hard to part with the illusion of safety that the preserver afforded, but I fumbled with the clips and eventually managed to untie the bands with trembling fingers, removing the device and wedging it into a rock nearby, for whatever good that would do. I rubbed my freezing fingers until they felt a little warmer, took a deep breath, and found my first good handhold.

At first it was slow going, though not particularly hard, once I realized it was just a matter of concentration, patience, and planning. Most of my trouble was my own brain, which kept reminding me of the danger inherent in what I was doing, suggesting that I should stop it as soon as possible. Another problem was that the seaweed was slippery when it was wet and not particularly helpful in getting a grip when it was dry. And although it clung to the rock tenaciously, it wasn't exactly built to hold the weight of an assistant professor, no matter how regularly she worked out, so I couldn't use it like one of Indiana Jones's conveniently placed jungle vines. It just took up space in the good cracks I wanted to use and shifted and moved on the rocks too. But

I made progress and was starting to get the hang, if you will, of how to test each step I was about to make. I was even starting to take pleasure in the challenge, a real satisfaction in being able to focus and channel my fear away, when I noticed a slight bulge that ran right around the length of the cliff. I vaguely recognized that it was just some kind of intrusion of one rock into the surrounding stratum, a vein that had been injected during the birth of this particular formation by volcanism or upheaval or something else grand and geological. It wasn't the composition or the formation of the rock that made me pause: it was the physics of it all. I had to stop and think about this, and a little of the panic that had possessed me began to seep back into the pit of my stomach.

The bulge wasn't big and its curve wasn't too steep, but it was just enough to make me realize that the rock was curving out over the water, whereas it had been curving in and upward to the top for the first part of my trek. This meant that, for a while, more of me would be hanging back over the water than leaning toward the rock and comparative safety. I knew it was just a matter of shinnying up as far as I could, reaching past that outcropping, and continuing on as I had been. It, logically, should only have been a minor setback, but it took everything I had left in me to face this new challenge. It was the idea of leaning back, even a little, over the water and danger when every bit of me had been devoted to leaning in, clinging like kelp, and working toward safety.

Every little antique mammalian cell of me that still preferred tree climbing to that silly, newfangled trick of walking on two feet knew that this was not a good idea. My toes were too short, even if they weren't encased in my sopping sneakers, my fingers didn't have the strength or the nice padding they should have for this kind of antic, and my nice, straight back just wasn't flexible the right way anymore. I would have given almost anything for a prehensile tail at the moment, even if it was just for balance. Somewhere down the road, about four million years ago, we had traded in all that lovely, built-in climbing gear for bipedalism and big brains, and it struck me now as a stupid, sorry mistake.

I was starting to get tired and trembling now out of fatigue rather than nerves alone. If I couldn't use the physical attributes I wanted, I'd have to make do with the big brain, and I'd have to do so quickly.

I gauged the next set of handholds as best I could, and then, thinking as little as possible, I pushed myself up, until most of my torso was over the bulge. I reached up and grabbed my next left handhold, then pushed myself again, seized my right handhold and swung my left foot up to a secure spot, before I remembered that most of my mass was over the ocean. My goal—the top of the cliff—was almost within sight. I slipped back, a cry escaping my lips, as the blunt toe of my sneaker slipped off the shallow step. I scrabbled desperately, trying to find a toehold that would support me, my face pressed against the rough, warm rock. My foot caught, slipped, then caught hold of another, sturdier bit of ledge, and I shoved myself up, hearing the little pebbles and grit I dislodged rattle down the face I'd just come up, plopping into the water, unheard over the waves. Two more steps up, and I could see the slope formed a large step, large enough to pull myself onto and lean back.

I was nearly at the top of the cliff, the last flat edge before the drop down to the water, and I let myself rest here, now safe. I could feel the sun's heat trapped in the rock, and I clung a little closer, trying to warm myself up. It was almost as if the rock beneath me was moving, because I was trembling from head to foot, not a bit of me still. I rolled over to my side and rested a moment, and when I sat up, I had to brush away the sand that had stuck to my sweaty face. I brushed off my hands and saw that I was cut and bleeding in several places; my fingertips were raw and stung like hell. I knew when I stopped shaking from nerves and exertion, I was going to feel every ache and pull I'd inflicted on myself. I would have to wash out those cuts good, I thought, as I got up, so they wouldn't get infected. . . .

I almost laughed when I realized that for the first time I'd been able to plan ahead, not in terms of inches or handholds, but actual time, a future that was not concerned with tumbling into the ocean. And then I did let out a war whoop, all self-consciousness burned away by adrenaline and achievement. I clambered up the two low shelves to the very top of the cliff, luxuriating in the feel of the ground under my feet, and I stomped my foot just for the pleasure of feeling the rock's solidity.

A line of large boulders marked the edge of the property, and a few feet behind them was a small chain link fence, probably put up by the land owners to keep people from tumbling off the cliff. You could almost tally the changing centuries, I thought giddily, by the way the edge of the cliff was marked off. Eighteenth century and earlier, you're on your own; if you're too stupid to see the edge of the cliff, well, that's the last time you'll make that mistake. In the nineteenth century, you get the polite notice of the large boulders, which don't do anything to detract from the view. And in the civic-minded, cautious, and ever-so-litigious twentieth century, I thought as I reached the fence, you get protection built in for you. I turned and looked out at the horizon, jolly pleased to be able to have something else to look at besides granite three inches away from my face. It was time to get out of here.

Ordinarily, I would have regarded a fence, any fence, as inviolable, but now, it was a minor inconvenience, a slight, meaningless barrier between me and my car, me and getting home to a warm shower and dry clothes. I pushed myself up with both hands, and fell back suddenly, my arms trembling from fear and exertion. A minor setback, it was to be expected, I told myself blithely. I tried again and succeeded this time, hauling up one leg easily and swinging myself over. I landed lightly on the ground, again feeling the elation that comes with having saved your own life.

I took two steps before I realized I was in back of the Bellamys' house, and then slowed down. When I saw that one of their cars was in the driveway, I sped up and began to run to the far side of the yard to my left so that I could hop the fence back onto the public road. I made it about two-thirds of the way across the lawn when an unholy noise erupted from the direction of the house, a racket like stampeding cattle and baying wolves. It was accompanied by the ominous metallic slither of chains.

I'd forgotten all about the Bellamys' dogs.

Two enormous animals came bounding toward me, huge shadows in black and gray, covering the area of the yard with terrifying speed. Their barking grew louder and more frenzied as they tore toward me. I froze for an instant, stunned by the sight and not knowing whether I could make it the rest of the way to the fence before they reached me or whether my movement would only goad the dogs to a greater fury. Then sheer panic took over and I fled, the fence my only goal, running as fast as I ever had in my life.

Chapter 8

I TRIED TO HAUL MYSELF UP THE FENCE, BUT MY ARMS were too tired, and the fence was taller on the street side of the yard than by the cliff. It was just another foot, but it was enough to thwart me. Clumsy and weak from exertion, I flung myself at the fence, but my arms just wouldn't respond. I couldn't make them work, and my sneakers were just too wide in the toe to fit into the small links of the fence. I tried again, fear an excellent spur, and succeeded in hanging on this time. I managed to get a toe wedged into place when I felt a savage pull on the leg of my jeans, and with a cry I came down off the fence.

"Down, Monet! Down, Matisse! Get down, now, both of you!"

I landed in a heap, blurs of black and a glint of sharp white teeth too close to my face. The things that overwhelmed me were purely the physical, the damp heat and smell of the dogs' breath, the heavy tread of clawed feet on my legs as I put my hands up in front of my face. I know I screamed but couldn't hear myself over the barking—

"I said down! Now, damn it!" The shrill voice came again.

And suddenly, the dogs were off me. When I felt fresh air again, I dared to put my hands down and scrabbled away until my back was up against the fence. I tried to stand, failed, then finally shoved myself up, shaking so hard I could barely manage to stand up straight. I leaned against the fence for support and tried to catch my breath.

Claire Bellamy was kneeling; she held both dogs by their collars and was letting them lick her face. "Good babies! What good dogs! You're so good! Yes, you are!"

That shocked me more than a bucketful of cold water would have done, which, come to think of it, I'd already experienced once today. "Good dogs? My God, lady, they just tried to kill me!"

Claire looked over at me, her smile vanished. "You were on their territory! They were only doing what dogs are supposed to do! What the hell are you doing in my yard?"

"I didn't mean to . . . I came up the cliff. . . ."

"What were you doing out there? This is not a public way, you know!" Then her face changed, flushed even darker red. "You sent the police over here yesterday!"

I couldn't even remember yesterday. "What? I didn't—"

"Yes you did! They came over to ask about the noise I heard yesterday morning, and that was after I spoke to you about it! You sent them over here!"

"They were asking me about—"

Not interested in my explanation, Claire suddenly noticed I was shivering. "Why are you so wet?"

"I told you, I came up the cliff. I was in a boat, the fuel tank . . . had a hole in it, so I had to ditch it, and I ended up on the—"

Her mouth, usually agape, was now positively round with disbelief. "What in God's name were you doing in the boat?"

I raised my hand to point to the Chandler House behind me, across the street. One of the dogs whuffed.

"Be quiet, Matisse. Well?"

"I was trying to see the Chandler House from the water, to . . ." What had I been thinking? "To see it the way people would have seen it back when. . . ." I licked my lips trying to get hold of myself. "Back when people traveled more by water, around here. I borrowed Aden Fiske's motorboat—"

The blood drained from Claire's face. "Aden Fiske's motorboat?"

I nodded. "There was all this fuel in the bottom, and I jumped onto one of the rocks and climbed up the cliff. I promise you, if I could have landed anywhere else, I would have."

"You borrowed Aden's—and it was leaking gas? You climbed up the cliff—you might have been killed!"

I nodded, thinking about how many times that made today. "Yeah."

"Look at your hands, they're a mess! You're serious about all this!"

I shrugged. Claire seemed to be having a hard time stringing the story all together. It was starting to seem unreal to me too, so I couldn't blame her much.

"Come up to the house, I'll help you get them cleaned up."

Then she let go of the collars. The two dogs, which I now recognized as standard poodles, stood up and stared at me. I tried to remember everything Bucky had ever told me about dogs, tried to remember whether wagging tails were good and whether teeth meant welcome or danger. I curled my fingers into fists, as much to steady myself as to remove the invitation of easy targets. But I realized that Claire was right: The dogs were playing. One of them stretched his front paws out in front of him, then bounded away a few steps, looking at me expectantly. I had the distinct impression that he was smiling, if such a thing was possible.

"No, Monet, this lady's—Emma's?—not going to play with you. You boys go lie down. Go lie down."

To my surprise and shattering relief, the two dogs trotted obediently back toward the house. And now that both the animals and my imagination were under control, it seemed to me that the poodles shrank down to, well, normal large dog size; my tattered nerves had turned rambunctious pets into slavering monsters. It had been a real fright though, and it took me a minute to realize that I should start moving myself.

"Come on. I'll get some hydrogen peroxide for those cuts. They look nasty."

I looked down at my hands and saw that my scrapes had been torn wider when I was pulled off the fence. The air stung, and I picked another small, sharp piece of barnacle out of my pinky.

"The dogs didn't actually bite you, did they?" Claire asked as we walked down the yard. "I had them just as they got to you, I didn't see them snap at you at all . . . after . . . you fell."

I noticed that she didn't say how I fell, but I was pretty sure she wasn't the one who pulled me off the fence. She wasn't particularly big, but to keep control over two athletic animals, I realized, she must have some considerable strength. "No, I don't think so."

"Good," she said with nervous relief. "I didn't think so, but I wouldn't keep animals like that. I couldn't. I have two small children and I do a good deal of entertaining, so there are people here all the time. I couldn't have dogs that would actually hurt anyone. I mean, you were in their territory, but M and M wouldn't actually attack anyone. They're very obedient."

I repeated mechanically, "Yes, I understand I was in their territory, by accident. No, I don't think they bit me," just so she would stop going on about it. I just wanted to get out of there and go home.

My bland statements seemed to reassure Claire, who was now positively chatty as we reached the back steps to the house. "Why don't you just—"

She paused outside the door and I knew that she was worried that I would drip. I decided that I didn't need to see the inside of the Bellamy house all that badly. "No, I'll get your floors muddy."

"No, no, come in. You can wait in the kitchen. I'll get you the first aid kit. Lie down, babies. Go to bed."

Monet and Matisse immediately went under the porch, to sturdy wicker dog beds with well-worn cushions. "Their outdoor beds are getting nasty, almost ready for the dump," she said, as she pulled open the sliding glass door.

"Just replace the pillows, they'll be fine."

She wrinkled her brows. "Well, they can have new indoor beds and the old ones will come out here. We don't want those stinky things hanging around."

Oh, good, I thought. Conspicuous consumption for the pets. But then I saw that that was small potatoes compared with the orgy of consumer display that was the interior of the Bellamy kitchen. Considering the state my own was in, it shouldn't have surprised me that anything else would have looked better, but this was straight out of a showroom. It was all straight lines, stainless steel, stone, and hardwoods, all blended into a professional-grade performance area for the knowledgeable home cook and her equally educated audience. A restaurant kitchen forced into Colonial Revival décor.

"Wow," I said. "Those cabinets are gorgeous."

Claire raised her eyebrows skeptically and looked around, considering. "Yes, well, cherry is fun, but I'd be happier with oak. It'd go better with the tile. This was all here before us, but I do like the clean look."

Clean was the operative word here, apparently. For a house with two large dogs and two small kids, I couldn't see a thing out of place. No dishes in the sink, no crumbs from breakfast, no boxes of cereal lying around. No footprints on the floor, no fingerprints on the stainless sink and faucet. No dog hair.

No dog hair? How could that be? She did mention that the dogs slept inside.

I didn't have long to ponder that new mystery as I had another one to consider while Claire went to the bathroom: Why was she being so solicitous of me?

When she'd come over to complain about the noise that my crew and I were supposedly making so early in the morning, her attitude had been one of wounded long-suffering. Now, once the specters of trespass and dog bites had been put to rest, for the moment, she was being positively chummy, trading home design tips, inviting me in to drip in her kitchen.

What had happened to bring this about?

As I stuck my head into the living room to see what that was like, it came to me that perhaps she was just scared into humanity, driven by fear that someone was trying to break into her house or cut across her yard or something. Hmm, lots of antiques crammed onto surfaces and a forty-two-inch flat-screen plasma display television over the mantelpiece, the kind that always stopped Brian cold in the mall. Where once it was the fire that was the center and focus of family life, now there was a television over the cold dark grate. Lots of money there, I reckoned.

But it wasn't real money; the furniture itself was generic modern Colonial Revival. In fact, I realized that the television was the only truly expensive thing in the room; the antiques weren't valuable, although they were arranged to give that impression. The longer I looked, the more I saw that there was a lot of taste but not a lot of cash in that room, besides the television.

And people who are confrontational to begin with don't usually back off because they are in the middle of a conflict. Claire shouldn't have been subdued by the violence of our meeting; she was in the right, she was safe with her dogs, and I posed no obvious threat. She should have been in her element. No, it must be something else.

Something else that scared her.

I tried to think back over our conversation to pinpoint where the shift had occurred. I returned to the kitchen and inspected the view from the window over the sink. I touched the neatly folded dishtowel next to the sink: it was still damp. Perhaps this is where Claire had been when she first saw me in her yard. She would have seen . . . I let my eyes unfocus, trying to imagine what Claire would have seen. As she dried dishes or washed the counters, glancing out the window at her expensive view, Claire would have been startled to see a figure coming up over the cliff, beyond the fence that delineated her domain. She would have watched as I tried, twice, to hop the fence, seen me hesitate as I got my bearings. Perhaps that's when she put down her towel, folding it automatically, and came outside. She would have seen me begin to beat it for the far side of the yard, toward the safety of the public road and then she might have realized that the dogs had also detected me and begun their race.

She begins to run, I hit the fence, the dogs corner me, she arrives in time to keep them from playing too roughly. Fine, at this point, she's still defensive, she's confrontational, she's still Claire as I've gotten to know her.

I gripped the sink, trying to remember how the conversation went. She demands to know what I'm doing there. I tell her I came over the cliff, she gets angry about the police coming over here—why was that? And we didn't keep talking about that, despite how angry that made her. She asked why I was shivering, I said I'd been stranded in a boat that was full of fuel and climbed out. . . .

No. I told her I'd borrowed Aden Fiske's boat. That's when things changed. She'd gone positively pale when I mentioned Aden's name. Aden, who she thought was my boss. I wonder whether—

"Here we are!"

I jumped, then sighed deeply. Claire had appeared suddenly from the hallway, her footsteps muffled by the wall-to-wall carpeting. My already overextended nerves were not up to any more surprises.

"I had to find another bottle of hydrogen peroxide. It's like the kids drink it or something, we go through so much of it so quickly. Maybe you'd better. . . ." She proffered the bottle and some cotton balls to me.

I poured a little of the liquid onto the cotton, gritted my teeth, and dabbed it onto my other hand. My eyes welled up and I blinked tears away, taking a deep breath. "Man, that stings," I said, watching the foam subside. I did the other hand, and it was no more fun than the first. At least the scrapes were clean for now.

Claire put the first aid box onto the counter, opened it, and handed me some bandages. I tried to pull the paper wrapper apart at the edges, but my fingers were shaking too hard to get it on the first try. I noticed how dry my mouth was. "Could I trouble you for a glass of water?"

She hesitated, then got a bottle from the fridge and poured me a glass. I could tell she wasn't keen on the idea of me prolonging my visit.

"Thanks." I took a sip, then surprised myself by drinking half of it at once. "That's good. I appreciate the Band-Aids. I suppose I've got to go tell Aden what's happened." I watched her. "I'm not looking forward to that."

"Why not?" She refilled my glass, her face quite blank.

"Well, I borrowed his boat this morning, and now I've got to tell him I had to jump ship, leaving his boat full of gasoline out there. And a life preserver. Odds are, he won't let me borrow anything again." I smiled weakly.

"I'm sure that—" She looked about nervously, and I wondered what she was so sure of.

"I was kidding," I said. "It's just that no one likes to pass on bad news."

"But I'm sure . . . he'll . . . I mean, it was an accident, after all. You couldn't have known the boat was going to . . . was . . . that you'd have trouble. He can't blame you for that."

"I'm sure he won't—"

"It wasn't your fault. In fact, it might be his fault! He shouldn't have been letting you use the boat if there was something wrong with it."

"I'm sure it was an accident," I said. An accident on his part, anyway: Those holes were deliberately punched into the fuel tank. But trust Claire Bellamy to take comfort in finding fault in the matter. "It's just that we'll have to notify the Coast Guard, so they don't freak out if someone finds the boat empty. I'm sorry, I'm just completely worn out. I should be going now. Thanks again for your help."

"Certainly. I . . . good luck with the, ah . . ." She gestured across the street, toward the Chandler House and I thought she was going to say, "Good luck with telling Aden," but she paused. "Good luck with the, ah, dig."

I whipped my head around, tact and discretion burned away by the adrenaline. "The dig?" I barely managed to keep the surprise out of my question.

"Yes, isn't that what you call it?"

"Yeah, I guess. . . ." She was wishing me luck with the dig, the thing that was the blot on her social landscape? The thing that was robbing her of sleep and adding to the density of noisome tourists? "I guess . . . we'll be back at work to-morrow, if the police say it's okay."

"Yes, the police." She seemed to consider, then spoke in a rush. "Well, it would probably be a nuisance for you to fill up your holes and everything, so you shouldn't worry about that for the weekend. I mean, you really can't see so much of it from here, and we'll just whisk people inside and out to the back."

I couldn't have been more surprised if she'd suddenly grown a second head. "I . . . appreciate that. It certainly makes my life easier." I decided to make a run for it, before she changed her mind again. "Thanks again."

I walked down the steps and hurried out the side gate, all too aware that Monet and Matisse had lifted their heads to watch my departure. I held my breath until I was safely on the other side of the gate and the latch dropped down, equally aware that Claire Bellamy was watching me too. I sensed rather than heard the kitchen door close silently behind me.

As I crossed the road to the Chandler House, I could see that Daniel was talking to Aden in the parking lot. "—been threatening to do it for ages. I just hope you mean it this time."

"Trust me, Daniel." Aden ground out the cigarette he'd been smoking.

Doubt was written large on Daniel's face. He saw me coming toward them, gave me an odd look, and took my arrival as an excuse to cut the interview short. Aden's face flickered annoyance and then slid smoothly into a welcoming smile. It was so quick a transformation that it was barely noticeable. Then his smile faltered and turned into a worried frown when he saw that I was soaked through and my hands were covered in Band-Aids. "Emma, what happened to you?"

"There was . . . someone punched a hole in one of your fuel tanks. I had to ditch it off the Bellamy's property. I'm sorry, Aden."

"How could that have happened?"

"Aden, I think someone stuck a screwdriver or something through the tank on purpose. When the first one was empty, I switched over, and after I opened the vent, it began to spill out. It's anchored out there but have you got any idea who might have—?"

He was silent for a long moment. "Emma, I'm very sorry that this happened. I can't imagine how it might have . . . all I can think of is that a lot of unsavory things happen down at the marina. Perhaps it was just vandalism, perhaps it was something directed at me. I don't know, maybe I took someone's parking space inadvertently. It's equally possible that someone tried to sabotage someone else's launch but got mine instead. I'm only sorry that it happened to you. Are you all right? Nothing broken, nothing . . . irreparable? How did you get ashore, if you ditched by the Bellamys?"

"I climbed up the cliff."

"My God." He stepped back. "But then, how did you get

past those two dreadful dogs, what are they, Mamet and Baudelaire?"

How strange. Someone like Aden would make a point of learning the names of the dogs, I felt sure of it. It felt like he was playing for time. "Monet and Matisse. I didn't get past them." I shivered. "But Claire got to me in time, though she claims they wouldn't have done any damage, that they were just playing." I looked him straight in the eye. "She was surprisingly nice about the whole thing, once she'd heard what happened. She even wished me luck with the dig. I suppose I have you to thank for that?"

He shrugged. "No, not at all. I had a chat with her; I think we've reached a sort of détente, in the matter of the dig. But she should be nice, that's only what neighbors should do."

"I think we should call the Coast Guard, shouldn't we?"

"Yes, and then I'm going straight to the marina, to see if I can't get some answers to this. But," he looked at me, "maybe you need to get to the hospital? Let me take you there now."

"No, no, I think I'm all right. Only tired and shaken. I just want to go home and take a bath. Maybe take a nap."

"Maybe take a Valium," Aden agreed. "Good God, what a morning. You're sure you're okay?"

"Yes, thanks." Valium sounded like a nice idea, but it wasn't actually part of my medicine chest. Aden came up with it pretty casually, though.

"Well, then, I'll see you tomorrow. Take good care of yourself. We don't want anything to happen to you before the end of the dig."

"Thanks, Aden."

He walked me over to the car and waited patiently while I got the key into the lock. I sat down, frowning at the cold fabric chafing against my skin. I waited until he returned to his office, and then went to see if Detective Bader was still on the site. He was, but when I gestured to talk to him, I realized that we would be directly beneath Aden's window. The curtain moved, so I suggested we go away from the crime scene to talk.

"What happened to you?"

I told him the story and he frowned. "I'll look into this. I don't like the way things are going around here. You're not badly hurt?"

"No, but I'd like to get going and change out of these things."

"Sure. Let's fill out a report too, when you're feeling up to it. I'll let you know if I find anything. Just . . . be careful."

I nodded and thanked him. Back in the car, and functioning on autopilot now, I pulled out of the parking lot. I got about two blocks along when I had to pull over, just for a minute, because another fit of the shakes came over me. I rested my head on the steering wheel and took some deep breaths until I thought I could drive again.

I sat up, turned the key in the ignition, and frowning, turned it off again. I lifted my foot from the brake and shifted, awkwardly resting it on the passenger side seat so that I could examine my leg. Okay, I wasn't seeing things. I reached down and poked at the four little tears in the bottom of the leg of my jeans, just above the ankle. Playing, my ass, I thought. Those dogs play rough.

I turned again, squelching against the vinyl seat, and hit the ignition. Claire had been scared into concern and politeness, and I was beginning to suspect that it was Aden Fiske who had scared her. I didn't know what was going on, I thought as I pulled off the verge, but it was big enough to involve sabotage and the possibility of death. Whatever it was, one thing was for sure. I was done with the eighteenth-century point of view for a while. No more messing around in boats.

Chapter 9

I PULLED UP INTO THE DRIVE OF THE FUNNY FARM TO see the students more or less doing as I'd asked. They were sitting outside with their dishpans full of water, washing sherds. I noticed that they'd taken some of the sawhorses to serve as drying racks, setting window screens up on them. I noticed with some jealousy that they'd had lunch and the drinkers had had beers. Sitting in the sun, laughing, nattering on, and working, they all looked pretty normal. And there was little or no chance that I could sneak past them without revealing that I was soaking wet. I was just glad that Brian wasn't home to see me like this.

I got out of the car and tried to keep my demeanor as careless as I could. "Hey guys. How's it going?"

They all looked up and waved. Joe frowned. "Emma, what happened to you?"

"I took a swim."

"You took a swim." Bucky stood up, looking like she'd bitten into tinfoil, pained and disbelieving.

"Yep. Pretty embarrassing."

"Yeah, but how'd that happen?" I noticed that Meg was looking at my hands, which I stuffed into my pockets.

"I was motoring past the Chandler House and Aden's fuel tank sprang a leak. I decided not to stick around. Man, was that water cold."

"Not exactly the best time for swimming in New England," Dian said.

"I wasn't under the impression that there was a good time for swimming in New England. Brian goes to the beach only for the sun; he wouldn't get near the surf if you paid him. It's that thin Californian blood of his," I said. "Let me get changed, and then I want to take a look at what you've got done today."

I thought I'd made it into the house without further comment, but then didn't hear the door slam behind me. My sister had followed me into the kitchen, and she had been followed by Meg. When Bucky realized that she wasn't alone with me, she gave Meg a guarded and irritated look. Meg returned the favor. I realized that each of them, based on our previous history together, believed that she was one who might be able to get the full story from me.

"I'll be down after I grab a shower," I said, but I was mistaken if I thought that would put either of them off.

"What happened out there, Emma?" Meg said. Bucky glared at her.

I dropped my bag onto the kitchen table and began to head upstairs. "I'm freezing. We can talk after I get changed."

"You never would have put out without checking everything first," Bucky said, following me. I might have been able to put Meg off, but apparently Bucky still thought that she had the right to follow me into my bedroom more than ten years after I left the family home. My sopping sneaker laces seemed all but welded together, but I finally managed to work them apart. I pulled off my wet things, down to my underwear. My socks landed with a wet squish on the floor.

Bucky sat on the bed as I gathered up my clothes. "So?"

I ignored her and shut the door to the bathroom, stripping down—where to put the wet clothes? The laundry basket wasn't the place for them and I was about to use the tub; I settled for dumping them onto the closed toilet seat cover. I got the shower going and took a minute to check the bandages on my hands. I'd have to chuck them and then replace them after I got done washing up. I hopped into the shower, immediately grateful to feel how hot the water was; the linoleum floor had been no comfort to my cold feet. As I stood there, letting myself warm up again, I heard the door open and close.

I stared at the tiles in front of me. "Bucky, go away."

"Not until you tell me what happened today."

The tiles were in good shape, but the grout needed work. "Could I just have a minute?"

"Sure. You've got a minute, and then I call up Brian to see if you told him anything."

I stuck my head out around the shower curtain to glower at Bucky. She'd dumped my wet clothes onto the floor and was sitting on the toilet seat, using my hand mirror to check for blemishes on her face. She put the mirror down when it became too clouded to see anything.

"I mean, you guys tell each other everything, right?" The little wretch had the audacity to pull the wide-eyed innocent look that hadn't worked on me or anyone else with sense for years. "No secrets from each other, right?"

"I haven't had the chance to call Brian," I said. I pulled myself back around the curtain and into the shower; I was still raisin-fingered and wrinkly, but far less shivery. I washed my hair and began to soap off, not because I was dirty, but just out of habit: that's what you do in the shower.

"I'll tell him when he gets home; I've got work to get finished up today."

"I'll call him, then. He'd want to know."

Shit. I turned off the shower and stood there. "Go get me my robe, would you?"

I heard the door open and shut again and grabbed a towel. I blotted my scrapes carefully and had replaced the antiseptic and the bandages by the time that Bucky got back with my robe. Snatching it away from her, I pulled it on over my towel and found another towel to start work on my hair. Bucky sat herself down on her throne again, this time using my razor to get rid of a few stray hairs around her ankle.

"Stop that." I took the razor away from her and went back into my room. "Jesus."

She followed me. "Well?"

"There was a hole punched into the spare gas tank. I wasn't about to start the engine again and I wasn't going to just sit there, so I ended up climbing up some rocks to safety." No sense telling her about the dogs and Claire, I reckoned.

"So you don't think the punctured tank was meant for you?"

I stopped looking for clean underwear. "Of course not. It was some stupid prank, something that someone did down at the marina. Maybe Aden pissed someone off. Maybe it was just something that someone was doing because they were taking it out on the Stone Harbor Historical Society. It was nothing to do with me. How could it have been? No one knew I was going to use that boat."

"Except for Aden."

"How could he have known I would be interested in borrowing his boat? And he would have been supremely stupid to give me the boat he'd tampered with. Jesus, Bucky, leave it alone. It was a dumb accident that I got the boat first, that's all." I got dressed hurriedly and began to brush out my hair; Bucky was looking through the change on the bureau, sorting it out by denomination.

"Of course I'm going to tell Brian," I said, working out a huge tangle. "I will always tell Brian everything. I just think an accident like this doesn't need to be blown out of proportion."

"And he'd take it better when he hears it with a couple of beers in him and you looking dry and warm and safe and making light of it all."

"Yeah, well, there's no point in making things out to be worse than they are, my little drama queen, is there?"

She watched as I ran the towel over my hair again; there was a lot of it and it took some work to get it dry. I began on another tangle.

"You should cut that hair of yours. It's nothing but trouble."

"Thank you for your opinion. I happen to think long hair suits me."

"It doesn't, really." Bucky swept all the quarters in the stack into her hand and pocketed them.

"Do you mind?" I shoved the dimes away from my sister before she could get them too. "God almighty."

Bucky wasn't a bit deterred, and not embarrassed either. "It makes you look too old-fashioned, even just plain old. I think it's just vanity, or maybe it's something to put people off. You know, when it's all pulled back and all, it gives you a rather fierce look. Quite the disciplinarian, or maybe that's what you're going for." Now she was rooting around in my dresser drawers. "How old is this lipstick?"

"I don't know, last summer, I think. Could you please just—"

"I never see you wearing any." She tried it on, cocked her

head trying to decide whether she approved of the color. I took it away from her and shooed her out of the room.

"Enough. I don't need your help with my marriage, I don't need your help with beauty tips—" I called through the door.

"That's what you think."

"—And I especially don't need your help making trouble. God, Bucks, you really are a pain in the ass."

"You're right there; you're good at making trouble all on your own. And I'm not the one messing around in boats, Ratty."

"Yes, yes, trust me when I say the *Wind in the Willows* reference already occurred to me. Now just stop poking your nose where it doesn't belong." I thumped down the stairs. Meg was still in the kitchen and could hear Bucky's voice as well as I could as my sister called downstairs:

"Isn't that what everyone always says to you, Emma?"

I waited until Brian came home to tell him what had happened; there was no use in getting him worried at work when no real harm had been done.

"Isn't that the house with the big dogs you're always talking about? The ones that bark all the time?"

"Yeah. They were there, but the owner was too, so it wasn't any problem."

Bucky had come in just in time to hear Brian ask about the dogs. "You didn't tell me about any dogs," she protested. "What else did you leave out in the version you told me?"

"Nothing, Bucky. Take a hike."

I stole a quick look at Brian, who was frowning deeply. "Hmmm."

I told them about the change that had come over Claire

when I mentioned Aden. Brian didn't seem much more pleased, but at least he wasn't thinking about the dogs anymore.

"I wonder what happened there." He threw some diced carrots into the coleslaw that he was making.

"I don't know. I don't particularly care, either, now that I know she's going to be off my back."

After we ate, the seven of us sprawled around the porch, drinking beer until the bugs drove us inside, and I took the excuse to head up to my room early. I was unbelievably tired and flopped onto the bed, relieved at last to have a little space to myself. The day had been so chaotic that I felt as though I'd been through at least two days in the space of one. I was so tired I didn't even pick up the book I was reading, but turned out the light to think while I waited for Brian to get done in the bathroom. Who would have wanted to sabotage the boat? Did it have anything to do with Justin's death? I couldn't think about that now: I tried to occupy myself by making plans about the site, when we could get back out there. Putting two or three more units to the north of the house might reveal whether there was an outbuilding over there, perhaps a storehouse or a stable or something. There was an outline of a structure I couldn't make out on the insurance map, and it was worth investigating. Even if nothing appeared, the units would give us a couple of windows onto what was going on over there. Maybe there'd even be enough to talk the Chandler House people into letting me continue working on the site after this survey was done. Did I know for sure that Justin had been killed? Maybe there was so much blood because of. . . .

I yawned and was surprised to find that I'd closed my eyes. I rolled over onto my side, curled up a little, and went back to my plans.

If the outbuilding was near the way down to the water,

perhaps that's where a counting house was. Or maybe boating equipment was stored there, oars and ropes and such . . . I must remember to look into the possibility of renting a boat for the students at the end of the dig. Haven't been for a sail in, what, years . . . out on the water . . . in the sun. . . .

Something warm and soft pressed against my side and I started awake, legs shooting straight out. I heard a yelp and a thump and I realized that it was Brian; he'd kissed the spot just above the waistband of my pajamas where my T-shirt had hiked up.

"Oh God, Bri! Please tell me I didn't kick you," I said, sitting up.

"No, you just scared me. I'm sorry, I didn't know you were asleep."

"I didn't know I was either. I'm sorry, come to bed."

"Okay."

But instead of walking all the way around to his side, Brian climbed in over me, making more of a production of it than was actually required. There was some rolling around and a lot of kissing before he actually got over to his side, and then he sighed.

"Well, I'm wide awake now. I'm coming back over there. It's much nicer over there, where you are." He scooted over and rested his head on my stomach, looking up at me, and walked two fingers up my arm. "Much nicer."

"Hey!" I whispered, pretending to slap his hand away. "We can't do that, not with a houseful of people. . . ." But I wasn't all that sleepy anymore, either, and something about all I'd been through earlier in the day suddenly made Brian's suggestion that much more attractive.

"They're practically outside and Bucky sleeps like the dead. You can't tell me you never learned how to sneak around with boys without getting caught back in high school."

"I was a good girl in high school," I whispered, primly and a little untruthfully. "But I'm always ready to learn."

The next morning, I called Detective Bader and got the word that it was all right for me to return to the site. When I asked him if he'd learned anything, he only said, "We're pursuing every lead at the moment and treating the case as a homicide." An unreasonable part of me pouted, believing that having handled myself so well on the discovery of Justin's body, I should get more than that, but I thanked him and hung up.

Leaving Bucky again asleep in the car when we got to the site, I was surprised to see Perry Taylor was back at work. Her arm was in a sling, which she'd covered up with a pretty colored silk scarf, the sort that is sold in expensive museum shops. I'd given my mother one just like it years ago, as a birthday present. Perry looked surprisingly well for her ordeal, maybe a little pale, but she brushed off my concern.

"I'm fine, just a little shook up, you know? When I stop to think about what happened. . . ." She swallowed. "I decided I just had to get back to work. Put as much of that out of my mind as possible." Then she smiled. "The great thing is that they gave me some absolutely *outstanding* painkillers. I highly recommend codeine and acetaminophen for putting your cares behind you."

I laughed. "Good thing you don't have to drive, with those. If the bus route had changed, you'd be out of luck."

Bucky showed up then, looking a little groggy.

"There's always a cab, and Fee would be happy to give me a lift if I asked." Perry shrugged. "But I do enjoy the walk down to the corner. And I'm not the only one glad that the bus route hasn't changed. So's Daniel, that was a real victory for him and his father. A lot of folks at their factory would have been out of luck." Perry wrinkled her brow. "But I understand that you had a little mishap yesterday too. Are you sure you're okay?"

"Yeah, I am." I looked down at my hands, which were a sorry collection of scratches; I was down to just one bandage on the deepest cut. I lowered my voice. "It just seems as though the Historical Society is going through a really bad time at the moment. First with you, then Justin, and—"

Perry's eyes welled up and she caught her breath. "I just can't believe that," she said. "I mean—Justin? Who in God's name would want to hurt him? There's no reason, no reason at all." She wiped her nose on a little old-fashioned lace handkerchief.

"I'm sorry, Perry," I said.

She was finding it difficult to stop crying, and it was obvious she'd been doing a lot of that lately. "No, Emma, it's not your fault. We live in an ugly world, and it looks like it found its way to Stone Harbor at last." She put her hanky away. "It's going to be a private service, just family, a few close friends. His mother is in a state of shock."

"I can imagine."

She checked her watch. "Damn. Almost time for the first group; there's no chance they'll stay away today, that's for sure. I thought we would still be closed, but after two days already, Fee is ready to go berserk. How's my mascara? No raccoon eyes?"

"No, you're good," I said. "Time for me to get down to it too."

Perry turned to go, and I heard an odd little clicking noise. Bucky heard it too, but judging from the puzzled expression, she couldn't place it either, so we went and found the others ready to start the day's work.

It took us all a while to settle into it. The students couldn't help looking over to the area where Justin had been when they went to sift their soil. There was nothing left to show that there had been an investigation there, save footprints that weren't ours and trampled grass, muddy in the areas where Justin had been: Someone had hosed down the area to remove the last traces of blood. It was more than enough to be suggestive.

The rhythm of work eventually took over, and when the visitors began to peep over the fence, or line up along the barricade, that provided the rest of the necessary distraction. It occurred to me as I answered the questions that all of the visitors could be divided into distinct categories, based on how each group perceived the past. Some embraced it, because they thought that it was a better time—more elegant, more polite, more religious, simpler, less cynical, less vicious—than the present, though I could have given them examples otherwise in every case. Some scoffed at it, rejecting it for being unenlightened, brutish, ignorant, too false, too coy, too harsh, and I could have made arguments either way there, as well. Some people wandered through the house tour, eyes glazed over, only there because it was on the checklist, or because they were supposed to, or because they couldn't find where they really meant to be; these treated the past as some people treat an older relative, visiting only out of duty or obligation, but taking no joy in it. Other people were eagerly lapping up every morsel, possibly because it fed their own images of the past, their own theories of local history, their own notions of what life should be like. Sometimes these were indiscriminate, never questioning anything they were told, never moving past the spiel of the tour; some of them, on the other hand, were combative, actively arguing with the guide over interpretations, dates, facts. There were still others who were there out of a sense of curiosity, some who were there because they got on the wrong bus, and some who just had a whim and decided to try something new. What you take from the study of the past, I decided as the crowds thinned toward lunchtime, was pretty much what you brought to it. As far as I was concerned, any difference between humans in the past and today and the future would only be a matter of degree.

The last of the crowd consisted of a young girl and her parents, who made as if to move on to more interesting sights in town. The girl balked, wanting to stay. She'd asked a couple of pertinent questions about how we date artifacts, and I let her handle the sherd of the day, a nice piece of eighteenth-century Rhenish stoneware with dark blue and purple glaze. I realized she was at the age, ten or maybe a bit older, when most archaeologists get the bug.

"Do you think you'd like to do this?" I asked at last.

She seemed to think about it for a minute. "It looks like hard work."

"It is, but it's a lot of fun too. You can learn a lot."

She cast another eye over the students, then nodded. "Yeah, maybe. I like history and that."

"Come on, Ashley, we're going to be late for lunch," her mother urged her. Over Ashley's head, she mouthed the words, "Thank you," to me, which made me glad I'd spent the time with her daughter.

As Ashley and her parents went past us, heading back toward the parking lot, I heard Ashley confide to her mother, "I think I want to be an archaeologist, Mom."

Her mother replied in no uncertain terms. "Not if I have anything to do with it. You're going to get a college education, missy!"

My face froze and I clamped my hand over my mouth. I was torn between horror, annoyance, and amusement. Meg and Rob were exchanging delighted looks and quickly shared the line with the others. Considering that between them they had four bachelor's degrees and three master's, and were working toward adding a few more letters after their names, I realized that, like the differences between past and present, the way people viewed archaeology was only a matter of degrees.

I told Bucky, who had just looked up and was unaware of the joke. "That's why I went into archaeology," I explained, grinning. "It was to avoid all the studying."

"That's stupid," she said, frowning. "People should know better."

"It's just ignorance, Megabucks. It's just silliness, it's no big thing."

"Still." My sister hunkered back down over her work. I sighed; she could be so impatient with anyone who wasn't similar to her, dismissing whole chunks of life as it went on around her because it didn't immediately appeal to her.

I sighed. "Hey, Meg, how close are you to wrapping up in that pit feature?"

"I'm almost done. Why?"

"I'm thinking that when you get to a good stopping place, I want you and Bucky to open up a couple of units over on the other side of the house. We've got permission to do one or two tests over there, beyond where the tourists are allowed, and I'd like to drop a couple of quick ones, just to see what that mark on the insurance map could be. Okay?"

"You got it."

Perry had finished up with another group of visitors around the back of the house. I heard Daniel Voeller's voice as he called to her. "Perry! You left these in the bathroom."

I glanced over and saw him hand her the brown bottle with her painkillers. She shook her head as she took them from him, and looked around, catching my eye. She shrugged, self-deprecatingly. "Thanks. I don't know what's wrong with me."

"Same thing that's wrong with the rest of us, I'll bet," Daniel said. "Take it easy on yourself, Perry. You've had a bad time lately."

"Thanks. You know, I really have. You just don't have any idea. Daniel, when you get done talking to Fee, could I have a word with you? It's about the. . . ."

She trailed off delicately and whatever it was, Daniel took the hint. "Sure. I still don't know what I can do for you, but when I'm done with Fee and before I see Aden, we can take a moment."

"Thanks. I appreciate it."

They both entered through the back of the house, and I got back to work.

It was interesting to watch how history was told at the Chandler House. There was a standard spiel to go along with every room, of course, and when the windows were open, the smell of grass and salt air and roses from the garden wafting over us, we could almost recite the history as the visitors got it by rote: Justice Matthew Chandler had built the house in 1723–24; his family was large, with as many as eight children living at home at one time with his wife and servants; that he was an important member of the community; that part of the house was burned in 1738, etcetera. But I noticed that each guide put a slightly different spin on his or her version of the house's history and what we were doing to add to it.

Fee emphasized the beauty of the house and the objects that would have filled it, now only partially represented by reproductions and similar objects. She tended to play up what I thought was a very romantic idea of the past and the house, although she didn't actually make any factual mistakes when it came to the family's history.

Perry also focused on the things in the house, but then added information about what the objects represented at the time, and filled in more of the town's history, so that the Chandlers were a part of the community. I did notice that her family's name showed up on more than one occasion: "Other families, including the Taylors, Bradleys, and Tapleys, would have had similarly fine wares." It was almost as if she was showing off her family's house, the number of times she made such comparisons.

And every time Perry came by that day, we heard that clicking noise again.

Ted, on the other hand, seemed to go the social history route, filling in the blanks that the others left behind, suggesting how the Chandlers would have made their money, what the harbor would have looked like filled with fishing boats, and how differently the wharf would have looked as an industrial area rather than a tourist area. He surprised me by adding Margaret Chandler to the narrative, pointing out that she would have been a busy person with her large family and the duties of the wife of an important man; he included the idea of how many servants would have been needed to run a house of this size or work in the family warehouses, even if he did suggest that Matthew was a capitalist ogre.

As for describing what we were doing, the guides usually hit the mark pretty well. Fee did throw out a couple of clunkers about what we could expect to find: furniture, clothes, meals still intact on plates. After I tried to correct her a couple of times between tours, she eventually just didn't bother anymore. I did tell the crew to put aside a marked bag containing the "artifact du jour," so that the guides could show the visitors without interrupting us.

Taking all the guides' narratives together, it wouldn't be such a bad picture of life on the site; one at a time, though, they left me with the idea that people were all leaving the site with a skewed idea of the history of the house. I'd heard

worse, though, and was pleased that this was a place where
the guides really took an interest in the past as something
more than an amusement park.

Apparently Daniel thought so too. He was leaning over
the sawhorse, taking us all in. "Wonderful what uses the past
is put to, isn't it Emma?"

"I suppose so." But I got the impression that he was being
sarcastic. "You don't think people should learn from the
past?"

"Oh, I do, I do indeed. It's just that everyone who works
at the house seems to enshrine history, and never learn from
it. I say you learn from your mistakes, and then forge on
ahead. Chuck the rest of it and move on with life."

"Pretty funny sentiments, for someone on the Historical
Society board, don't you think, Daniel?"

"Not at all. It's the perfect place for a little shakeup, to insert the thin end of the wedge. If I had my way, there'd be a
whole lot less of Fee's way of thinking, or Perry's for that
matter, and a whole lot more of Ted's. Use history to teach
people about how to get along with each other, not as a monument to one family."

"I liked what Ted said too, but he didn't seem to mind including a discussion of the Chandlers along with the rest of
it. It is their house, after all."

"Well, never doubt that Ted does everything to a very
specific end. He thinks of himself as an agent provocateur, a
political creature."

"Like you?"

Daniel laughed. "Ah, he'll never be the schemer I am.
Take care, Emma."

"See you Daniel." I checked my watch. "That's lunch,
guys."

I was glad to imagine that things were back to normal by
this time. It was a busy day, for everyone, with record num-

bers showing up to the house, and the foundation now fully exposed. The puzzle there was that it was clearly not the brick foundation to a house, as I'd thought there must be, but seemed to be a much less substantial structure. The uneven surface that we were uncovering also puzzled me; we were obviously still above the charred remains, and those were incorporated into some of the holes, making mottled fill. All I could tell was that it was done by human agency.

It was while we were eating that I noticed something unusual. I was keeping an eye on everyone, trying to gauge how their morale was, when I noticed that Bucky wasn't at all engaged with the banter as she had been the day before. She was sitting next to me, peering intently at one of the brightly colored flowers at the border between the beds and the lawn where we were eating. It soon became apparent that she wasn't so interested in the flower itself, but its occupant, a fat bee that was gathering pollen with workmanlike diligence. My sister's stillness was what made me remark the scene; it wasn't the laziness that she was so fond of, it was a focused tranquility that separated her from the outside world. Even when she raised her hand, it was almost meditative, and as I watched she slowly, with infinite gentleness, stroked the soft hairs on the bee's back. Before I turned away to answer Rob's question about our strategy for that afternoon, I saw her examine the yellow grains of pollen on her finger with the same deliberateness. I was glad for the interruption, reluctant that anyone else should see her or break the moment for her.

"Well, I think that after lunch, we'll take some photos of what we've got exposed so far and then move Meg and Bucky over to start the next set of units. You ready for the big time, Bucks? A unit of your own?"

"Sure, no problem." The words were flat; the magic of the moment with the bee was gone.

"Okay, good. Meg'll be there if you have any questions and she's the one to watch for a good example."

"I think I can get a good start today."

We looked at the map and considered the tree line that marked the edge of the Chandler House property and the now-empty Mather House. The units would go there to see if we could pick up anything that might have marked the boundary, or possibly identify any outbuildings associated with the landing. "Find me something good," I finished.

"What do you want, as long as I'm taking orders?" Meg asked.

"Another foundation would be good, but make it early. Pre-Chandler European, if you want."

Meg pretended to write down a lunch order. "Pile of old rocks, hold the elites."

"I'll be back around in a bit to see what you're up to."

I tucked the map into my notebook and we walked back to the main part of the dig, where quite a crowd had gathered. They were staring at the now-exposed brick foundation, too small for a house structure, too large and too close to the main part of the house for a shed. There was a nearly three-foot break in the line of bricks, which looked as though a doorway belonged there. There were still those irregular pits, spaced around the edge of the features and throughout the interior of the brick perimeter.

"Emma, can we get any shots from the upstairs windows?" Rob asked. "An overhead shot might give us a little better picture of what's going on here."

I looked up, shading my eyes. "I checked with Fee, and the two windows that we could use are blocked by pieces of furniture. I'll try to talk her into it, but they are covered with things, and it would be a production to try and move them. It's worth the effort though, you're right."

It took us a good forty-five minutes of fiddling with the

photographic work but I knew it would be worth it in the end, once we had the foundation recorded. I just knew that with a little work on the microstratigraphic level, we'd be able to say something interesting about what was going on here directly after the fire.

Bray Chandler wandered by the site right after we finished. Characteristically, after a grunted "hello," he stood and stared without a word, not asking questions, not offering insights. Remembering the discussion about Nicholas Chandler, I told Bray about what I'd seen in the records at the library.

"So I think that if you went back to England, to poke around the collections there, you'd be able to clear it up for sure. But it doesn't look like Nicholas was Margaret's son to me. It might be a family of Chandlers unrelated to Margaret and Matthew, but I doubt that."

He was quiet for a long time, and maybe I'd had him figured wrong; he was just taking things in, considering them. His next words were a surprise to me, though. "You won't tell anyone, will you?"

I laughed. "I won't be taking out an ad in the paper, if that's what you mean, but, yes, it will go into my report."

But whatever thought I had that he was teasing me was incorrect. "You can't possibly publish that! There's . . . there's no earthly reason to!"

I could feel the smile leaving my face as I realized he was far from being intrigued or amused. "Except for the fact that it's what I'm able to say at this moment is the truth. It's part of my work and I'm professionally obliged to publish it."

The garden gnome began to get agitated. "It's a detail . . . that's all, a minor, unsubstantiated detail that can't possibly make one scrap of difference to anyone."

It certainly seems to be more than a scrap of difference to you, I thought. "Right, so why get so upset about it?"

"It . . . it would upset my mother," he said. "She . . . she shouldn't like to think there had been any . . . irregularity in the family history."

I almost laughed again, that was so weak. "I'm sure that it wouldn't bother her. I mean, this was nearly three hundred years ago. Most people in the older generations are tickled to find that there's some juicy colonial scandal in their past; it's just fun to tell about and it doesn't hurt anyone—"

"It could hurt me," he muttered.

"—and we don't even know that there is a scandal. I'll keep researching and you never know. It might be a bureaucratic error, it might be a former marriage of Matthew's that I don't know about yet—"

"There was no former marriage; it doesn't appear in any genealogy I've ever seen."

"—or it might be a cousin who was adopted into the family. There are plenty of perfectly ordinary reasons for it to be there."

"But there may not be. Perhaps your professional obligations might keep you from printing things you can't verify."

"Are you kidding me? Theory accounts for ninety percent of our published material." But another attempt on my part to add levity to the situation was a little like trying to put out a fire with kerosene.

"You're not taking this seriously. You have no idea of the ramifications of this."

I sighed. "Then tell me."

All he said was, "It's personal. Deeply personal. And it will do a lot of harm."

"Well, if you tell me how. . . ."

"This is really none of your business and I advise you to keep your nose out of it."

Bray stomped off toward the house, just as Ted came around the corner.

"He's in danger of breaking his contract with his wife," Ted whispered, as if that would explain everything. It was abundantly clear that he'd been listening in to my discussion with Bray. I admit that made my answer snappish.

"Contract? What could anything that happened three centuries ago have anything to do with—?"

"They have an agreement. She has the money, he has the name. A name that opens a lot of doors around here, and that is very handy to her business. She's one of them venture capitalists. She funds his whatdoyoucallit, lifestyle, and he makes her a part of the family."

"That sounds a little clinical to me. I mean, you don't have to get married to do that."

"It's handy to be married, sometimes," he said cryptically. "The other part of the agreement is that he keeps his nose clean, and that is where he's been having a little trouble lately. Can't keep away from the ladies. And if any scandal should reach the ears of Mrs. Bradley Chandler . . ."

"He would lose his meal ticket. And here I am providing him with another reason, however slight, to worry about that." It was a matter of one scandal, however remote and insignificant, reminding him of his own peccadilloes.

"There you are. I mean, he could take a little more care. It's almost as though he wants to get caught."

"He probably regrets his decision now, I bet."

Ted shrugged. "Maybe, maybe not. He's not that complicated a person; he's probably just trying to have his cake and eat it too."

"Thanks, Ted."

I mulled that over as I went to take advantage of one of the principal amenities of the Chandler House dig: the indoor toilet. I had to admit that, as a site, the Chandler House did provide some pretty spectacular perks. For one thing, there was no poison ivy and little to worry about in the way of ticks; the lawns and grounds were always kept carefully manicured, thanks to the good offices of Jerry and company, for the visitors. The view of the water was superb and the gardens around us in the back of the house made for some first-rate lunchtime lounging, although we were always careful to keep our sloppy selves a bit off the beaten path. But having a clean indoor bathroom at our disposal really made a nice change of pace.

The toilet was, however, an afterthought in the old house, wedged in under the staircase in the hallway and next to Aden's office. You had to be something of a contortionist to use it, and it wasn't made any easier by the fact that I was as usual festooned with various tools stuck on and in my belt and crammed into my pockets. Still, it was with a good deal of satisfaction that, when I washed my hands prior to peeing—a habit borne of many years working near poison ivy—there was actually some genuine dirt on them. This meant that I'd actually spent some time messing around with the stratigraphy, my nose in the dirt, and that meant today was a good day.

I was just sticking my trowel back into my belt when I heard Aden's voice right behind me. I jumped, but then realized as I bumped my head that there was barely room in the bathroom for me, and that his voice was being carried along by one of the air ducts.

"—pretty sure we would have seen the money by this time, after our last little conversation, Fee."

"Aden, I don't know what the problem is. I can't understand—"

"But I think I do understand, Fee. We both know, don't we, that you've been short of cash lately? Times are difficult and you told me yourself that your investments went the way of the dodo. You've had to dip into capital, as we' say, haven't you? Only there isn't so much of that either, is there? This job means a lot to you, doesn't it?"

I could barely make out Fee's voice. "You know it does."

"It would be difficult for an aging . . . person . . . such as yourself to find another job, especially in this economy, wouldn't it?"

The strain in Fee's voice was audible through the ducts. "Aden, what do you want from me? You know I didn't take it and you've already—"

"You know what I want. I want my money back."

"It's not your money, Aden."

"But you know, I've come to think of it that way. You're the one with the books, you find out where the money could have gone. By, shall we say, Friday? Yes, I think so. I think that would do nicely."

Fee said something that I couldn't make out. Aden laughed.

"I wouldn't have thought you'd have known that word, Fee. But I'm sorry to say, it's not the first time that it's been applied to me. Friday then. Or we start going through official channels."

I was about to duck out of the bathroom when I heard his door slam. Fee was hurrying back to her office. I waited another moment before I quietly let myself out of the bathroom and sidled past Fee's closed door.

I was still looking behind me, making sure that no one had noticed my too-hasty exit from the building, when I bumped into something. Ted was standing right behind me. I gasped.

He took my arm and quickly led me back around toward the front of the house, away from where the students were working on the units, away from where we had collided, which was right under Aden's window.

"That was quite an earful, now, wasn't it?" His eagerness made me queasy.

"I . . . I wasn't—"

"I know. But maybe you should. There's a lot you don't know about what's going on around here, and maybe you should know."

I smoothed out a wrinkle in my sleeve, putting as much as my feeling about intentional eavesdroppers into my reply as I could manage. "I'm sure it's nothing to do with me."

"Sure, but wouldn't you rather know why you went for an unexpected swim yesterday?"

I eyed him distrustfully. "And just what do you know about that?"

"Only that it happened. Anything else, well, they're just my theories. If you want to hear them, and it might be good for you to do so, come have a beer with me after work and I'll fill you in. It will only take a minute. I'll tell you about some of the history the Historical Society doesn't trot out for the public."

Chapter 10

"I'LL SEE," WAS ALL I COULD MANAGE. I WANTED TO get back to work, away from these people who, for some reason, were so eager to reveal each other's habits to me.

Ted was trying not to look eager at my halfhearted response. "If you're interested, I'll be by my car about five." He left.

I scurried back to the site, trying to gather my thoughts. I gnawed on a pen cap, which didn't do much to quiet my pounding heart, and neither did what I saw next. Perry Taylor was walking along the lawn with Daniel Voeller, deep in conversation. Whatever it was must have been fairly intense, because at one point, Daniel paused and looked around before he began talking again, low and close to Perry. I wondered whether Perry was aware of how tightly her fingers were wrapped in the fabric of her skirt. They parted, neither looking entirely satisfied.

Daniel walked toward the house, and I jumped a little when our eyes met. I acted as if I had been staring into the distance and then waved at him as if only recognizing him now. I could feel my cheeks warm, and it had nothing to do with the sun; both of us knew that I had seen him and Perry.

"Meeting with Aden," he said as he walked past me to the house.

"Have fun," I said, and then asked Meg a quick and unnecessary question about her progress, just to give me some cover. It was then that I decided I would go see Ted after work.

Meg and I had been able to finish marking out the new units and taking the sod, when Bucky was free to start up. Meg described what she was seeing so far—no intrusion of the twentieth-century features below the surface, and the apparent lack, so far, of anything but late-eighteenth-century materials.

"Meg, would you come with me? I want to have a look at the insurance map. Buckwheat, why don't you finish up the paperwork?"

There was no response from my sister; she was already hunched over her clipboard, closing out her notes on the first part of the site she'd worked on. She was taking to the habits of fieldwork as if she hadn't just started learning about it three days ago.

Meg and I walked out a bit, toward the fence that marked the edge of the site near the cliff. "I just want to make sure you know this isn't a baby-sitting job. I want you to get a quick look at this area, and I know you can juggle that and keep an eye on Bucky, if she needs it."

"She'll do okay; she was doing fine with the unit I helped her on."

I nodded. "I don't want to spend a lot of time out here, but as long as we have the chance. . . ."

"Right. Quick and dirty. It'll go faster without the audience participation from the tourons too."

At the end of the day, everyone was finishing closing up the main part of the site and locking the tools away, when I found Bucky chatting merrily away with Perry, who took every opportunity to drop by and follow our progress. That was also unusual; my sister seldom took the trouble to be social, and Perry—the epitome of what our mother had hoped Bucky and I would be—was definitely not Bucky's cup of tea. A little too overly mannered, a little too cute. But, I reasoned, Perry was a decent sort, if a little self-centered, and it was possible that Bucky was growing into a few social graces. It was well past time for it.

"—just past the center of town. It's really simple," Perry was saying.

"Good deal. Thanks," my sister said.

"Sorry to break this up," I said, "but I've got to get you off home, Bucks. I've got an appointment to get to."

"No problem, we're done." Perry waved her cast. "I've got to get going too. Doctor's appointment."

She looked really worn and drawn to me. "How's your arm doing?" I asked.

"Still hurts like a bear, but that shouldn't be too bad for too much longer. I'm not looking forward to the physical therapy, though. I hear it's pretty grueling." She grimaced and I said good-bye.

I dropped Bucky off at home, then rushed back to meet Ted in the parking lot of the Chandler House. He was leaning on the back of his car, a dark blue Dart that was spic and span. He'd never have to worry about getting his trousers dirty. Again, I thought that I really should do something about my ancient Civic. Ted offered to drive.

"Are we heading for Shade's?" I asked. "They have a pretty good bar in there."

Ted snorted. "I wouldn't be caught dead there. Batcha

snobs. No, we're just going down the street and around the bend to the Little Green Bar."

The part of town we ended up in, literally down the point from the Chandler House, was probably one of the oldest in town that was still standing, and, after the first prosperous generation, it had developed into a working-class neighborhood. Those two factors in mind, it had taken the hardest use over the years: Tiny houses that were built before the Declaration was signed were squeezed between early-twentieth-century triple-deckers with a porch on every floor. All the houses were butted right up against the street with no room for a front yard, though almost every house had at least one windowbox full of blooms. Many were sporting the Stars and Stripes in anticipation of Independence Day, and the near-universal choice of flowers—red geraniums, white impatiens, and purple petunias—also seemed to reflect that sentiment. I realized that some of the flags were looking tattered after having been outside continuously for nearly a year.

The bar was close to the water, a little brick joint with a green door and a couple of neon signs in the high, tiny windows. Ted pulled over onto the dirt verge.

"The original bar was painted green, so when it burned down, the name stayed, even if the owner decided brick was a better idea," he said. His faults aside, Ted did know the town history.

"You don't mean that the original burned down back in the fire of seventeen-thirty-eight?" I said doubtfully. "It can't be that old."

"No, but I bet there was a bar or a tavern or something here then too." Ted pulled the door open and held it for me. "A place for the sailors and fishermen to hang out."

"Makes sense."

"This place burned down in the nineteen-forties. And

again in the nineteen-seventies; that's when the brick came in."

"Good idea." I had to pause in the doorway, the difference in light was so great and the smell was overwhelmingly of old beer and stale cigarette smoke. Inside was nothing remarkable: a television suspended over the bar broadcast the baseball game, and I noted that the Red Sox were playing Cleveland; a mirror behind the bar was doing its best to reflect the backs of the lines of bottles—mostly blended whiskeys, bourbon, gin, and vodka—and struggling through a thick layer of soot or grease to do it; there were three optics, all for national-brand domestic beers. There were only two other drinkers, sitting in a booth, besides the bartender. Ted was the only one wearing a necktie, and he pulled it off and stuck it into a pocket as soon as we sat down.

Ted hesitated. "What'll you have? I don't know as they're set for anything fancy. . . ."

"Draft is fine for me," I said.

Ted looked pleasantly surprised. "Two drafts, Bill."

Bill got the beers by feel, as he clearly wasn't going to tear his eyes away from the game. They were cold and the glasses were clean, and it was nice to be out of the sun.

"So tell me about your theories," I said after we'd had a chance to wash the dust away.

Ted pursed his lips, almost as if he were belatedly trying to decide whether to keep them closed. "I wouldn't go so far as to call them theories. That's too big a word. Call 'em hunches, and you'll be closer to the truth." He took a small, neat sip of his beer. "And my hunch is that the Historical Society is a lot of things to a lot of people, if you know what I mean, but the biggest thing it is, is window dressing."

"How do you mean?"

"I mean it makes people feel important when they really aren't. It makes them feel like they're a part of the town, you know, or the neighborhood, when they're not. And it makes them seem respectable, when there isn't enough decency in some of them to fill an ant's Dixie cup. Window dressing." He reached over and adjusted one of the cocktail napkins so that it fit squarely on the top of the pile on the bar.

I nodded. "I was wondering about all that myself. There does seem to be an awful lot going on, between the town and the Historical Society, right about now."

Again he demurred. "There is and there isn't, that I know for sure. Some of it's just Aden flexing his muscles, you know, and some of it's a real problem, or will be, somewhere down the line. Aden does that, likes to have his power felt, every once in a while, and sometimes he's more obvious about it than he should be."

I'd never heard anyone criticize Aden Fiske so openly before, though it seemed that plenty of people would have liked to. Then I recalled Daniel's assessment of Ted as a political creature and wondered what his motives were in telling me any of this. "Who does he want to feel his power, do you think?"

Now he was certain. "I don't think: I know. It's that old guy, Voeller. It doesn't have anything to do with the bus routes, it has to do with the factory. The two of them act like the town is their private playground. Carving it up between them, trying to outdo each other. It's a game, and they don't much care about how it affects anyone else."

I took a sip of my beer. "You don't think much of Aden."

Ted shrugged. "So he writes me a check, so what? The guy's a runt. I don't mean like, small physically. I mean he's got a runt's attitude, always needs to be the one on top, always needs to act like he's everyone's friend. But he's not choosy about how he builds up his side; if he's got something on you, he'll use it." He took another sip of beer, maybe moving the level of it down an eighth of an inch. "I don't buy the nicey-nice from him."

"So you figure that's why someone punctured the fuel tank in his motorboat?"

Ted looked solemn. "Probably. Hang on a sec." He leaned over and called to Bill, still engrossed in the game. "Hey Bill, you know anyone got a beef against Aden Fiske?"

Bill's voice was a low growl and he answered while still glued to the set. "Do I know anyone who doesn't?"

"Yeah, okay, what about someone willing to act on it?"

"You mean the Tapley House?"

"I mean someone did his boat."

That drew Bill's eyes away from the game. "Let me ask around, okay?" He noticed I was there for the first time and gave me a look like he was wondering if I was the health department. "Who're you?"

Ted answered for me. "Archaeologist. She's working down at the house with me."

"Archaeologist?"

"Yeah, you know. The study of man's past?"

"Huh." Bill turned and regarded me as he might any curiosity. "I woulda thought Teddy here'd be more interested in the study of woman's past—oh, Jesus Christ!"

The Indians had caught a pop fly and effectively ended Bill's participation in the conversation. I had to steel myself against watching the game, much as I wanted to, and focus on the conversation.

"Don't mind him, he's okay," Ted vouched for the bartender, who was moving in on the television set as if his presence would goose the Sox lineup. "He hears anything, I'll let you know."

"What was that I overheard about Aden's money?" I was

assuming that Ted had heard too, but he didn't seem to mind that. "Some gone missing lately?"

"I don't know. Market crunch hit a lot of people around here pretty hard, everyone's short. I doubt it's his money though; I think if anything, Fee was talking about Chandler House takings."

"Would she have taken it, do you think?"

Ted stopped to take another tiny sip. He rearranged the glass so that it was exactly in the center of the coaster, which was aligned to be parallel with the line of the bar. He began to say something, thought better of it, then tried again. "Fee's pretty upright about most things. I don't think she would've taken it."

"Most things?"

He pursed his lips. "Her business, not mine to say. Not Aden's either, when it comes down to it, the sumbitch." He glared darkly at the top of the bar. "It's not right, how he carries on." He snapped out of it. "But there are plenty of folks who might tell you more about Aden's antics, along with Bill, here. Another person, you probably heard of her. Lives down on the common in that house. You know, the one with the stripes."

It was pretty hard to miss "the one with the stripes," as it stuck out like a candy-colored zebra in the middle of all those monochromatic cubes, a flower child among stolid burghers. "Who is she?"

"Janice Booth is a painter, does mostly seascapes. She is pretty well known, in her circles, but you know, she'll never get rich. Well, that house has been in her family since they built it there, and she's hung on to it with a death grip, specially the last couple of years when the taxes shot up so high. She's got some other artist-types living with her, paying rent, which is just about tolerated, and that keeps the roof over her head, if not actually leakproof. She's well liked around here, does some volunteering at the schools to teach kids about art, you know? But she and Aden got about as much use for each other as Bill there's got use for the Yankees, and something came up a couple of years ago when her place was getting a little rundown. Since the house is technically part of the historic district, there are rules about maintenance and that sort of thing, and Aden took the opportunity to give her some trouble about it. If anyone heard anything about someone with a grudge, she might have."

Ted took another, almost dainty, sip of beer and grinned humorlessly.

"Aden offered to buy her place, right after he smacked her with the regulations. But Janice is not the kind to roll over and she's not the kind to neglect the fine print. All she had to see was that it was required that the house be painted in the colors previously approved by the historic district; it didn't say anything about the house having to be all in one color. So she painted every other clapboard of the sides on the street one of the colors: yellow, gray, white, blue, brown, red. It looks kind of nice too—she wasn't going to sacrifice her sense of color or anything—but you notice that the sides of the house where she has the garden, where she and her 'paying guests' spend their time is all one color—she's no fool. I guess it helps with her light or something."

I was a little in admiration of Janice already; that's the sort of thing that Bucky would have been able to do and get away with. I could never do something like that and have it work out. At the same time, it didn't seem to fit with the present circumstances.

"Does the boat really sound like the kind of thing she'd do?" I asked. "I mean, that's more like an issue of her being able to live her own life, on her own terms."

Ted scratched his head. "I don't know, but I wouldn't put it past her. She's got a mean streak, if you cross her, and

Aden's done that. She ran with a pretty rough crowd when she was younger, too, got into all kinds of things she don't talk much about." He leaned over, confidentially. "She lived in New York for a while, back in the nineteen-seventies."

As if that told me exactly what she was capable of, I thought, trying not to smile. I stored that remark away for my friend Marty, who was constantly amazed at the way outsiders, particularly Bostonians and their neighbors, perceived her native city. Of course, she never did anything to change their bizarre misconceptions—she actually seemed to foster as many as she could—but that was her prerogative, I guess.

"What kind of crowd? What kind of things?"

"Politics, some. They called themselves anarchists, but who knows? It was the early seventies."

I stored that away for later. "She ever have cause to be down by the harbor? By the boats, I mean."

Ted sucked in his cheeks while he decided how to answer me. "She has a little motorboat. She does seascapes, remember. But that doesn't mean anything."

"What about Justin? I mean, that's the thing I can't understand." Everything I'd read in the paper or heard on the news confirmed what I already believed, that he wouldn't have hurt a fly or been mixed up in anything that should have ended in being shot in the head.

"I have no idea." He looked at me slyly. "Why don't you ask your friend, the cop?"

"Detective Bader?"

"That's the one."

Ah. Maybe that was it; Ted thought that he might be able to find out something extra and off the record from me. "He's not about to tell me anything. The man's like a clam with laryngitis."

Now Ted started getting a little antsy. "Well, who knows?

Maybe if you hear something, you'll let me know. And maybe if I hear anything. . . ."

He let the thought trail off, almost as if his faith in me as a source was also drying up. I nodded. "Thanks, I appreciate it. No, let me get this," I said as Ted pulled out his wallet.

Ted was aghast at the suggestion. "Oh, no. I've never let a lady pay for her drink and I'm not about to do it now." Then he smiled to take away some of the reproof. "Even if she does play in the mud all day."

The next morning, I stopped in to greet Fee, and she asked if I'd seen Aden.

"His truck's here, and the alarm was off when I arrived, so he's around here somewhere. I want to ask him about some of the arrangements for the Chandler family reunion."

"I'll keep an eye out for him."

She thanked me, and after I saw that the crew was settled, I followed along after Meg and Bucky. I was a little surprised to see them staring at the uncovered units. Not studying them, just, well, looking, which is different. Something seemed to be stalling them.

"What's up guys? Something wrong?"

"I don't know," Meg said. "I don't think so. But the cover tarp was missing and I'm trying to see if anyone screwed around with the units."

"Missing?" I asked. "But you guys weighted it down last night, right? It didn't just blow away." But even as I said it, I could see the rocks were still there, some tumbled into the unit, some still scattered about the edges of the unit. "I don't see anything else amiss here."

"Maybe one of the guards moved it, for some reason, after we left?" Bucky said. She didn't sound much impressed by her own suggestion, however.

"They shouldn't have done," I said. "But I'll ask up at the house, just to make sure. Don't worry about it for now, just get to work. Dress up that wall, would you, Bucks?"

She leaned back and scrutinized her work. "Isn't it straight? Damn, I thought I had it. The light under here wasn't too good in the late afternoon yesterday."

"She's starting to learn all the excuses, isn't she?" I asked Meg.

The graduate student nodded. "Taught her myself. Need the right tools for the job."

I was about to hike back to the side of the house when I decided that it would be a good idea to have another look at the broken-down fence that sporadically divided the two properties on the far north side of the Chandler land. No sense walking all the way back only to have to return if I could just do it now. I pulled the enlargement of the insurance map out to see if there were any other features that I could identify that might indicate whether there would have been any earlier structures or fence lines out that way. It was also a good excuse to clear my head for a moment and take in the view. When any site director tells you they're going to do some thinking, the thinking will get done, but there's a better than fair chance that they're taking a scenery break as well.

"Hey! Hey, I got something! Hey, Emma!"

It was Bucky, and she was running toward me, Meg following hard behind her.

"What is it?"

"I don't know. It looks like a fish hook or something, but it's on a chain."

She held it out to me, a little out of breath, and inwardly I cringed. I hurriedly looked over at Meg, who looked as uninformed as I, but she shook her head. She didn't even need to be asked my unasked question: Whatever Bucky had found, had she taken it out of its place *in situ*, in the ground, which would have given us the most information about its context, the place it was found, and its original date?

My sister caught the look. "It came out of the screen, I found it while I was sifting. But I know exactly where it came from. In the new level, I mean."

"What is it?" Meg tried to peer over Bucky's shoulder.

"I don't know, I can't tell." She handed the object to me and I took a look at it.

There was dirt crusted to it still, and it was a hook of some sort, but something that had never been used to catch fish. I brushed a little of the dirt away and blew off a bit more, not wanting to be too rough with the object, which appeared to be a set of three links attached to a small hook. The dappled light under the trees wasn't ideal, but I could tell that it was made of silver.

"Is it a necklace, or from a belt of some sort?" Meg asked.

"The hook seems too big for a necklace, the chain's too small for a decorative belt, I think," I said. "It's small, it looks ornate, I think it's silver, and I do think it was ornamental. Jewelry, maybe."

"What about a watch chain?" Meg asked.

"Um, I don't know. Possibly. It seems to me that a watch chain would be attached more securely. This hook has a fairly loose curve, if you know what I mean. For taking something on and off frequently."

That's when the penny dropped for me and for Meg too, at almost the same time. We struggled to find the right word, our excitement mounting as we got closer to the object's identity.

Meg stomped her foot, as if that would help her flagging memory. "Oh, what is it, one of those waistband thingies, with all the stuff—"

"Yeah," I answered. "The Victorians brought them back into style, cult of the household, but they've been around since the Egyptians—"

"You know, that lecture at the ASAAs last year. What's her name?"

"Right, that's the one. And that slide she showed, the portrait of—who was it?" I turned to Bucky, as if she had the answer, but my sister just looked blank.

"The woman in the portrait was wearing blue; was she sitting or was she standing . . . ?"

I shouted: "Chatelaine!"

"No, I think it was Elizabeth something."

"No, I mean the object, not the speaker." I turned to Bucky. "It's possible you've found part of a chatelaine."

My sister frowned. "Oh, good. What's that?"

I noticed Bucky had been watching the exchange between me and Meg with some excitement, some confusion, and a little hurt. She felt left out, and now was the chance to bring her back in.

"This is good stuff, Bucky, personal stuff. And that's what this is all about, as far as I'm concerned. If I'm right about what it is, it's also something that belonged to a woman." I looked at it and back at Meg, who nodded. "Silver, right? That's high status. Could have belonged to someone here, maybe even Margaret Chandler herself. Can you show me where you think it came from?"

Her face lit up. "I can do better than that. I had just cleaned up that wall you were complaining about—"

"Tell me it didn't come from the wall," I said quickly. If it came from the wall, well, it was just that much less likely that we could establish which stratum it had originally been in.

She shook her head vigorously. "It didn't come from the wall. It was the first bucket of soil of the new level, after I'd cleaned the wall up and threw it out. I didn't see anything in the wall stuff at all." There was an enthusiasm in my sister's voice and carriage that made my heart swell. There were so few times in my life that I'd seen her so excited, and the thought that it might have had something to do with what I was teaching her was thrilling.

I gave the links and hook to Meg, who promptly removed a small plastic bag from her shirt pocket and sealed them up tightly in it. We began to walk back toward the units when something caught my eye. A bit of blue, under some leaves in a little dip by where an old oak had been tipped over and the roots exposed.

"Guess I found where the tarp got to," I said. "Probably some kids hopped the fence, came to smoke or something and they dragged it away to sit on. Bucky, give me a hand, so we can spread it out to dry."

It was probably the excitement of the chatelaine chain that made me less alert than I would have been ordinarily. The fact that only a section of the tarp came away when I pulled it should have been the next clue that something wasn't right; the tarp wasn't just stashed away among the roots, or weighted down with a few rocks; it was a dead weight. When I pulled the free corner of the tarp away, the fetid, all-too-familiar smell almost knocked me over, and I dropped the tarp and staggered back for reasons having nothing to do with that. Out of the corner of my eye, I could just register the fact that Bucky had stumbled backward to the ground, where she turned and retched.

"Oh, God, Emma! What is it?"

I heard Meg's words but couldn't answer. I was transfixed by the face, that awful bloated face, and the realization that I knew who it was, wrapped up in the blue tarp and tucked into the hollow of the uprooted tree.

"Emma, what the fuck is it?"

It was the growing hysteria in Meg's voice that finally

made me able to draw my gaze away from the horror on the ground in front of me. I stepped back again, swallowed, and tried to speak.

"Oh, God," I heard Bucky moan from the ground. Her back arched and spasmed and I knew she was sick again.

"You're okay, Bucks," I said mechanically, unable to draw my eyes away from the sight.

"Emma!"

"Meg, it's okay," I said numbly. "It'll be okay. It's only Aden. It's just that he's . . . dead."

Chapter 11

OF COURSE I'D LEFT MY CELL PHONE BACK IN MY bag, which was at the main work area. I decided it was just as quick to go up to the house itself and call from there; it was more private than calling in front of the students and a dozen tourists. I made sure that Meg and Bucky were okay, moved them back toward their units, and headed for the house. Mercifully, for I was feeling rattled and a bit cowardly at the moment, Fee was leading a tour through the house and Perry was somewhere in the garden. Ted wasn't on today and I had the office to myself. Stabbing at the buttons with cold and shaking fingers, I found myself in the distressing situation of hitting buttons out of order, having to start again, and then, sure I was able to dial 911 correctly, found that I was left with no tone at all. Cursing, I realized that I hadn't also hit a "9" to get out. I finally made the connection.

With a nightmarish sense of déjà vu, I realized that I was relaying almost exactly the same information that I had when I'd called about Justin, but there was little hope that I was dreaming about any of this. And the fact that, after hanging up, I could now reach into my wallet and find the card that Detective Bader had given me merely cemented the reality of it all. I dialed his direct number as quickly as I could, and for once, luck was on my side.

"Detective Bader," came the terse reply.

"It's . . . it's Emma Fielding." I could barely recognize my own voice, wondering who was doing the talking and the thinking on this end. It surely didn't feel like I had any real part in it.

Before I could figure out how to announce my news, he said, "What's wrong?"

"Aden Fiske is dead."

"Where?"

"The wooded area next to the Chandler House. In one of my tarps," I added, as if that would be significant to him.

"Have you called emergency response?"

"Yes. They're coming."

"Good girl. Okay, I'm on my way. Emma?"

"Huh?"

"Emma, are you okay? Are you hurt?"

"I'm not hurt . . . just feel a little. . . ." I couldn't find the right word to describe it.

"Okay, do me a favor? Take a couple of real deep breaths, slowly let them in and out. Can you do that for me?"

"Uh. Yeah." I gave it a try, and my head cleared a little.

"Good. Sit tight and I'll be there right away."

"I'll . . . I'll be out back. I have to tell the students to stay put. Make sure everyone's okay."

"Just stay away from the body, all right? Keep everyone else away too."

"Yes. I know that." The annoyance in my voice reassured me and Bader too.

"Good girl."

And I knew I was starting to get a grip because I could feel my teeth gritting when he said "good girl" again.

Meg, Bucky, and I waited by our second set of units, trying to look as inconspicuous as possible. I had to tell Fee after her tour, of course, and she went pale at the news. "There's got to be some mistake," she said in a hurried whisper. "You found Aden—?!"

I assured her that it was true and then, after a hasty conference with Perry, they decided the best thing would be to close down the house and inform the board. Perry had to sit down, looking as if she would faint, and I watched as she fumbled in her purse for her painkillers. Once again, it took her a while to find she'd left the little brown plastic bottle on one of the filing cabinets in Fee's office, and she swallowed the pills from shaking hands. At least finding her a glass of water and putting out the CLOSED sign kept Fee busy, but it did really seem as though Perry relished being tended to a little more than the situation called for. Eventually I was able to sneak away and deal with the crew.

"Wrap up here and go home," I said. "Get cleaned up. Don't worry about the rest of the day. In fact, don't worry about anything. I'll be back as soon as I can."

"What about us?" Meg said. Bucky still looked green, but a lot steadier.

"If you don't mind, let the others take the truck. You'll have to stay with me, at least until Detective Bader is done with you." I found I couldn't muster a grin as I said, "You know how it goes; it shouldn't be too long."

So the three of us were standing there by our new units, quiet and uncomfortable, when Bader arrived. He took a few Polaroids of the tarp and the surrounding area, looking around carefully, but there seemed to be even less to see than with the discovery of Justin the other morning. He emerged from the wooded area and spoke briefly to the other officers and the ambulance crew, who had just arrived, and then called the state police lab.

"What was he doing out here?" I asked. "Was he meeting someone?"

"Maybe he was being taken away, at gunpoint," Meg offered.

"It's no use speculating until we've had a closer look," Bader said. "We have to look for other signs of blood, footprints, a struggle. We can't tell about other wounds, defensive or otherwise, on him until the autopsy."

"We . . . his office should be checked," I said. "The door's been closed since I got here this morning. Maybe he was in there last night?"

"We'll find out," Detective Bader said shortly. "What was his schedule yesterday?"

"You'd have to check with Fee," I said. "I know he had a bunch of meetings with people."

"Like who?"

"Daniel Voeller and Bray Chandler both came out to the house, I know that much." I recalled the conversation I overheard in the bathroom. "Oh!"

"What is it?" Detective Bader seized on my exclamation like a terrier on a rat.

I took a deep breath. "I heard a conversation, coming through the duct. I couldn't help it. As far as I could tell, there seems to be some money missing. Maybe it's just an accounting error," I said, feeling my face go hot. "Fee and Aden were talking about it. Aden . . . used some pretty strong language with Fee. It sounded like he was threatening her with something."

"Ah," was all he said, but there was a gleam in his eye.

"I don't know what it was about," I said in a rush. "It could have been anything, but. . . ."

"But." He carefully made a notation, and then arranged

for Meg and Bucky to talk to two other officers. He turned back to me. "Why don't you tell me how you found him?"

I ran down the story. By this time the crime scene technicians had begun their work on the area immediately surrounding the body, just out of our sight.

"This is one of your tarps?" Bader asked.

"Yes. It was missing from the units when we got here."

"You put it there last night?"

"Yes, same as always."

"What time did you leave?"

"About fourish. The historic site closes at five." I remembered my meeting with Ted. "I met Ted Cressey back here, about five. We went to get a drink."

"Cressey?" He noted that too. "Okay, that's it for now. I'll go talk to the rest of the staff. Anyone who isn't here today, who usually is?"

"Ted has his day off today," I said. "I don't know the name of the new guard, but he's around somewhere. Can you give me a call later?" I blurted out suddenly. "Let me know what you find out?"

"I'll let you know when you can return to work," he said.

Case closed on that front; I could understand wanting to be closemouthed about the investigation while it was still in progress, but surely, he could let me know how things stood? It wasn't as though I was just some casual observer here, really.

He cleared his throat. "You might also be careful about locking up at home tonight, if that's not a habit with you." Bader gave me a look that I couldn't quite identify, but his words made me nervous.

I shot a look at Bucky and Meg, who had finished giving their stories and wandered back closer to us, Bucky was now staring at Bader fixedly. "Why? This can't have anything to do with me?"

"These murders do seem to be occurring right near where you're working," he said.

"Yeah, well, that's probably just because we're working in the areas of the site that are least visible from any other area," I retorted. "It's just a coincidence, that's all."

Bader seemed inclined to let my vehemence slip by. "Just never hurts to be cautious, that's all. Now, if you'll excuse me."

Once again, it was more like he was giving us leave to depart rather than booting us off my site. We walked slowly out to the parking lot; Bucky was hugging herself, Meg was silent and tight-lipped.

"How you doing, kiddo?" I asked my sister quietly.

She rubbed at her wrist. "Better. I can't believe I threw up."

"Perfectly natural response. I almost did myself," I said.

"Yeah, but . . . you should see some of the things I see," Bucky protested. "Cases of animal abuse that would break your heart. That always bothers me, but I don't get physically sick over it. Nowadays."

"Probably because you have to expect that at work, sometimes. And you can do something about that," Meg said shortly. "Nothing anyone can do about what we saw back there."

It took me a minute to pipe up with the answer she was expecting. "You're right, Meg. It's up to the police now." But my mind was racing. Maybe Bader was right. Maybe the bodies had something to do with me or my work. If it was something to do with me, I certainly couldn't think of too many gestures more hostile than leaving corpses where I could find them. I shuddered, but the notion was ridiculous. Just in case, it certainly wouldn't hurt to make sure, though. Keep my eyes and ears open, ask the odd question, strictly in the course of my own work, naturally. . . . "She's right, Bucky. It is up to the cops now."

I could tell that Bucky didn't like taking advice or comfort from Meg; as much as they seemed to get on, there was a sense of competition between them that was growing by the day. "Yeah, probably," she said grudgingly.

By the time we got back to the Funny Farm, I'd made a few decisions, not the least of which was that I was not going to sit back and wait to find out if the bodies were someone's idea of a calling card. I got the crew together, and we barely knew how to look at each other, the situation was so strange. For the second day in a week, we were forced from the site because of a murder at the Chandler House.

"We're in a singularly bad position," I said. "We can't go back to the site for a couple of days, at least, so I want to know what you're up to. Do you want to work on the artifact processing and cataloguing—in which case, we will be the first crew ever in the history of the world to actually have that done by the time we leave the field—or would you feel better taking a little time off? It's entirely up to you. I'm going to call Brian and make some plans; I'll be here all day.

They decided to work until lunch, and then get cleaned up and head into town, en masse. "Maybe we'll catch a whale watching trip or maybe go over to the museum at Boxham-by-Sea," Dian said. "Something to, you know. . . ." She shrugged uneasily and looked away.

"Cleanse the palate," Bucky offered.

"Yeah."

"Sounds good. We'll decide what to do tomorrow later on tonight, okay?"

They all nodded silently, looking very sober and a little bewildered. I mean, what are you supposed to think under these circumstances? There is no real cure for that kind of strangeness, stress, and fear heaped the one upon the other; there's only time and distraction and gradual acceptance, with any luck.

Dian's mention of the museum gave me an idea. I went into the house and made an appointment to speak with a Dr. Spencer, one of the fine arts curators at the museum at Boxham-by-Sea, which was the town just to the north of Lawton, visible from the Stone Harbor coast. If anyone could give me information about the object I believed to be a chatelaine, the folks there would.

I came back out and heard something really strange; Meg and Bucky were arguing over an artifact. An argument between two of the most stubborn and opinionated people I know was probably to be expected; what was strange was that my sister was calling up some truly obscure examples from deep within the archaeological literature. It was nothing a neophyte should have been acquainted with.

The Chin was directed at Meg now. "Yeah, but I thought that Lancer said that these kind of things dated to 1700."

"He did, but those data were later found to have been erroneous because the settlement at Millville wasn't actually settled until twenty years later."

"Emma?"

"Sorry, Bucks. Meg's right. Where'd you pick up on all this, anyway?"

She shrugged, not pleased that I wasn't taking her side. "You know. Around."

I gave her a doubtful look and told everyone that it was time to start putting things away, if they were going to quit for the day.

Bucky wanted to take off into town on her own, in my car, saying she'd be late and that I shouldn't wait up for her. "Where are you going?"

"I'm just going for a walk, get something to eat, clear my head. I won't be late."

"Do me a favor? Just don't wander around anyplace that looks too dark, too empty. Keep an eye out, all right?"

She shifted from one foot to the other. "Emma, you worry too much. I'll be safe as Fort Knox."

I still didn't like it, but I couldn't very well put a leash on my sister, as much as I might like to. "Okay, don't stay out too late."

"Just like I said." I tossed her the keys and she took off. I went in to call Brian.

Brian was unusually quiet when he got home a while later; no one felt like cooking, so I called in a couple of pizzas. Once we'd finished eating, we went up to our room to talk. It was warm and stuffy up there; the porch was more comfortable, but too public. He asked me about what happened and I told him, leaving out the bit where Detective Bader suggested we be more than usually cautious. No sense in getting him more riled than he already was. His silence worried me the most now.

He just nodded and sighed and took my hand. I tried to think of something happier to talk about, and realized we hadn't seen our best friends since their honeymoon.

"You know, we should have Marty and Kam over this weekend," I said.

Brian grimaced. "I don't know about that."

"Why not? You said he's back at work since the honeymoon, right?"

"Yeah, but I kinda wish he wasn't."

"Oh?" Brian and Kam have been best friends since graduate school; they've known each other even longer than Brian and I have known each other. This was the first time I'd heard Brian say anything like this with real seriousness.

He shrugged. "He's been a dickhead at work. He quit smoking."

"Kam? You're joking! But . . . that makes everyone cranky, doesn't it?"

Brian shook his head. "It's not just that, though. Something else is on his mind. He won't say what's wrong and I'm inclined to let him stew in it until he gets over it."

"Well, that's not a very nice thing to say."

Brian scowled. "He's not being very nice."

"I can call Marty though, right? Maybe she'll know what's going on." Then again, I realized that my friend, whom I'd known since our undergraduate days, had only called me once since she'd returned from her honeymoon. I should have been inundated with pictures, plans, gossip, the whole nine yards, long before now. Maybe something *was* seriously wrong. . . .

"Sure, call Marty. Whatever."

I decided I'd better tackle this head on. "You're being pretty grumpy. What's up?"

"Nothing."

"Okay." I got up and made as if to leave, knowing he'd speak up.

He sighed.

Here it comes. . . .

"No, not nothing. Emma, I'm worried about you. I don't want you messing around too much at the site."

"Brian, I'm not messing around. I have to be there, it's my project. I have to talk to the police, for obvious reasons. Before, I gave them the pictures of the site so that they could find whoever killed Justin. There is no extra Emma presence in that situation, other than what is expected of a good citizen. I promise, I'm not doing anything exciting—"

He broke in with an irritated gesture. "Yeah, look, I know we've used that word before, to talk about things I don't really even want to think about. I can't do that anymore. I *won't* do it anymore. I don't want you getting yourself hurt. I don't want you getting yourself killed because your job takes you to weird places and places you near weird people."

I tried humor. "*Honey*. I've been to your Christmas parties and the folks *you* work with—"

He was in no mood for it, though. "Em, I'm trying very hard to be serious. I'm trying to be reasonable and you're being flippant about it. I don't appreciate it."

I leaned against the doorway; all of a sudden our room, which usually felt like a nest and a haven, felt like the site of a cage match. "I'm sorry. I don't like it either, that's why I'm making stupid jokes. But I'm not going to not do my job, just because of something that has nothing to do with me."

He leaned back against the bedstead looking defeated. "But how do you know it won't have something to do with you? If there's someone with a grudge against that place, those people, and you're seen to be connected with them— jeez, Emma, you've been in the local papers, already—then why doesn't that make you an obvious target? Especially if they want to make a big, public gesture. You're a large, slow-moving target, as far as they're concerned."

"But I don't think it is just people with a grudge against the historic site," I said. "I think it's much more likely that—"

He slapped the bedspread with a bunched fist. "Damn it, you can't even leave it alone when you claim it has nothing to do with you! Emma, I don't want you going back there."

That hung between us for a long while.

"Just wait a few months," he pleaded. "Come back to it after they've found whoever's responsible for killing Justin Fisher and Aden Fiske."

More silence.

He folded his arms. "I really think that would be best."

I came over and sat on the bed, where the old wooden floor and the braided rag rug unaccountably held my attention. "Well, I don't. I've got a schedule. I've got other people whose jobs are in my hands. I've got work at the end of this summer that I've got to do, and then it's time for classes. What am I supposed to do about that?"

I waited a long time for his reply.

"What if I ask you not to go?" Brian was very quiet now. "Really ask you not to go, like it means as much to me as the promises we made to each other when we got married?"

I pulled at one of the tufts on the chenille spread. "You can ask, but I don't think you have a right to."

"I don't have a right to not want you to get hurt?" he exclaimed. "What the hell is that about?"

I looked at him. "You don't have a right to use how I feel about you against me like that."

"Well, what else am I supposed to use?" He stood up, really agitated. "Logic isn't working! You'd laugh in my face if I said 'I forbid you to go.' What else am I supposed to do to keep you from getting yourself killed? Huh? You tell me what you think would work, because I believe I've got every right in the world to want you safe. I think I'm being a freaking prince about this, all things considered. And I'm only saying this because I love you."

I threw my hands up. "Yeah, I *know*. All I'm saying is that this isn't like bungee jumping. I'm not doing something stupid just for kicks, I'm trying to do my job. I'm telling you, if all these things had happened in broad daylight, if there were drive-bys, that would be one thing. But this is all happening at night, after everyone's gone."

"Yeah?" Brian nodded unhappily. "What about the motorboat?"

"That was a mistake, it wasn't meant for me—"

"And that is just exactly the kind of mistake I'm worried about!"

I tried to be as patient and understanding as I could. "Brian, I'm only out there for another couple of weeks. I'm out there with a crew, several hundred visitors trooping past us, landscapers roaming over the landscape, and so on. We are in the center of town. I'm not going to go poking around where there's trouble. I'm not looking for trouble. I've got my phone with me, I've got my sister with me. I'm going to do my job. I won't stay there after work. I'll come straight home. I think that's enough. I think that's fair."

There was a long silence hanging now, spreading out like a chasm between us. "I guess I'll have to be happy with that," he said at last, but he was far from satisfied. "Look, one thing. I know we've been leaving the alarm system off at night with the students downstairs, so they could come and go as they wanted, but I'm going to feel a whole lot better if we move them inside and set the alarm, okay?"

I chewed the inside of my cheek. "Where are we going to put them? The dining room isn't done, the living room is a warehouse—"

"We'll put them in my office. It will be tight, but if I move some stuff around, there should be room enough for them and their stuff. It's not like they're going to be penned in there forever; they'll just be in there to sleep at night. And there's an air conditioner in there; they won't feel so crowded if it's nice and cool."

I really thought that he was overreacting, but it was something I could live with and it would be a gesture to Brian that I really was taking his concerns into consideration. "Okay, I'll let them know about the plan; do you need some help getting things moved around?"

"No." His forehead wrinkled. "Look, you've just got to tell them not to touch the stereo or the albums, okay?"

"Brian, I am sure they wouldn't hurt—"

"Emma, those things are my pride and joy. Please—unless you'd like to move the kids into your office? In with your books?"

I hated anyone being near my work or books—it might look chaotic, but there was a method to the madness. "No, it's too hot up there," I said hastily. "I'll tell them."

"Fine, I'll get started. Give me about an hour to get things ready."

I went around to the front of the house and climbed up onto the porch swing, pushing myself off from the railing with my toe. The dry, dusty boards of the porch felt comforting beneath my tired feet, solid and reassuring.

Brian and I hadn't had to have the discussion that most of my married archaeologist friends inevitably had, about being out of the country for long periods of time, or working in areas that were dangerous because of the political situation or the physical environment itself. I knew very few archaeologists who were married to archaeologists, or who stayed together more than a few years: It just didn't work out well when both partners were in the field at different times of the year, or worse, competing for the same jobs. We'd been lucky, for the most part, since almost all of my work has been within spitting distance of home, and even when we'd been a dual-house household for a while, it was only lonely, not impossible. Now I found myself weighing my career—something I considered to be more of a vocation—versus my marriage, and I can't say that I liked it much.

I knew I had to give Brian a lot of credit; he'd always understood when I'd had to be away from home, sometimes for weeks on end, and he was always supportive. He'd been there with me through my dissertation-writing stage and the first massive job hunt, two periods of my life that taught me a lot, though I'd just as soon forget what they did to my personality at the time. Even now, with a house torn apart and my sister visiting, he still didn't blink an eye when I suggested letting the four graduate students stay with us, even though he'd heard about what disgusting habits archaeologists could evince while in the field—the drinking, the bizarre ways of combating boredom, the sex, the lack of hygiene. So it wasn't like he was kicking up any extraordinary fuss. And to be fair, he was worried about me.

But I was worried about me too. And if I were being fair to myself, I'd been there for him too. It was mostly the contract work I did while we were still at Coolidge that kept us fed while he finished his dissertation, and I did more than my share of the cooking, uninspired and can opener–based as it was, when he had a deadline or crunch time. He sometimes had to take off for meetings across the country, sometimes with less than a couple of days' notice, and I did my best not to bitch too much about that, even though it seemed a little unfair when I knew months in advance what my schedule was like, and he had plenty of time to get used to the idea. There were times when I realized the sort of chemicals he occasionally used at work were highly dangerous, and a tour to see the emergency eye-baths, showers, and other safety protocols hadn't done much to reassure me. What did put me at ease, most days, was that I knew how careful he was, how good he was at his job.

And, damn it, I was good at my job too. And I was careful, I didn't want to get hurt or worse, any less than he. No way. Did he have the right to ask me to stop because of something beyond my control?

It was the creaking of the chains against the S-links in the roof of the porch that told me I was going too fast, that the swing wasn't made for the kind of workout I was giving it. I slowed down to a more leisurely pace and tried to take the same calm approach to my thoughts as well.

He did have the right to ask me, and I was obliged to listen and give serious consideration to what he was saying: I owed him that. What happened after, though, was up to me. There were times when I could oblige Brian and did so, happily. I wasn't certain that this was one of them, however. I couldn't stop my work because he was afraid for me, any more than I would stop because I might be afraid myself. It wasn't any risk that I was taking, it was something outside me, beyond the project and nothing to do with me, and I refused to let that stop me from doing my work. Whatever else Brian might have to say about my decision, he at least had to realize that it was mine alone to make.

And I realized that whatever happened after having made that decision was up to us both. I had faith in us, in our ability to sort things out, and was willing to bet that we would be okay. I was ready to take responsibility for my decision now because I knew my reasons and I had considered what Brian had to say. It was the only honorable thing to do, and I could live with that, I hoped.

It did, however, occur to me that there were others who had a stake in this, for whom I could not make such decisions. I had to talk to the students about what they wanted to do.

I stopped by the fridge on the way out back and pulled out a six-pack and a soda for Joe. They were out by the barbecue, trying to get a fire going. I couldn't understand what all the fuss was about, but then saw Dian toss aside a piece of wood with a bit of leather and realized that they'd been trying to light the fire without using matches. A cheer broke out when the embers spread into small licks of flame, and then they started to add some larger kindling. I wished I'd been out here too, setting fire to things and forgetting what had sent us home early again.

"Now that you have successfully captured fire, can I talk to you all for a minute? It shouldn't take very long."

"I hope not," Dian said. "I have to invent the wheel and writing before we go to bed."

"That for me?" Meg asked as she took the beer from me and started passing them around before I could answer.

"Have a seat, everyone." I handed Joe his soda.

"This sounds serious."

"It is," I said. "I want to know what you all think about going back to work at the site, what with the trouble there and all. The murders."

The students exchanged worried looks and sat down without another word.

"I'm going back to work Monday. I've thought about it a lot, and once I get the okay from the police, I'm going to finish up the job. It's only a few more days, all told. I want to know whether any of you are willing to come back with me. If you're not, I will completely understand. I will say that again: You are under no obligation whatever to go back to work at the Chandler House if you are not one hundred percent comfortable with the idea. I will not hold it against you, and neither will anyone here, I know." I looked around at each of them, letting my gaze linger on Meg just a little longer so that she would get the message. There was to be no unnecessary bravada about this.

They exchanged uneasy glances.

"But . . . Emma," Joe said. "It has nothing to do with us, right?"

"That's a matter of opinion, but that's how I feel about it. What do you all think?"

"We're all there together, during the day," Dian said.

The others nodded.

"There are lots of tourists there during the day, too," said Rob. "The murders happened before the site was opened, right?"

"We haven't actually seen anyone with a gun. I mean, not like some places," Meg finished hurriedly. "There's no threat directed against us."

"I want to find out where the brick foundation leads." Rob threw another large stick onto the fire.

"Okay," I said. "Me too. So business as usual, then, Monday?"

"Yep."

"Sure."

Joe slurped some of his soda off the top of the can. "Hang on a minute. Is Brian going to let you go? I mean, he's pretty cool and all but—"

"It is not a matter of anyone 'letting' Emma go, Joe. What century are you from? Let her go." Meg's tartness made me wonder about what kind of conversation she'd had with Neal on the same subject.

He threw a piece of bark onto the fire. "I don't mean 'let'; you know what I mean." Joe turned to me. "Brian isn't wicked happy about it, is he?"

I wondered whether I should mention that it was none of anyone else's business, then realized that his question deserved an answer. "No. Not particularly."

"Well, what if we made up some rules?" he suggested. "Just to be on the safe side."

"Like what?" Dian asked.

"Like, no one goes out to the site alone," he said.

Everyone stared at Joe—he was showing evidence of real leadership all of a sudden. "Well, there's no particular reason for anyone to be out there alone, or after dark, is there?"

"I suppose not." Meg didn't look like she was happy about putting restrictions on anything, though.

"All right then," I agreed. "That's good, that's sensible. And I've got a new cell phone. I'll keep it with me and turned on."

Again, the students exchanged another look. "Emma, I'm pretty sure we all have cell phones," Dian said. "This is the twenty-first century, after all."

The others nodded, looking at me quizzically.

"I happen to know what you all get paid, so you'll excuse me if I'm a bit surprised. You mean I'm the last kid on the block to have one?"

"I don't have one," said Rob, "but I mostly rely on sticking close to Dian and screaming really loud if I have to."

"You do have a computer, right?" Dian asked me. "How about television? You heard of that?"

I narrowed my eyes at her. "Smartass. Okay, that's agreed then, and a very good suggestion on Joe's part. And we just all keep an extra eye open for trouble then, and we're all set." I told them about Brian's idea about moving into the main house and said that it was pretty much a deal-breaker for me. They readily agreed to it, and I thought I saw a look of relief cross Joe and Dian's faces. Good, I thought. They're taking this seriously too. They invited me to share another beer before they began the move into Brian's office, but I declined, saying I needed some time by myself.

I went up to my office and shut the door. As always in the summer, it was hot up there, under the roof, and I went through a ritual of turning on window fans to get the air moving. I rifled through my CDs, a small but growing collection since I'd purchased a portable player for my office—a real splurge for me—until I found something that suited my mood. Or rather, the mood I wanted to have; I was still in turmoil, but needed to get some work done and reclaim some peace of mind. I finally decided on J. S. Bach as I turned on the computer and plopped myself down in the chair. There's nothing like listening to the music of a period for putting you in that time's mindset. Without knowing anything about the correct musicological terms, there was something about the framework, the structures of the music that helped me think about non-tangible things: Motion, emotion, behavior, all seemed to be keyed in with the cadence and the sound of the antique instruments. It worked for me, anyway.

I didn't even look at my notes or drawings, I waited for the music to take over and began to jot down my ideas: a brick structure that was not part of the dwelling, an irregular surface of planting holes with a lot of rodent disturbance, glass shards of too wide a diameter and too fine a thickness to be a drinking or serving vessel. A rage for symmetry, and none where there should have been some. Trouble in town, and possibly on a wider scale.

I leaned back, my eyes closed, and waited for the allegro passage of his concerto in D major for three violins to end before I started to add it all up. Okay, if I went with my initial instinct of it being a garden, something that was put up after the fire, that was still okay. The glass could be bell jars, used to protect fragile plants, although those might have been better used in a greenhouse. I'd have to look it up and double check that. The bond of the brick structure seemed to be similar to that of the house—although the bricks were a different color and texture from those in the house—perhaps that suggested a garden wall? Built to be a balance to the other wing, the one undamaged by the fire? That was fine, but why not just rebuild the lost wing?

I dug out my field notes and tried to do a rough estimate of a date based on the pottery and other artifacts that I recalled seeing. The redware wasn't much help—made since time immemorial and still made today—and without a vessel form, it's sometimes tricky to pin down its exact time of manufacture. But there were a couple of pieces of creamware and one tiny bit of porcelain that might be dateable by its decoration. Okay, the "garden" wall was certainly built after the fire; the sherds and such also postdated the fire, at least by a short time. So the sequence was the wing burning, the debris being cleared away, and the wall and a garden being installed after that, then used for a long time before the wall was dismantled and the garden eventually abandoned.

I flipped to the front of the notebook, where I'd begun a rough timeline of what was going on in the household and what was happening in the town. I'd have to check other sources to see what was happening in the regional and global spheres, but this was a start. Here we are: Margaret had the last two of her eight surviving children earlier in the year that Nicholas died and a new barn was built to house the new carriage—that was listed on the tax bill as well the following year. Another year goes by, and a neighbor's diary discusses the Chandler's work on a new house on the point. Now, did this simply mean that they had begun work on the garden wall, or was this a different house altogether, possibly the Mather House? I knew that they had built many houses in Stone Harbor through the years, the parents and then the succeeding generations, both to live in themselves and to rent out. I felt like I was on the edge of something, if I could only keep pushing along these lines. . . .

The fire in town in 1738 hadn't really reached as far up as the Chandlers' house, which was the only one built that far north at that time. They owned the whole point up there, where the Bellamy House and the Mather House were now too, selling off the two outside lots sometime after Matthew Chandler's death in the late eighteenth century. Was the fact that the wing of their house had been destroyed a coincidence or was there some connection between the two events? I tried to recall what I'd read about the fire in town, which was described as starting during a scuffle in one of the seedier places in town; it was generally viewed as God's wrath against license gone too far, but it also threatened a good number of the ships and wharves. If Matthew Chandler had been a justice, was it possibly some retribution against him too? He had a wharf and shares in many ships . . . but I was probably reaching. I needed better proof that there was a connection.

For the moment, I was happy with the garden theory, although its existence as such a prominent structure was still a puzzle. The Chandler family was growing and could have used another wing of their house easily. Aha—but the addition and its rooms! They would have provided the needed space! Even though the downstairs had been renovated into a ballroom of sorts in the nineteenth century, the ell had been built to provide more serviceable space in the eighteenth. But why build toward the water? Why not balance the house's architecture?

Brian was still downstairs reading when I decided to knock off. He said he'd be up in a while, but he didn't show any signs of moving. I tossed and turned for a while, then fell asleep, finally, just as I'd decided there would be no sleep that night.

Chapter 12

BRIAN REMINDED ME TO BRING MY CELL PHONE with me the next morning, when I reminded him that I'd be visiting the museum at Boxham-by-Sea. I replied rather shortly that it was already in my bag; I was capable of learning a new trick, even at my advanced age. I guess my feelings were still hurt that he didn't come up to bed when I did the night before. After he got out the door, I pulled myself together, and dropped Bucky off in downtown Stone Harbor, telling her I'd meet her at the library around noon, before I headed off to Boxham-by-Sea.

Business was thriving in Boxham today, I noticed as I walked along the water; good. Then I frowned: A car honked at a tourist who had paused in the middle of the street to get a better picture of the harbor. As I had recently moved into the area, I understood what drew people to these historic towns: the beauty, the history, and the people were well worth the visit. But, lapsing into the complaint of locals everywhere around the world, why did tourists leave their common sense behind when they went on vacation? The laws of physics do not also go on holiday; cars do not pass through you because you are a visitor, the sun does not burn less brightly because you have the day off. I wished they would take the care that they took when they were at home.

Just like you do when you are on vacation? a little voice inside my head asked. Like stalking strangers through cemeteries at night and going into bars in the bad part of town? And what about the time that you—?

Shut up, I told myself amiably and reasonably. I turned down Shield Street so that I could find my way to the museum.

As hard as I tried, I still wasn't on time. After I gave my name to the receptionist at the desk, I tried to stop panting and pull my sweaty shirt away from my back without being obvious about it. A few minutes later and I started to wonder whether Dr. Spencer wasn't just making me wait because she was put out with me for being late. Eventually a harassed-looking woman in a nice blue suit came striding purposefully toward me. As she drew closer, I could see that she was probably my contact—the badge around her neck was one clue—and that her day wasn't going smoothly either. Her blonde hair, longer than mine and reaching well below her shoulders, was loosely caught up in a barrette behind her head, but it seemed to be slipping, letting little tendrils escape, curling from the humidity. She stuck out her hand and began introducing herself before she even made it up to me.

"You must be Dr. Fielding, hello, sorry I'm running a little behind." She pumped my hand briefly, twice, and immediately turned around to head back to where she'd emerged from. I had to trot to catch up with her again. "Mary Ann Spencer. Actually, I forgot your appointment was this morning. Good thing I was just working on some cataloging, or it would have been a bigger problem." She looked down at her left hand, which was covered with drying blue ink. "Damn. I guess that pen is dead." She pulled out a crumpled linen handkerchief, and before I could protest, started to rub at the stains vigorously. "Well, it's still blue, but no longer wet." She stuffed the ruined handkerchief back into her pocket, without noticing that she'd left a smear of dark blue ink on her periwinkle suit.

I snuck a peek down at my right hand, to make sure she hadn't gotten any ink on me.

"Right, we'll just head back to my office, and you can show me your find." She showed her badge to another guard, led me past a door that said STAFF ONLY, and we went down a corridor of anonymous closed doors. Presently she stopped in front of one of the doors, pulled out a key, and opened it. In the office, there was a desk that was barely visible under piles of folders; even the phone and desk lamp were covered with Post-It notes. The rest of the room, another table, three other chairs, the window ledges, and the radiator cover, were all stacked with books, papers, folders, and empty diet soda cans—at least I hoped they were empty. It was like the kind of bookish chaos I'm always apologizing for in my office, but this place had even me squirming with unease.

She cleared off a section of the table by removing a pile of papers and sticking them on top of another pile on the floor, which immediately slid over. She cleared off two chairs the same way, and invited me to sit.

"Ow!" The straying barrette had finally shaken loose and was now dangling off one strand of hair. She unfastened it, untangled it, and then, impatiently, gathered up all of her hair and clipped it again. It was a pretty messy job, with strands of hair humping up in disarray, but at least now it was all out of her way. She sat down and immediately kicked off her shoes. Apparently, things were pretty casual in Dr. Spencer's office.

"Let's get a look at your hook, then." To my infinite relief, she pulled a pair of clean white cotton gloves from a boxful, and pulled them on. "Don't want to let the skin oils damage the metal," Dr. Spencer announced didactically.

Not to mention the ink, I thought. I pulled out the box and removed the plastic bag with the hook and its two links. The third, twisted link lay at the bottom of the bag.

She took the bag and held it up to the light. "Oh, yes, I see what you mean. It certainly looks like silver, doesn't it? Something gave this a good hard wrench, to pull it apart so. May I?"

I nodded, and she carefully slid the metal hook out of the bag and onto a small square cushion that looked as though it was stuffed and covered with flannel. She trained a strong light down onto it and pulled over a magnifying glass on an arm, delicately beginning to examine the hook and its plain links.

"I think you're right. It is silver, and I'd be willing to guess that it's come from a chatelaine. Probably something that belonged to a woman, judging by the fineness of it; I think it is probably too small to have been for a watch or a man's seal or anything like that. I'm also guessing that it was part of a multiple-element chatelaine, not the kind that was made for carrying the household keys or a large pair of scissors. It was meant to carry a variety of small items—a thimble, perhaps, an etui or needle case, maybe a small pencil, that sort of thing. Decorative and useful at the same time. The meaning changed over time—you know they date back to the Roman and Egyptian times?—but since this is eighteenth century, it's meant to be more decorative and petite. Some of the examples you see from the later nineteenth century are huge, real monsters."

I nodded. "So it would have been valuable as a piece of jewelry?"

"Oh, yes. In fact, I think you were very lucky to have found it. For one thing, there is the value inherent in the metal, not to speak of the fineness of the workmanship. Probably lots of sentimental and symbolic value too; if you think of these things as a cross between a Swiss army knife and a charm bracelet, you'll get a good idea of how they were viewed. For another thing, if whoever had owned it had lost more of it—the clasp or the main jewel—she would have turned the place upside down looking for it."

"The way that someone will look harder for a gold coin, but won't bother so much over a copper one," I said.

She nodded. "It might have been a gift from a husband, and it was emblematic, if you will, of a lady's position as queen of her household."

"Queen of little enough, in those days," I said half to myself. The light caught the silver and gleamed brightly.

But Dr. Spencer disagreed. "I don't like to write that off so easily. Don't forget, there was tremendous power to be found in the home. People like to think of colonial ladies being immured in the house, but just stop and think what was going on at all those endless tea parties. Gossip, matchmaking, a political hint dropped from one husband to be transmitted to another over the tea and via their wives—no, I think there was quite a lot going on that we just don't know about. It just wasn't written down all that often. Who's going to give any attention or credence to women's gossip, after all? But it had its uses, and its power too. Remember *Dangerous Liaisons*?"

She picked over the links and squinted at them carefully. "Okay, definitely sterling silver, most likely of English manufacture—"

"How can you tell? Is there a mark that I missed?"

"No, no mark. It's just that it *feels* English to me, as opposed to Continental or colonial. You just get a knack, develop an instinct after a while, you look at enough things. Where did you find it?"

"At the Chandler House."

"Was it from a good . . . I don't know what word you'd use." She ran her fingers through her hair and smoothed out a tangle. "We'd say provenance, to describe where a thing was found and how it might have gotten there—who owned it, that sort of thing."

"We use the English pronunciation—provenience—or context. All they mean is where it was found and what it was found with and how old it is."

She nodded recognition.

"Yes, I think so," I said. "I think it is an early-eighteenth-century stratum."

"And there were wealthy women there at the time? That was the first generation of Chandlers, wasn't it?"

I nodded. "Margaret Chandler might certainly have been rich enough and important enough to have had such a thing. I think she was the only one old enough and rich enough to have had one at the time."

Dr. Spencer looked out the window a while, thinking. "I can recommend a few books to look at, if you like, to compare this with other chatelaines. Of course, those won't have been broken and buried, like this one was."

"Oh, I know. Museums prefer to deal with whole objects." I looked over her shoulder and studied the object. "I wonder what would have been attached to that hook."

"Difficult to say. A lot of objects were made attached right to the chain, not meant to be removed. Perhaps a key to a cupboard or a clock or a jewelry box? A seal? Something pretty and personal and valuable."

I looked through the magnifying glass at the little bits of

metal. Smooth, silver-gray, rounded, and shiny, they were actually pretty plain, but when you knew what they were a part of, suddenly they contained all sorts of meanings.

"We don't even know if it belonged to the Chandler family, do we?"

I shook my head. "It might have belonged to a guest or a visitor."

The curator looked at the links. "I don't know how you can stand not to have the whole thing, now, not be able to study it all, to touch it, get to know it."

I couldn't help but laugh. "You've got the light of greed in your eyes, Dr. Spencer."

"Please, call me Mary Ann. Of course I do. It's the best job in the world, this one. I get to have all the things. And pretend they're mine." She shrugged again, but she was smiling this time, which did a lot to mitigate the squalid ambience of her room. "Of course, I get to use all those gorgeous, yummy adjectives too, to describe them. It's all things and words, with me."

"Come out to the site some time. I'll be happy to show you how we make do with just the broken pieces."

"Oh, thanks. I couldn't." She heaved a theatrical sigh. "All those poor, fractured darlings out there, lost in the ground, lost to time? It would break my heart."

I was pretty sure she was kidding, but you couldn't ever be certain. I replaced the chatelaine fragment in its bag and gathered my map and my pack, making ready to leave, when Mary Ann Spencer's sudden question stopped me.

"Tell me, how's Perry Taylor doing? I heard she had some trouble a week or so back? Actually, I won't beat around the bush. I heard the whole Historical Society is having the heaves, even before the other murder was announced on the news last night." She looked at me. "You don't know anything about that, do you?"

"No." I wasn't permitted to say anything, but a simple negative seemed the easiest answer. Nothing official had been said about Aden's identity yet; the authorities were waiting until they had informed his family. I said slowly, "It's been very difficult there lately. Perry seems to be doing better. Still a bit shaken up, as you might imagine."

"Naturally." Dr. Spencer gave me an odd look.

"Do you know Perry well?" I asked.

There was a long pause. "That's a very interesting question."

I hadn't really thought so. "Oh?"

She went over to her desk and gathered up a pile of papers, tapping them against the surface to order them. It didn't seem to do much good: One of the papers caught her eye and she removed it, putting it back into the piles on her desk. Then another stuck out the wrong way and she scrutinized that, then the one under that, and finally came to the conclusion that none of the papers actually belonged together at all. She set them aside.

"Do I know Perry well? I'd say I knew her better than most, to be honest."

There was another pause and I got the distinct impression that Dr. Spencer was milking it for dramatic effect.

"How's that?"

"She applied for a job here, just before she began at the Historical Society. I knew her so well that I saw to it that she didn't get it." She smiled briefly, without humor, as she rummaged in her pocket for the broken pen.

Holy snappers, I thought. She kept Perry from getting a job? "And why was that?"

"We went to the same college for undergraduate. Were actually in the same department for a while."

"And then she changed departments?"

She threw the faulty pen away and it hit her wastebasket

with a sharp clunk. "Yes, she did. She did indeed. You see, she was asked to leave."

Another pause so pregnant it might have been feeling the pangs of labor.

"And why was that?"

She straightened some other papers. "That was because Ms. Perry Taylor was caught cheating."

"On an exam?" It was a little like teasing a secret out of a second grader.

"On a term paper. She got bounced from the department. It wasn't the first time, you see. It was a miracle she didn't get kicked out of school. There were a lot of quiet little conferences with her people, possibly even the family lawyer, first with the chairman, then, I heard, with the dean, possibly even the president. Someone told me that at one point, her bags were packed and ready to go, but I don't believe that. Not for a minute. It was about that time that Ms. Perry Taylor—"

Every time she said Perry's full name, it was accompanied with a sarcastic side-to-side rocking of her head, in time to the syllables. Perry's name had become a byword for something ugly to Mary Ann Spencer.

"—suddenly developed an interest in business studies, and left American history entirely alone." Dr. Spencer's face was quite red now, and I could see a few reddish blotches appearing near the base of her throat. "This was the girl who always said the past owed her something. Business studies."

"Wow."

My limited encouragement was hardly necessary at this point, however: She was on a roll. "You might say so. And then, gall upon gall, after a respite of a year or two after graduation and a suitably restrained M.A. in art history, she shows up here, applying for a job with our American Fine Arts section. I was here, by that time. Oh, I was working on my dissertation at night, but I was here and happily settled in—even though Perry is a year or two older than me, I beat her into the market; no distractions of a changed major, you understand—and I felt that I simply had to speak up and let the hiring committee know what I knew—"

All through her descriptions, I recognized the unassuaged bitterness of graduate school competition. Who finished soon, whose degree came from the better school, who got the job first.

"—It wouldn't have been right for me to keep my mouth shut."

"I suppose," I said, "but people do make mistakes, when they're young. Even—"

"I'm sorry," she interrupted with concentrated steel in her voice. "I don't care who you are. I don't care how much of town your family owned, or how much you think the world revolves around you. You don't get to cheat and get away with it. You just don't."

Well, all right then.

"God, is it getting warm in here?" Mary Ann asked.

"Maybe a little." But I was thinking of the heat of emotion and not the temperature of the room.

She rubbed at her throat and swallowed. "You know, I think they put some kind of nut oil in the salad dressing in the museum restaurant. They always swear that they don't— too risky to serve something like that—but they must have. Every time I have the salad for lunch, I come out in hives." She thought about that for a minute. "But I didn't have the salad today. I had the salami."

I shrugged. "I hope it's not serious."

She shook her head. "No, it never is. I mean, not more than a nuisance. But I'm boring you, going into my health issues. I hate indiscretion in new acquaintances, don't you?"

I looked at the curator, recalling our conversation, but decided that she hadn't actually been ironic. "It's hard to deal with that."

She nodded again. "Those are the keys to museum work: discretion and order."

I gazed around the upheaval that was her office, but still didn't detect any irony in her remark. Carefully packing up my chatelaine and its fragment of chain, I thanked Dr. Spencer again and set off to complete my other errands.

Chapter 13

I DROVE BACK DOWN TO STONE HARBOR, INTENDING to spend the rest of the morning at the courthouse. Even in this more modern section of town, there were traces of the past. There were a couple of churches that were early nineteenth century in date, and sat prim in their white clapboards, steeples straining to the skies in the attempt to find a little space vertically, as the old common area had been filled in with shops, houses, and businesses. I had a vague recollection that this had been the original center of town, but that there had been a fire in the first part of the eighteenth century and the common and churches had been moved closer to the point and the Chandler House. In the center of town, a couple of blocks from the waterfront, there were a few brick structures that looked as though they had survived from the eighteenth century, warehouses perhaps, or storefronts, but were now legal offices and restaurants and antique shops. Things got a little seedier in the area close to the courthouse, and the people loitering around the buildings there usually looked unhappy or preoccupied for whatever reason, and were generally less garishly dressed than those on Water Street. With any luck, by the time I finished with my research, I would be one of the few smiling faces. But I had to find my sister first.

The library was a tall red-brick building, daunting Victorian Italianate with big granite steps, the very picture of what I imagine libraries should look like: imposing repositories of human knowledge. Maybe that was a little overly dramatic, but I always felt as though nothing bad could happen in a library. A lot of very good things had happened in them, as far as I was concerned, and so I was happy to make the stop.

I saw Bucky sitting at one of the empty tables, poring over one book, a stack of others sitting on either side. A librarian walked by and addressed her by name and I realized that this was where she'd been coming, all those times she'd left for downtown. The books on one side of the table were all on beading and jewelrymaking. The books on the other side, presumably ones she'd finished with, were all about archaeology. This explained her disagreement with Meg, a quick read of old sources and not the later ones that refuted them. I was instantly struck by a jealously competitive feeling: Archaeology was mine. But Bucky had the time, she had the lack of responsibility, and more importantly, she'd had the impetus to follow up on things about which she was curious. I sighed and walked up to her.

"Hey, Bucks."

She looked up after a moment; my words had taken their time penetrating the closed world of her consciousness. She blinked as she recognized me.

"Hey, Em. What are you doing here?"

"Working. Want to get some lunch?"

"Sure, just give me. . . ." She held up a finger and then it seemed as though she were diving off the high board, back into the book, and she might as well have been diving into deep water for all she noticed me. She finished the page she'd been working on, and then the final paragraph of the chapter, and closed the book. "Just wanted to finish that. Okay, I'm set."

Again, I felt a stab of jealousy because I knew that once my sister had read something, she never would forget it. She had a kind of eidetic memory that I would have killed for. I'd always been good at school, and worked my butt off to do it. Bucky had been tested when she was a kid because she seemed so much slower than the others, never doing very well at her work. To everyone's surprise she tested off the charts for her age. She was skipped a couple of grades to try and coax her into achieving her full potential with harder, more challenging work, but the simple fact remained: When Bucky wanted to do well she did, and when she wasn't interested in it, no power on earth could convince her otherwise. I'd been envious of her skipped grades, too.

"What are you in the mood for?" I asked once we got out into the fresh air. The warmth after the air conditioning was like walking into a sauna, but it felt good. "I'm buying." That was to make up for my unsisterly feelings in the library.

"How about lobster rolls?"

"You are a bad date, aren't you?" I groused. I wasn't feeling that guilty. "Okay, I know a place."

It was actually closer to the courthouse than to Water Street, but it didn't make any difference. The place was packed, and we had to hover over a couple who were loitering over their coffee and paid bill until we could snag their booth. After a bit of a shuffle, where we both went to sit on the same side of the booth, I let Bucky take it.

"What's wrong with the other seat?"

"I just don't want to look at anything that spidery," she said, jerking her head back toward the lobster tank that bubbled away in back of her.

"You don't mind eating them," I pointed out.

"Just as long as I don't have to deal with the legs." She shuddered and made a face. "Yuck. Have I told you lately how much I hate Ma for naming me Charlotte? In grades K through six I was constantly reminded of both my wretched name and spiders. It was always, oh, Charlotte, *Charlotte's Web*—"

"It's a great book, Bucks."

"Yeah, unless you're a screeching arachnophobe. And the thought of a talking spider, I don't care how nice she was, just about sent me screaming, foaming, into the wild blue yonder. I considered becoming an astronaut, on the chance that there were no spiders in outer space."

"Yeah, and then you read *Starship Troopers*."

"Stupid book," was all she said. It was tough for her, because Bucky loved science fiction and particularly Heinlein.

We got our food in record time and wolfed it down. I automatically pushed the chips I didn't eat toward Bucky; she was already eyeing them anyway.

"You know it was Perry's earrings making that clicking noise? It's because she doesn't make her headloops close enough to the bead. If she did that, they wouldn't make so much noise. She should get better pliers."

"Oh." Why on earth did that grab her attention? I sighed; why did anything interest my capricious sister? "I thought they were antiques or something. They look old."

"No, reproductions. She made them. There's a place downtown, she said." She looked up from the chips. "Maybe we could go sometime?"

"Sure." It was unlike Bucky to suggest an actual activity

that we could do together. "Just name the date. You want to come with me now? I'm just going to be a half hour at the courthouse, checking something out, then I'm heading home."

"Sure, whatever." She licked the tip of her finger and caught up the last few crumbs of my chips, seeming more interested in cleaning her plate than my offer.

I was getting to know the courthouse pretty well and knew right where to head for the records I wanted. Shelves of tall volumes in red and brown leather were at the far end of the room with the probates and wills. I looked for the volumes that covered the years I was interested in, 1738—when Nicholas Chandler had died—and 1772, when Matthew Chandler had died. I pulled down the first volume and found what I was looking for.

"See here." I pointed to a page that was covered with cramped lettering. "This is Nicholas's will. He wrote it just before he died, it seems, and he was about twenty. He was born about 1716, then. That was several years before Matthew and Margaret Chandler were married."

"So they had a kid out of wedlock," Bucky said, growing interested.

"I doubt it. I mean, if he had been born six months *after* they were married, say, I could believe that. But people of that class didn't go around having a kid, waiting a couple of years, and then getting married. It just didn't work like that in those days. No, this is something else."

I could feel my excitement growing, the way it always did when I was chasing down a clue. "Look at his will. It says that he left things to his children and wife, but also to his brothers and sisters: tokens, money for gloves, mourning rings, that sort of thing."

"So?"

"Look at the names of his siblings."

"Thomas, Rupert, Carlisle, Lydia, Seaborn—hey, that's a name?"

"Yep. The first couple of names are from Margaret's family and the third is from Matthew's side; I've seen them in genealogies. Seaborn, though, that's different. He might actually have been born at sea, but whatever the circumstances of his birth, it is a Chandler name we know was associated with Matthew and Margaret. So it looks like Nicholas is definitely one of our Chandlers. This is the document that Bray is probably working from." I chewed the inside of my lip for a second. "I wonder if there is a connection between Nicholas's death, the wing of the house burning down, and the fire downtown. I'll have to think more about that."

Bucky's face was screwed up in concentration. "So was Nicholas Matthew's son from another marriage?"

"I don't know, maybe."

"From an illicit affair? But would you think that Margaret would let her husband's bastard be raised in her own house, with her own children?"

"It's possible; I believe she was that kind of Christian."

Bucky thought about it for a minute, and I could almost see the gears turning as she mulled over the problem. "Did they adopt in those days?"

"Yes, but not necessarily the way we think of it. There wasn't always a formal procedure, and families took cousins, orphans, all sorts of people into their houses. They didn't necessarily make legal distinctions, either, between in-laws. Your sister-in-law was your sister, etcetera. If we could find a document that Matthew signed, officially announcing his intention to raise Nicholas as his son, that would be one thing, but there didn't need to be. Now let's check Matthew's will."

Sure enough, it was right there, although with the long

list of children's names, it wasn't surprising that I had missed it there the first time. "Check this out: Thomas gets the real estate and the first son's portion—that's primogeniture for you—and Margaret gets her widow's third—"

"Her what?"

"In a lot of wills at the time, the eldest son got a third, including the land, if there was any, and the wife got a third, and the rest of the children divvied up the rest of the estate, unless some other provision was specifically made. In this case, we see that Thomas, the eldest son of both Margaret and Matthew, gets the lion's share, and the rest of the kids, including Nicholas, share in the last third." I furrowed my brow. "But wait. This will was written before Nicholas's death. Why wouldn't a lawyer like Matthew have drawn up another will? This is strange."

I glanced at the date of the will and saw that it did in fact predate Nicholas's death, but that it had been filed in the year of Matthew's death, decades later. Any will that had been found at his death would be here; there was nowhere else I could look, without some other clue.

"Maybe they couldn't find a later will at the time of Matthew's death," I finally decided. "Or maybe that one was misfiled; all sorts of things happen to keep official documents from ending up where they should. At least from this we know that Nicholas was not being given the eldest son's portion, as he would if he were legitimate."

"So if we know that Nicholas was older than Thomas—" Bucky began.

"It seems reasonable to believe that Nicholas was adopted," I finished. "So Bray Chandler can't be descended from Margaret and Matthew, and he might not even be related to Matthew at all either."

"Isn't Bray going to be pissed about this? He seems pretty wound up about the whole thing."

"The name is his legally, of course; it's just a matter of blood." I bit my lip. "Though that seems to be the thing with folks around here."

"Pedigree is that important? I mean, maybe in a competitive show animal. . . ."

I thought of my conversation with Ted. "You know, I'm beginning to wonder if that isn't a fairly good description of Bray, at least as far as his wife is concerned. I think it's very important to him, and I wonder if Aden didn't know it too."

Bucky shifted her weight, looking uncomfortable. "Yeah, but that isn't a reason to, you know, kill someone. Is it?"

"I think we'd both be surprised."

We were both quiet for a moment. Then Bucky leaned over the book, straining to see something. "Where does it list what he had?"

"What do you mean?"

"I thought you said that wills listed what people owned when they died."

"Not wills. Probate inventories. Those are separate documents and they are usually more detailed. They were taken after someone died, sometimes years after, if the estate was complicated. Those are in another section and I think we'll leave that for another day. I'm beat."

"How do you know all this stuff?" Bucky said suddenly. "It's like you have to know about these whole other worlds. All the information from other times and places, whole other lives and philosophies."

I put the books on the trolley to be returned. "A lot of years of work and practice, Bucks. That's all."

I was getting a goodish dose of the Chin now; Bucky was annoyed with me and I wasn't sure why. "But it's more than that. It's like you belong here, you know what I mean?"

I did; I knew what she meant and I believed her too. I was just a little disconcerted to hear something that sounded so much like admiration and envy coming openly from my little sister. I suspected her questions were related to her reasons for spending her vacation with me; perhaps she was unhappy with her personal life. "I belong here among the dusty old books?" I joked feebly, trying to lighten the moment. I dusted my hands off on the back of my jeans; the red from the record books had bled off in crumbly dust onto me, making me feel a bit like Lady Macbeth. Will all the perfumes of Arabia never sweeten this sibling rivalry?

"You know what I mean."

"Yeah, I do," I conceded. "I'm lucky, is all. I found a good fit and it worked out for me."

"You get all the good fits, don't you?" Bucky almost sounded angry. "Husband, job, even a town that suits you."

"It takes a hell of a lot of work," I said curtly. "And it takes being honest with yourself about what you want to get out of life. Now, let's get going."

But we didn't make it out of the courthouse then. I saw Daniel Voeller down one of the other aisles, scrutinizing one of the much more recent deed books. I pulled Bucky down the aisle after it and gestured for her to be quiet. We both pretended to be studying a book, facing away from the main walkway, until we heard Daniel leave.

"What was that about?" she asked.

"I want to see what he was doing here. He's not the type to be doing deed research on his own; he's got lawyers for that."

We went down the aisle where Daniel had been and found the book he'd been reading, still out on the table. It was closed, but I noticed that it hadn't closed tightly: some of the pages were still not settled back into the bulk of the book. I stuck my finger in and opened the book to the page I thought he'd been looking at.

"That's it," Bucky said.

"How do you know?" I shot back.

She licked a fingertip the way she had done to fish up the last of the chips and pressed it against the page before I could stop her. You really shouldn't treat documents like that, no matter how modern they are. She picked up a fine hair and held it up for me to see.

"A lot of people have brown wavy hair," I said, and Bucky made a face at me. "But that's the right page."

"How do *you* know?"

I had been glancing at the street names. "These are the properties that are immediately adjacent to the factory that Voeller's father owns, just to the north of the Chandler House, north of the Mather House. He's trying to see who owns them." I read the name of a corporation that I didn't recognize: "Stone Harbor Investment Properties." "It looks like the Voellers want to expand."

Bucky wasn't thrilled about waiting for me while I nosed around Stone Harbor Town Hall, but I found out at last that, much to my surprise, the owner of the Mather House wasn't Perry Taylor. I had automatically assumed it might be she, mostly because she kept mentioning how much property her family once owned in town and Dr. Spencer's remarks also suggested that. And the owner wasn't Bray Chandler, either, whose wife's income might have been enough to own such pricey waterfront property. Much to my surprise, the owner of the Mather House was the supposedly strapped Fiona Prowse.

Saturday morning was gorgeous and, having slept until nine o'clock, I was in a terrific mood as I went downstairs. Brian sat on the counter, outlining his day's plans for the dining room floor while I cleaned up the kitchen. I had just started another pot of coffee as Bucky came down and settled in blearily with the *New York Times*. I put a cup in front of her. A grunt and a couple of slurps later and she felt equipped to start the crossword puzzle.

"Not much of a vacation, Bucks," Brian said. "I mean, being out in the field, and with all that's going on. . . ."

She rattled the paper. "Mmm, well. I haven't been bitten or peed on or puked on. I haven't had to shove a thermometer anywhere embarrassing and haven't had to worm anyone for days. As far as I'm concerned, life is good."

Quasi slunk into the kitchen and regarded her cautiously. She directed her next words to him.

"Doesn't mean it won't happen by the end of my stay, though, big fella."

The cat put his ears back and went right back to wherever it was he'd come from.

"What are you going to do today?" I asked. "I suppose it's too much to hope that you're going to stick around and help out with the housework?"

She filled in another clue. "I'll do some and then I'm off. I've got a date with Phil."

Phil? "Who's that? When did you meet him? What do you know about—?"

Bucky stared at me from over the paper. "He's one of Jerry's landscapers. I don't know anything about him except that he's cute and he was giving me the eye too. We're just going for a walk downtown and get some lunch, that's it. Any other questions, Mother?"

"Bite me." I messed up her hair. "Get out of here. Have fun."

She smoothed the newspaper and took up her pen again. "Oh, I've got hours yet."

I took the pen out of her hand.

"Hey!" She looked up, annoyed.

"If you've got hours yet, you can help with the laundry.

Or, alternatively, you can help Brian with the flooring. Your choice."

"They wouldn't make me do laundry at Beach Club Piña Colada on the exotic Caribbean island of St. Debauchery," Bucky grumbled. She finished her coffee with a resigned look, though.

"Then you shouldn't have booked in at Camp Fielding. Which one is it?"

"Just let me get some toast and then I'll do the laundry." She popped some bread into the toaster. "There are nice long breaks in between loads. I can get some reading done."

"Longer breaks in between for cleaning the bathroom," I corrected her.

She made a face like she'd just drunk sour milk. "God. Okay, flooring. But if I get a splinter and it turns septic and no one notices and I get gangrene and die, it will be your fault."

I considered briefly. "I can live with that."

The students wandered into the kitchen, all ready to make the most of their free time. They were mostly all washed, except for Rob, who still looked bleary, as though he could use another hour in the sack.

"Have you got anything on for this weekend, Emma?" Joe asked. He took a piece of toast from the toaster and Bucky didn't even protest.

I wiped up some crumbs. "Nothing beyond the usual household scrabble. You?"

"We were thinking of driving up to Portsmouth. It's going to be a nice day, you should come."

Brian abruptly excused himself and put his dishes into the sink, and went into the dining room. We could hear lumber being shifted about and a metal measuring tape being used.

"Thanks, but I don't think so," I said carefully.

"Emma hates New Hampshire," Bucky offered, from around her slice of toast. She didn't look up from the paper.

The students looked at me quizzically. "A whole state?" Meg asked.

"No, I don't . . . Bucky, it's not that I. . . ." I was momentarily flustered. "I've just got a lot of things to get done around the house today. You guys go, have fun. Check out the museum, learn something for a change. The shops are funky, too. It's a great city."

"Okay, if you're sure." The students exchanged quizzical looks and then realized they weren't getting any more from me.

"Yeah, thanks. See you tonight."

They dumped their things into the sink, and since it was Rob's turn for dishes, things went quickly if not antiseptically, and they were gone in a few minutes.

"That was remarkably indiscreet," I told Bucky, who was still engrossed in her puzzle.

"What? Oh, who cares? Ah!" She scribbled in a long clue. " 'Grandiloquent.' Nice one. Hey!"

I'd pulled the crossword puzzle out from under her, leaving a long pen mark across the page. "I do. I emphatically do not need you bandying my private life, my past, in front of my students. There are some boundaries that I wish to maintain there."

"God, you are such a prude. Everyone makes mistakes. Would it hurt them to know you have one or two lurking in your past?"

"They are completely aware of my human fallibility," I said. "You don't work on a dig and not get to know a little too much about people. That, however, was an exceptionally painful time in my life and I have no wish to revisit it, especially with my students, most of whom were probably in diapers at the time."

"They're only a little younger than I am, Emma. I was thirteen."

"And not old enough to know anything about it either," I said. "So just leave it."

"Okay, whatever. God, you're uptight."

"It's something I cultivate." I shoved the paper back toward her again, but she folded it up and put her dish into the sink. "Now, is your dirty laundry in some kind of pile that a non-Fielding would recognize, or do you want to pick it out for me?"

"It's everything on the right hand side of the bed. The left side of the bed is still clean."

I was right; anyone who wasn't a member of the family wouldn't have seen a difference in the piles of clothes strewn about the floor. The clean stuff was what someone with a good sense of humor and a fair amount of imagination might call folded, meaning that they were comparatively flat and layered, though showing no trace of ironing. The dirty clothes were balled up into tight little knots. I had once used a similar plan myself, but out of respect to married life had made an earnest attempt to put the dirty ones into a hamper and the clean ones into a closet or drawer. It often worked, and I was surprised at how much room it left for moving around on the floor. Bucky still hadn't learned the advantages to using a bureau or a closet. I don't know why both of us had no use for such furniture; it just never seemed important.

As I gathered things into my clothes basket, I noticed that Bucky's wastebasket was full, which struck me as unusual, even after a week. Most of her trash never would have made it to the basket and would be lying around in crumpled ring around it. I also recognized the cardboard boxes and the labels that were on them. The name on them, however, was my own. Then I saw the stack of books on the side of the bed and realized that they were all new and all dealing with beading and Massachusetts history. I stormed downstairs.

"Bucky!" I yelled to make myself heard over the power saw.

There was a crash followed by a clatter and swearing as the whine of the saw died away to a loud, metallic whirring. I entered the end of the dining room that had a floor, albeit covered with sawdust and tools. Bucky was trying to look innocent, even if she didn't know what about.

Brian was trying to ease the saw blade off the plank and was not having much luck. "Damn it, Emma, why'd you have to shout like that?" He gave me an angry look and finally got the plank off the table. "I could have busted the saw blade!"

I held up the boxes for my sister to see. "Do you mind telling me what the hell this is?"

I held out the cardboard shipping flats and had the satisfaction of seeing Bucky look really guilty before I got a double dose of the Chin. Her eyes went steely, she crossed her arms, and she set her jaw.

"I ordered some books online," she said defiantly.

"Yeah, I know you did. Using *my* account. On *my* computer. In *my* office."

"So?"

"So? So how much did you spend? What were you doing in my office in the first place? How did you figure out my passwords? And what gives you the right to—?"

She waved that off. "I was going to tell you. I'll pay you back, it's only like forty bucks."

"Ha!"

Bucky went purple. "Like you never take any of my stuff!"

I crossed my arms over my chest. "Who'd want your stuff?"

"Oh, I found that pile of cassettes and CDs up in your office, the ones you borrow from me, when you come down to visit Ma. For someone who gets all snotty about classical music, you seem to have a real taste for alternative rock."

"You said I could borrow some!"

"Some is the operative word there," Bucky corrected, flushing now. "And that was the first time, five years ago! You keep borrowing them, and you never give them back!"

"Well, that's not the same as using someone else's credit card without asking!"

"Cool your jets; I said I was going—"

"God, I am so glad I am an only child!"

Brian sounded so pissed off that we both stopped and turned to him. "The only thing you two ever do is fight with each other! I thought sisters were supposed to be best friends, or something."

My sister and I stared at him as if he were slow. "Fat lot you know," Bucky said to him, holding up a hand for me to talk to. "I'm out of here."

"Where are you going?" I demanded.

"I'm going on my date, remember? I'll be a couple hours early, but wandering the streets is preferable to this."

"Fine," I yelled after her. "Just tell landscaping boy not to leave his wallet in his coat while he goes to the men's room, or he might discover he owes a fortune to an online bookstore!"

Bucky ran upstairs, and came back downstairs a moment later, having changed. The door slammed and Brian and I were left alone together.

Chapter 14

BRIAN MADE A CLUCKING NOISE. "YOU KNOW," HE said, "I'm usually jealous of you two for having each other, but now. . . ."

He was just teasing, but I was still mad. "Did you hear what she did? Ordering all those books and charging them to me?"

"Yeah." He shrugged. "Look, she was just fooling around on the computer. She thought she could figure out your password at CyberBooks, and then ordered some books while she was there. She said she'd pay you back."

"Only after I confronted her!"

"Are you sure you're just not ticked because she brought up whatshisname?"

I was silent for a moment. "You can say his name."

"You're not just pissed off because she hinted at the existence of Duncan?"

"No. I'm fine with that."

"You're so fine with it that you don't like to visit his

home state? Is that fair? He dumps you and then cheats you out of a scholarship, and you're the one who has to pay the price? Anyway, doesn't he live in Michigan now?"

"I don't know, I guess so. He didn't . . . cheat me. Not really." But that's not what I was going to say.

Brian knew it was still a sore subject. "Honey, that was more than ten years ago."

"Yeah. I thought I loved him."

"You probably did love him."

That simple statement smarted. "And now I feel like an idiot because of it. I don't fall in love with creeps."

"Then there must have been something worth loving in him," Brian said. He set the saw aside. "That doesn't mean that I won't pummel him if I ever meet him."

"Brian—"

"I'm serious. He hurt you. I don't care how long ago it was."

"He was just immature and . . . and weak," I said. "That's all."

"So you'll let him off the hook, but not yourself?"

"I just hate thinking of myself being young and vulnerable."

"Never regret that, Em. That's what pasts are. Lots of events that make you who you are. And I love who you are, so don't ever regret that."

"You know, you're right." I stuck my hand in the back pocket of his shorts. "Come here."

I had just tilted my head up for a kiss when a movement caught my eye.

Bucky stood in the doorway of the living room. "Jeez, you guys can't be left alone for a minute, can you?"

"Nope," Brian said. "Go away."

Bucky laughed at him.

Brian wasn't laughing. "I'm serious. I'll give you twenty

bucks if you'll leave right now." He pulled me closer, even as we both realized that the moment was slipping away from us.

"Where am I supposed to go?" she said. "You guys live in the middle of nowhere. I walked for nearly five minutes and didn't see another living soul, not a house, not a car, nothing. Besides, I need to take a shower."

"You should have thought of that before you went storming out." I squirmed out of Brian's embrace. "Look, you've still got hours, yet. Before you bother with a shower, just help Brian with that pile of planks. If you get that done, and then get washed up, I'll give you a lift into town."

"You could just give me your car."

"Not a chance. I've got things to do today. And Brian needs the truck."

He caught my eye, about to protest, but didn't say anything when I winked at him. "I'll pick you up after, too, Bucks. Come on. Just help with the housework like you said you would."

"Oh all right."

An hour later, I got the second load of laundry started and was waiting for Bucky to get done in the bathroom so I could get started there. Brian had finished cutting the first lot of lumber and was now putting it down, hammering away noisily.

"Cool. You're making good progress."

He grimaced. "I'm channeling a lot of pent-up sexual energy at the moment. It's tough with a house full of people." He grabbed me by a belt loop in my shorts and pulled me close again. I patted his arm.

"Well, don't channel too much. I'll get Bucky out of the house and then we'll have at least lunchtime until she gets fed up with her date and calls for a ride back."

"So that was your plan. Not bad, Fielding," he said, nodding approbation. He has this way of raising one eyebrow that is very sexy. It made me glad of my decision.

"Just looking for a little advance warning, is all. Can you make it that long?"

"Yeah, but don't push it. Or rather, you can push it far enough to pick up some mud-pie ice cream at Krazy Kones on the way back."

"You got it." I bent over to kiss him.

"I'm ready," Bucky called out from upstairs.

Brian sighed and picked up a hammer. "I can't wait until all the kids are out of the house."

After admonishing Bucky to call if she didn't like the guy, to stick to public places, and to not take any crap from any-one—all of which was met with a resounding "Haven't you got better things to do?"—I stopped by the ice cream place to pick up the requested quart. On the way back, about a mile down the road and up a slight rise, I saw that a closed-up restaurant, which for three months had had the parking lot full of contractors' trucks, was now showing signs of be-ing completed. A new sign was hanging over the door: LAW-TON YACHT CLUB AND TIKI BAR. Smaller letters beneath that announced WATER VIEWS FROM OUR DECK.

Since we were about two miles from Lawton's minuscule marina and nowhere near the river or other body of water, I felt compelled to pull over and check it out. The sign was made of richly carved wood with gold leaf that suggested yacht clubbiness, but the rest of the name was odd enough to make me think that this could be something quite different.

As I got out of the car, I noticed a young woman squat-ting in the doorway, sweeping something into a dustpan. A smell of fruit left too long in the sun and the whizzing of a few interested flies informed me before I saw that she was cleaning up a squashed apple. There were several stains on the ground already, which suggested this was not the first time she'd had to perform this duty.

She looked up at me, squinting against the sun. "Grand opening's not until tonight."

"Oh, thanks, I just was curious about what was going in here, that's all."

She straightened up. "It's a bar."

"Yes, well, I got that much. Good name."

"You can come in and look around if you want."

"Sure—oh, wait, I can't." I hooked a thumb back toward the car. "I've got ice cream melting."

"We've got a freezer."

Whatever she lacked in loquacity, she made up for in hair; she was about five two but her hair streamed down almost to her knees. She was very finely boned, and I had to wonder whether the hair didn't actually compose most of her weight. It was something to see, however, a glossy raven sheet that almost looked like a cape on her.

"Okay, thanks." I got the ice cream from the car and handed it to my hostess, who put it into a small refrigerator behind the bar. "I'm Emma."

"Raylene."

I looked around the room. In addition to the bar, which stretched halfway down the room in mirrored Victorian splendor, there were about ten dark wooden tables. The walls were painted a dusky blue that built in a relaxing twilight; there were a few framed pictures and mirrors, but nothing that stood out enough to jar. Big windows and low interior lights. It was all ornate enough to proclaim a status above an ordinary grill or fried fish joint, but casual enough to warn the onlooker that there was no stuffiness to be found here. A beautiful staircase, a wooden relic from some other building, I felt sure, led upstairs.

"Dinner's down here, every night but Monday. Drinks and snacks upstairs and at the bar all the time."

"It's gorgeous." She saw me hesitate, so I added, "I guess I was expecting something more . . . I don't know. Grass huts or anchors or something, to judge from the sign out front."

"Upstairs. Come on."

I followed Raylene up the wooden staircase to a doorway at one end of a hallway. A velvet rope and stanchions blocked off the rest of the hall. "Out here."

"What are the other rooms?" I nodded at the rest of the doors that lined the hallway.

"We live here."

"We?"

"Me and my old man." She stopped to announce his name reverently, almost as if I should have heard of it. "Erik the Red."

She didn't explain whether the "red" referred to his hair, the state of his bank account, his politics, or a sunburn, so I shrugged and followed her. On the deck patio, there were several things that immediately caught my eye. There was in fact a bar with a grass roof over it, and about fifteen different kinds of rum, two optics, and an array of ceramic coconuts, tikis, and other paraphernalia for exotic drinks. There were two of the most hideous mock-Hawaiian velvet paintings I had ever seen hanging behind the bar. They probably dated to between 1955 and 1965, and depicted women wearing nothing but grass skirts and exotic flowers in their hair. I was pleased to see another, in equally poor taste, over the doorway we'd come in. This was of a strapping youth, wearing a colorful loincloth that was two sizes too small, astride a surfboard that seemed to be, well, either a wish, a promise, or an extension of something else. If you're going to be tacky, at least be non–gender-specific about it.

On one end of the deck was a telescope and an apple crate turned upside down. Raylene watched silently as I climbed up onto the crate and peered through glass. It was trained on the Lawton marina, which was reduced to HO scale in the eyepiece. Aha, the water view. At the other end of the deck was another crate, this one half-full of bruised apples. It was directly over the spot where I'd first seen Raylene sweeping. I asked her about this crate.

"Erik hates apples," Raylene offered, but it left me as much in the dark as before. She turned to go back downstairs. "Come back sometime." She handed me a couple of coupons that said FIRST TIMER. "First two drinks are on us."

"Wow, great, thanks. We will." I followed her back downstairs and got my ice cream. "I didn't know there was going to be a bar in here. I suppose I missed the advertising or something."

"We didn't advertise."

"Oh?" I found myself being as economical with my words as she was.

"Won't need to. People talk." She shrugged, as if she didn't much mind one way or the other.

"You know, I've got an idea." I told her about Brian's upcoming birthday and asked a couple of questions.

Her slow smile lit up her face like Christmas lights. "No problem. I'll keep a table for you."

An hour and a half later, Brian and I were eating semimelted mud pie in bed.

"Hot sex and cold ice cream," he said. "A good combination."

"I actually prefer them this way, in sequence, but I'll try anything once," I offered, licking the back of my spoon. "Stop hogging the carton."

Brian passed the carton back to me, and just then, the phone rang. "I'll give you three guesses as to who that is," I said, around a mouthful of ice cream. I gave Brian the carton back and he handed me the phone. "Better ice cream interruptus than some other alternatives I could imagine, though."

I hit the TALK button. "Hey, Bucky. How's it going? What do you mean, how did I know it was you? It was sisterly intuition, what else?"

"Her impeccable timing," Brian muttered. I poked him in the arm and he grinned, pulled on his robe, and went into the bathroom. He took the rest of the ice cream with him, but I guess he'd earned it.

"I'll be down to pick you up in about forty minutes. Well, go to the bookstore or something. I need to shower, that's why. I was helping Brian with the housework. Yes, that is what we call it these days. Sit tight, I'll be there soon."

After a quick shower, a kiss, and a nibble, I hit the road for town. The bright sun that had scorched the morning was vanishing behind thick clouds, illuminating their edges until it was finally completely hidden. It smelled a bit like rain and the wind picked up as I parked in the last open spot in the lot on Main. I hustled down toward Water Street and the Book Bin, where I'd told Bucky to meet me.

For some reason, it has always struck me that it is easier to envision the past in a place that is cloudy rather than sunny, in winter rather than summer, and by night rather than day. Maybe it's because the amount of visual stimulation is lessened, the shadows are longer, sound is muffled by snow, and with one good squint, a crowd of modern tourists can be transformed into a generic throng, from any time at all. The fact that so much of the downtown still maintained cobblestone sidewalks and brick paving in places helped. The buildings didn't hurt either, as there were still a lot of

early-nineteenth-century structures, even some eighteenth-
century architecture left; warehouses and shop fronts were
now restaurants and shop fronts, ranging in style from the
plainer symmetrical patterns of the earliest part of the eighteenth century, to the more ornate columns and wooden trim
of the later part of the century, all the way through the eclec-
tic and fantastic revivals of the Victorian era. On the water
side of the street, there were vendors of hot dogs, ice cream,
and handmade jewelry hoping to attract the tourists who'd
come down to look at the sailboats as they skirted Sheep's
Head Island or go on a whale-watching tour or were getting
off the tour buses for a fifteen minute pee-and-scenery
break. The salty air was intoxicating and it seemed that, for
just a minute, everyone else was also caught up in their own
reflections about the sea, the past, the lure of Stone Harbor.

A large woman in flamingo pink shorts and a turquoise
top and matching baseball cap and fanny pack walked past
me with her sunburned brood; no amount of squinting could
transform her into period garb. "I suppose we could find a
museum. If we had to. There's one over in Boxham. It's going to rain and we've been to all the souvenir stores here. At
least we'd be dry," she concluded reluctantly.

"There would be a gift shop, too," reminded her friend, in
canary yellow.

"I suppose. C'mon, kids, we're going to a museum," she
called. Moans and whining followed. "Clam up, it's good
for you."

I fled into the Book Bin and nodded at the owner, Alice.
She was even taller than I was, just shy of six feet, and had
wiry black hair caught up in a knot on the back of her head.
She wore, as she always did, baggy cotton trousers in a vi-
brant blue pattern, a loose crinkly maroon shirt with a draw-
string neck, and Birkenstocks. She had a silver pendant
around her neck, a curled-up cat on a leather thong.

"Gonna rain soon," I said.

"That's always a help. It drives them in, and sometimes they even buy something."

I picked my way past the recent best-sellers and the local interest section to find Bucky at the nonfiction shelves, checking out a collection of essays on natural history. "Hey."

"Hey."

"So how'd it go?"

She shrugged, but it wasn't a happy shrug. "There'll be no second date."

"Any particular reason?"

"He was boring."

"You said Joel was boring. You thought a landscaper would be more of a thrill than a software engineer?"

She shrugged and I decided that I didn't really want to know what kind of thrills Bucky had been shopping for. Phil was, as Bucky had pointed out to Brian, young and tanned and extremely well-muscled.

"All he talked about was mulch and how much money he makes and going to the gym. And the great parties he and his friends have, where they drink lots of beer and do shots and get hangovers the next day. Oh yes, and how they go looking for hot women."

"Charming."

"And tactically stupid, particularly if you are telling this to someone who asked you out."

"Well, at least you gave it a try."

"Grand consolation. I've decided I'm off the whole male species."

"Wouldn't be the first time. Are you about done?"

"I'm just going to decide about this one. Give me a minute?"

"Sure. I'll be over in the history section."

She waved at me, already back into her book, and I

strolled around for a moment. Because Alice kept a small section of used books dedicated to the town's history, I headed over there and was surprised to see Bray Chandler in deep discussion with a dark-haired woman of about forty or so, their heads close together.

"Bray, how are you?" Even as the words were out of my mouth, I realized my mistake. They hadn't been talking but caressing each other passionately.

Bray turned dark red as he recognized me. "Uh, not bad, Emma." He pointedly didn't introduce me to his companion, but that didn't faze her in the least.

"This another one of yours, Bray?" she asked, giving me the once-over. Her glance was as frosty as her words.

"Uh, this is Emma Fielding. She's an, uh, archaeologist—"

But his friend was having none of it. "Sure, Bray. And I'm Mary Queen of Scots. Save it for your wife."

And with that, she turned on her heel and marched out of the store. Bray followed, after glaring at me venomously. "Mind your own damn business," he said to me over his shoulder.

I only said hello, I thought, and gave his back the rude, two-fingered salute I learned in England. Alice caught me doing it, and raised her eyebrows, but then repeated it herself as Bray slammed the book he'd been looking at on the counter right in front of her before following the other woman out of the store.

"What was all that about?" I asked, walking toward the counter.

"Apparently Bray's peccadilloes are starting to pile up and I think Miss Thing thought you were the competition."

I thought of his unkempt appearance and petulant personality and wrinkled my nose. "Trust me when I say absolutely not. Besides, he's married."

"Oh, yes, he is. Doesn't slow him much down, though."

Bucky joined us, putting her selection down on the counter. "Well, he must have solid gold boxer shorts, because I can't see anything else attractive about him."

Alice shrugged. "Never mind boxer shorts. Before I even considered sleeping with him, he'd have to have a solid gold—"

"What was he was looking at?" I asked hurriedly. I picked up the book, a used copy of a history of Stone Harbor by Reverend Joseph Tapley. "Are you saving this for him?"

"I thought of you, after I put it on the shelf, but Bray grabbed it before I could put it behind the counter. You want it?"

"You bet!"

"Let me get that." Bucky checked out the penciled price on the flyleaf. "This will about cover my computerized pilfering."

"Bucky, I shouldn't have—"

She nodded. "And I shouldn't have either. I got it, Em."

"You got your Binge Card?" Alice asked me. "I can stamp it for you and give your sister the discount."

"Great, thanks." I handed my Book Bin Book Binge card to her and she stamped two more little books onto the already crowded space. Only three more spaces, and I'd get ten bucks off my next purchase, but I had to keep reminding myself it wasn't like that ten bucks was free. Even if I kept Alice in rent every time I walked in there, I was still surprised that people only wanted money for books. Not body parts or firstborns or souls. Just money. It always seemed like a steal to me.

Detective Bader called later that afternoon. Brian handed me the phone, his lips tight, but he didn't say anything. And

Bader wasn't just calling to tell me when I could get back to work.

"I'd like to ask you a few questions about something we found."

I could feel my heart begin to pound. "Something near Aden's body?"

Brian scowled and went back to his work. There was a long silence from the other end of the line.

"I can answer anything you like," I said as neutrally as I could, "but it might be possible that I could help you a whole lot more if you tell me what you're looking for."

There was another brief pause before Bader reached his decision, and when he began to speak, I let my breath out as quietly as I could, not even aware I had been holding it.

"It was homicide." Detective Bader's voice was gruff, as if it was a compromise for giving me this information. "Aden Fiske was shot twice through the head, once at the base at close range, then another in the left temple, very close to the head to judge by the tattooing, the powder marks I could see on his neck. It was a smaller-caliber weapon than that used in Justin Fisher's death. No brass was recovered, but it was definitely a different weapon than that used in the Fisher case."

"Really." I mulled that over. It seemed the two cases must be connected, somehow, but this made it more difficult.

"It was very cleanly done; perhaps he went willingly with his killer, perhaps he was unaware that anyone was behind him. There was no sign of a struggle, no defensive wounds, no disturbance to indicate a fight. We think that he was shot just about where you found him, sometime late yesterday, then loosely rolled up in the tarp. You saw for yourself that the killer didn't take great pains to conceal the presence of the body. I think your tarp was just an afterthought for the killer, though I don't know why he bothered."

"Why do you say that?"

"If he was going to dump the body, there was no need for the tarp; he would have brought something. If the killer was sending someone a message, there would be no need for concealment."

"Sending someone a message?"

There was a pause on the other end of the line, and I realized he wasn't talking about bread and butter notes on floral stationery. More than that, I wondered whether he was thinking that they were directing that message toward me.

"It has some of the characteristics of a contract killing, but there are problems. Like the attempt to hide the body—why bother? That's unusual. The casings being cleaned up. Someone didn't really know what they were doing."

"But you think it was someone different than Justin's killer?"

"Different weapon—probably at the bottom of the harbor, by now—and a different MO. A different lot of things. And there was something else."

I held my breath again. He was telling me so much. . . .

"Fiske's keys and wallet were missing. They weren't on him, they weren't in his office. But his vehicle was still in the parking lot. He drove an old Ford pickup. Liked to pretend he was a gentleman farmer, but the truck was really more of a classic antique than a working vehicle."

"Was his office disturbed?"

"I think so. You know that he was a neatnik. Well, now it looks a little less neat, more like a normal desk. Someone, probably the killer, was rifling it. Looking for something."

"The Chandler House alarm didn't go off that night?"

"No, but if it was never set, we wouldn't expect it to. What it looks like was that Aden left his office under his own steam, and then the killer came back and did a thorough job of looking for something. And then just walked out."

"Looking for what?"

"I can't say at the moment. Fiona Prowse thought that Aden had already arrived at the house the day you found him, so she didn't think it was strange the alarm wasn't on when she arrived at work."

And she did make a point of asking me whether I'd seen Aden on the site, I recalled. "What was it that you found?"

"A copy of a piece of paper," he said. "It looks old—the original was anyway. This copy was found crumpled up in Aden's home office wastebasket. When I brought it to the lab, they gave it a once-over, told me what they knew, and then suggested I contact someone who knew about the Chandlers. And it was either someone at the Historical Society or. . . ." He didn't need to tell me why they weren't on his go-to list.

"Or me.

"Right. Can you take a look at it for me?"

"Do you want me to come over now?"

"I'll stop by the site Monday. You can take up your work by the side of the house again, then, if you feel up to it."

"I'm up to it. I'll check with the crew, but if they're not up for it, I'll be by anyway."

"Fair enough."

I was glad to know more about what was going on; it was just a relief, not that it did anything to inform me about what was happening at the Historical Society. Of course, Brian wasn't going to be thrilled about this, but maybe if he could see it the way I did, that a closer relationship with the police was going to be in my best interest, he wouldn't get too wound up about it. After all, it wasn't as though I was looking for trouble, and helping the police was in everyone's best interest.

I whistled the first few bars of the fourth movement of Beethoven's Fifth Symphony as I grabbed a broom and began to sweep the kitchen floor.

The next morning, I decided that the best way of starting off Brian's birthday on an indulgent note would be to go to Wendy's Bakery, way the heck over on the north side of Boxham-by-Sea. Crossing two towns might sound like a lot of trouble to go through on a Sunday morning, especially for a no-no like doughnuts, but then, you've never had a doughnut like these. They're so tasty you could eat a dozen before you notice it and so fresh you're not left with that greasy feeling around your lips all day, which makes for a deadly combination. I made sure that I would beat everyone else out of bed, and, fueled only by the delight that comes with doing something unexpected and nice, took off.

Wendy didn't look as though she was very happy to be awake—her hennaed beehive hairdo was leaning off to one side, like a heavily shellacked Tower of Pisa—and I was careful not to let my own unusually good mood annoy her. There's nothing worse than some bright, cheery thing in your face first thing in the morning when you're up only by the grace of autopilot and your body's still convinced you've got another hour left to sleep. She cast an evil eye at the teenyboppers in front of me—when did eighteen-year-olds get so young?—who were chattering away, one hundred and twenty beats a minute. I wondered who told them that sweatshirts and pajama bottoms made suitable daywear, and whether they really thought it was appropriate to leave the house with baseball caps on over their uncombed hair. Even I had combed my hair before donning my Red Sox cap.

When it was my turn, I ordered two baker's dozens of the juiciest and a large cup of coffee for the ride home. The bags in one arm, keys and the coffee in my hand, and a chocolate cruller stuck in my mouth, I elbowed the door open and almost bumped into the incoming patrons. The little do-si-do I had to do to get out of the way took me away from my car, but, overflowing with the virtue of doing good deeds so early in the morning, I waited patiently for the beleaguered unshaven father with a stroller and dog and two toddlers to get out of the way. It looked like Mom was having a morning to herself today, if she was lucky.

I glanced over to make sure I wouldn't bump into anyone else, and a movement in a car caught my eye. A woman was leaning over and kissing someone in the driver's seat. The driver she was kissing, I realized, was Fiona Prowse.

Well, it's nice to know there's someone in her life, I thought. Someone outside the Historical Society.

The kiss broke. Our eyes met. Hands still not free, I gave her a nod of my head and as much of a good-morning smile as I could around the cruller stuck in my mouth. It would be nice if for once the people from the Chandler House could see me when I wasn't dirty or bending over or loaded down with equipment. Or doughnuts. I guess my first presentation and my talk at the family reunion would be their only chances to see me at my best, I thought as I juggled my way into my Civic.

I was concentrating on getting the bags settled in the passenger seat and my cruller out of my mouth before it broke, when I was started by a sharp rap on the window. Fee was there, red-faced, and I balanced the doughnut on top of the coffee lid as I rolled down my window.

"Morning, Fee. Sorry, I had my hands full back there. Wendy's is great, isn't it?"

Fee's mind wasn't on pastry, however. "You have to forget what you saw back there."

"What I saw back where?"

She reddened further. "You know, just now. In the car."

The penny dropped for me. "Oh . . . okay. Really? No problem, but. . . ."

"I understand that young people nowadays are a little more casual . . . about such things, but I am not. I prefer things to stay . . . quiet."

"Sure, Fee, fine." But I was thinking to myself, if she hadn't made anything of it, I wouldn't have given it another thought. If she hadn't been kissing someone in public, no one would be the wiser.

It was as though she'd read my mind. "Gracie is sometimes impulsive. That doesn't change things for me, for either of us."

I was starting to get irritated. "Fee, I already said I would keep it quiet, and I will."

"See that you do." She pursed her lips. "I take this very seriously. This is the sort of thing that could make a lot of trouble. For everyone involved."

And just what does that mean? I wondered. I simply nodded again and watched her retreat to her car, fists clenched and shoulders rigidly held back, before I brushed the crumbs off my lap and took off for home, my mood considerably deflated by the experience.

Brian was there, waiting at the door for me when I got back. "Did I read the note correctly? Did you really go all the way to Boxham? For me?" He was bouncing up and down as he held the screen door open for me.

"For you, for everyone. Happy Birthday, sugar." I gave him a kiss on the cheek, just knowing the coffee hadn't done much for my breath, and handed him one of the bags.

"Chocolate-frosted cream-filled?" he said even as he dove into the bag like a raccoon into a dumpster.

"Four of them, top of that bag."

"You spoil me."

"Not nearly enough. The least I could do, after giving you a houseful of strangers for the day."

"You okay?" He peered at me as he got a couple of plates down from the cabinet and started setting them out one-handed while he began eating his breakfast.

"Yeah, just need another cup of coffee." I'd promised Fee, and I'd keep my word even if I didn't think there was any real cause. In fact, the entire incident had taken me so off-guard that it had never even occurred to me to ask Fee about the Mather House. Although the house was run-down, the land itself was a gold mine. Why did she hold such valuable property if she was so broke?

Brian had decided that he wanted a quiet dinner out with me and Bucky for his birthday treat, and that evening, the parking lot outside Shade's was packed. Since we were early, Bucky and I volunteered to snag a place in the bar while Brian parked. The pickup was a little out of place outside the restaurant, standing out a mile amid the upper-crusty imported sedans. My car wouldn't have been much better, and since it was hemorrhaging fluids, might have been worse.

The maître d' led us to the last two seats at the bar, and I settled back to survey the landscape. We had been told that the dress was "casually elegant," which is a pretty broad definition. All the men were in jackets, most with ties, and the women tended to run to very smart, very understated separates or dresses for the older ones with the kind of consummate accessorizing that I could never manage unsupervised. There wasn't a lot of jewelry to be seen—discreet pearls, a good brooch, a heavy gold choker here and there—but some of the rings were real knuckledusters, diamonds big enough to ice skate on. Bucky and I played a couple of quick rounds of "who's had what done," calculating the cost of the cosmetic surgery done on each face until the bartender came over to take our order. Bucky was better at it than I, since I'd lost some of my edge in university life. She still saw enough of it in her partners' swanky Connecticut veterinary practice.

"Good evening, ladies. What can I get for you?"

"House chardonnay," I said.

"Excellent," he responded. "And for you, madam?"

" 'Scuse me." Bucky reached over the guy next to her and grabbed the wine list. "What I'm looking for," she said as she ran down the page, "is a big, nasty red. Dark fruit, chocolate, tobacco, not too heavy on the tannins." She scrunched up her face, made a fist. "Something with balls."

I gave her a skeptical glance, and almost said something disapproving. The bartender nodded gravely, and nearly smiled.

"I can recommend a couple of excellent zinfandels that might do the trick."

"Surprise me. Just pick one that shrieks 'big, blowsy peasant girl, the village strumpet,' and that'll do fine."

"Right away."

"What was that about?" I whispered. "You couldn't just order something like other people?"

"What, like your mimsy little chardonnay? Please. How milquetoast can you get? At least I take a little interest in my liquor."

"I don't recall ever hearing a wine described as 'the village strumpet' before."

"He knew what I was after. And I'll have more fun with mine than you will with yours."

The bartender put down my glass of chardonnay. I took a sip and it was very nice. If Bucky's was the village tart, mine would have been the melancholy spinster aunt, but it suited me just fine. I didn't like wrestling with my wine.

He set down a glass in front of Bucky, so dark that light didn't pass through it. I was almost willing to bet that bullets wouldn't have passed through it. She took a look at it, swirled it around with more vigor than I thought prudent, and took a sip. She didn't slurp or anything, just lingered over it and closed her eyes. "That's it, that's the stuff." She opened her eyes. "Rookhaven, right?"

"Exactly. Their Mignon vineyard, in Sonoma. I think you'll find that there's just a hint of—excuse me." His lecture was curtailed by a call from the end of the bar.

"Eucalyptus," Bucky said.

"Huh?"

"There's a flavor of eucalyptus in it."

"And where did you gain all this expertise?"

"I have friends who like wine." The way that she buried her nose back into the glass told me.

"You mean Joel."

"Maybe." Bucky stayed immersed in her glass until something at the other end of the bar caught her attention. She put her glass down abruptly. "Hello! Will you look at this little beauty! What a little darling she is!"

"Huh? Bucks, what's with the silly antipodean accent?" I tried to look where she was looking but couldn't figure out what was going on.

"Lovely skin, just gorgeous!" she continued in broadest Strine. "Shiny, in fantastic shape for one of her age. Just watch out for those claws, mate! She'll get you, whap! quick as anything, if you're not careful. And just look at those teeth. . . ."

Just then Brian appeared. "Place is jammed tonight. High Rockaway Pale Ale, please," he told the bartender. "Why is Bucky talking like the Gator Guy?"

"Who?" I said.

"Crazy guy on TV who tracks reptiles and teaches about them. I think he retains more of his lizard brain than most of us, but he's pretty good at what he does, you have to admit. Oh, I see."

At last the bartender had moved out of the way and I could see where Bucky's attention was so focused. An older couple was seated at a table directly opposite the bar in the dining room. She was maybe in her well-preserved forties, while her male companion might have been deep in his seventies, maybe older. At first I thought my sister was talking about him, as he certainly had a reptilian cast to him: compact, tanned, and lizard-skinned, hooded eyes that were a little bulbous, and a slow gaze that was unnerving even from this distance. Steely gray hair was threaded through with white, and a good deal of this also showed where his white shirt opened at the neck under his jacket. An image of Mediterranean tycoons immediately sprang to mind, and I got the impression that while he might be old, he was still a powerful man.

But Bucky had been talking about the woman, and now I could see why. She was as carefully maintained as any of the other women in the room, Bucky and me excluded, of course; we couldn't be considered maintained by any stretch of the imagination. She was more metallic than they, however: shiny, hard, sharp. She had piles of dark hair, and wore it proudly in cascades down the back of her head. Her fingernails—the claws to which Bucky had alluded—were longer than the taste embraced by most of the crowd here, and were an unabashed scarlet, as were her lips. Her teeth were very white against tanned skin and it wasn't difficult to imagine this couple at expensive island resorts in winter because you don't get a tan like that by putting the laundry out on the line or raking leaves. She wore heavy gold at her wrist and throat, as well as on her fingers and ears, and it was clear that it was genuine and expensive. She had a tall clear drink with a lime wedge in front of her and looked concerned when her companion signaled the waiter for another round. She put her hand on top of his and he kissed it fervently.

I found that I was the only one still absorbed by the couple in the far corner. "Whew, big money in here," Brian said, taking it all in after he took a sip of his beer.

I rested my hand on his back. He liked his dining on a more casual note and was never entirely at home the few times we'd been to really good restaurants with our friends Kam and Marty. He always went for the food and the company, though.

"Except in this corner," Bucky said. "We're the intellectual elite."

Brian smiled and relaxed. I tensed up, annoyed that she should be able to say something so obvious and silly and have it reassure him like that.

"Evening, Dr. Fielding," a voice said from behind us.

Bucky and I both turned around, saying, "Evening." We looked back at each other crossly.

Daniel Voeller, dressed very elegantly casual in a black silk suit and a cobalt-blue shirt, was standing behind us looking puzzled. "You're not both archaeologists, are you?"

"Perish the thought," Bucky said, with the conviction of an oath.

Not much nicer, I laughed too. "Nice to see you, Daniel. No, my sister, ah, Carrie, is a veterinarian. And this is my husband, Brian Chang. He's got a real job too."

Hands were shaken. "Are you having dinner tonight?"

"Yes, I'm about to join my father and stepmother over there." He indicated the couple I'd just been contemplating. "A little family celebration. Dad likes to get out every once in a while, though his health isn't the best. Delilah tries to keep an eye on him, but it's beyond anyone's capabilities, I fear. Especially tonight."

"We have a stepmother like that. Looks after Dad." Bee-bee was just five years older than I, and though we would never have a great relationship—we were just too differ-ent—I had to admit she made Dad cut down on the red meat he was so fond of and made him exercise enough to keep healthy.

"I'm just here to fill him in on things at the factory, what's up with his pet projects. We're a team, Lila and I. She watches the home front and I take care of the family biz at the factory. He's worth every bit of our efforts. He's an amazing guy."

"Oh, yes?" Daniel seemed so unguarded and enthusiastic that I was surprised.

"Self-made man, immigrant story right out of Horatio Al-ger. Came from nothing, made everything. If only his health wasn't so shaky. It's the one thing his money can't do." He caught himself. "But I'm getting soppy."

I offered him a way out. "How's Charles tonight?"

"He's well. He'll be along later." Daniel leaned in and said confidentially, "He likes to limit his exposure. You know how it can be with in-laws."

Brian nodded gravely. "Amen to that."

Bucky hit him on the shoulder.

Daniel laughed. "Well, I just wanted to say hello. I must get going."

"Enjoy your meal, Daniel."

It was only when our appetizers arrived a short while later that I began to wonder about the Voellers celebrating so soon after Aden Fiske's death.

There was one more chance encounter that night. Having gorged ourselves on fresh seafood served up in a simplified French style, we had decided against coffee and dessert right away. I was following Bucky out when I noticed a familiar form at the bar. I promised Brian that I would only be a moment. "I've got one more treat for you," I said, by way of apology and inducement. "I'll be two seconds, tops."

"I'll get the truck," he said, resigned. He let go of my fingers reluctantly. "Emma, please don't be long."

"I won't." I walked up to the bar, where Detective Bader was talking with the bartender, lingering over a plate of the oysters Florentine that Brian had liked so much.

"—then she sent him down to the pantry to find a left-handed whip. Kept him looking for hours."

They both laughed at that, and I saw my chance.

"Good evening, Detective Bader."

"Eh?" He turned around, and although his smile faded, it didn't entirely disappear. There was a wary look in his eye. "Well, hello there, Ms. Fielding. How was your dinner?"

I thought it was an odd question to start with, but figured that even detectives get to have some time off too. "Very nice. Actually, it was excellent. We don't often get meals like that."

"I could eat like that every day, if I wanted to." He patted his stomach proudly. "But I've got to watch myself, so I limit it to just once a week. Otherwise, I ask Sandra to keep her eye on the fat."

I could tell he was dying for me to ask. "Who's Sandra?"

"My daughter. She's the chef here, isn't she, Rich?"

The bartender nodded.

"Wow, I guess you would have to watch it," I said. "I'd be the size of a house."

"She can cook anything you want, better than anyone. All she has to do is taste it, just once. It's amazing how she does it, and worth every penny I spent sending her to Europe when she was training. You should see what she can do with just a couple of fresh onions, a little olive oil, and—"

Apparently I'd found the one topic that kept Detective Bader talking.

"—and the best decision that Walter Voeller ever made was to hire her. You here for an occasion?" he asked. "I haven't seen you here before."

"No, it's a little too rich for my blood," I said. Detective Bader's daughter worked for Walter Voeller? The name just had to be connected with Daniel's family. "It's my husband's birthday."

"Well, you couldn't have done better. Though you know, if Sandy wasn't who she was, I sure as hell wouldn't be in here every Saturday night. Couldn't afford it."

I was about to ask him the questions I had, about what he wanted to show me, but thought better of it. I knew as well as anyone that it was nice to be able to get away from the thought of work for a while; I was sure as a police officer, Detective Bader had an even more difficult time. But at least, his work wasn't actually living at home with him, even for a couple of weeks. "I just thought I'd say hello. I'll see you tomorrow?"

Again, that guarded look shadowed his face. "Sure, first thing."

"You enjoy your dinner."

"I've been looking forward to it since last week. You have a good night."

I nodded to the bartender and hurried out the door. Brian and Bucky were waiting in the pickup, the engine running.

"See, I wasn't too long," I said as I slammed the door and buckled my safety belt.

"No, that's good. Now what's my surprise?" Brian said.

"I'll tell you the way to go."

I directed him to the Lawton Yacht Club and Tiki Bar. The smell of rotten apples was still present by the door, though fainter. Brian looked at me, doubt writ large on his face.

"Trust me," was all I would say.

The look on his face when we entered the crowded bar and dining room encouraged me; then, when his puzzlement going up the stairs changed to glee when we reached the roof, I knew that I had it exactly right. The tiki torches were lit, the bar was aglow with the strings of chili-pepper Christmas lights, and Raylene met us with plastic leis in one hand—for Brian to wear in lieu of a party hat—and a pot of coffee in the other.

"What can I get you folks?"

"I'm driving," Bucky announced, putting a package that was flat and about a foot square down next to her chair. "So I'll just have a coffee."

"How do you take it?"

"Black."

"And for the birthday boy?"

"Uhhh. . . ." He was still trying to take it all in, a gaping grin of amazement spreading across his face.

"I'll have a mai-tai," I said, throwing caution to the wind along with my usual request for a bourbon or a single malt.

"Me too. Wow," Brian said as Raylene went to get the drinks. "This place . . . it's. . . ."

"I hoped you'd like it," I said. "We haven't found a place yet, you know, that was really . . . us."

"This is good, this is close," he agreed.

Bucky took a sip of her coffee. "This is your sort of place, Em? Really?"

"Why not? It's an amalgam. It's got a good menu, but doesn't take itself seriously; it isn't trendy or theme-y; it has a quiet place to eat and a place to get rowdy, inside and out, all of which I appreciate. It successfully combines these theoretically opposing qualities in a pleasing new fashion. I should say it suits me down to the ground."

"Thanks for the lecture." Bucky gave me a sour look. "I just meant I didn't have you figured for girl drinks."

"Ha! Shows how well you know me. Once in a while, I do something wacky. I learned that from you."

"Gee, thanks; turn my rebellion against human hypocrisy into an excuse for umbrella drinks. In any case," she handed the package to Brian. "Happy birthday, Bri."

"Hey, thanks a—" He had the wrapping torn off the package before he could finish, though, and he was agape when he saw what it was. "Whoa, Bucky! How did you know?"

"I did a little nosing around." Bucky was inordinately pleased with herself, though.

Brian held up the album for me to see. There was a disgruntled-looking young man with a mop of messy hair on the cover.

"It's Bob Dylan, *Highway 61 Revisited*," he explained. "Very hard to come by. Wow, thanks, Buck."

"Bob Dylan? Doesn't his voice drive you crazy? I can hardly listen to him," I said. "And I thought you were listening to reggae at the moment?"

"Dylan is always appropriate." Brian looked at me, pity and disapproval in his eyes. "And when you write lyrics like that, you can have whatever damn kind of voice you want."

"Yeah, but I thought you had that one already," I said. It was a good guess, anyway; he seemed to have every album in the world.

"That's a reissue. This is on the Columbia label, with an alternative version of "From a Buick 6" on side one. In near mint condition. This is something special. Bucks, are you sure—?"

"I got it for you. I don't care about vinyl, you dinosaur."

"Oh, man, thanks." He leaned over and gave her a hug. I

was glad the drinks and the cake I'd asked Raylene for came at that moment. Once the candle was blown out, I invited her over for a piece of cake. She joined us and after a few bites—still not much of a conversationalist—I decided to ask her about the apples.

"Erik doesn't like them," she said.

"I know, but why does he have so many up here?"

"He drops them off the roof."

By this time, Brian was interested too. "How come?"

Raylene finished chewing, then took a deep breath. "He gets up in the morning and drops an apple off the roof. If it hits the ground, he knows gravity is still working, and he has to go to work." She thought about that, nodded, satisfied, and continued eating her cake.

"Oh" was all I could come up with. Bucky nodded, as though it made perfect sense to her, and then reached over to pick one of the chocolate rosettes off my slice of cake. I rapped her knuckle with my fork and she retreated.

"Is Erik around tonight? Maybe he'd like some cake too," Brian suggested.

"He's down the boat tonight." Raylene finished up, nodded thanks, and left.

"Anyone understand any of that?" I asked.

"What's not to understand?" Bucky and Brian both said.

Later on that night in bed, waiting for the excitement and the sugar to wear off, I confessed to Brian. "If I'd known you wanted that record, I would have gotten it for you." But I didn't even know what such a thing cost. A lot, probably. "But you said you wanted to get the cell phones, and I went with that."

"I wanted the phones. I think they're a good idea." He raised himself up on his elbow. "What's this all about?"

"Bucky gave you something I didn't even know you wanted. I gave you . . . household appliances."

"You're not jealous, are you?"

"Yes," I said into the pillow.

"You shouldn't be."

"Well, why not? You guys speak the same language, she knows things about your work that I don't know. You guys hang out and never get into fights. You catch bottles of water you don't know she's throwing. She gives you good birthday presents. I don't like it. It has to stop now." I turned my face so I could see Brian, who wasn't smiling at my last joke.

"Yeah, we can hang out. We like each other. She's a different person, so naturally our relationship will look different than yours with me."

"But you look like you're having more fun with her."

"She is fun. We do get along. But you give me what I want every day of my life. Bucky and I don't have a history, the way you and I do. We don't have to be so careful with each other."

"Oh, great. You have to be careful with me."

"Shush, you know what I mean. Couples have to be more careful with each other, to stand up to the long haul. She doesn't have to live with me every day. I don't know how she thinks, like I know you or you know me. I wouldn't trade that for a whole stack of Dylan. That's why I wanted the phones, so we could be in touch, so I could feel like I was looking after you, so you could call me whenever you wanted. It's the only lifeline I can give you and not look like an idiot. Besides, she's not worried about a mortgage or keeping up two cars or renovating a house. It's easier for her to be frivolous."

"I know she likes you," I grumbled. "A whole lot."

He fluffed up his pillow and puffed up his chest. "And it's right she should. I'm a hell of a guy."

I smacked him.

"Well, I am! Aren't I?"

"Yes, you are. You just don't have to be so smug about it; I'd hate to have to tell Bucky how you eat cold leftover mashed potatoes right out of the fridge."

Brian grinned, then turned serious again. "Who was that you were talking to, on the way out?"

"It was Detective Bader. He's the one working on the case."

There was even less humor in his voice now. "And what were you talking about?"

"I was just saying hi." Brian knew there was more, so I told him. "When he called yesterday, he also asked if he could show me something. It has to do with the Chandlers."

"So even after all you said on Friday, you're still going to mess around with the case?"

"I thought you'd be happy. I mean, if the cops are talking to me, then that means they'll also be keeping an eye on me, right?"

"The killer might think so too."

"Oh, man. I can't win, can I?"

"Arrgh! Emma, it's not about winning. It's about staying alive. Do you know what I wished for when I blew out my candles?"

"No, and you can't tell me. It doesn't come true, if you tell."

"Well, let's just put it this way. I'm looking forward to spending my birthday with you next year, too."

"God, Brian. I'm doing my best. What more do you want from me?"

"Just a little common sense, that's all."

"Well, I'll work on the common sense, if you work on treating me like an adult." I flopped around onto my side, my back to Brian. He leaned over and put his chin on my shoulder.

"I'm sorry. I love you."

"I love you too, babe. I'm sorry, I just can't. . . ."

"Shh. We're both tired. We'll talk about it tomorrow."

But the celebration was well and truly over.

Chapter 15

M Y EYES FLEW OPEN; IT WAS LIGHT BUT THE ALARM
clock hadn't gone off. I almost never beat the alarm
getting out of bed. Brian wasn't next to me anymore.

He came into the bedroom quietly, dressed except for his
socks. He was looking in the bureau when he must have
sensed that I was awake, for he turned around and looked at
me. "Morning."

"Hey, babe," I said. "You're up early."

"Yeah, I've got to get in to work early today. A lot I need
to get done."

Oh God. "Look, about last night. I probably said things
the wrong way—"

"I understand what you were trying to say. I understand."
Thank God.

He pulled on his socks, not really looking at me. "I just
can't talk about it now. I've got to get going, okay?"

Oh no; he was still upset. "Brian, look, I just want—"

"No, Emma, it's okay. Right? I've just got to get going.

Bring your phone with you today, all right? I'll have mine
with me. I've got to run." He pulled on his sneakers and then
leaned over and kissed me. I kissed him back as hard as I
could, trying to interject as much heartfelt concern, love,
apology, and a plea for understanding into it as I could, but
he broke it off much too quickly for me. "Look after yourself, okay?"

I grabbed his hand. "Brian, I love you."

"I love you too. More than anything."

He left. Brian almost never varied his routine if he could
help it. I didn't know what to make of it, but I wasn't real
happy about it.

Maybe I shouldn't go back out there.

Too late, the logical part of me reminded myself. You've
already told everyone you would go.

I can unsay it.

Do you really want to? Go out today, see how you feel.
Decide tonight when you aren't worried about so many
other things.

Like my marriage disintegrating?

Don't be dramatic—

I don't think I am being dramatic; this is a big-ticket discussion Brian and I are having.

—and don't confuse the issue. Deal with today and you
can reevaluate the situation later.

That was the logical thing to do, but like most reasonable
and logical things, it wasn't easy.

When I went downstairs, I saw there was half a fresh pot
of coffee waiting for me, and I seized on it with all due
haste, thinking that Brian must still love me, at least a little
bit. I drank a cup down, as hot as I could stand, and then immediately had another cup. I poured the rest for Bucky, who
was just feeling her way down the stairs, and then put an-

other pot on. I stuck my head into Brian's office after knocking and saw that the crew was up. I left the cereal and bread out after I got something for myself and tried to wave a piece of toast under Bucky's nose.

"Uhnn." She batted at it and retreated further back into her corner, her hand over her eyes.

"You'll be hungry later on."

"Don't care. Coffee."

It was nice, having them all crowd around the table to scarf down the food, and then get the lunches made. It was nice, to have that bit of normality around us there, but it didn't last. We were out of the house promptly.

"Okay. I give," I told my sister in the car. "How did you find out about the album?"

"I nosed around a little." She took another sip of coffee from her travel mug. "Had a look through Brian's collection last time I was here, talked to a few people who knew some people."

"Any of those people named Joel, by any chance?"

"Maybe." She leaned back and pretended to sleep, and I kept quiet untll we got to the site.

It also seemed as though the elements conspired to distract us from whatever bad memories the week before might have held for us. A perfect morning for work; if mornings could start closer to ten or eleven, I would have been even happier. A fresh breeze off the water reassured me that the heat wouldn't be too bad today, not enough to get in the way of work. Even though we were all back working at the side of the house, there was plenty of room, and I was convinced that the concentrated effort would bring us down to the bottom of the charred layer, and maybe down into whatever might have been there before the Chandlers had built their house. But the crime scene team was already out there ahead of us.

Stuart Feldman was loitering by our part of the site when I arrived, passing the time of day with Perry. Ted was nearby, reading a book on a folding chair before the first tour of the day started.

"Say, do you mind telling me what you're looking for here?" Stuart said.

I gave him the rundown of what we were looking for and how we were piecing together our evidence, the documents, the stratigraphy, the artifacts, the architecture, the history. "But I suppose you remember all this."

He nodded. "It's pretty much the same as what we're doing here."

"Yeah, everything except the consequences," I said.

"You might be surprised." He paused. "You ever think about training in forensic bioarchaeology?"

I was taken aback. "Me? But I'm not qualified . . . I could never. . . ."

"Like I said, our work is essentially similar, but you'd have to do some training, there are courses. Brush up your osteology, do some work on the safety protocols and the legal aspects; depending on your experience, I'd bet you could get certified. If you're interested."

I didn't know what to say; the thought had honestly never crossed my mind.

Feldman spoke again, hastily. "Only if you're interested. It's not for everyone, that's for sure. But we are always looking for more help, even on a part-time consulting basis."

"I don't know. I don't know if I could do that," I said slowly. I looked at him. "It's a wild idea, though. I'll think about it."

He handed me a card. "Well, if you ever do, let me know.

I'll tell you where to get started on your certification. No pressure."

"Thanks. That's really . . . I mean, it's always nice to be asked, you know?"

Feldman laughed. "Yeah, I suppose it is. Well, I'd better get back to it. Take it easy and thanks for the tour."

"Sure, any time."

About 10 A.M., the breeze dropped off and the heat became blistering. I tried not to watch as Detective Bader approached the site; perhaps he didn't want to speak with me at all. Still, it was with a quiet sense of excitement that I realized that he was gesturing for me to meet him on the lawn below the house. He mopped his head with a handkerchief; a big guy like him would definitely be feeling the warmth of the day. As he walked from the crime scene, he tucked the hankie back neatly into his blazer pocket.

I put my notes down and tapped Meg on the shoulder, letting her know that I would be away for a few minutes. It wasn't too surprising that Detective Bader led me over to one of the trees that was next to the street side fence, well away from the crew, well away from the crowds, well away from the house.

"I hate to take you away from your work, but I've got that paper to show you. The one I mentioned the other day?"

"I'd be happy to help, if I can."

He pulled a folded piece of paper from his pocket. It was a photocopy, but one that had been the result of putting the original the wrong way around on the glass; the paper only showed half of the original, cut off midway down the page. He handed it to me, saying, when I hesitated, "Go ahead. It's a copy I made of the original photocopy, if you know what I mean. You can touch it."

I took the paper and looked at it. It seemed to me that the original photocopy had been crumpled. The original document it showed was old, maybe as old as the house, and darkened with age. The cursive handwriting seemed to swim before my eyes for a moment; some of the lettering had faded over the years, there were one or two blots, and there was a peculiarity about the way the tails of the letters were formed with an abrupt jerk upward that took a while to get the hang of. When I focused on the first word, however, I could make it out well enough to realize that I was reading a sentence that began in the middle, part of a letter. I read aloud:

"—though it can scarce matter now about the Boy's parentage. What is important is that you have promised to give him your protection, raise him as your own, and that, along with his own deeds, will determine the kind of Man Nicholas is to become. This is the last favor I shall ever ask of you, Mr. Matthew Chandler. It is a great one, but I realize that you would undertake it for his sake, as well for the sake of the memory of his Father and me. It is better this way; if he had grown older here with me, he would have grown into the City's vices and perhaps mine too. Perhaps this way, it is not too late. Your grateful Servant Sarah Holloway."

There was no date. I didn't recognize the name or the handwriting from any of the documents I'd been studying, so I didn't know why Detective Bader was giving it to me.

"It looks eighteenth century," I told him. "I can't tell too much more than that."

"But it looks like . . . something that was real?"

"Yes. It looks genuine, but I couldn't say better unless I looked at the original. Where did you get this?" I said.

"From the wastebasket in Aden Fiske's home office. Did you know it had been broken into the night of his murder?"

"No, I didn't."

"Broken in is probably the wrong word. There were no signs of a forced entry. Whoever killed Aden used his keys.

Not the sort of thing you are careless with, particularly when you have as much to guard as he did."

"The historic site and his house," I suggested.

"More than that. Aden Fiske was a blackmailer."

"You're kidding me." Ted had said something like it at the Little Green Bar, but I hadn't considered it seriously.

"If I were, it would reduce the number of suspects I'm suddenly considering."

"How do you know he was blackmailing people?" I could tell that I was pushing the limits of his tolerance for telling a civilian anything to do with an ongoing investigation, and I held my breath until he reluctantly answered.

"We got to his house and found that a fire had been set in his home office. A pile of files, letters, photographs, a lot of things were smoldering in the fireplace. Someone had taken a hatchet to the filing cabinets and managed to get one of them opened. Most of the files from that one were burnt in the fireplace—"

"Does that mean you can narrow down the suspects in some way—by alphabetical order or something like that?"

"I wish. His filing system wasn't that well organized. I got the impression from the way things were organized that there is a larger collection, hidden away somewhere. What we found were mostly photocopies like this one. Apparently the murderer didn't think to look in the wastebasket."

"You said 'a larger collection'?"

He nodded and looked out toward the water.

"A safety deposit box?"

"There's no way to tell at this stage. But Aden wouldn't have been stupid enough to keep the originals at home. He didn't even have an alarm system."

"Maybe he believed that whoever might want to get at him knew that his files were protection enough. Maybe they were worried that he might have some kind of 'dead-man's switch,' in case he died. You know, a lawyer who would mail a letter to the paper on the news of his death, or something like that."

"You have a very devious mind, Dr. Fielding." He looked down the way we'd come, toward the site at the side of the house. "We've considered all that. But it didn't do him any good in the end. It does make me think about the trouble you had with Aden's outboard."

I chewed that over, thinking about Bray Chandler's claims to be descended from Margaret and Matthew Chandler, now utterly refuted by this letter. A letter that Aden had in his possession and perhaps even held over Bray's head.

I told Bader about Bray Chandler's claims. His face grew more and more stern, and I realized that Bray wasn't the only one whose secret I also now knew. Fee and Grace, Perry's history of cheating at school, Ted's prying and spying. Even the Voellers' competition with Aden seemed all too sinister now.

"What will you do with all the evidence you've found? I mean, about other people's blackmail-able activities?" I asked.

"It depends. A lot of the stuff we found was just . . . personal. Some of it wasn't, but we'll have to see."

I remembered from childhood that "we'll see" was an all-purpose conversation ender. I couldn't afford to let it end now. And I'd promised Brian I wouldn't.

"What about the vandalism? Perry's hit and run? Any ideas about where they might all fit in?"

"Hmmm, well. Perry Taylor's hit and run isn't part of this story."

"How can you be sure?"

"Trust me. We're still looking into the vandalism though."

Once again, his reluctance to speak about police matters

was frustrating, but I couldn't allow it to stop me now. "Detective Bader. I'm not sure how to say this, but . . . there were two bodies found here at the house. They were found, both of them, right next to where I've been working. Is there any chance that this might have more to do with me or my work than—?"

"So far, this all looks like it's focused on the Historical Society and Aden Fiske," he said briskly. "I would just suggest you take the usual precautions."

We were walking along the fence that ran down the street side of the house. I noticed that Ted had followed us out onto the lawn, pausing here and there at some of the garden beds, as if to pick out weeds or deadhead past blooms. He was straining to hear us. If Detective Bader noticed, he gave no indication. Eventually Ted gave up and returned to the house, his hands stained red from the geranium blossoms.

When we reached the edge of the property at the water, we turned and walked back up the slope until Detective Bader halted at the turnoff for the crime scene. A loud "woof" came from across the street and I realized that a pair of canine eyes were following us closely.

"Piss off, Matisse," I called. I turned back to Detective Bader, who looked amused. "If you let me see the original, maybe I could say something more about it."

"I'll let you know. Thanks for your help; I don't want to keep you any longer."

I couldn't just leave it at that. "Did you ever find out about your U.S.–Mexican War troops?"

"Yes, I did." He hesitated. "You know, I really appreciate it when someone tells me straight out that they don't know something. That's the mark of a professional." And with that, he walked away.

Okay, it might not have been what I was looking for, but

maybe it told me why he'd brought the Chandler paper to my attention, rather than to the museum or someone else's.

Aden a blackmailer? Whew, that made a lot of sense. A lot of ugly sense. I couldn't think of too many things worse than holding someone hostage with their own indiscretions. It certainly went a long way to help me understand the state of relations between the town and the Historical Society. The only problem was, it also widened the field of suspects, as Detective Bader said, not only in terms of Aden's murder—and Justin's too, for that matter—but the strikes against the Historical Society as well. It might be that all of the vandalism and other problems were the result of several different perpetrators, not just one. It did feel, though, based on the people and where I'd found them, that it had to do with the Chandler House. And maybe even the people associated with it.

It was with some relief that I returned to my work. Although the house was still open for visitors, most of the grounds outside the immediate perimeter of the house were not, as Detective Bader and the lab crew were still working out by the northern part of the site. That did not stop, however, many people from gathering on the street side of the fence to ask us questions, and we were pretty busy for most of the morning. A little too busy, in fact, because I heard a soft curse from Joe around ten thirty.

I gently extracted myself from a gentleman who was telling me about his family history ("Since you're sort of an antiquarian, you might find this interesting," was how he had started, too long before), and went over to see what the problem was. It turned out to be a simple matter of a mislabeled feature number that involved a lot of erasing, renumbering, and cross-checking the drawings he'd made yesterday, but it seemed to hit him hard. His dark hair was soaked with sweat so that it stood up. Between that and his dark eyebrows against his pale skin, he looked rather like an anxious Muppet.

"It's not like I've never done this before," he said.

"You know, you could just be tired. Are you thinking about what's been going on around here lately?" I indicated the northern part of the site, where it was still possible to detect the movement of the crime scene squad over there. "That could shake anyone's nerves," I pointed out. "Completely natural."

He shrugged, then shook his head. "No, not really. It's horrible, but . . . don't take this the wrong way, will you?" He lowered his voice even further. "It's kind of interesting, too, you know what I mean? I mean, to see it from a distance. With Justin, it was hard to take. I knew him a little and it was really creepy. The violence, everything. I didn't feel that way then. But with Aden, I know it is terrible, even if I don't know him, but I can't help feeling a little curious about it all." He put his head in his hands. "Oh, God, I sound like a shithead, don't I?"

I stared at the side of the house. "No, I understand what you mean. I can see how it would be interesting, out of the ordinary for you. I don't think you have to feel ashamed of that. But you seem to be taking a few clerical errors too hard today. Are you sure you're not just upset about the murders?"

He looked up, but his shoulders slumped. "No, it's not that. And it's not just the paperwork I'm screwing up. I mean, yesterday? I didn't catch the edge of that planting hole until I was centimeters down into it."

"It was irregular and mottled, that's what makes it hard to see. I mean, not that you shouldn't try hard, but it's not the end of the earth, if you'll excuse the pun."

He wasn't convinced, though. "I just can't seem to get into it today. This week. I keep making mistakes."

I nodded. "But you keep catching them and correcting

them, which is a good start, a good sign. Everyone has an off moment or two. Just take it slower, and you'll find your groove again."

"This morning you told everyone to pick up the pace," he muttered.

"Right. Well, you know what I mean. Go quicker, but slowly and carefully."

That at least brought a grin from him. "Okay."

Although I knew what Joe meant, I was one hundred and eighty degrees away from where he was, right on top of my game today. Because we were all forced by the investigation to work on our original set of units, I was caught up on the eternal paperwork, and had begun to think of where we might put an extra unit on this side if we had the time, which wasn't really likely, but it was nice to be able to think ahead.

"That's lunch, folks," I announced a while later. "Clean it up and lock it down. Pick a spot in the shade and I'll be with you in a minute."

Lunch flew by, and we were soon back hard at it. Even though Joe seemed a little disheartened by missing the transition and by the frustration of trying to get the surfaces cleaned, everyone else had had a pretty good day. In fact, I felt quite confident now that the wing on the other side of the house was original and not a later addition: Our garden wall was the anomaly. There was some reason for them not having built this wing again, and I knew I would eventually find out why.

"Time to wrap it up, guys," I announced, after I realized that the sun was moving a lot faster than I'd given it credit for. "Good day, everyone."

Joe gave me a defeated look, his face sunburned and lined with unusual concentration and fatigue, as he went around and collected the tools that were lying about.

"You'll get it back tomorrow, don't worry about it," I said to him.

Joe nodded, accepting my statement, but still not believing me. He looked past me and suddenly his face changed from hangdog to puzzlement and then into a big grin. "What are you doing here?"

"I'm helping close up," said a familiar male voice. "Isn't that what it's called?"

I looked over my shoulder and was surprised to see Brian putting half a brick onto a corner of the tarp that he and Meg were handling.

"I figure the extra hands don't hurt at the end of the day," he said, looking up at me.

"And the extra eyes, either?" I said in a low voice so only he could hear.

He shrugged. "I'm not so much keeping an eye on you as seeing for myself what is going on here. Call it reassuring myself that there's nothing going on I don't know about."

"Okay, I can live with that," I announced, then frowned. "Just pull that corner a little tighter, would you? It's crooked."

He smiled. "Aye aye." He turned and said to someone behind him. "Pull that corner tighter, would you Kam?"

"I believe that is what is known as passing the buck," Kam announced. He was dressed casually—casually for him, at any rate—in a crisp white shirt and jeans that were pressed. I saw Dian frankly checking him out, intrigued by his refined English accent as much as by his form.

"Hey you!" I gave him a hug. "It's been weeks! How was the honeymoon?"

"Oh, it was lovely, thank you very much. And it was nice to get away from work."

"Kam! I can't believe you!"

He looked pained. "Honestly, Emma. What am I supposed to tell you? You'd be no happier if I'd merely said that I thought that the hotel was worth every penny, would you? And if you're fishing for the lurid details, you'll not have them from me. My wife, however, is in the car, and you may have some luck there." A funny look crossed his face, a kind of worried indecision I'd never seen him before.

I ran out to the parking lot, to see my oldest friend Marty sitting in Kam's Jaguar XJR. Something was up, though, because I know how much Marty likes surprises and couldn't figure out why she hadn't come out to see me. She was sitting in the car, the door opened and her feet on the ground outside the car, her head low. I picked up my pace when I got a glimpse of her face; she wasn't made up. Something was wrong.

As I got closer, I saw she wasn't dressed up, not even in designer casual, which was another shock to me. What she was wearing looked like the sort of thing that Kam might have worn to the gym, a T-shirt that looked as though it might have been ironed—a thought that nearly made me giggle—and a pair of sweat pants that were rolled up almost a foot to reveal worn-out sneakers. She looked up and I realized that Marty's face was drawn and her eyes were red.

I ran to her side. "Oh my God, Marty! What's wrong? Tell me."

"Oh, Emma. I'm so pregnant!"

"Marty, oh, sugar! It's all right." I drew her into a gentle hug because, tiny as she was, I had never seen her look so fragile. I pulled back to look at her. "It is all right, isn't it?"

"Yes, it's all right, it's fine. We're very happy." And then she started to cry as if her heart was breaking.

"What is it? What's wrong?"

"We were going to tell you, I wanted to tell you in person. But I just keep throwing up. Oh, God, I've been so sick. I've never been this sick. I feel like I've been throwing up things I ate twenty years ago."

"But everything's all right, isn't it? I mean, what's the doctor said?"

"She said I'm fine, if you can believe that. She says it might be better in another six weeks or so, but. . . ." She shrugged tiredly.

"But it might not."

"I'm hungry all the time, but I can't keep anything down. It's awful. It's not just morning sickness, either. Motion sickness, smells drive me crazy these days, even things I used to crave make me ill. And I look horrible."

"You don't look horrible. You just feel that way because you're not made up."

"Trust me, that's the last thing on my mind right now. I just pity Kam, having to see me like this. At least I can avoid mirrors."

"It's not that bad, I'm telling you. You just feel out of sorts."

"I'm not the only one. Kam gave up smoking."

"So I heard." And now it all made sense. "Good for him."

"I'll tell you, Em, that hasn't been easy for him and if that weren't bad enough, he's really stretched at the moment."

"Work has been tough?"

"That, always, but it's hard for him to be the kind of person he's used to being, lately. So many changes, so many things to think about."

"What with the baby and all."

"It's more than that, Em." She put her hand on my shoulder and leaned in to me, even though no one was around. I was instantly transported back to our days as undergraduates together, sharing confidences. "Please don't tell anyone else. Even Brian, I mean."

So it was serious then. "Okay."

"He's worried about bringing a baby into this world," she whispered.

I nodded. "I can imagine. But you can't wait for the perfect time to have a baby, there never is one. It doesn't work like that."

"I know, I know. It was time, as far as I was concerned. I mean, my folks, well, they were actually telling us to go for it, practically as soon as we were engaged. My sister threatened to have his baby if I didn't—but you know my sister."

"I do."

"And his mother is so excited by the thought of it, she nearly pees when she walks past Baby Gap. That's helped a lot, but—"

"But it must still be pretty scary for him. For you too."

She nodded. "It doesn't bother me so much; I just know everything will be all right. Kam would never worry about himself, it's the thought of a family that he won't always be able to protect that drives him nuts."

I thought about Brian's reaction to my returning to the site. "He'll be okay."

"I know." Marty cocked her head to one side. "I mean, it shows, how very excited he is, though. He's already talking about putting the little one's name down for Winchester. I think he's a couple years early for that, though."

"And assuming the baby will be a boy," I agreed. "A little eager, is Kam? But there probably isn't so long a waiting list at your old school. What was the name of that juvie hall you attended? P.S. Three-to-Five?"

"He'd sure as hell learn self-defense, if I sent him there. Or her. And she'd swear like a champ, too."

"The best of both worlds: an American high school and an English public school. That's real training for life."

Marty started to laugh, then clamped her hand over her mouth and reached for a plastic grocery bag.

I stood aside, not knowing whether to try and help or give her some space. "Anything I can do?"

"I'll be okay in a—oh God."

More unhappy noises followed. I went into the house and got her a paper cup of water.

"All right now?" I handed the cup to her.

"Yeah, for the moment, anyway. Thanks, Emma. I need you to be my friend now."

"You got it." If I hadn't felt the tears starting then, I would have for certain with her next words.

"And you'll be a godmother, right? Promise me."

"I promise." I hugged her again, carefully. Then I made a face. "Oh, man. I thought it would be years yet before I had to worry about someone calling me "Aunty Em, Aunty Em." I've been dreading this day, but since it will be for you. . . ."

Marty drew herself up and looked as dignified and reproachful as she ever did, and it did me good to see it. "Emma, please. No child of mine would be that obvious."

Chapter 16

WE GOT HOME AND GOT OUR GUESTS SETTLED IN the kitchen. I claimed the shower first, pleading company to be entertained, and ran up to the bathroom. After I shucked off my clothes, I thought I could hear laughter downstairs. I grabbed a quick shower to cool off; I'd also hoped to scrounge the time to tease out another stray thought or two about the paper that Bader had showed me, but that well was dry, for the moment. I went downstairs in an even better mood than I had been and was a little surprised when the conversation stopped as I entered the kitchen. Everyone—students, friends, family—was lolling around the kitchen, crowded on chairs, the floor, the counters, looking far too relaxed and chummy.

"What? Why did you all clam up when I came in?"

"No reason," Bucky said in a tone that suggested that there was plenty of reason. Everyone exchanged grins and I began to get worried. "I was just telling them about the time we went to Montreal."

Oh damn. "Which time was that?" As if I didn't know very well.

"The time with Grandpa Oscar. The time you brought your trowel, you know, just in case, and set off the metal detector." She turned to Dian. "Airport security guards don't like trowels and don't like wise-ass teenagers."

"I wasn't a wise-ass; I was just explaining why I had the trowel with me. It wasn't my fault he didn't understand I wasn't just going to dig up some monument and take stuff home."

"Our luggage got searched," Bucky offered. "Oscar thought it was pretty funny, though we thought that Dad and Grandma Ida were going to blow a gasket."

"And what brought that up?" I asked.

Brian smiled. "Well, it was just the four-clunk-Emma-tracking system. Boot one, clunk, boot two, clunk, pants, big clunk, shirt, small clunk, shower goes on. We can track your progress pretty good from down here."

"Lovely."

Quasi liked Kam very well, which was not surprising, since it had been ascertained in an early, ugly incident that Kam was hysterically allergic to cats in general and to Quasi in particular. When Quasi made as if to jump into Kam's lap, Kam merely said, "Do your worst, you, my little bête noir. I took my antihistamines before I came."

Quasi yawned hugely and settled for rubbing against Kam's knees, leaving a trail of long white and black cat hairs clinging to his meticulously pressed jeans.

"Good God, that cat's like a porcupine," Marty said. She was doing a lot better now, with a glass of ginger ale in one hand and a pile of oyster crackers in another. "I'm sure he can just shoot those damn things like missiles at a distance."

"Porcupines don't shoot quills," Bucky said. "But I wouldn't give Quasi any ideas, if I were you."

"What do you guys want to do about dinner?" I asked.

"Well, the only reason we're here is because Marty thought she had a better-than-average chance of getting a hot dog for dinner," Kam said.

"Miss the hot dogs in the city, huh?" I said.

"I'm not going home to visit for another month, but I can't wait that long. And since I don't know any of the vendors in Boston, I thought this would be close enough to hold me."

"Well, I'm flattered you consider us a tolerable second to the guy down the street from the Met," I said. "I think we can help you out there. But just give me fair warning if you decide a dog with everything is one of those old favorites that is suddenly going to make you hurl, okay?"

"Deal."

"Joe, give me a hand with these?" I handed him a plate of salad and a plate of buns, took up a big platter of meat, and then bumped the screen door open with my elbow, holding it for the student.

"I don't want to keep you from your shower," I said. "But I wondered if you'd made plans for next summer yet?"

"Emma, I'm still trying to get through this summer." His voice was heavy with fatigue.

Oh man, he thought I was trying to rub it in or something. "I know, it's a long way off, but I'm already starting to block out field time, and I wanted to know if you'd be available."

"As far as I know." His face brightened. "Sure. You've officially got first dibs. Thanks."

"Good. I'll keep you in mind when I plan the schedule."

We heard Rob shout from the house. "Shower's free, Joe."

"Thanks!" he called back. He rolled his eyes. "God, I was afraid I'd be next. Rob has so much goddamned hair that he always leaves about a pound of it behind in the tub."

"And that is officially more information than I needed," I said. "Go on, it's better than no shower at all."

I watched as Joe headed back into the house, a little bounce in his step that hadn't been there earlier.

After dinner, the wind changed and the muggy air started to lift. Maybe it was the wind, maybe it was the smoke from the fire, maybe it was the amount of garlic that Meg and Brian loaded into the barbecue, but the bugs were mysteriously absent as the sun went down, leaving the sky tangerine and pink in the west, blue overhead, and dark violet in the east. As the shadows lengthened and merged, sunlight was replaced by the flickering orange glow of the fire.

It all started out ordinarily enough, but sitting around a campfire at night changes things. Bright sun that lights everything evenly allows for distinctions that aren't as easily made by firelight. The wavering semidarkness alters status, blurs age, evokes stories that are common to us all, or at least makes a space where it is easier to relate to those stories. It could be because telling stories around a fire at night is one of the oldest shared communal experiences, and we yearn for some lingering memory of that, or it might simply be because, by firelight, we are reminded of just how little our human distinctions matter, how much closer we are to our roots than complicated cultures suggest. A fire under a starry sky changes the way people look, the way they seem, and the way they behave. The darkness grants license; the magic of fire, largely lost in the modern world, provokes daring. There is something dangerous in seeing people, friends or strangers, by firelight. It can deceive. It can reveal. It is illuminating.

The tenor had been set in the house and it was officially

"pick on Emma night." Many cultures have something like a Twelfth Night tradition, where those who are usually in charge are temporarily made fools, deposed by those they govern. It was fun, it was good for morale, and I was fully prepared to go along with the teasing, not minding that the memories that people were sharing were all of me at something less than my best.

Besides, I was completely outnumbered.

"I can't believe she was that boring," Dian was saying. The pop of a burning branch punctuated her observation.

"I was, completely," I confirmed. "Within whiskers of being a prig."

"You never had detention?" Rob was incredulous. "Never skipped school?"

"Never dared to," I said, taking a sip of beer. But I also never got caught when I did dare to do something. But those times didn't really count, because they were usually when I was out in the field with Oscar, and that was different. "Bucky was the one who made up for both of us."

"It's true," my sister said. "But it didn't make much difference to me whether I stayed after school and read, or went home to read. It was later on, when I really started to get bored, that was the problem. Emma saved my ass a couple of times, kept me from getting caught."

"I didn't want to," I protested. "I didn't think you should be leaving the house at night, after you were supposed to be in bed."

"Yeah, but you didn't squeal either. And you had the credibility that counted when it mattered."

Meg nodded: Loyalty was important.

I knew the time Bucky was thinking of. She'd fallen out of the tree that was outside her window. I'd suspected for some time that she was using it as a means of illegal egress and entrance, but this time, she'd busted her arm. I was home for one of the last times, it was Thanksgiving break of my senior year, and I heard the crash. I was up late on the phone and ran outside, beating my parents by an instant.

Spying my sister sprawled on the ground, I'd said, "Bucky, I said I'd take care of it!"

"Take care of what?" Dad had asked.

"There were some kids from school," Bucky had said. "I didn't even see who they were."

"I was just going to the door, to turn on the light," I'd said. "And Bucky fell out of the window."

"They were going to TP the house. I guess I leaned out too far when I yelled at them."

Mother and Dad looked at me and I nodded, astounded by the speed with which she'd invented the lie. They weren't thrilled with the notion that our lawn and trees might be the target of the toilet paper treatment, but they would have been even less pleased to know that Bucky hadn't been home snug in bed as they thought she was. Something changed between us that night, something that made us more friends than sisters. A mundane event with longterm repercussions.

I was thinking about that when I realized that the subject had changed. Joe was talking, Joe who seldom offered much in the way of conversation. Joe had been talking the whole time I'd been remembering.

". . . he bought me my first bike and taught me to ride. We went out almost every weekend."

I knew a little about this, that Joe's father had died when he was just twelve. I realized what was happening when I started to get tired, sitting on the ground and leaning against Brian's legs as he sat in a lawn chair and was reluctant to move, even to shift my weight. Joe was telling us about a bicycle ride he'd taken recently, over three hundred miles, camping along the way, over the course of a week. He said he'd been taking it fairly easy, which I found difficult to believe, though I couldn't have gainsaid him.

"That's when I learned that you see the land in a whole different way than you would in a car," he continued. "You get very familiar with the landscape when you're pedaling up all those hills and feeling every change in every microclimate—hot and steamy in one place, and chilly with a breeze one minute later. You start thinking about how farmers and ranchers think about the land, in terms of wind and vegetation and grade, and a lot of little things start to make sense. I go out and it's like being with him again."

It was more than I'd heard from Joe the whole summer, and suddenly I saw where he had focus, how he saw things, in the hard, the physical, the concrete. Direct experience was what fueled him. I filed it away to make the most of it when directing him later in the semester, or with his master's thesis.

Around and around it went, everyone picking a story to tell, the care with which they chose them showing that they all felt it too, that there was communion around that fire. It was like building a rope bridge over a chasm, each step important and a link between the last and the next, one after the other, until it was completed. Or maybe it was like building a fire, feeding the thing between us, already so fragile, so elusive that we didn't want it to die away or be extinguished by an ill-considered contribution. It wasn't the stories themselves that were important, or the questions either, it was the trust. I leaned back against Brian's knees and gazed at the stars through the smoke.

At last, we fell quiet. It was late and it had to end sometime, and it was better that it should be intentionally than have some wrong note jar and ruin the harmony. I got up and threw another stick onto the fire. "Well, it's late and I've got to get my beauty sleep. I'm heading in."

"And we've got to head for home," Kam announced. He helped Marty out of her chair, even though she was months away from showing yet. "Enough hot dogs, beloved?"

She nodded and patted her belly. "And the little one liked them, too."

"For which I am, on behalf of the car's interior, eternally grateful."

We all exchanged good nights, and Brian and I walked Kam and Marty out to the driveway. We said quiet good-byes, and Kam and Brian shook hands; a truce had been called or an understanding reached; perhaps now that Brian knew about the baby, some of Kam's worry was lifted. We lingered on the porch as the Jag pulled away and left us in the quiet of the night—crickets, ambient light from the center of town nearby luminous over the field across the street. We heard everyone come in the back, so we locked up and set the alarm. Brian and I went up to bed, neither feeling the need to talk.

We were the last ones up; the students had decided to come in. After I confirmed that they'd doused the fire, I ran into Bucky as she was coming out of the bathroom.

"Okay. I get it now," she said, as if she was here to observe me. Maybe that was why she'd come to visit in the first place.

I paused outside the doorway. "What do you get?"

"I get the attraction. Of what you do. Why archaeology means so much to you."

"Oh?"

"Psychology aside?"

"Please."

"Well, maybe just a little psychology. At first it was just because I thought you were misanthropic, but you're not really a hermit. Studying the past, that allows you to think about why people do things without getting too messy. Too personal. Possibly a reaction to Ma and Dad's divorce."

"Interesting." I cocked my head. "And here I thought I was in it for the money. But I was into archaeology well before they split."

"But then there's the influence that Grandpa Oscar had on you, when we were growing up. And it's because it gives you the chance to build these communities. That's important to you."

"Yeah. It is."

"And you know something? It's just as important to them too."

I mulled that over, hoping she was right. "You want to know the real secret? The real reason I became an archaeologist?"

"Why?"

"It was the only job I could think of where I could read someone's diary and get paid for it."

"Every job has its perks. Good night, Emma."

I gave Bucky a hug. "Goodnight, kiddo."

I got up early again, reluctantly, but I wanted to make the most of my time to check out some of the names I'd come across yesterday, to see if I could figure out what Sarah Holloway meant to the Chandlers, and what her connection was to Nicholas Chandler in particular. It seemed likely that he was her son, but while it seemed that Matthew Chandler had been ruled out as his father, it still seemed that there must be some strong tie to bind him to the Chandlers, if she was able to persuade them to take him. Nothing came up, but that didn't do anything but make me more curious and more determined to ferret out the real story.

At least the fieldwork seemed, thankfully, to be answering more of its own questions. Not the one that really perplexed me, though: What had kept the Chandlers from rebuilding the wing that had been destroyed in 1738? I spent a little time with that one too, before I went downstairs for breakfast. The fire that had razed part of Stone Harbor in the same year was confined to the waterfront, well below the Chandler's house. Official sources attributed it to a malicious servant striking out against his master, something that had gotten out of hand. What was more interesting was that although the man in question, Pike Fisher, was working for William Bradley, the Chandlers' warehouses had also been badly damaged. More interesting still was whether Pike Fisher had been associated, as the diary of the Reverend Tapley suggested, with pirates. Pirates had been a plague to the coast at the time of the fires, and I wondered if they hadn't been part of the "roguish band" that Tapley suggested Pike Fisher was involved with. The pirates had been chased away or captured by a group of Stone Harbor citizens before they could do any further damage. Fisher had been the only one charged with the crime, in the end, and there was nothing to suggest that he was responsible for the fire at the Chandler House or Nicholas's death.

I was sure the incidents were somehow related, but at the moment, I didn't have the information necessary to put them all together. The only thing I could do was go back out to the site and keep digging. The archives would still be there, ready for more plundering, when I got done. The other thing that popped unbidden into my head was whether there wasn't some distant connection between the events nearly three hundred years ago and the events of the past week. Fisher was Justin's last name, too. But surely there couldn't be any relation between that distant past and the present? Then it occurred to me that everyone connected with the

Historical Society seemed to have a closer relationship with the past than most people.

I realized that I should ask Ted and Fee, who were both taking a break in Fee's office.

"Depends on which source you check," Ted said instantly. "There's lots about pirates in general, in Massachusetts in the eighteenth century, but only two references to them in Stone Harbor then. One is Tapley's book—the entry you saw—and the other. . . ."

"What?" I looked between him and Fee, who were both shrugging.

"Well, there's a footnote to one of the town histories that was written in the nineteen-twenties. It's to a source that we haven't been able to locate yet, but it suggests that they might have been connected with the fire of seventeen-thirty-eight."

"What's that say?" I asked eagerly.

"Well," Fee said reluctantly—she still wasn't speaking much to me—"there's a paragraph about the fire of seventeen-thirty-eight and the footnote says, "See Beecham, eighteen-sixty-seven.""

"That's it?" I looked at both of them.

"That's it." Ted looked pleased that I should be as flummoxed as he was.

"Okay, well, thanks." I went back out and stared at the pocked and pitted area beside the house for a while.

The remains of the wall were fully exposed now, and the pits seemed to be at the same level, though it was clear that some later ones had been moved around. The afternoon was consumed with another orgy of picture-taking and pencil-gnawing, which did nothing to relieve my headache.

Chapter 17

AFTER WORK THAT DAY, I GOT BRIAN TO TAKE Bucky home with him and start dinner, so that I could stay late with the crew and finish the photography. On my way home, I stopped by the striped house that had been a thorn in the aesthetic side of the Stone Harbor Historical Society for a couple of years now and had my first good, close look. Actually, I'd paused a couple of times before, getting the project set up, but now I didn't mind if anyone caught me looking. In fact, I was hoping that Janice Booth herself would be there.

She was on the side of the house, working in the garden, a prodigious pile of weeds and cuttings a testimony to her labors that day. She was a big woman with short blonde hair shot through with gray; it looked as though she'd cut it herself with dull scissors. She resembled Bray, and I wondered whether there wasn't a family connection there. Her features looked as though they had been molded by a kid with modeling clay, overexaggerated and a little mannish, but her skin was flawless, soft and glowing like porcelain that had been handled with loving care over the generations. She was wearing a pair of enormous denim overalls, a man's collared shirt that was daubed with blue and green paint stains, and a straw sunhat so large that it could have served as a beach umbrella with little modification. A low growling took us both by surprise and alerted Janice to my presence.

"Calm your liver, Franklin." She spoke to a nearby shrub and then turned to me. "You want something, or just looking at the house?"

I was still trying to see what was making the noise. "Um, I guess I was hoping to talk to you, if you're Janice."

"Yeah, I'm Janice." She began to get up, with some effort.

I raised a hand. "Oh, don't stop working on my account."

She took my hand and I helped her up. "I'm stopping on my account, don't worry. You want something to drink? It's as hot and steamy as Satan's jock."

"Um, sure, thanks." I tried to keep that particular image out of my mind.

She jerked her head toward the gate, indicating that I should come in that way. "I'll just be a second. Come on, Franklin, I'll get you brushed."

Another growl came, this louder than the first, and a long-haired miniature dachshund waddled out from under the rhododendron. He was showing a lot of gray around the muzzle and a bright green harness didn't seem to do anything for him besides make him look like one of those long, bulging mozzarella cheeses tied up with string. He took two little steps toward me and began to growl louder, showing his upper teeth. I sighed; my animal karma was for the birds lately.

This time, Janice didn't bother trying to be polite about it. "Franklin! Cut that shit out, you fat, hairy hot dog! Show some manners, for gossakes!"

Franklin did show some manners, however reluctantly, and at the sound of his mistress's voice, lumped himself over to where she stood, his face turned up beseechingly, panting and thumping his tail.

"Don't mind him. It's the heat. I'll be back in a second."

When she did return, she was holding two paper cups of lemonade in one hand, spilling a lot of it, and carrying a brush in the other. Franklin immediately began to jump against Janice's legs, yipping like fury. She sloshed lemonade all over herself, cursed again, and thrust the now half-empty cups at me. When I took them, she immediately knelt down and brushed Franklin, who rolled around under the brush in a frenzy of excitement. Finally, she'd had enough and paused; Franklin yipped again, and it was funny to watch his stumpy little legs as he jumped.

Janice shook her head. "No, that's all for now. Go ahead, go get dirty again."

The dachshund wagged his tail a couple more times in an attempt to coerce her through cuteness, then heaved a giant sigh and lumbered back into his den under the rhododendron. I saw the glint of an aluminum water dish under there and heard sloppy lapping.

"He's a spoiled little beggar," she said, but the smile on her face told me the whole story. She reached for a cup. "So. What can I do you for? You don't look like the sorts who usually come to buy some of my work."

"I'm sorry, that's not why I'm here."

"I didn't think so. Well, come have a look anyway. You might want one someday."

I followed her into the house, which wasn't anything like what you'd expect from the outside. The front room, which would have been the parlor at one time, was painted differently on each wall—one mocha, one white, one sea-foam green, one gray—and this was her gallery. There were no

shades on the windows, just white sheers that didn't keep
out the light and also contributed to the feeling of being on
the beach, as they billowed in the breeze. Janice's paintings
were here, and though I don't know much about art, apart
from the portraits that tell me about who I'm studying or
which Dutch painters depict seventeenth-century pottery,
her work made an impression on me. I did recognize that
they were abstract, and though I couldn't have told you
whether they were any good from a technical point of view,
I did know what they made me feel. There wasn't anything
that might be recognized as a wave or a cloud by its form,
but the colors, the *movement* of the shapes and brushstrokes,
if you will, instantly transported me onto the ocean. Nothing
was depicted as it looks in nature, but every part of it suggested what it represented. I'd seen that water before. You
could smell the salt spray.

"Wow," was all I could manage.

"That one's not bad," Janice conceded. "Sure I can't
tempt you into buying one?"

I glanced at the price sheet on the wall and swallowed.
"You can tempt away, but my bankbook will be adamant,
I'm afraid." I looked back at the canvas. "But some-
day. . . ."

"Someday then. You wanted to know about . . . ?"

"Someone—Ted Cressey—said you could tell me about
Aden Fiske—"

"The man was a prick of the first water," Janice said
matter-of-factly. "What else can I do for you today?"

"You weren't overly fond of Aden, then," I said.

"Let me count the ways." She gave me the once-over.
"What's your interest in all this, anyway?"

Her bluntness was catching. "I found him. He was the
second body I found in a week, and I'd like to make sure that
this is more about him than me. That I'm not the next body."

That seemed to satisfy her. "I'm sure you've heard some of the stories by now."

"A few strong opinions, but no real particulars." I didn't feel too bad about my fib; I needed more information.

"I'll give you a list. You've noticed the house? That's Aden, all over." She crumpled her paper cup. "He tried to enforce some stupid-ass historic district regulation about colors, something that shouldn't even have come up because I was in the house long before that rule was made. I didn't have the money to do the job the way he wanted it; what I did have was a bunch of paint samples and a friend who explained the letter of the law to me; no one said anything about where the colors had to go on the house." She exhaled noisily. "It was all personal, of course."

"How's that?"

"This house is all I have, and everyone knows it. I get by, with the tenants, and I can do my art, and that's all I ask of life. Aden, the big real estate magnate, decides he's going to do me a favor and buy it from me. At a bargain price, of course." She got another glass of lemonade from a sweating pitcher on the table. "I told him to shove it. He raised the price, something to within spitting distance of fair, I guess, but I'm not going to sell. Ever.

"He tried some other petty shit, like trying to hassle the tenants, get them to move out, even tried to dig up some of my bad, old past to hold over my head." She smacked her lips. "He forgot that my nasty reputation is also my stock in trade. It didn't do a bit of damage to me; hell, I prolly sold a couple of paintings on the strength of it. That kind of thing."

"Nice guy."

"Go to his wake tonight and you'll see that I wasn't the only one glad to see him take the big dirt nap. If I'd have been able to come up with some way to do it myself, I just might of."

"So you didn't do it?" I asked, surprising myself. Janice's bluntness was infectious.

But Janice didn't take a speck of offense. "No. I'm not much for that kind of thing—"

So she *sort* of goes in for it? I wondered crazily.

"—I think that people generally get what they deserve in the end, but Aden was pushing it. It was fun, kind of, to watch him get worked up and try to figure out what he'd do. He had a kind of cunning that was hypnotic, kinda like a cobra, but you can't watch it for long and not start to worry about who it was aimed at. That's why I would have, if I had the mind for it. He hurt too many people."

"The wake is tonight? That seems kind of quick."

"Well, you got two choices there. Either those in charge wanted to make sure the bastard was going into the ground and staying there, or someone wanted things pushed along so there would be as little attention paid to the manner of his death as possible. Take your pick."

"That's not very reassuring."

"Hell, at least you know for sure that Aden is dead. Lot of people probably trying to lift the coffin lid and sneak a peek, just to see for themselves." She gave me a sideways look. "You could ask your friend Doug Bader; he might know."

"How do you know I know Detective Bader?"

"Same way you knew to come to ask me about Aden: Ted Cressey."

"Well, he's not my friend. He's not likely to tell me anything." That was an interesting thought, and I made a note to pursue it as I got up to leave. "I appreciate your time. And thanks for the drink."

"Here." She shoved a handful of postcards into my hand. "I'm part of a show in another week. Come by and check it out."

"Sure, thanks again."

* * *

I'd decided I'd better put in an appearance at the memorial service for Aden. Brian didn't want to go and wasn't thrilled about me going, but I convinced him that nothing much could happen at a funeral parlor. I was also curious to see who would show up to what must surely size up to be a pretty significant public event.

As I told Brian, I didn't expect to be too long, just enough time to stop by, pay my respects, and get out. When I saw the line of people waiting to get into the funeral parlor, however, I knew I would be a little longer than I predicted. Cars packed the street and a couple of uniformed officers were directing traffic and waiting by the door. Whew, I thought, Aden was that big a noise in Stone Harbor.

I found a parking space a couple of blocks down—there was no hope of pulling right into the funeral parlor's lot—and hiked back to get into the line, glad that the overcast was helping mitigate the warmth of the evening, which was a little like walking through clam chowder—muggy, salty, and body temperature. Another couple joined the line behind me, and it was clear that we would be the last ones in the hushed queue as it shuffled forward to the doors and the wake itself. It's one of those situations where you're not trying to overhear anything, but such lines are so quiet that it almost can't be helped.

"It is just so sudden," said a woman in back of me to her companion in a whisper.

"I know, honey, I know," came the low reply.

"I can't believe it, I just can't—"

"It's okay, honey."

"If I can only get through this, I think I'll be okay."

"I'm right here with you. You're all right, honey."

"I just can't believe the bastard's gone. Thank God."

That took me up short: Did she actually say, "thank God"? Reflex made me imagine that I'd probably heard wrong. But no. The consensus was that Aden was a black-mailer. I was still unprepared for just how many lives he had affected, and how strongly. I was about to learn.

Honey's friend was a little more cautious. "Let's just get through this, let's not get our hopes up, okay, honey? Just a few minutes more, I promise you."

"I just can't believe it's over."

"Honey, we're not out of the woods yet. Just keep your voice down and maybe we'll know in a little while. A half hour. That's not long, is it? You can do that."

"You're right, a half hour's nothing. Not after what he's put us through." The bitterness in Honey's voice was almost tangible. I wondered what brought it on.

By this time the rapidly moving line had taken me to the steps of the building itself, and I looked around to see whether there were any other wakes being held at the same time as Aden's. There weren't. Honey and her friend had been talking about him. Aden's eccentricity and bonhomie hadn't been convincing on every front.

The viewing room was very crowded. I signed the visitors book and looked around to see whether I recognized anyone. Daniel and his partner, Charles, were in a corner, but so far away that it was impossible to join them, even if I had been able to discreetly catch their attention. Fee was closer by, and I did catch her eye. She smiled briefly in acknowledgment and then immediately turned away to speak to someone beside her; Grace was nowhere in sight. Perry was chatting quietly with several people I didn't recognize but thought they looked like her; members of her family, I decided. She looked completely done in. Her face was drawn, her eyes were swollen, and the rest of her face was pale. I wondered whether her arm was bothering her and realized I had no idea how long she'd worked with Aden, who I knew had been a friend of her family's. It looked a little like she was holding court, accepting the concern of others passing by with practiced grace.

Ted Cressey was wearing the coat and tie he wore every day to the historic house. He was off by himself—so far as anyone could be said to be by himself in that crowd. No one spoke to him, and he didn't attempt to speak to anyone there; when I nodded to him, he only smiled without any gladness or indication that he felt any emotion at all. The smile did not reach his eyes, which kept wandering over the rest of the crowd, not so much looking for anything as keeping track of what and who he saw.

I couldn't quite suppress a feeling of dislike for him, but it was by following his gaze that I saw the scene before the rest of the heads swiveled around to catch it. The Bellamys were leaving, practically stumbling over each other in their rush to get away from the wake. Mr. Bellamy, who I remembered from one of his early morning complaints over the Chandler House fence, was sweating profusely despite the frigidity of the air conditioning. Claire was hyperventilating so that I thought she might be ill, but I saw her tighten her hold on her husband's hand and shoot him a look of unadulterated joy as they fled the room.

"A little premature for that, if you ask me," said a voice behind me. I turned, but couldn't see anyone I recognized. Apparently the sentiment was shared by most of those present.

I tried to identify who was in the receiving line and saw only a lone gentleman in front of the closed casket shaking everyone's hand. I would have thought that the Fiske family would have been larger, considering the number of people here. The crowd was dark in summer mourning, warm in spite of the air conditioning, and . . . wary. There were a great many bouquets near the casket, I saw, but in glancing at the cards, I realized that almost all of them were from organizations—the PBA, the city council, the Historical Society, that sort of thing—and none were from individuals. There was nothing on top of the closed coffin, where the family tributes usually sat, save for a bunch of daylilies, which bore no label at all. It was a strange choice of flowers, I thought.

"I'm very sorry for your loss," I said to the older man in the black suit, when it came to be my turn. "I worked with Aden at the Chandler House."

"Thank you for coming. The family asked me to let everyone know that there would be a brief ceremony following the viewing tonight."

"Oh, then you're not—?"

"I'm Elliott Amberson, the director here. The family asked me to represent them tonight."

"Oh." I looked at him, but he didn't offer any further explanation.

"It will be a very brief service."

"Well, thanks."

I paused briefly in front of the closed casket and then moved along, but there was very little space for me to move into: The room was packed. That was why I could hear Honey hiss, "Fuck you, Aden. You got exactly what you deserved."

I knew I couldn't have been the only one to have heard her, but perhaps it was shock that kept anyone near me from commenting or even gasping. Honey's companion took her by the arm and all but dragged her out back the way we'd come in. I wedged myself into a tight space near the head of the coffin. With a nod from Mr. Amberson, a lectern was brought out for the clergyman, and the service began.

It was immediately clear that the minister was no one who'd known Aden Fiske. After welcoming everyone, he ran down a list of Aden's achievements in town, all on quite a grand scale, and launched into reading a few psalms. I looked around to see how the other mourners were taking this, and realized that no one seemed to be paying attention to the funeral. The eyes of almost everyone in that crowded room kept wandering, and every time someone moved near the door, he or she was watched like a hawk. There were more people looking around at the crowd then there were looking at the minister, and because of the odd emotion in the room, anxiety and fear and expectation, I was now among them, trying to figure out what was going on. From my vantage point, I could see that there were a lot of worried faces, a lot of unhappy faces, but no genuinely sad or grieving faces. There wasn't a damp eye in the house and more than that, there was a palpable tension that seemed to increase as the minister wound his way through the last lines of the Twenty-third Psalm. When it became clear that he was finishing up his service, it was as though everyone in the room was holding his breath. I had to be the only one who didn't seem to expect something else to happen, and when the funeral director again thanked us for coming on behalf of the Fiske family, there was a pause, everyone looked around at everyone else, and then there was a huge, almost communal sigh. Whatever had been expected had not come to pass, though I couldn't have told you what everyone was anticipating.

The room emptied as though a vacuum had been opened on the other side of the door. It worked out that Daniel, Charles, and I, coming from the two separate corners of the room, ended up next to each other near the end of the exodus.

"Quite a turnout, wasn't it?" Daniel said.

"Yeah. Didn't it all seem a little strange to you?" I asked.

He paused. "All funerals are a little strange, I think," he said finally.

Charles snorted. "You must be new to the area," he said, dismissing Daniel's guarded comment.

I nodded. "I am, at least to Stone Harbor."

Daniel sighed and shook his head at Charles, who rolled his eyes and turned away. "I think Charles was just trying to say that most people around here knew about the feud between Aden and his family. I think that was what you were picking up on."

"Oh yes?" It seemed apparent to me that the rest of the town was siding with Aden's absent family.

"Long time ago, details lost or distorted in the mists of time. Terribly unhappy man."

"Oh. Maybe that explains why he tried so hard with the people he worked with. You know, to be so . . . jovial."

Daniel gave me a hard look. "Yes, I suppose you're right. Good night, Emma."

"Good night, Daniel. Charles."

"Night, Emma."

As I headed back to my car, I could hear Daniel admonish Charles, who stood near the door flipping through the guest book. "Well, I think everyone in town would be interested to see who signed in, is all," Charles retorted.

I had my key in the lock when Daniel called out. "Emma, why don't you join us? We're going for a drink at the restaurant."

Curiosity got the better of me. "Sure. Which restaurant?"

Charles laughed. "Why, the *only* restaurant!"

I still didn't understand.

"Shade's," Daniel said. "See you there in a few minutes?"

I waved and they took off. The street was almost empty by the time I got into my car, as if everyone else had fled. It had all happened so quickly that I was surprised that I hadn't heard the squeal of rubber on asphalt. I got in and locked the door, glad to be getting away from the most unpleasant wake I'd ever been to.

Chapter 18

I PULLED UP TO SHADE'S AND PARKED, THEN CALLED Brian to tell him I'd be a little later than expected.

"See?" I said to him. "Look at me using my phone and everything. All charged up, a real modern girl."

"I'm glad, that's why we bought them. Take care, okay, babe?"

"Sure. See you soon, sugar."

I hit the wrong button twice before I managed to turn the thing off.

Daniel and Charles were already at the bar. Rich the bartender nodded at me. "Chardonnay?"

"You've got a good memory. Actually, I'll have a glass of the Rookhaven zinfandel."

He nodded and poured me a glass of the same dark wine my sister had ordered on Sunday night.

Daniel nodded approvingly. "That's a good label. We were out at their Sonoma vineyards, what was it Charles? Two years ago?"

"That's it. That was a wonderful trip."

"My husband's from California," I said, "but we almost never make it that far north. His folks are in San Diego."

"You must visit wine country, next time," Charles said. He took a sip of his martini and fished out one of the olives. "You'll love it."

"I don't get much time for vacations," I said. I took a sip of the wine, and it made me pause. It was everything that Bucky had said, and I was amazed at what I could taste when I really paid attention to it; her outré descriptions even started to make sense now. "I'm teaching through the school year, then digging in the summer. Conferences during the holidays."

"Grim," Charles said, munching his olive. "All work and no play."

"Well, this summer's certainly been no picnic for you," Daniel said, and I sensed we were getting down to the reason they'd invited me along. "What did you make of the wake? You said you thought it strange?"

"Well, people certainly weren't at their best, were they? I mean, even for a funeral."

"You mean the Bellamys," Charles said matter-of-factly. "If you ask me, he's about three baby steps away from a stroke. One more setback, and he'll lose what little hair he has left. Bought that place across the street from the Chandler House, and then lost his job over some funny business before the buyout. He's working at the factory now, but it will be macaroni and cheese for their overstimulated little darlings for another couple of years, till they get their feet back under them again."

"Oh?"

"He's doing all right at the factory," Daniel said, trying to balance out Charles. "Been working his tail off in marketing. Won a nice prize at the company Christmas party. Big flat-screen television."

Aha, I thought. That explained that little anomaly in the Bellamy's living room.

"And isn't *she* awful?" Charles said to me. "All drama, all the time. Comes from being overbred." He leaned in close to me. "Diminishes the brain size. Her and the poodles both."

I stifled a giggle, then composed myself with the sobering notion that Mr. Bellamy's "funny business" had gotten them into Aden's clutches somehow. Was Claire's complaint about our early morning noise just a distraction, because it was actually one of them trying to get at Aden when they ran into Justin instead? The thought gave me the willies, and I took another sip of wine before answering Charles. "Well, something Aden said to them certainly got them off my back about the dig."

"Aden was an evil little cockroach. They were probably just there to make sure he was really dead. Like practically everyone there."

"Charles."

"Danny, it's *true*."

"So why were you both there?" I asked. "I didn't get the impression that you were his biggest fans."

"I didn't like him and I didn't like working with him," Daniel said, "but I was there because I was a member of the board. I was at the wake out of respect, not that anyone else would have noticed or believed it. I believe in appearances."

"But you don't even seem particularly interested in history. I guess I don't understand why you'd put so much time in on the board as you do, if you don't." And money too, presumably, I thought. Takes both to be on the board of anything.

"He doesn't, does he?" Charles said. "I do, though. I love

antiques—I'm in the business, you know? Fabulous. I went for the show, of course—who wouldn't want to see that freak show?—but also to keep up my contacts. I wonder what will happen to all of Aden's goodies, now that he's gone?"

"Charles, you are impossible."

"Danny, at least I'm honest. You were there for the sights, too." Charles gave Daniel the hairy eyeball and turned around on his stool, ignoring us.

"Yes, I went because I was on the board and because I do like to keep an eye on what's happening in town. My father is deeply involved in several businesses and with the community, and I do the legwork he can no longer do. As far as the Historical Society goes, I'm not very impressed with how it teaches history. I don't much care at all about the past—the future is what matters to me—but Dad does care. He was offered a position on the board, for obvious reasons, but his health prevented him from taking it. He asked that I sit in his place. Aden wasn't thrilled—there is, pardon me, was, no affection between him and Dad—but I'm sure he thought it was worth it to keep an eye on his rival, one way or the other."

"Such intrigue." Charles rolled his eyes.

"Business is partly intrigue, and so is politics," Daniel said mildly.

"Didn't Ted Cressey used to work for you, your father, I mean?"

"Oh God. Cressey is a toad. He's a smart guy, don't get me wrong, but he spends so much time scheming for things he could more easily get through hard work. It's tiring, really, trying to figure out what he wants. Playing one of us against the other." He took a large sip of his whiskey, which I recognized as a good single malt when Rich poured it, though a generation older than I could generally afford to quaff.

"What will happen to the board, to the Chandler House, now that Aden's gone?"

"The board will elect a new chair. My money's on Bray Chandler, if you want to know. Then we'll start a search for new managers for the Tapley and Chandler Houses."

"Oh, so it's not going to Perry then?" Charles said. "Speaking of high drama. I misspoke earlier; La Bellamy has nothing on Ms. Diva Perry."

"No. Charles, can I get you another cocktail?"

It struck me that Daniel's offer had more to do with trying to shut Charles up than with anything to do with thirst. He gave him a pointed look, which Charles ignored.

"Oh, yes please."

I asked, "Perry wants to be director of the Chandler House?"

"She asked me about it the other day. Aden had been planning on retiring, and she wanted to know what her chances would be if she applied. Frankly, I think she could use the money. I had to tell her it wasn't up to me, but . . . I didn't think the board would think she was fully qualified."

"Ah." I thought about what I'd learned from Mary Ann Spencer. I saw that Daniel was watching me closely. I suspected he knew all about Perry's dodgy academic past as well.

"Well, you're right, she could use the money, that's for sure," Charles said. "Trust fund's about dry after Daddy's illness."

"It sounds as though she could use a break to me," I said. "I mean, with all that's been happening to her lately. The murders at the house, not to mention the hit-and-run attack—"

"Emma, please! Don't tell me you're still buying *that* fish tale!" Charles said, putting down his glass. "Oh, no, no, my dear. One of my very close friends was working the night Perry was brought in and he told me she said nothing about the mysterious dark car she's told the rest of us about. Not a bit of it! He says she broke her arm falling off a ladder. Trying to clean up that old white elephant house of hers, I suppose."

"What?" I didn't believe my ears.

Charles nodded. "You don't know our Perry. If she says that someone nearly ran her over, you can bet it was much more likely that someone drove by and waved hello. The stupid girl has to be the center of attention, and frankly, a near-fatal attack reads much better than mere clumsiness, doesn't it?"

I didn't know what to say; I took a sip of my wine and thought of Detective Bader's words: "The hit and run isn't part of this story." He must have found out in the course of his investigation that Perry hadn't been run down.

Charles was just warming up to the subject and began demolishing the olives in his fresh martini. "So she gets no pity votes for me, if you're asking my opinion."

Daniel wasn't asking and pointedly brought the discussion around to the original subject. "As for the site manager, I think if Fee Prowse wants the job, she'll get it. Nothing electric, but she knows the site as well as anyone."

And if what I heard was true about her, then Fee could use the money too, I thought. Was that a motive for murder? Aden had threatened her, it sounded like, too, and then there was the business with the Mather House. . . .

"Fee!" Charles snorted loudly. "As if everyone didn't know about her pussyfooting around with Grace Fisher! If you'll pardon the expression."

Daniel was truly angry, for the first time. "Charles, everyone doesn't, so keep your mouth shut."

"Gracie." My mind raced back to the sidewalk outside Wendy's Bakery. "Gracie is Grace Fisher?"

"If you do know," Daniel said, "then I hope you'll respect her wishes."

"I do. It's her business."

"It's everyone's business," Charles said, under the influence of tee many martoonies.

"Charles, leave it," Daniel said in a voice that was dangerous.

"Fine." Charles took the hint that he'd pushed it as far as he would get away with.

Daniel turned back to me and leaned close. "It's not as open a secret as Charles makes out. She's . . . made some decisions and I think she should be allowed to live by them. It's terribly important to her."

"Sure, I can understand that."

"She's of a certain generation; she's been very careful to live her life a certain way and she deserves that right."

"I agree."

He sat back, relieved, maybe believing he could trust me.

"Grace is related to Justin, isn't she?" I asked.

Daniel nodded. "Distant cousin, I think. All the Fishers around here are connected, one way or another."

I filed that away for later consideration; it was worth thinking about, especially in light of the Fisher who was charged with setting the fire of 1738. More immediately though was the question of whether Fee wanted Justin away from the Chandler House because of her relationship with his cousin. And when getting him fired didn't work, the next day he was found dead. I found him dead.

"I wonder whether Detective Bader knows as well,"

Daniel said. He looked me straight in the eye. "I wonder what he knows."

"I couldn't tell you." I realized that sounded as though I wouldn't tell him. "I mean, I honestly just don't know."

"I just thought you seemed to be in contact with him quite a lot."

"That may be, but he's not told me anything. Less than what you can get from the paper," I said.

"Hmmm." He settled back into his seat. "Emma, are you hungry? Do you want an appetizer?"

Daniel seemed to want to persist with his questions about Bader. "No, actually, I've got to run soon. Thanks anyway."

"I hope you won't mind if I order something, then."

He and Charles, who had stopped ignoring him by this time, conferred and ordered a plate of bread and tapenade.

I was just getting ready to depart when we were joined by the woman I recognized as Daniel's stepmother. She was dressed entirely in black, with slim-cut Capri pants, a sleeveless turtleneck, sandals, which set off her red nails and lips—and the heavy gold on her fingers, neck, and wrists— to perfection.

She kissed Daniel on the cheek, then she and Charles air kissed twice, neither much interested in disguising his dislike for the other. Daniel introduced me to her.

"I don't want to keep you," I said. "It's nice to meet you, Delilah."

She seemed amused by me. "You too, Emma."

I reached into my purse for my wallet. Daniel protested before I could remove it.

"Please, Emma. This is on us."

"I couldn't."

"Of course you can," he insisted.

"Silly!" Charles said. "Don't you know? Danny's father owns Shade's."

"Oh. Well, I knew there must be a family connection, I just didn't put it all together. . . . It's a very nice place." I wasn't certain what to say on hearing such news. "Well, then, thanks for the drink."

Delilah regarded me with a faintly contemptuous smile. "Any time, Emma."

As I turned to head out the door, I caught a glimpse of the party I'd left at the bar. Charles was chatting with the bartender. Daniel and Delilah were watching me, speaking quietly; they paused and smiled when I looked back. I couldn't help feeling a little chill run up my spine as the door shut behind me, and I walked into the sultry night.

I got into the car, wondering why everyone was so interested in bending my ear about what was going on at the site. They were certainly interested in giving me their side of things. It wasn't such a stretch, I realized. They either wanted to find out something that I might have learned from Bader, who did seem to spend a lot of time near me, if you didn't know that it was mostly just with regards to what I knew, or they wanted to give me information that might color what I passed along to him. I thought about what Mary Ann Spencer had said about the importance of social gossip, and realized that I was seeing the living proof of her statements.

Chapter 19

B Y THE END OF THE NEXT WORKDAY, I WAS BEGIN-
ning to believe that we were hitting everything we
would from this field season. There was always hope, of
course, but there was so much to finally map out that it
would take us a good deal of our remaining time to do it.
Brian stopped by again, to help close up, and I was glad of
that, because my head was spinning with all the details I had
to keep straight to help the graduate students figure out what
they were looking at.

The Chandler House was also in a whirl, with the threat
of two hundred visiting Chandlers and Chandler-descendants
looming on the horizon, just a few days away. Trouble struck
when Perry discovered that the last of the bunting that was
meant to be draped on the house was torn and dirty, just after she'd brought it out for the scaffolding team to hang.

"Someone must have just shoved it into the bag last time,
and never bothered about fixing it. I'll take it home tonight."

"Hey, I've got to go out to the farmstand anyway," I said. "Let me give you a lift." I was curious to see what she would say in the course of our drive, now that I knew a different version of how she'd hurt her arm.

Perry shook her head. "That's okay. I'm getting a ride with Fee."

"Fee's at the caterer's now, working out the tent issues. I don't mind."

"Okay, thanks. I'll see you back here about four then? I'm going to have to leave early if I'm going to get it all done by tomorrow." She giggled. "Ted's going to hate me."

"He'll get over it." Any kind of attention seemed to be okay with Perry, I thought. It seemed as though Charles was correct in his assessment of her.

"Great. I'll just help get things packed up, and I'll see you back here." She paused. "Damn it, this means that the scaffolding can't come down until tomorrow morning. We hoped to have it down by now."

I shrugged. "As long as you can remove it in time for the reunion."

I sent Bucky home with Brian again, explaining why I would be late. "I'm just going to give Perry a hand. I'll pick up some corn to roast too, on the way back." I promised.

I helped Perry with the heavy box of fabric and got her settled into my car. We drove past the common, struggling to make our way against the tourist traffic on foot, buses, and cars. We were held up while someone tried to back a camper the wrong way down a one-way street, which kept us practically parked in front of Janice Booth's house. There were as many tourists taking pictures of the striped house as there were people snapping shots of the common, with its green grass, colonial homes, white church, and waterfront.

"Look at that, would you?" The bitterness in Perry's

voice was like acid eating through metal. "It's just a travesty, the way some people treat what should be respected."

"I think Janice keeps the place up well enough. She's just got a wicked sense of humor, that's all." I was able to maneuver past someone parked halfway across the intersection before the light turned, and breathed a sigh of relief as we got onto the wider road up the coast and out to the edge of town. It's funny how you seem to hold your breath in traffic and let it out when you get through the snarl; the word "congestion" is most appropriate.

"There's not a damn thing funny about it." Each word sounded as though it was a dry twig snapping in half. I shot a glance across to the passenger's seat. Perry had one hand overlapping the other in her lap, the knuckles white as the cast on her left arm, and fingertips red with the pressure. Her lips were pinched with disapproval. "This town, its past, is something to be cherished. Not mocked."

"I don't think Janice was mocking the town so much as she was trying to stick it to Aden."

"Aden might have had his faults; I'm the last person to say he didn't. But he did care deeply about historic Stone Harbor."

"I don't know," I said. We had turned inland from the coast and were almost at the edge of Stone Harbor, near its shared border with Lawton and Boxham-by-Sea. Here the houses were interspersed with fields. "I'm beginning to think that Aden treated the past as something to use against people."

"What do you mean by that?" she said sharply. "Aden worked as hard as anyone to preserve the past. He had an obligation, we all have, to look after what was built up for us. You look after the past, and it looks after you. You should know that, of all people."

I'd never heard anything quite so silly in my life. The past might not be dead, as Faulkner pointed out, but it sure as hell wasn't up to looking after the present. It was something to learn from, something to inform you, but there's no way I'd call it a living force, as Perry seemed to be doing. That kind of idealization was just sickly sentiment, as far as I was concerned. "Maybe he did care about preservation, but he had a nasty habit of using people's histories against them."

"So I've heard," she said slowly. "Not very nice, some of the stories that have been going around."

"From what I've heard, there were a lot of people who Aden was blackmailing. A lot of people who would have been happy to see him dead."

"Hmmm. I guess I'm just trying to think of some good in the man. Now that he's dead."

Trust Perry to ennoble something that was past. Her whitewashing of Aden was as obnoxious to me as Janice's house was to her.

We passed the farmstand, and I pulled down the road that led to the old Taylor place. A rambling old house, it was carefully maintained but clearly had seen better days. The lawn was overgrown and the gardens were getting weedy.

"You'll have to pardon the decay." Perry laughed. "I've not been too handy with the lawnmower since the accident."

Her use of the word "accident" rather than "mishap" or "rundown" caught my attention, and I couldn't help poking at her story a little. "Have the police found anyone yet?"

"No. I'm afraid I wasn't much help in terms of giving them a description. It all happened so fast." She took a deep breath. "I don't like to think of it."

I nodded, unsmiling. "Of course not. Let me give you some help with the bunting."

"Thanks, Emma."

I pulled the heavy box out of the back, and Perry opened

her front door. The smell of old house—aging wood, polish, and the habit of centuries—washed over us.

"Just tell me where the washing machine is. I'll bring them straight there, so you don't have to lug them any more than necessary."

"That's okay, really. You can just put them anywhere."

"No, really. Which way to the washing machine?"

"Just down here." Perry led the way down to the basement, crowded with boxes. "Forgive the mess. I'm afraid my father was an inveterate collector. I've only had the chance to go through about a third of his stuff since he died last year. It's amazing what gets left behind to be sorted out."

I deposited the swags right into the washing machine. "I know. It's always a surprise when I see the tangle of legal documents that get left behind after someone's death."

She put her finger to her chin. "That's right, you study those, don't you?"

"All the time."

"Well, come up. You can at least let me give you an iced tea."

"Thanks, that would be great. I can't stay long, though." But just to be on the safe side, I called Brian to let him know I would be running a little later than expected.

She filled the glass from the pitcher in the fridge and handed it to me. Her kitchen seemed to be a time capsule from the 1940s, crowded with pieces of furniture and implements that were even older, probably handed down through many generations of the Taylor family. It had a comfortable, well-worn, much-loved quality that more than made up for the dated equipment. The windows let in lots of light, and Perry pulled down a yellowing shade to keep it from heating the room up too much.

"I can't believe what we've all been through in the past

week or so. It's hard to believe that the family reunion is still ahead of us. Other years, we're never allowed to forget."

I nodded. "Your hands will certainly be full. Ted says that you're expecting about two hundred people all together?"

"I think that's right. He's in charge of the invitation list." There was more than a trace of contempt in her voice.

"And Bray Chandler is taking over where Aden would have been in charge?"

"Yes, so far as I know." She looked at me sharply. "You've been talking with Ted a lot lately?"

I shrugged.

"Well, anything that comes out of his mouth ought to be taken with a grain of salt. Everyone knows what a talent he has for spying and creating gossip. I suppose that you knew he worked for the Voellers before he retired. He made very little secret that he was 'keeping an eye' on Aden for them while he worked at the Chandler House." She shook her head. "He has absolutely no sense of loyalty. Not a shred."

"Do you think the Voellers—?"

"I have no idea whether they actually put him up to it, but I suspect not. Daniel is nice enough, though I don't put anything past that stepmother of his. But I do know that Ted is in bed with that hateful Booth woman."

I gaped.

"Oh, I don't mean literally, though that's possible too. They've always got their heads together, plotting and scheming." She shuddered. "They're just so nasty, the two of them. Look, what else can we talk about? What have you found out about the site lately?"

"Well, I did a little research on the broken bit of chain that we found. It was silver and . . ." I realized what I was going to tell Perry next, thought better of it, and then immediately changed my mind back again. "I took it to the

Boxham-by-Sea Museum. Showed it to one of the curators there."

The transformation that Perry's face underwent was impressive. At the mention of the museum, her jaw tightened. By the time I got to the word "curators," her face had gone red. And then she recovered herself. "Oh, I suppose you spoke to Mary Ann Spencer?"

"Hey, good guess." I was watching her closely now, to see what her version of the story would be.

Perry shook her head. "Not really. It was either her or the assistant curator, and since he's only there half-time now, it wasn't much of a guess." She caught my eye. "Mary Ann's an interesting person. Odd little ways about her."

I nodded. "Her office was in a state."

"She's never been very tidy, not since I've known her. We were in school together for a while." There was a pause and I watched her carefully, wondering what she would say. "She and I . . . don't have a wonderful relationship. Let's just say that there was a slight misunderstanding over whether she'd actually broken up with her boyfriend when I started dating him. Left some bad blood between us."

"Oh, I see. That would do it." I didn't see, really. I now knew how unreliable Perry was, but I didn't have any idea about Dr. Spencer or whether her story was the exact truth either. Graduate school and its competition does strange things to people, and who knows what the real story was?

"God, when you live in a small community—and I don't care whether it's a town or a college or whatever—there are just so many things going on just below the surface." She smiled grimly at me. "But I guess you've learned that by now."

"I'm afraid so." I set my glass on the wooden counter. "Thanks for your help."

"Thanks for the tea. I'll see you tomorrow?"

"You can bet on it."

It wasn't until I got halfway home that I realized I'd left the camera behind at the Chandler House. Cleverly trying to keep it out of the sun and away from where the tourists watched, just in case it should grow legs, I'd put it under one of the shrubs. I was damned if I was going to leave it out all night, so I turned straight around and headed back.

I pulled up in the deserted parking lot and saw that the scaffolding to put the bunting up was already in place. No one seemed to be around though, and I figured that perhaps they would return tomorrow to hang the swags and flags and such. I knocked on the door, in case Fee or Ted were still around, but no one answered. I thought I saw a shadow cross the inside doorway, but when I cupped my hands around my eyes to look more closely through the window, I realized that it must have been the waving tree branches on the other side of the house. I rang the bell and no one answered. I heard nothing from inside, and a quick glance across the street suggested to me that the dreaded Bellamys were off someplace: their house was dark and the family minivan was nowhere to be seen. Presumably Matisse and Monet were idly surfing the shopping channels while the rest of the family did something educationally uplifting. But I wasn't going to be bothering them anyway. I only wanted to take a nice picture of the site while I could get directly overhead. I hurriedly removed the tarps from the units as best I could, stashing them away so that they were well out of the frame of the shot I wanted, and then considered my upward route.

I really only thought about it for a moment; it was one of those situations where the repressed teenager in me starts to get impatient and point out that it's easier to get forgiveness than it is to get permission. I know that I was thinking a little about the other night around the fire, when I recalled all of Bucky's stunts as a kid, and how I had always been a scosh envious behind my disapproval. I suppose I was also bridling a little bit about Brian having come out to the site that day, and the days after. As much as I appreciated what he was trying to do, the idea that he thought I needed looking after rankled. Most of the time, I'm able to be mature about these things.

This time was Oscar's fault, I decided. The only time I'd hesitated, when he'd offered to get me a banana split for dinner, I said, "Ma doesn't like me to." Oscar mustered as much patience as he could. He nodded gravely, scratched under his beard, and said, "Em. Your mother's not here."

The scaffolding looked pretty sturdy. There was no one around; the Chandler House was set far enough off the common to keep my activities hidden from any suggestible young people, and the roof would shield me too. I didn't want them to get the idea that what I was doing was all right for just anyone; I was, after all, a highly trained professional. I slung my camera strap over my head and tucked it around to my back so it wouldn't get bumped, made sure I had an extra roll of film in my shirt pocket, and wiped my hands on my jeans preparatory to grasping the rung over my head.

I stepped up onto the first rung and made good progress up past the first floor. It was only at that point that I started to realize just how narrow the climbing area was and how sweaty my hands were getting. Funny how that sort of thing only comes to one rather too late, well after the moment at which an idea that seems like a gem at the time is past recall. I concentrated on moving up, promising myself that I didn't need to go all the way to the roof, just up high enough to get a nice overall picture of the site. A handful of photos, five or six minutes max, and then I was out of there, safely on my way home, and no one the wiser.

I could feel my hand, slick with sweat, slip against the rust-pocked surface of the rungs. I redoubled my hold and gasped.

Highly trained *archaeologist,* that prudent and tardy little voice in my head reminded me. Not trapeze artist or chimpanzee.

Shut up and concentrate, I told myself. Hurriedly wiping my hands off again, I continued upward, a little shaken.

I made it up to the top and then realized that the peak of the roof was in the way of the best shot. I couldn't get what I wanted if I stayed where I was, so I considered climbing back down and trying again in the morning. This of course risked righteous rejection by the scaffolding folks and the ire of the insurance-conscious Fee. It probably wouldn't happen.

My other option was to climb out onto the roof. The scaffolding wouldn't be there tomorrow evening and a picture from the upstairs window just wouldn't work as well as what I had in mind. So I kept going.

It didn't seem like such a long step from the scaffolding to the roof, but suddenly aware of the nearly three stories of open space below me and the lack of safety lines or nets, I paused and felt a wave of vertigo wash over me. It was a small step, but an important one, as they say. I didn't really need these pictures, I told myself. They weren't that important.

Chicken, jibed a little voice in my head. This one sounded remarkably like Bucky.

There really was nothing to be afraid of, I reassured myself. It is purely a matter of will over fear. I focused my concentration, and wishing that my hands didn't slide around quite as easily as they did, took the large, half-jumping step

over onto the roof. It was roasting up there, in spite of the
clouds that had darkened the sky all day, and the smell of hot
slate and tar was quite strong. It was like stepping onto a hot
cast-iron skillet. The heat instantly surrounded me, and I felt
like a drying piece of beef jerky.

Once my heart stopped pounding so hard and I had the
chance to catch my breath, I was immediately rewarded. I
had a magnificent view of the harbor and was just in time to
see the evening flotilla as the boats headed back from what
should have been a fabulous day's sailing. The site below me
was becoming a little overshadowed, but it didn't matter.
The great thing was that the planting holes, which seemed
randomly placed on the ground, from up here appeared to
demark two sides of a snakelike walkway. I made a note to
check the artifacts from those areas, to see if we were getting higher concentrations of mettling material—broken
pottery, pipe stem fragments, shells—that might have been
used to form the path itself. I snapped a few shots, getting
the ones I most wanted, and then realizing I was getting carried away, decided it was time to get going.

It was at that moment that I heard the front door slam in
the house below me.

I froze, trying to decide what to do. Anyone who'd come
in from the front would have seen my car out in the parking
lot and might be wondering what I was doing here. Embarrassing but not fatal; I would simply indicate that I was up
on the roof, explain myself, and we would all have a good
laugh. That was the sensible course of action.

I half-scuttled, half-crawled over nearer to the front of the
house and the main entrance. "It's only me! I'm on the roof.
Don't worry, I was just—"

The alarm in the house began to go off, nearly causing
me to jump out of my skin and almost break potty training.
It was looking decidedly as though there was more trouble

brewing here than my potential embarrassment. But perhaps I had only startled someone into setting off the alarm?

I went back to the other side of the roof to the scaffolding, determined to get down from there as quickly as possible. I might just make it down before the police arrived, and that would suit me just fine. I already had all I could do to explain my presence on the site after hours; it wouldn't help me any to be found clinging to the scaffolding of a house whose alarm is alerting the local law enforcement that there is an intruder.

I admit that I was feeling pretty shaky; the alarm was a particularly obnoxious noise and it seemed as though its main purpose was to drive any potential burglar insane. I was also starting to get vertigo again, merely from the act of being where I should not, when I should not, with that great view reducing itself to a pretty background on which I could splat myself if I wasn't careful. But I am usually pretty good at concentrating first and having a hissy fit second; that's why it took me rather too long to realize that it wasn't my imagination, but the top step of the scaffolding was farther away than I remembered.

It was the shuddering of the entire structure that finally drove it into my brain that the scaffolding was actually moving away from my foot as I reached out for it. I risked a look down to try and find that damned rung and saw, far below me, a taut rope tied around the bottom of the scaffolding. I spent two or three precious seconds following the line of the rope over to the shrubs and trees that blocked most of the view of the Chandler House's air conditioning plant and storage shed from the Bellamy property, when I should have been using that time to get back onto the roof or get the hell down off there.

My pause narrowed my range of choices. I had to get

back onto the roof or else be pulled down with the rest of the scaffold.

I scrabbled back toward the comparative safety of the roof and watched as the scaffolding lurched away. The knot slipped, and I heard a heavy car tear away, unable to see it from my side of the roof. My heart was in my mouth when I realized what might have happened: I was lucky to get back onto the roof. Although the scaffolding didn't collapse completely—it only swung away from the house, with the resisting screech of bending metal, listing against a massive oak tree. There was no way that I wanted to be on it.

Any thoughts of leaping from the roof into the trees or shrubs were stillborn; it was still too far away for me to make it to a tree and maybe climb down. It had been a good number of years since my last tree-climb, too, and I didn't trust my shaking hands or my frazzled nerves that far anyway. That sort of stunt only happens in the movies, and there wasn't an awning or hayrick around when I needed one.

My heart beat so hard that I was almost dizzy, and I was trembling so hard that I thought I might fall if I wasn't careful. Someone had deliberately tried to pull me off the roof along with the scaffolding. It was little enough consolation to hear the wail of sirens in the distance over the persistent screech of the house alarm. Someone really had tried to kill me.

Chapter 20

I WAS GLAD TO GET OFF THAT ROOF. THE HEAT WAS still strong, even though the sun was going down, and I couldn't help but feel toasted by those low-raking rays. Between the sunset and the warm air trapped under the roof, I was probably lucky not to—

"Emma! Are you listening to me?"

I was brought back to reality by the sharp insistence of Detective Bader's question. "I'm sorry?"

"You're sure you didn't see the car? Color? Make, plates, anything?"

"No, I'm sure. I was kind of distracted at the time."

"And the driver?"

"I didn't see anyone. I heard the door slam, I hollered, then the alarm, and I suppose there was an engine after that, but couldn't see anything from where I was standing." I took another sip of the water that he'd given me; it seemed as though I could still feel the heat from the slate tiles on my face.

"Are you okay to drive yourself home?"

I looked at him. "Yeah, I'm fine."

"Good girl."

I frowned. "You know—"

Bader didn't even notice I'd said anything. "If you're sure, you can get going. Just do me a favor, okay? Don't climb up on anything higher than a stepladder, until we find whoever's got it in for you."

I got home a little later and went upstairs looking for Brian. I found him flaked out on our bed, and for a moment, it looked as though he'd grown a huge, furry black beard. Quasi was sleeping on his chest, curled up as nice as a pie, with his head resting under Brian's chin. At the sound of my soft, scuffling footstep, the cat woke instantly, and glaring at me as best he could with his one good eye, opened his mouth in a soundless protest. He slunk off to become part of the shadows under the bed, only leaving the room when I was out of the doorway, tail low to the ground, slithering around the corner.

Brian sat up and stretched and smiled. "I was getting worried about you."

"You're not going to like this." I confessed where I'd been and what happened and got ready to take my lumps: I'd been stupid and done something I'd promised I wouldn't and I was lucky not to be dead. His smile fading, he listened to the story, growing more and more pale as it progressed, silent the whole time.

After he confirmed that I was indeed unhurt, he asked, "So you climbed up on the scaffolding, without permission, to take pictures of holes in the ground?"

"It wouldn't have been any safer if I'd had permission—"

"But it would for the simple fact that there would have

been people around. Maybe whoever was in the house wouldn't have been there, right? This is what you promised me, that you wouldn't be out at the site alone, isn't it?"

"Yes, and it was stupid of me. I admit that and I'm sorry that I scared you. But I only meant to be there for, what? Less than a half hour, tops. And I wasn't doing anything, you know, to do with the murders. I was just trying to do my job."

"That apparently doesn't worry the killers, does it?" I began to think he was going to wear a trough in the floor with his pacing.

"What do you want me to do, Brian? I could stay away from the site, yes, fine. But what about the courthouse? There are all kinds of criminals lurking around there every day, not to mention some fairly upstanding citizens who also happen to have motives for the murders. Do you want me to stay away from there too? What about the library? Oh, hell, what about the whole of Stone Harbor? Should I just stay out of a place because something bad happened there? Or do I go on about my business, taking ordinary precautions, and try to carry on with my life?"

"I'm just saying, I can't be with you all the time—"

"Brian, I know, but even if you could, what good would that do?"

"I could be there, look after you?"

"How?"

"What do you mean, how?"

"I mean, I understand your instinct in this, but . . . Brian. What could you do?"

"What does it matter? Someone tried to kill you and I'm not going to just stand by and wait for it to happen."

"Brian," I said again, as gently as I could. "What could you do about it?"

"I think being there is a good start," he said stubbornly. "There's safety in numbers."

"There are numbers, at the site, during the day. Yes, I made a mistake, and I'm really, really sorry for it. But are you planning on going with me to the library? To school, come the fall? You can't be with me every second, you know."

"I know. But it would make me feel better, if I'm there with you."

"Brian, how long have you been taking self-defense? Like I am, with Nolan?"

There was no answer.

"How many fights have you ever been in, in your whole life? I mean, counting in high school, on the street, whatever?"

I already knew the answer and so did he. "A couple. I can handle myself."

What I wanted to say was, sweetie, you've only got about thirty or forty pounds on me, you're just about six feet, which doesn't make you very physically imposing for a guy. You don't have any kind of physical training, not even a mean instinct, at all. You work in a lab all day, listen to music and write about it at night, and you've never been in anything more serious than a scuffle in your life. It would have been realistic, it would have been logical, and it would have done no good at all. Worse than that, it would have wounded the man who was the love of my life, who only wanted me to be safe and was willing to do everything in his power to ensure that. He was as aware of these facts, these realities, as I was, and to say them out loud would have done nothing except make him wish that he was something other than he was, which I couldn't stand.

But even touching on the subject as indirectly as I had had bruised his ego, and he did what anyone would do in that situation. He got angry.

"Emma, look, I love you, but taking a handful of lessons with Nolan doesn't make you Wonder Woman—"

"I know that."

"—and it doesn't, frankly, do a lot to reassure me. I'm just afraid that it's going to make you cocky, that you'll assume that you can handle more than you can."

"Brian, I—"

"And since you can't even seem to remember to bring your cell phone with you or keep it charged or learn to stay off the fucking roof, things that any twelve-year-old can manage, you'll forgive me if I'm not as impressed as you think I ought to be."

"I had my phone with me, it was in my bag."

"It has a belt clip."

"Being on the roof at the same time that anyone was in the house was an accident."

"It was an accident on your part. Not on the killer's and that's what you seem to forget. His will in this matter." He took a deep breath. "I think this is where you ask the cops for some protection."

"I don't think it works like that. I mean, they're not going to assign me a bodyguard or anything."

"No, but if they think that someone who is a potential witness is endangered, they might take an active interest. Talk to them. Please."

It wasn't so much a request as a demand. It was Brian's starting offer for letting me off the hook for the moment. "Okay. I'll do that."

"Good. I need to get some space from this for a while. I'm going out for a bit."

"Brian—"

He took my hand and shook his head. "My office is full of graduate students, there's no room in here for us to talk,

much less for me to think. I'm going to drive safely, I'm going to think, I'm not going to do anything stupid. Don't
worry. I'm mad and scared and I need to figure out what to
do about it."

"You can't do it here?" I was almost pleading.

"Hon, there's no space in this house to think anymore. I'll
be back in an hour or two."

He gave me a kiss, and I was absolutely miserable. I
heard him go downstairs, heard the door slam, and he drove
away, mad, for the first time in our relationship. I was at a
loss.

I went downstairs and found Bucky already in the
kitchen.

"Whoa, must have been a good fight."

"Come off it, Bucky. You haven't got the faintest idea and
I'm not in the mood for it."

"You don't think I can hear you and Brian arguing? I'm
in the next room!" Suddenly she was engrossed in the mag-
nets on the refrigerator, rearranging them into an unlikely
tableau where the fish appeared to be swimming among various famous paintings. "So. Is he coming back?"

I stared at her, but she was serious. She actually thought
that Brian was leaving me. "What do you mean? Of course
he's coming back."

She looked sheepish and a little defensive. "Well, it was a
pretty big fight. . . ."

"Yeah, it was. So what?" Then I realized what she was
getting at. "Okay, Bucky, guess what? This is what a mature
relationship looks like. Brian's upset and I can understand
that; this is not an easy thing to figure out for either of us.
He's not running away from anything, and neither am I.
He'll be back later, after he's had a chance to think."

"You sure?"

I gave her a disgusted look; I had used up my diminishing

stores of patience for the night and had none left for her in-
direct questions about relationships. "Yes, I'm sure. Look,
we'll sort it out because we both want to. Good relationships
don't just happen. When you hit a bad patch, you don't just
dump it and look for something else. You duke it out as
fairly as you can, you stop and get your breath before you
say something stupid or hurtful, and you try to find the solu-
tion that benefits everyone, okay? I mean, it's absolutely
worth it, but it's bloody hard work." I plopped myself down
on a chair. "You should try it sometime. You might be surprised at how things can go; it might simplify your life
some."

I suppose I shouldn't have said that; we weren't really
talking about her, but I was mad and she was being dense.
Bucky only shrugged, arranged the speckled trout magnet so
that it looked as though it was studying a Corot, and pulled
the refrigerator door open.

"So why do you keep nosing around the site?" Bucky
asked as she fished through the fridge. "And don't tell me
you're just going out there because of work. You just can't
seem to keep yourself away from it."

"I do it because I can," I said tiredly. "Because I should if
I can."

"That's it?" My sister emerged from her exploration tri-
umphantly holding two bottles of beer aloft. "It's not because you're bossy and you're a control freak—"

"I'm not bossy! I am authoritative and well-organized," I
said.

"Insisted the control freak." Bucky sat down and slid one
of the beers down toward me. I caught it, just as the base of
the bottle left the table. "So it's not because of those two
sterling traits, not because you want everything settled and
orderly, preferably to your standards and expectations.
Maybe it's because you're nosey—"

"Curious is a better word." I opened my beer and then passed the church key down to Bucky, intentionally tossing it a little short of where she could reach it.

"—or because you're good at investigating things." Bucky ignored the church key and removed the cap from the beer bottle by jerking it sharply down against the edge of the table. If I had tried it, I would have broken the bottle.

"Hey, watch the table! Jesus, Buck, just because the house is a mess doesn't mean you get to treat the furniture like it's disposable!"

"What did I do? There's no mark!" Sure enough, there wasn't so much as a nick in the aged oak wood. I scowled at her. "It's all in the wrist. Right, where was I? Right, you're good at investigating things."

"Yeah, so?" I crossed my legs and drank deep from my bottle.

She peered at me curiously, like I was something suspended in a jar of formaldehyde and not her sister. "Why do you get defensive when I'm telling you you're good at something?"

"I'm not." I uncrossed my legs and sat up straighter.

"Yes, you are. You curled up like a hedgehog. Hell, why shouldn't you be good at it? You have a natural talent, something that Grandpa Oscar was able to foster, something you've honed yourself over the years. Archaeology is something you love, and you're good at it, it's in your blood, so why not?"

"Why not what?"

"Why not admit to yourself that you investigate these other things because *you like it*?"

I looked away from her. "What do you care what I say or don't say?"

"Because I'd like to see you, just once in your life, admit that you're doing something because you like it and not strangle yourself with rationalizations that only account for a small part of the story. Big words you're bound to use, like 'obligation' and 'morality,' sound so much more noble than 'I like it,' don't they?" She began to wheedle. "C'mon, Em, admit it, I'm the only one here. You like prying into other people's business—that's a professional requirement for you—you like the idea that you can catch a bad guy, you like doing things you're not supposed to be doing and all under the oh-so-high-toned rubric of responsibility!"

"Bucky—"

"You get off on coloring outside the lines, you love the idea of doing something naughty, all in the name of being a good citizen. Come off it yourself. Just say it for me once, Em."

"Bucks, you couldn't have picked worse timing," I said. I put my nearly untouched beer bottle in the sink and left the kitchen for my room. I changed into my workout gear and went to the gym.

I don't bother working out when I'm in the field. I could say it's because I'm getting all the exercise that I need, but really, it's usually because there's just no time and I'm too damned tired. I do move around more when I'm out in the field, but it's hardly aerobic and never sustained. Somehow, though, even just sitting and thinking and answering questions for eight hours leaves my muscles aching by the end of the day, don't ask me how it happens. So it actually felt pretty good to run a few laps in air-conditioned splendor and lose some of my tension.

It was just as I was starting to warm up, put on a little speed, and really get into the effort that I almost heard him sneak up on me. That in itself was a minor triumph, just realizing the split second before he spoke that there was a *presence* beside me. So it was a great credit to me that I didn't fall on my butt, that there was just a prickling at the back of my neck, and I had already started looking to my right as I heard the words.

"Good evening, Dr. Fielding."

The voice was something coming from the bottom of the ocean, very soft, very deep, and profoundly elemental. Old as rock and just that hard. It was the voice of command, and I found myself running through the simple phrase looking for some order to obey before I got hold of myself and managed a grin. "Good evening, Nolan."

It was always "Nolan" with him, never "Mr. Nolan" or anything else. I didn't know whether it was his first name or his last name, but that's how everybody in town knew him too, so there was never any confusion. Neither was there any confusion about what the lack of an honorific might mean: In Lawton, across the world, for all I knew, the one name contained its own title of respect.

"Not used to seeing you here during the summer. To what do we owe this honor? Surely it's not in response to my message."

I glanced just above my shoulder, meeting Nolan's eyes. They were a green hazel, and I'd learned to my cost that while they were very attractive eyes, it didn't do to get too wrapped up in looking at them. Nolan was perfectly capable of exploiting every hesitation and weakness; he was teaching me to guard against them in myself and use them against others. He was a better teacher than I was a pupil.

"Tough day today."

He dismissed that immediately. "Has to be more than that. You'd be at home otherwise. What's going on at home?"

There was no point in trying to bluff Nolan; he has a state-of-the-art, built-in bullshit detector. Besides, he knew all about me. That was one of the prerequisites for taking me on as a student; getting to know me well enough so that he could identify my Achilles' heels.

Sometimes I hated Nolan quite a lot.

"It's too crowded," I said. "Brian and I are fighting." It felt strange to say that word again. We had arguments, sure; every couple does. But this was a no-doubt-about-it fight.

"Ah. About the business at the Chandler House."

He wasn't even breathing heavily as he matched my pace and dissected me. I wasn't surprised that Nolan knew about the Chandler House and I wasn't surprised that he expected that it would have an impact on me. I expect that he also knew that wasn't even registering on my "I Love Nolan" meter.

"Yup."

"Tricky. I can't help you with that."

Which made me wonder . . . "Is there something you *can* help me with?"

"I'm not sure yet."

Fatigue and frustration made me stupid. "That's a first."

I regretted that as soon as it left my mouth. Nolan had an account he kept in his head, where unnecessary remarks, sarcasm, or repeated stupidity accrued and made for a tougher workout when next we met. Nolan was as good an accountant as Fee was.

Maybe he was taking my present situation into account as well; he simply responded, "That's the mark of a professional. To admit when you don't know something. You should know that."

The little rebuke stung, especially as Detective Bader had recently paid me that particular compliment. "I do. I'm sorry."

"I know. Come to my office, Dr. Fielding. I'll buy you a bottle of water."

We trotted over to the side of the track where Nolan's office was. He always called a client—student, victim, whathaveyou—by courtesy titles before a lesson. After that brief interlude, the lesson began, and he inevitably found the nickname that was most galling to her and used it as a goad and a provocation. He almost never called anyone by their first name. A very high tribute was to be called by your last name only, during a lesson. I hadn't heard mine yet.

Framed in the door of his office, I was struck by the fact that Nolan resembled the letter T, serifs and all. His posture was superlative and relaxed, his shoulders were ridiculously broad in comparison to his waist and hips, and he had very small, almost dainty, feet, on which he moved with catlike grace and speed. They certainly didn't feel small when they were kicking your legs out from underneath you. Like many men of short stature, he was a little vain—the first thing he did before reaching into the fridge was to glance at the mirror and smooth the last of his graying hair into place—but unlike most short men, he never extended the fact of his height to his behavior. Being a tall woman, I often run into a lot of attitude from guys who aren't any taller than I am, and I'll tell you frankly, there is nothing more tedious. Outside the schoolyard, no one cares. It was a relief that there was none of that in Nolan.

He handed me a water and settled into the chair behind his desk, indicating that I could take a seat opposite him. Nolan gazed at the wall a moment, then drank off half of his water in one go. "You drinking enough water at work?"

"Yes."

"Good. Even when it's not hot out, your body needs water. Now, as for this other thing. I'm not hearing much about it."

I shook my head. "There hasn't been much in the news."

"I'm not talking about the news. I'm sure you realize that it is not only professorial types who are coming to me for training?" He paused while he drank the rest of his water, and got another out of the fridge. "I do get a very wide spectrum of the community, shall we say? I see who's in the weight room because they want to be fit, and who's there because they might need to beat the tar out of someone in their professional life. Sometimes on one side of the law, sometimes the other."

I gaped. You just don't think about that sort of thing.

"While it is understood that I know how to keep my mouth shut and that I don't ask too many questions when they're not needed, I will keep my ears open. If there is anything that I hear that will be of use to you, I will let you know."

I was struck by the magnanimity of his offer. "Thank you, Nolan."

"You might be very surprised to see who I work with." He tapped his Rolodex thoughtfully. "It gives one an entirely different outlook on our quiet little community. I can say that it both depresses and inspires me. If I ever retire, I could write a book that would curl your hair." He looked up. "Did you ever think about cutting yours, by the way? I think that braid makes all-too-useful a handle in an unfair fight. Also," he studied my face, "I think a shorter cut would do a lot for adding character to your face."

"Thanks, I'll think about it." I took a big sip of my water to cover my irritation. Everyone had an opinion about my hair. I liked it the way I had it.

"I have a late student tonight," he said, standing. The conference was over.

"Thanks for your help, Nolan. I appreciate it."

"My pleasure, Dr. Fielding. Of course, I expect to see you back here as soon as you are done with your outside work. Krav Maga waits for no one."

"Oh, yes. First thing."

"And you could stand to leave one or two beers in the re-frigerator at the end of the day, you know. I happen to know that you don't actually spend your time digging ditches and leaping through the trees, Red."

I flinched; there was the hateful nickname that had haunted me all my life.

"And watch the sunscreen; your nose is getting a little burnt. Now, if you don't mind. . . ." He glanced over my shoulder. I turned and saw Delilah Voeller, in sneakers and workout gear, her hair pulled back into a ballerina's bun, and sans makeup. She glanced at me sharply and nodded recognition as I squeezed past her.

"Ah," Nolan said. "Good evening, Mrs. Voeller."

I wondered again about the power of gossip—let us call it unofficial news through alternative channels. So far, most of the help I'd been to Detective Bader, apart from telling him what I'd observed on finding the bodies, had been because I'd seen things or heard things he didn't have access to. In the past, if you put Nolan in the role of a fencing master, say, Ted Cressey as a gardener, and Fee or Perry as house-keepers, all of a sudden, you could start to see how information was communicated faster across fences and by the village pump than by broadsheet. Thing was, as useful as it was, it could also work against me. Participating in that net-work, especially in the course of searching out the killer—or killers—could be dangerous, because the information might not be true. Or it might be handed my way to deliberately mislead Detective Bader. A lot of people seemed to think that he and I had exchanged much more information than we had. I thought it made me a rather likely target, just as Brian had suggested. But I also counted on the fact that I was much more in the middle of all this information than the murderer or murderers were, and that worked for me. At least it was a spur for me to try and put this together, before he or she decided I'd heard too much.

Suddenly I was thinking about the fragment of the chatelaine Bucky'd found at the site. I suppose it was my contemplation of things historical, but also seeing Delilah Voeller at the gym, that made it pop into my thoughts. While basic human behaviors and emotions hadn't changed much, the reasons for them had changed quite a lot. Once upon a time, the chatelaine might have represented the woman's power in the home, but what had made it possible for me in the twenty-first century to get out of the home and away from the side of the cow also made it my responsibility to look after myself while I was out in the world. My power was not to be found in my husband's name or reputation—my own name and my own reputation were sufficient, thank you very much—and neither did my protection lie solely in him. If we were able to negotiate our relationship as equals, it meant that my physical safety was my job too. The problem with this modern arrangement was that all of the protocols hadn't been worked out yet; it was still too new to our culture to have been completely and successfully negotiated.

Apparently Delilah Voeller, who according to Daniel was a partner in her husband's business affairs, thought the same way. That kept me thinking until I felt the crunch of the gravel of our driveway under the tires.

Brian called soon after I arrived home. I knew he was mad, but Brian wasn't the kind of guy to punish someone by scaring her. All he said was that he needed some time to think, he'd get dinner out, and he'd be in later. I did wonder whether he might unconsciously be giving me a taste of my own medicine, by not letting me know exactly what was going on, but then I was tired and out of sorts.

I showered and read up in bed for a while, and against

every instinct and inclination I have to working late at night, I fell asleep.

I woke up a while later; the clock said it was close to three-thirty. The bedside light was off and after an instant of panic, I realized that Brian was in bed next to me. Relief flooded through me, and I was able to calm myself by listening to his own slow, regular breathing. I thought about waking him up and then rejected the idea; he hadn't woken me up, it was late, and it seemed that one of us should get some sleep tonight. I realized that he might not have wanted to wake me up because he still wanted time to himself. Maybe he didn't want to talk to me. Maybe he was still angry, maybe he wasn't, but I was too much of a coward to wake him up and ask.

I thought about how easy it might be to excuse myself from working on the dig any further this summer. No one could blame me, and some would say that I was making a wise decision. But I couldn't leave work just because something nasty had happened there. Nothing to do with me, I was taking all the right precautions, and I was reluctant to be shifted on such circumstantial grounds.

It just wasn't in my nature to leave. And I didn't know if Brian could accept that. I didn't know if I could have, if I were in his shoes. I didn't know how to be fair about this.

My head ached. I rubbed my forehead, moving very slowly so as not to disturb Brian, and tried not to watch the clock as it seemed to be frozen in time. I stared blankly at the closet door and realized that I'd been shot at, beat up, and threatened in a variety of ways in the course of what I thought of as my work. It had been horrible; you can't even imagine the place your head has to be when you are struggling for your life unless you've actually been there. The uncertainty of it all, the choices you are forced to make, never knowing if what you do will make the situation worse, is grim beyond words. Physical confrontation is fascinating and terrifying and even if you are good at it, which I am not, you try to avoid it if you possibly can. Clinging to the side of a rock, worrying about being dragged out to sea to drown, even what had happened on the scaffolding, I could still remember how afraid I was, even if it was only an intellectual recollection of what I'd been through; the emotional impact was fading, thank heavens.

Wanting to reach out for Brian, without knowing whether he would want me to, seemed worse to me at this moment than any of those situations.

Chapter 21

I SPENT THE MORNING OF JULY FOURTH THROWING notes together for my talk. The students took off, leaving the house quiet again. By the time I'd figured out what to wear, gotten angry at Bucky for not having to work on the holiday, and achieved a kind of détente with Brian, it was time to go.

At the historic site, there was a uniformed officer in front—Officer Lovell—and another one back in the crowd. "For public safety," Lovell had told me, but I thought the reasons were probably a lot more specific than that. The Bellamys had decamped, presumably, in the face of so many Chandlers. Monet and Matisse were barking their heads off, jumping as far up the fence as they could manage. Bucky wandered over across the street and started talking to them. She stuck her fingers in through the fence before I could stop her and fondled them. They licked her fingers, delighted at having met a kindred spirit.

"What good doggies you are! Yes, you are! You're just

bored, aren't you? Oh, you're good babies. You be quiet now. Go lie down, be good."

After one more ear scratch each, the dogs obediently trotted away and were quiet. I gave Bucky a disgusted look, mostly for having shown me up, but also for having managed to sound so much like Claire Bellamy.

"They're nice dogs. Real smart," was all she said when she returned. Her face was all innocence save for the little smirk she was unable to conceal. "You know, they were used for hunting in France?"

Bitch.

Behind the house on the lawn, Perry and Ted were armed with trays of the famous, even notorious, Chandler punch, circulating among the guests. I'd heard only that the recipe was supposed to have been handed down through the generations and included, among other ingredients, both brandy and rum and a number of spices. Perry and Ted both stopped by Bucky, Brian, and me a couple of times. I refused each one, not liking to drink before work. Bucky made a face at me and remarked that it was nice not to have to work when everyone else was playing.

"It sure would put you into the swing of things," Ted said, and he was right. The party was going full force, after the hastily improvised ceremony marking Aden's passing was over. I suddenly thought I had a good idea of how the Chandler House might have looked during its heyday, lights from every room, light from torches and candles outside, the salty breeze making them all flicker.

After refusing Perry's offer again, I heard my cue to hit the stage, so to speak, in the big meeting room. "Good luck," Brian whispered.

"Thanks," I said, but my mind was already on my presentation. I went upstairs and started my lecture.

The talk went very well, although I was a little nervous doing it. It wasn't stage fright; far from it. I'd done a thousand of these sorts of things and still get a little excited about doing them. And frankly, the situation couldn't have been better set up for a good reception: The members of the Chandler family had been well fed and had made several toasts and were now pleasantly situated to hear me tell them interesting and scandalous things about their ancestors.

No, what I was worried about were the people I knew were in the audience who wouldn't be so pleased about the news I had. I saw that the Bellamys were in fact present, had been invited as a courtesy; they weren't going to be thrilled to learn that what I'd found not only warranted more research, but with a larger area to be opened. Bray Chandler kept darting dirty looks at me every time our eyes met, and I wasn't ready to forget how upset he was by the fact that his ancestor, Nicholas, might have been something less than the legitimate offspring of Margaret and Matthew Chandler. I'd also spoiled one of his trysts and now that he would probably be made director of the Chandler House, my chances of doing more work there were diminishing. Fee had barely spoken to me since that day at Wendy's Bakery with Grace, and she too would be put off by the thought of more fieldwork, and now I wondered what kind of shenanigans she was pulling with the old Mather House, especially when she was supposed to be broke. Perry, who now knew that I'd spoken to both Dr. Spencer and Daniel Voeller about her, kept smiling too hard and chattering too excitedly for someone wholly at ease. Daniel himself was watching me with a focus that I knew had nothing to do with my talk and more to do with my supposed discussions with Detective Bader. Ted was passing around a tray of miniature desserts and avoiding my glance. Only Janice Booth seemed the same as

I remembered her the day in her garden and studio; eating with titanic gusto, whispering to her near neighbors, Franklin clutched to her bosom.

Most of them were short on cash, all of them had a reason to want Aden quiet or dead. All of them potentially had access to guns, I thought suddenly, reminded of the hunting photo in Aden's office. And I still had no idea whether Justin's death was a part of this as well.

It was about the time that I was talking about what properties the Chandlers owned in Stone Harbor, what percent of town actually owed them money, the financial stuff, that a thought dislodged itself for my consideration. What if Aden hadn't been marched into the wooded area at gunpoint? What if he had been going somewhere intentionally and the killer had followed him? There wasn't much there, just the old Mather House, the vacant lot, and then, a ways down, the Voeller factory.

I stumbled a little in my talk, lost my place, and then riffed a little on the slide of an account book until I could catch my place and reconstruct my train of thought. I finished up by offering my tentative theories about the garden wall and the Chandlers' failure to rebuild that wing of the house after it had burned.

"My next goal is to start going through other diaries and town documents to learn what I can about the fire of seventeen thirty-eight and whether it might have anything to do with the destruction here at the Chandler House and Nicholas Chandler's death. With a few more specifics—things I never dreamed I'd have to know about when I began this project—"

There were a few appreciative laughs here.

"—I hope I'll be able to piece together this puzzle and add another chapter to Chandler family history. For the moment, if you're interested in possibilities, I'm wondering

about this: What if Nicholas died when the wing was destroyed? Is it possible that Matthew and Margaret Chandler,
not wishing to let the death of one of their family members"—that was a sop to Bray—"go unobserved, rebuilt to
the back, with the addition you are now seated in, and put in
a permanent memorial to Nicholas, in the form of a garden?
Remembering how useful a garden was to colonists, containing plants for food, medicine, beauty, and pleasure, and
how meaningful the natural and the built landscape was to
them, is it so hard to imagine that they also planted rose-
mary for remembrance and pansies for thought? I think it's
possible.

"But of course, that can all be answered only with more
work and more study. Thank you very much and enjoy the
reunion."

I answered the questions that followed as well as I could.
I might have been a little brusque, eager to chase down my
thoughts, but people were already filing down the stairs and
outside to get back to drinking in preparation for the fireworks that were about to start. I wrapped up to enthusiastic
applause, and went to find Fee. I had to ask her about the
Mather House and trusted that the crowd would keep her
from responding violently to my sensitive questions.

Unfortunately, Daniel, Perry, Ted, and Bray were all clus-
tered around her, finalizing their plans for the end of the
event, so I had to just brave it out. I came up with as good a
ruse as I could, and plunged in. None of them left after they'd
finished, and I had made it clear I wanted to talk to Fee.

"Say, Fee? I had a question for you."

She eyed me maliciously. "Go ahead."

"I haven't had time to do the deed research on the Mather
House, well, not carefully anyway. The past five or six years,
it passed through a lot of hands, but it's now in the hands of
the Stone Harbor Investment Properties, and that seems to

be something you know something about. That might be another good place for me to do research and I figured I should check with you about who to approach about working there."

The others frowned; it was an odd thing to ask at such a party. Fee took a deep breath and took me by the elbow a few steps away from the rest.

"Why do you keep doing this?" she asked desperately. "What do you want from me?"

"I don't want anything from you, Fee. I just want to know what the deal is with the Mather House, because I think Aden might have been heading there when he was killed."

She looked around; the others were quite obviously paying attention and the uniformed cop was within sight. Her lips tightened, but then relaxed. "I might as well tell you; it's going to come out anyway, sooner or later. Aden gave me the money to buy it. To keep it in my name, although it really belonged to him. That's why we set up the company."

"Why?"

"I don't know. He said taxes, but you could never trust Aden about anything. I went along with it. . . ."

"Because he threatened to tell . . . about Grace unless you did."

"Yes."

"I see." Taxes? Aden wouldn't have to worry about taxes and if he did, he'd have about seventeen tax attorneys to help him out. He wanted a blind for some reason, but why?

A secret place to store his files.

Fee continued. "I don't know what will happen now, who it will go to, now that he's . . . gone. But the will would have led people to find out about my involvement. So there's no harm in telling you. I just don't know what I'm going to tell the authorities when they come to me."

"None of it will have anything to do with Grace, though," I said. "There's no reason to bring that up."

She didn't look much relieved by this. "You're right. Now if you don't mind. . . ."

I thanked Fee and went back to find Bucky and Brian.

Bray, Daniel, Ted, and Perry had circulated back into the crowd, getting people settled in for the fireworks and handing out more glasses of punch. The crowd was starting to become loudly jocular as the night grew quickly darker.

I found my sister standing near the back of the gathering, trying to get a little breath of air. She'd already finished her second glass of punch, had started a third, and was holding another one in her other hand. Her eyes were bright and she was getting into the spirit of the party.

"Emma, you did so good!" she announced, throwing her arms around me. "Your talk was just great!"

"Thanks," I said, surprised by her enthusiastic response. "I'm glad you liked it. Brian around? I've got to find—"

"He's in the can," she announced. "I was saving this punch for you. The spices are a little overdone, but it's not bad."

I took it absently. "Thanks. You know, I just found out something very interesting. You know the Mather House? Aden owned it. Why wouldn't he have told me? I asked him about it and he kept putting me off. Jesus, I wonder if he had the rest of the files over there. It would be a big enough space, with no one to bother them. No one even knew it was his, really."

"Wow! You should mention that to Bader. Wouldn't it be great if you hit on something?"

"Yeah, it would be nice, but I mostly just want this behind me."

Bucky gestured to my glass. "You going to drink that?"

"Here." I handed it to her. "I'm going to find a Coke or something, I'm dying of thirst."

"Don't be long, the fireworks are about to start."

I had only gone about ten feet when I ran into Bray.

"Thanks for flouting your half-baked theories all over the place," he growled. "You never stop, do you?"

God, but I was sick of him. "You know, I can't help but think that you are overlooking a couple of rather obvious things here."

"And what is that, Dr. Fielding?" Bray's untidy beard bristled, making it too easy to imagine a tall pointed red felt hat on him. For all he and his wife seemed to be anxious about appearances, they might have worried about his dress a little more. And that was saying a lot, coming from me, a poster child for the fashion impaired.

"Two things. The first is that, even if Nicholas Chandler had not been a Chandler by birth—and I believe he was, though not through Matthew—he arrived in this country very early and was a part of a prominent family. Surely that counts for something?"

"Perhaps."

"The more important fact is that of your first name."

"Bray?"

"Bradley. The Bradleys were also one of the first families in the town, who arrived even earlier than the Chandlers. Nicholas, whoever else he might have been, was good enough for them to marry one of their daughters. So you should remember that you are descended from them as well." And if pedigree counts, as it seemed to for Bradley, then that fact was even more significant.

He nodded slowly. "Perhaps." This was a little less depressed than the last "perhaps," though, and I began to believe that I had shown Bray a way out of at least one of his problems. Keeping it in his pants and being unhappily married weren't things that I or anyone else could help with. He wandered off without another word, which suited me just fine.

The first volley of fireworks went off, scaring the hell out of me. I needed to find the ladies' room too, but a drink and a rest first. I didn't make it too much farther, when I heard my sister's voice.

"Emma! Emma, come here! Please!"

I turned back, and saw that Bucky was clutching her head. "What is it?"

"I don't know, something's wrong. I feel sick."

"Sick like you're going to throw up, or sick like something else? Do you need your inhaler?"

"No, it's not that . . . I don't think so. I feel dizzy and my stomach . . . ohh, man, can we just go home? I feel really ill."

"Okay, no problem. It's probably just dehydration or something. Maybe you just drank the punch too fast."

She was sweating and looked greenish on the dully lit lawn. "No, it doesn't feel like . . . just get me to the car. Please?"

No time to look for Brian now, I decided. I'd get Bucky settled into the car and then collect him. "Okay, here we go."

I looked down at her and was really worried now. Bucky was stumbling as often as she took a step. We were almost to the parking lot when she collapsed.

I tried to pick her up. "Jesus, Bucky! What's wrong? Get up, can you? Can you get up for me, and I'll get you into the car?"

Despite my pleading, she just sat there on the gravel, drooling a little, and the little hairs on my arms and neck stood right up. I looked at her face and her eyes were funny, the pupils too small for the minimal amount of light outside. My stomach contracted; she was badly ill. As soon as I could get her to the car, we were going to hightail it for the emergency room.

"It's not . . . I can't . . . Emma, what's wrong . . . ?"

"I don't know, Bucky—"

She slumped forward.

"Oh, God! Bucky . . . Carrie? Wake up, hon, okay? You've got to wake up for me. You've got to do that now!" I shook her hard and got a moan out of her. I shook her harder and saw her eyelids flutter.

"Don't do this! Wake up!" I screamed. "Wake up, Bucky! I'm going to get help, just wake up!"

She moaned and I felt her hand tighten on my arm. "The drink."

"What?"

"Something . . ." Her head rolled and I couldn't hear what she said. I thought I would shake her head off, before she opened her eyes again.

"What did you say?"

"Bitter." She fell over and I couldn't wake her up. I rolled her over onto her side, just in case she should get sick, and realized that I needed help; I couldn't carry her to the car myself. . . .

The phone! I grabbed my bag and found the cell phone. We were just close enough to one of the lights in the parking lot that I could actually read the buttons. I punched the on key and waited for what seemed like an eternity before the screen registered. I almost screamed when I read the screen.

No signal.

I flung the thing away from me and ran back to the crowd to find Brian. I found Officer Lovell instead, thanking providence for that. I had to shout to make myself heard, but he got the idea that something was wrong immediately, and followed me as I all but dragged him toward the parking lot. He used his radio in a second, then started to go through the CPR protocol.

"What happened to her?" he asked as he worked.

"I don't know! She said it was the drink."

"What did she have?"

"Two or three glasses of the punch! That shouldn't be enough to do this! Look, I don't know if this is important, but she's got asthma."

"Okay. What's her name?"

"It's Bucky!"

"Bucky! Who gave you the drink, do you know?"

She didn't answer this time. Not even to cough.

Lovell kept going through the motions. "Okay, an ambulance is on the way."

I was feeling sick with dread. "I'm going to get my husband."

He was sweating as he worked. "Make it quick."

I ran back, but couldn't find Brian in the crowd. It was one of the most terrible experiences in my life. Try and remember when you were a kid and got separated from your mother in a crowd, then multiply that panic times a thousand, and you'll get the idea. I could feel myself starting to hyperventilate. I couldn't see very well in the dark, the crowd's faces only occasionally lit up by the glare of the fireworks. I couldn't even hear myself calling for Brian over the noise; some joker had brought a sound system with the "1812 Overture" and was blasting it away. Faces glowed red and green and blue and none of them were Brian's.

I found Fee and Daniel and shouted to them. "Have you seen Brian?"

"Who?"

"My husband! Have you seen him? My sister's really sick and I—"

They exchanged a worried glance. "Perry just left too,"

Fee yelled over the noise of the happy crowd. "Said she didn't feel well. I hope it wasn't the smoked salmon—"

"No, she said it was her arm," Daniel shouted. "Going home to take a painkiller—"

A painkiller? Oh sweet Jesus! I stared at them in horror and grabbed Daniel's arm. "Tell Brian she's in the parking lot! Tell Officer Lovell, I think Perry put painkillers in Bucky's drink. She's gone to—"

Another volley of mortar fire exploded around us. Daniel nodded, but I wasn't certain he'd heard all of what I said. Fee just looked confused, but I couldn't waste any more time. I began to shove my way through the crowd, going as fast as I could get bodies out of my way, until I reached the edge. I stumbled, but regained my footing on the fly, pounding as far as I could toward the tree line, the sound of simulated cannon blasts and clanging church bells filling my ears.

I was practically running blind; it was only the last bursts of the finale that gave me enough light to find my way through the woods, once I got past the familiar track to the second set of excavation units. I could feel the branches cracking beneath my feet, could feel brambles and undergrowth tearing at my clothes, but I kept charging right through. I only paused when I could see the ambient light of the town a little more clearly: I was coming to the edge of the wooded area.

I slowed down to a quiet creep now; I could see a light bobbing ahead of me, moving deliberately toward the Mather House. With any luck, whoever it was—and by now I assumed it was Perry looking for the last of Aden's files— hadn't heard me over the noise of the fireworks display. I could just barely make out a female form by the door to the house; the flashlight was now on the ground by the door, and I could hear the clink of keys as she tried them in the lock.

I tried to think of what to do—should I call out to her?

Should I go back and tell Lovell? There was no time. I crept closer and closer and realized that this was not a time for finesse or patience or calculation; like Brian had said, sometimes the trick was knowing when to use brute force.

There was also no time to worry about whether she had a gun.

I ran the last couple of yards, and as she turned, I lowered my shoulder and slammed her into the door. That was a mistake, because I didn't hit her quite right, and I felt something in my shoulder pop. I also felt the door buckle underneath us, and for a split second worried that it would collapse, but it held.

Perry was quick; she stomped her heel into my foot and drove her elbow into my ribs, throwing me off balance. I was too close to her and didn't fall back. My foot hurt like blazes though, and it only made me madder. I grabbed her left arm, the one with the cast, and shoved it as hard as I could against the door. Perry screamed and brought her right hand, bristling with a fistful of keys, around. She missed my shoulder, but I could feel something sharp tear across under my chin.

This time I did step back. She dropped the keys and reached into her bag. I didn't wait to see what she would pull out. I grabbed her shirt at the shoulders with both hands and pulled as hard as I could, setting my foot against hers to act as a fulcrum. There was a ripping noise. Perry fell forward. She sprawled out onto the leaf-strewn walkway, the beam from the flashlight spilled on the ground, glancing off her disheveled shirt and hair. Her hands were still underneath her, however, and I couldn't see her bag. I could, however, smell lighter fluid.

She rolled over even as I darted toward her. I snatched the bag away from her and she struggled. I sat down on her chest, my knees pinning her shoulders. She struggled still and threw me off her as my hands closed around the grip of a pistol. I pulled it free from the bag as Perry rolled away. I got to my knees, and Perry scrambled to hers, just as I checked that the safety was off and aimed it at her. I stood up slowly, unable to control my trembling.

"What did you give her?" I shouted. "What did you put in my sister's drinks?"

"I thought you'd get at least one of them," she said in between heavy breaths. "But if she got one, and that slowed you down. . . ."

The drinks were meant for me?

Perry seized on my hesitation. "Do you really want to be here with me, when your sister's back there . . . ?"

"Tell me what was in the drinks!" The gun felt so heavy in my hand. It was larger than the one that Meg had showed me how to use, but the principles were essentially the same. I could see Perry watching my shaking hand, the barrel of the gun jerking but still pointed at her. "You tell me now, or I pull the trigger."

She hesitated.

"Tell me!" There was no mistaking the hysteria in my voice or the conviction either. Perry's eyes never left the gun.

"It's in the bag."

Not taking my eyes off her, not dropping the pistol, I groped with my left hand for the flashlight and set it upright, then rummaged through her purse. I found the can of lighter fluid, and put it aside. I rummaged around until I could ascertain that there wasn't another weapon in the bag. My fingers curled around a plastic pharmacy bottle and I pulled it out. I risked a quick look: 60 mg codeine and 300 mg acetaminophen. There were the little warning stickers plastered all over the label; the one with the stylized martini glass caught my eye and almost made my knees buckle.

"Is this it?"

She shrugged. "Yeah."

"Good," I said, thinking hard. "Now take off your shoes."

Perry had the audacity to be shocked by my demand. "What?"

"Do it *now*!"

I picked one up and threw it as hard as I could into the tangle of briars and trees to the right of me, then did the same with the other, only aiming in the opposite direction. I stuffed the pills and the can of lighter fluid into the purse and gave a last look at Perry. I wanted to slap her, I wanted to choke her, I wanted to hurt her, badly, but I had to keep my head. Bucky needed me now.

"You had better start praying my sister doesn't die."

I picked up the bag, backed away a few steps, and began to run back toward the Chandler House.

Chapter 22

I COULDN'T EVEN CATCH ENOUGH BREATH TO SPEAK when I got back. The ambulance had arrived, Brian was waiting there, and so was Detective Bader in addition to two more police cars. I thrust the brown plastic bottle into the hands of one of the EMTs. "She . . . will she be . . . ?"

"We're going to the hospital right now. Do you want to come with us?"

"Yes! No—Perry! I can't!" I turned to Brian. "You go . . . I have to—please!"

He took one look at me and got in the ambulance without a word. I saw him take Bucky's hand as the door shut and the ambulance took off.

I leaned over, hands on my knees and tried to catch my breath. Perry's bag slid down my arm and landed heavily on the gravel; I was glad I'd put the safety on the gun before I stuffed it back into the bag midflight. I didn't want to arrive amid a collection of cops brandishing a large pistol.

Detective Bader came over to me. "What happened?"

"Perry's by the Mather House. That's where . . . Aden's files are, I think. She was going to go through them, destroy them, maybe."

"Is she still there? Is she armed?" Bader gestured to other uniformed officers.

"She won't have gotten far. I took . . . her shoes." I took another deep breath. "I took one gun from her. I don't know whether she's got another. I don't think so."

"Where's the weapon you took?"

I nodded at the bag by my feet. "In there. Uh . . . my fingerprints will be on it."

Bader looked grim. "I . . . didn't hear a shot."

"I didn't need to fire it."

He didn't say anything about my choice of words, just gave instructions to the other officers, and they headed into the woods. I started to feel where I was hurting, but all I cared about was whether the ambulance would be fast enough.

"You're bleeding," Bader said. "You should get that looked at."

"Yeah, I will," I said. I wiped at my chin and could feel the warm trickle of blood smear the back of my hand. It looked almost black in the dim light of the parking lot.

"If she'd caught you a little lower," he said, "It could have been a lot more serious. You'll need to get a tetanus shot. Maybe stitches."

"It hurts like hell, but I don't think I'll need stitches. And I get tetanus boosters every five years; for archaeologists it's just like getting an oil change." I listened hard but could no longer hear the ambulance's siren.

He grunted. "What happened back there?"

I told him about my idea that Aden wasn't led into the

woods, but was going somewhere deliberately, and then talking to Fee.

"Everyone I was worried about was right there," I continued. "And then when Bucky got ill, and I heard that Perry had taken off, I realized that she might be heading for the Mather House, to see if Aden's files were there. She had his keys, she was trying to get in when I found her."

"Found her?" Bader had a frown on his face.

My shoulder still ached, and I wondered if I'd done anything permanent to it. Maybe I shouldn't have dismissed his offer of medical attention quite so abruptly.

"All I cared about was finding out what she'd given Bucky. I thought it might be her painkillers, but I had to be sure—wait! There's a mortar and pestle in the kitchen display in the back of the house! She crushed them there and then put them into the glasses of punch. I was just glad that Lovell was there when Bucky collapsed. I could barely think straight."

By this time, Bader's radio crackled something I couldn't make out. He responded, then turned to me. "They got her. Picked her up in the basement, no shoes, flashlight, piles of folders around her. Blood on her feet, on the papers. She was trying to tear them up."

"I think she was planning to burn that batch too, same as in his home office. That's why I took the lighter fluid away from her." I fidgeted, wishing he would just hurry up and finish with me.

"Good girl."

"You know," I said irritably, "I know you mean that as a compliment, and I appreciate that, but to some people, 'good girl' sounds like you're talking to a dog or a child. It's patronizing."

Detective Bader didn't say anything, just sort of sucked

his teeth. Then I guess he saw that my mind wasn't really on Perry Taylor or feminism. "Sorry. I'll keep it in mind. How about I take you to the hospital?"

"Yes, please." The wave of relief that rushed over me was almost big enough to surf on. "Can we . . . hurry?"

We got into the car and, as if in apology, I told him about the company that Aden had put in his and Fee's names. "That's when I began to realize that it was the Mather House and not the areas I was working on that was the important part. That was just coincidence."

"Another coincidence was that Perry was never run down by a drunk driver or someone who had a grudge against the Stone Harbor Historical Society." The blue light on his dash flashed and bathed his face in its weird strobing glow.

"I know," I said. "I heard."

He glanced over at me, but didn't ask how I knew. "Thing was, she had to set up a payment plan with the hospital because she had no insurance."

I nodded. "So she was the one who was siphoning off the money from the historic site accounts." I recalled what Mary Ann Spencer had told me about Perry's degree in business. "Everyone was talking about how little money everyone else had. And the tourists usually pay cash for their tickets and souvenirs."

"I think that's what we'll find out. I wonder if she'll also confess to the vandalism at the Tapley House; those incidents seem to have dropped off about the time that Justin Fisher was killed."

"He probably caught her coming out of the Chandler House when she shouldn't have. He just got in her way." As I said the words, I realized that I had also gotten in her way, and she'd tried to poison Bucky to slow me down when I'd inadvertently told her where Aden's files were. "Can't we go any faster?"

Detective Bader didn't answer, but we sped up, and soon the hospital was in sight.

Chapter 23

BUCKY LOOKED LIKE GRAY DEATH BY THE TIME WE were able to take her home late the next day. I knew she would be better when I told her that I'd called Ma and Dad and Beebee, and that they'd be down for a visit the following weekend. Separate days, of course.

"You can't not tell your parents your sister's been poisoned," I argued. "It isn't right."

"What they don't know won't hurt them," Bucky muttered. She stroked Quasi absently; he bore it tolerantly and then she scooped him up and cuddled him, nuzzling into the back of his head. He took that too, for nearly thirty seconds, before he strained to get away, pushing at her chest with all four feet, and then jumping off her. He slithered under the bed to repair his dignity. "Or, better yet, you could just tell them that I'm in a coma or something. No visitors."

"*Bucky.*"

"I know, I know. But don't say anything if I play up needing long naps and lots of quiet."

"I won't. But you could even be home by then, tomorrow, if you want."

"No, I'm good here. I'll be out of bed tomorrow, I think. I can't stand lying around anymore, which is saying something. And you won't have to wait on me anymore, either. I'm sorry you'll be shorthanded on the site, though."

I picked up an empty orange juice glass. "It won't be too bad. You going to make a habit of it? Helping me out every summer, I mean?"

She made a face. "Nope. Once is enough. I couldn't do what you do. I'm not patient enough."

"But you're patient enough to sew an animal's insides back together."

"That's different. Maybe I'll come down and talk to you while you get dinner going."

"Good. You up to peeling a few spuds?"

Bucky pretended to be faint. "Pass the smelling salts, I feel another attack of the vapors coming on!"

"I'll give you the vapors. Need a hand getting up?"

"No, I'm good."

I watched her get out of bed and make her way downstairs, then felt something at once soft and solid hit my ankle. I looked down to see what of Bucky's crap was in my way and saw Quasi bang his head against my ankle again. I was too stunned to do anything, and before I could stoop to try to pat him, he slunk down the stairs like smoke following a draft. However grudgingly, however probationary, for some reason, he had accepted me into his pride.

Even better and far less surprising than that, things between me and Brian were back to normal too. It felt so good that I didn't acknowledge to myself what I knew deep down in my heart of hearts: We were better now only because the threat of danger was now gone. Our mutual relief was so great and so welcome that I put off worrying what might happen should the issue ever come up again.

I picked up the empty sandwich plate, thinking about relationships, how complicated and how necessary they were, and how much hard work they required.

"You know, you really should get your hair cut short," Bucky called up to me as she descended the stairs.

I followed her downstairs and decided that it was more than time for me to give Bucky the advice she'd come for but not yet actually asked to hear. "Great. Fine. So long as we're talking makeovers, I'll make you a deal. I'll give short hair a chance if you give Joel a chance. A real chance. You up for a little psychology?"

She rolled her eyes. "A very little. My gratitude doesn't stretch as far as it used to."

"I'll say. Okay, I think that keeping people, including a decent guy, at arm's length—through hiding out in books or focusing on animals or being cantankerous—won't keep you from getting hurt. Maybe it has something to do with Ma and Dad divorcing."

She paused on the steps. The Chin was nowhere to be seen. "I've been hiding out in books and animals since before they split."

"Yeah, well, just be sure you're not just letting some little stuff get in the way of what could be a pretty good thing, okay?"

Bucky shrugged. "Hey, it's no skin off my ass. If Joel turns out to be a real freak, well, I can just dump him again." She continued into the kitchen. "Your hair will take a couple of years to grow back, at least."

"Fine. So is that a deal?"

"I s'pose so."

"Good. Because guess who else I invited to dinner on Friday night?"

"Joel." She exhaled heavily and leaned against the banister, but didn't really look mad or disappointed. In fact, she was almost smiling. "You're such a bossy bitch," she said. But affectionately.

I nodded. "Rhymes with control freak."

Later that weekend, while Brian was out to pick up some ice cream for the invalid, I was being blackmailed over the phone.

"You can either get down here now, and give this newbie the glowing recommendation that I deserve, or you can forget working with me. Ever."

I sighed, not in the mood for any of it; I'd had enough of blackmail for a good long time, even the tame stuff that Nolan tried. He meant it all the same. "Just put her on the phone. That way I don't have to get off my ass."

"Put her on the phone? That's rich. That's pretty good. No, I think we both know that there's nothing quite as reassuring as a face to face, and from what I've seen of you lately, your ass could use a little time off the chair."

That was a lie and we both know it, but there was no way he was going to tell me how well I'd done, even if he was asking me to do him a favor.

"You can tell the newbie just how I saved your bacon. You'll like that, you'll sound tough."

"Nobody saved my bacon but me. And I am tough. I am one tough mutha." I was sure that Nolan could hear my grin through the phone. "Fine, you win. I'll be down there as soon as I can."

"Sooner." Then there was a click as he hung up.

I checked in on Bucky, telling her I wouldn't be more than an hour. She was fine, however, didn't look up from the stack of books she was reading, even to scoff at my suggestion of putting on the alarm while I was away. "What, is Perry going to stage a jailbreak?"

I stuck out my tongue, glad that she was feeling good

enough to give me some sass, and hit the road. There was little traffic, and I got there earlier than I expected.

"Thanks for coming, Dr. Fielding." As always, in his office and upon greeting, Nolan was the soul of politesse. If
you could ignore the hard bands of muscles that seemed to
cover every inch of him, from his earlobes down, I suspected, to his little toes, the odd scar here and there, and then
imagine him in a suit instead of sweats, it would have been
no problem to imagine him taking tea and making polite
conversation. So long as he didn't inadvertently crush the
porcelain handle of the teacup into powder between his
overdeveloped thumb and fingers.

"Nice haircut; very . . . whatshername? *The X-Files* . . .
Agent Scully. Takes years off you."

"Thanks. But I don't see why I couldn't have written you
a letter or just let the other person call me," I grumbled.

"As I've told you before, we get all sorts in here. Kids
who want to be Jackie Chan, guys who want to think they're
hard, guys who are hard and need to keep that way, little old
ladies who've decided they've been too scared for too long.
I do my best to help all of them, according to their needs.
Even smart-aleck archaeologists who get themselves in over
their heads."

"I did exactly what you taught me to do, even if it wasn't
textbook form. I made a decision, I didn't overanalyze, I got
in, I got out." I was a little miffed; I suppose I had been hoping for a pat on the back, but with Nolan, it was more likely
that any pat he'd give me would result in bruises.

"Getting yourself into the situation in the first place is not
what I taught you to do." He seemed to consider. "But I have
five sisters, and if one of them, even one of the loud ones,
was in the kind of trouble yours was in, I suspect I would
have done the same thing. You get points for that, Fielding."

Fielding. I felt as though he'd just pinned a medal on me.

"Maybe next time, you won't take so damn long about it."

"Maybe." I restrained myself from making a face, knowing that any sarcasm on my part would result in a worse time of it when I came in for my next session. "Maybe there won't be a next time."

Nolan threw back his head and laughed, a noise that was like a jet breaking the sound barrier. "That's a good one."

I shrugged. It wasn't all *that* likely.

"In any case, I'm here to make sure you get what you need. Just in case there is a next time." He looked past my shoulder and nodded approval. "Here we are then, right on time. Good evening, Dr. Chang."

I whipped my head around to see Brian standing behind me, wearing a new pair of sweat pants and new sneakers. "Brian! What are you—?"

"You mentioned that I'd never had a self-defense class. I figured, why should you have all the fun?"

"I wouldn't call it fun," I said, glancing hurriedly over at Nolan. He seemed to be preoccupied with papers on his desk. "Most of the time, I don't even know what I'm doing. It's pretty tough going."

He took my hand. "Well, I can take it if you can."